Christmas
FROM THE HEART

A Collection of
Christmas Romances

Christmas FROM THE HEART

A Collection of Christmas Romances

Boatman ❋ Mattis ❋ Pitts ❋ Pura ❋ Wells ❋ Wyse

ELK LAKE PUBLISHING INC

PUBLISHING THE POSITIVE
Plymouth, Massachusetts

COPYRIGHT NOTICE

Cover and Interior Design: Derinda Babcock
Editor(s): Cristel Phelps, Linda Rondeau, Deb Haggerty

Stacy Boatman represented by Dunamis Words Literary Agency
Jenny Louwes represented by Credo Communications
Jessie Mattis represented by Golden Wheat Literary Agency

PUBLISHED BY: Elk Lake Publishing, Inc., 35 Dogwood Drive, Plymouth, MA 02360, 2021

LIBRARY CATALOGING DATA

Names: Boatman, Stacy; Mattis, Jessie; Pitts, Sally Jo; Pura, Murray; Wells, PeggySue; Wyse, Amos (Stacy Boatman, Jessie Mattis, Sally Jo Pitts, Murray Pura, PeggySue Wells, Amos Wyse)
Christmas from the Heart—A Collection of Christmas Romances / Stacy Boatman, Jessie Mattis, Sally Jo Pitts, Murray Pura, PeggySue Wells, Amos Wyse
408 p. 23cm × 15cm (9in × 6 in.)
ISBN-13: 978-1-64949-405-4 (paperback) | 978-1-64949-406-1 (trade paperback) | 978-1-64949-407-8 (e-book)
Key Words: small town, candy-making, search for identity, Christmas plays, Cozy, sweet, clean, holiday love story, Jesus
Library of Congress Control Number: 2021947575 Fiction

TABLE OF CONTENTS

TO OUR WONDERFUL READERS

These romance novelettes are for your enjoyment. They are more than tales of human love, for each story celebrates the purest of love found in Jesus Christ, God's gift to the world.

What better time of year for Christian romance than Christmas?

We've been through, and continue to struggle with, the worst pandemic in a century. Our lives have been turned upside down and inside out, but not only with the economic and physical impact of COVID. Unrest and division abound. Anger is evidenced in every arena of life.

We at Elk Lake Publishing pray you will seek God's comfort this Christmas season, remembering he has not abandoned his creation, for Scripture assures us his love endures forever.

As you trim your tree and wrap your presents, we hope you will offer up a prayer for Peace on Earth and Good Will Toward Men. Take some time from your busyness this season to remember God's goodness.

May these stories stir your heart as you let the warmth of God's love fill you.

From all of us at Elk Lake Publishing, we wish you a Merry Christmas and a Happy New Year.

SNAPSHOT: A LAKE DIAMOND CHRISTMAS ROMANCE

STACY BOATMAN

CHAPTER 1

Everly Frost parked her car at the neighborhood ice rink in Diamond, Minnesota. Fluffy snowflakes floated down from an indigo sky, creating an ideal backdrop for the winter engagement photoshoot. She pitched a canopy tent to protect the expensive camera and lenses from precipitation and set to work assembling gadgets. The muffled ring of her phone emanated from her coat pocket, chiming the ringtone set for Melody, of Melody's Portrait Studio.

On the other end of the line, distant voices and mechanical beeping were audible. "Everly, you'll have to cancel the session. Ow, ow, ow," Melody cried out.

Fear cascaded down her spine as visions of Melody, trapped in her upturned car, or slipping on the ice and gashing her head, and an array of other calamities flashed in her mind. "What's going on? Are you okay?"

"I broke my leg skiing. Or as the doctor put it, 'I *shattered* my tibia.'" She puffed a huffy breath. "Who puts a wooden fence at the bottom of a ski hill? I can't be the first person to crash into it. Would you believe I flipped over the thing? I did a full three-sixty. Landed flat on my back on the other side of the fence."

"Yikes." Everly grasped the tent pole, feeling woozy from the descriptive visual.

Melody bellowed a guttural groan. "I need medication!" she shouted to her unfortunate nurse. Then she panted a sequence of jagged breaths that made Everly worry her boss might hyperventilate. "I can't work for a while. I'll be having surgery."

"You take care." Everly could not take another minute of this ghastly phone call. "Don't worry about this photo session. I'll let the clients know." She glanced over her shoulder at the park entrance. They would arrive any minute.

"Thank you, Everly. I can always count on you."

"Wait." An idea was transpiring. "Maybe we don't need to cancel the appointment with the happy couple." This was Everly's chance to prove to Melody she was ready to step up from her role as apprentice and take on clients independently. Everly could use this opportunity to prove herself as a professional photographer. Melody would benefit as well by following through with the session. Canceling on clients was never good, especially at the last minute. "*I'll* take the photos. Their wedding is only a couple months away, so if we postpone the shoot until you've recovered, we risk them hiring a different photographer. There's not time to delay."

Shuffling noises sounded. A woman was talking to Melody. "This Dilaudid will ease the pain."

"You're a saint," Melody said—to the nurse or Everly.

"Melody," Everly said. "Are you okay with me taking the engagement photos?"

No answer.

"Melody?"

"Huh?" She sounded groggy. "I have ... to ... go." The call ended.

Everly needed to assume the answer was yes.

The sound of snow crunching under tires made her heart thrum a happy rhythm. This was her moment to shine. Stepping out from the tent, she watched an SUV park next to her car. She aimed her camera, ready to capture the man helping his fiancée out of the vehicle—

should the opportunity arise. Candid shots were always the best.

The guy stepped out, dressed more casually than expected. He had certainly dressed the part of an ice-skating date in his hockey pants, jersey, and skates slung over his shoulder. A helmet dangled from his fingers, and his other hand clutched a hockey stick. Okay, so he portrayed the sexy, athletic look. She could work with this, although it would be better for him to lose the black beanie. She snapped a series of photos as he headed toward her, trekking through ankle-deep snow. *Click, click, click.*

"Who are you?" he asked.

She lowered the camera. "I'm Everly. Your appointment was with Melody, but she took a nasty spill downhill skiing this afternoon, so you get me."

He tucked the helmet under his arm in another casual, ruggedly handsome fashion. The lights above the rink shone indirectly across his stubbled face, and snowflakes graced his dark eyelashes. She snapped a few shots. The fiancée would go nuts over these pics. "Are you from the local paper? I didn't realize a neighborhood hockey league was big news these days. Even in a town as small as Diamond."

"Wait." She dropped the camera against her chest with a thump, safely hung from her neck by the strap. "You're not the groom?"

"Do I look like I'm getting married?" He held up his gear.

Everly's face burned with embarrassment. In her eagerness to capture candid shots, she had photographed the wrong dude. "You're actually here to play hockey? You didn't just dress the part?"

He chuckled. "I'm suited up for an actual hockey game."

"Oh. I—"

A pickup truck, modified with ginormous wheels, roared into the parking lot, whipping figure eights and drifting.

"I suppose that is not your fiancée."

The hockey player laughed at her joke, lessening her embarrassment. "Nah. That's Reggie. Trust me. The only attraction I harbor toward him is platonic, and even that can be questionable." Soon a third vehicle entered the lot. This vehicle not only had giant wheels but was also lifted, cluing her in to yet another hockey player.

This couldn't be happening. "Hold on a minute. You guys can't play here. I'm doing a photo shoot on this rink." She needed to make these clients happy when they were settling for her over Melody. "You guys need to play somewhere else." Not usually an assertive type, she put her hands on her hips to show she wasn't budging. She could not blow this job.

The hockey player chuckled again, but this time his laughter was devoid of humor. "We *are* playing here. Just like we do every Thursday night."

"No, no, no! I called the city and tried to reserve the rink. They said first-come-first-served, and I was here first." The back of her eyes stung with the threat of tears. She would not allow herself to cry in front of this guy.

On second thought, maybe he would back down if she cried. *Hmm ...*

No. No crying. She was a professional. And she would not be intimidated by a man-child at the park who wanted to play a game with his friends.

Her heart sank as cars and trucks rushed into the parking lot, and guys lugging hockey gear marched toward the rink. "Excuse me," she shouted in a voice of authority. "This rink is closed. You can return in an hour or find another rink." The Reggie guy outright ignored her, plopping on a bench and lacing up his skates. She looked at the man in front of her—the guy she'd almost, sort of, established a relationship with. "Please." She looked into his brown eyes—which happened to be deceptively, charmingly warm, like a cup of hot cocoa—with a firm gaze, toggling between pleading and demanding.

He shifted his weight and looked over at his buddies littering the park with their giant bags and hockey gear. "Sorry, but like I said, we've been playing here every Thursday night. This is the only rink in town with boards." He did look sorry, but that didn't lessen her urge to punch him in the nose, right between those adorable eyes. He shrugged his shoulders, then joined his teammates at the rink.

Unbelievable.

She texted her clients and told them to meet her out at Lake Diamond instead. There was no lighting out there, so she'd need to swing by the studio to pick up equipment, including flashes and battery-operated lights. Oh, and a shovel in case there wasn't an ice rink cleared.

Tearing down her tent and apparatus, she choked back tears. Why was she always the one to compromise?

Like with her job. Although Melody was mostly fair, paying her well, teaching her every trick of the trade, she didn't include Everly's name on the website or give her credit for exceptional photos. Everly didn't protest only because she was grateful to be working for a woman so excellent at the craft.

Someday, Everly would summon courage to start her own company.

Ian Knight held his phone between his ear and shoulder. "Hey, Mom. What's up?" He sent off the email he'd been working on.

"Honey, you are the talk of the town."

"Um, what's this now?"

"At book club this morning, the ladies were passing around your picture in the paper. They were going on about how handsome you are. I have to agree. You look just like your father."

The comments were equal parts disturbing and flattering. "Back up a minute. What picture? I don't know about any picture in the paper." He flipped his laptop closed and held the phone to his ear with a firm grasp.

"Oh." Her voice pitched in surprise. "You were playing hockey. Well, not *playing*, but you were at the hockey rink, wearing your jersey."

"Ah, yes." He'd forgotten about the sassy photographer who'd mistaken him for a groom. And then attempted to boot out two teams of testosterone-driven men—a losing battle. He had felt bad for her.

"I was happy to see your helmet. I've heard about young men getting concussions on the ice. I hope you have a mouth guard too. I'd hate to see you damage those beautiful teeth your father and I spent so much money straightening."

"I have to see this picture." He opened the laptop and waited for it to reload. Meanwhile, his mom filled him in on the gossip she had learned at book club. Personally, he'd only engaged in small talk with these women, yet he could practically write their biographies. Beth was married to Barry and their children moved across the country, so they didn't get to see their grandkids enough. Ian's mom clearly stated she wanted to see *her* grandkids often. Lorna was a widow and sounded to Ian like the classic cat lady. There were a handful more ladies who he knew too much about for comfort.

He brought up the local newspaper's website, *Diamond Daily*, which, ironically, only printed weekly, since there wasn't enough news in this small town to fill a newspaper seven days of the week. Soon he was staring at his own face. *Oh boy*. Front and center on the community activities page. The guys would give him so much crap if they saw it. Which, to his relief, was unlikely. Not many people in his age group read the newspaper. "That is ... a big picture."

"It's an excellent photo. The photographer is an Everly Frost. I called the paper, and they said she was a freelance photographer who entered your picture. I'd like to hire her to take newborn photos of your sister's baby. Nadia says professional photographers are too expensive, but I insist. This will be Dad's and my baby gift to them. Could you have this Everly Frost contact me?"

"Mom, I didn't exactly hit it off with this woman. She might not be happy to hear from me."

"Don't be silly. She sold your picture to the paper, and it's a raging success. She should be thanking you."

"Huh. You're right." She hadn't asked his permission to take the photo or to put it in the paper—an infringement of his privacy. Although, aside from mild embarrassment, he wasn't bothered.

Shouldn't be too hard to find her. He could never forget her pretty face. She wore her makeup naturally and looked about his age—mid-twenties or so. Her light brown hair, streaked with blonde, fell in waves from her pale pink stocking cap with the pompom. She had been notably upset—her bottom lip trembled—but she had put on a brave face and tried to stand her ground, insisting they leave.

She had been right. She was the first to arrive at the park so had every right to the rink. Maybe he could have tried harder to stall the game. Talk the guys into hanging out at the brewery for an hour until her photo shoot was over. He sincerely hoped her session at the alternative location had been a success.

"All right, Mom. I'll do my best to locate this photographer." Giving her business was the least he could do to make amends.

"That's great, honey. I'll let your sister know. The baby is coming soon." His mom made a giddy sound. "My first grandchild will be a Christmas baby. How wonderful."

Ian talked with his mom a few more minutes then promised to let her know when he tracked Everly down. He would be sure to apologize and thank her for making him famous with the older ladies.

CHAPTER 2

Everly revealed the final products to the happy couple. Laura and Rob had selected save-the-date postcards, displaying a trio of pictures—Laura ducking behind a tree while a snowball splattered on Rob's shoulder, the duo making snow angels side by side, and the two of them ice-skating hand-in-hand. They had chosen a close-up, more classic pose for an 8 by 10 to hang above their fireplace. The shoot had been an absolute success. Everly could not be prouder. Aside from booking the clients, she had done this job all on her own.

"We love them," Laura said, gazing at the pictures, a hand over her heart and tears in her eyes. She looked at Rob with adoration and smooched his cheek. To which he returned a lengthy kiss on the mouth. The lovey-dovey stuff was almost enough to make Everly toss her cookies, yet the positive reaction had surpassed her expectations. Couldn't complain about that.

Melody hadn't heaped praise on Everly's successes. She was just relieved someone was picking up her slack during recuperation. Since her accident a couple weeks ago, Melody had dropped by the office a few times to do paperwork, but she had left the photo sessions and client interactions up to Everly. Melody wouldn't be back to work full time until after Christmas.

Everly used this time as a mock run of owning her own business, taking thorough notes along the way, paying special attention to detail. She had decked out the studio's waiting area and office in soft white twinkle lights, draped garlands of evergreen branches over the windows and doorways, and decorated a Balsam fir Christmas tree—delightfully aromatic—in the front window. Outside, the door was adorned in a classic wreath, complete with a giant red bow, jingle bells, and twinkling lights. Everly believed creating a homey, inviting environment would build trust with the clients while providing a glimpse of the photographer's creativity. A fun and simple way to enhance business opportunities.

"Would you like more tea or scones?" she asked Laura and Rob while packaging their photos and postcards.

"No, thank you," the couple said in unison. "Will you be the photographer for the wedding?" Laura asked, slipping her thin arms into the cranberry-colored wool coat Rob held up for her.

"I'll be assisting Melody. She should be fully recovered by your wedding on Valentine's Day."

"We'd like for you to do it," Rob said, hardly leaving room for negotiation. "Your pictures look natural. Candid."

Everly's chest and neck flushed, both from flattery and discomfort. Melody would never step aside for Everly to take over her clients, as long as the woman was physically capable. "I understand. I've enjoyed working with the two of you. I'll let Melody know your wishes."

"I want you to do it too," Laura said. "I love your style."

"I'd be honored to photograph your special day." Not exactly a promise. Not dishonest either. She would have to make this work. Melody would want to keep her clients happy, right?

As she pulled the door open for the couple, crisp air filled her nostrils with the refreshing scent of winter—freshly fallen snow and the anticipation of Christmas. She sent the clients off with wishes for a merry Christmas.

"Oh, we'd appreciate an online review," she said as they approached their car. *Mention my name,* she wanted to add.

"You got it," Laura said.

Downtown Diamond looked like one of the Christmas cards Mom mailed to friends and family each year. Colored lights wrapped around street lamps. Giant pots of Christmassy evergreen arrangements punctuated street corners. The tree in the park, standing about thirty feet tall, had been lit by the fire department at a lighting ceremony the day after Thanksgiving. Ian might not stay in this town forever, but Diamond would always be comforting to come home to.

After a long day at the office, he had decided to stop at Adelia's Bakery on his way home to buy one of those amazing frosted cookies. He parallel parked on the street not far from the bakery. Passing by a storefront, he noticed portraits in a window display. Melody's Portrait Studio. Why hadn't he noticed that before? Maybe that's where the elusive photographer worked. According to a sign posted on the door, the studio had closed five minutes ago, but the lights were on. Worth a try. As he reached for the handle, the door swung open, catching him off-guard, positioning him face to face with—

"Everly Frost." Wisps of her golden hair danced around her rosy cheeks, stirred by the chilly air. Delicate, shiny earrings dangled from her earlobes. She was so pretty. Just like the night of their run-in before the hockey game.

"You." She didn't appear to reciprocate the pleasure in meeting again.

"Ian Knight." He extended his hand, which she reluctantly shook. Her skin was warm and soft. "I was hoping to run into you again."

"I wouldn't call stalking me at work 'running into me'."

So, she was still miffed about the hockey team taking over. "Sorry for what happened out at the rink. You had every right to be there."

"Yes. I did." She crossed her arms and planted her feet firmly, shoulder-width apart. If looks could kill.

"Did you find another rink?"

"Cut the small talk. What do you want?"

"My mother saw my picture in the paper. Thank you for that, by the way." He posed in a dramatic reenactment of the photo. He waited for a reaction. A smile, perhaps—but got nothing. He relaxed into his normal stance. "Anyway, she wants to hire you to take pictures of my sister's baby."

Still no response. Then a flicker in her eyes betrayed the fact she was considering it. "Me or Melody?"

"You."

"How old is the baby?"

"Thirty-eight weeks? She'll be born any day."

Everly's eyes twinkled, and she finally smiled. "A Christmas baby."

"So, you're interested?" The icy air nipped at his fingers. He rubbed his hands together to warm them. "Mind if we talk inside?"

She looked over her shoulder, debating her answer. "We're closed now. But I'll give you a business card. Come on in for a sec." She went to a desk and grabbed a business card from a stack. "Ask for Everly when you call." She handed him the card but quickly snatched it back. "Actually, I'll give you my direct number."

This was going better than anticipated. Maybe he was getting a date out of this business encounter, thanks to Mom.

"Your *mother* or *sister* can reach me directly on my cell." His pleased reaction must have been written all over his face. She jotted her name and number on a sticky note and gave it to him. "What is your mother's name?"

"Yvette Knight. My sister is Nadia Hamilton."

"I look forward to hearing from them."

Everly practically danced into her apartment. Laura and Rob's photos were fabulous, and they wanted *her* to photograph the wedding. They were adamant, so they'd likely convince Melody to allow Everly to take the job. The cherry on top of her day was booking her own client. A newborn. At Christmastime. What could be more precious?

She turned on her electric fireplace, plugged in the Christmas tree lights, and played carols through her Bluetooth speaker. Her studio loft above Marinara, a tantalizing pizza place, more than sufficed for her needs. The view of Lake Diamond, directly out her window, made up for lack of space. Her loft was sandwiched between two more spacious living quarters, and her neighbors had become dear friends. Jade Powers lived above her business, the delectable coffee shop, Lakeview Brew. On Everly's other side, Levi Billings resided atop Firefly Gifts. He was a quiet type who wrote for *Diamond Daily*, was penning his first novel—often seeking Everly's opinion on excerpts—and played piano in his downtime, occasionally lulling Everly to sleep when his beautiful music seeped through her walls.

The obvious downfall of living above an excellent pizza shop was the tempting aroma of garlicky, buttery pizza crusts. She ordered the pepperoni and green pepper calzone all too often—tonight being no exception—and had gained an inch or two on her waist to show for it. No regrets. Every bite was worth the calories. After donning her comfy flannel pj's, she stretched out on her daybed and enjoyed the first delectable bite of cheesy, melt-in-your-mouth goodness.

She sent a group text to her parents and brother, informing them of her progress toward becoming an entrepreneur. Her mom and dad, both doctors in Minneapolis, were thrilled. They'd long ago accepted the reality that Everly was more the creative type and wouldn't earn an MD behind her signature. Her brother, Henri, followed closer in her parents' footsteps, working his way up to Nurse Manager of a burn unit.

Yet another way Everly differed from her family was in her desire to explore the country and, ultimately, the world. Her parents and brother were happy to settle down wherever they found work, traveling only on the occasional vacation. Everly, however, craved full immersion into a variety of settings and cultures—to experience the world through differing perspectives. Her goal was to capture those perspectives through photography. A whole story could be told through a simple snapshot.

Gaining Ian's sister as a client sparked confidence in her ability to start on her own, which would require relocating, since she couldn't compete with Melody in this small town. She could move anywhere in the world. A thrilling thought. Closing her eyes, she imagined the possibilities. Soon she dozed off, dreaming of the adventure awaiting her.

Music blasted, startling her from sleep. Her phone was ringing through the Bluetooth speaker. She wiped drool from the corner of her mouth and cleared her throat. "Hello?"

"I'd like to speak with Everly please."

"This is Everly."

"Hello, dear. I'm so pleased Ian found you." Everly jumped off the bed and ran her fingers through her hair, despite the obvious fact the woman on the other end of the line couldn't see her. "You have such a pretty name."

"Thank you." Wow. This lady hadn't wasted time contacting her.

"I'm Yvette, Ian's mother. The picture of him in the paper—so handsome. It's all the women in my book club can talk about. They think he should go into modeling."

Now it was Everly's turn to say something, but she didn't know how to reply. "Yes. He's very handsome." *Ugh*. Why did she say that? Those words better not get back to Ian.

"Just like his father. Anyway, as Ian told you, I'd like to hire you to take pictures of my daughter's baby. I'm going to be a grandma any day."

"How exciting. I'd be honored. Would you like to set up an appointment?"

Yvette laughed. "I wish we could plan for these things. Babies have their own timetables. Nadia is due December twentieth."

Everly opened her calendar. "I have availability the week after Christmas. I'll call Nadia to pin down a date."

"I don't think you understand. We want you at the birth."

Blech! Her stomach lurched, and she repressed the gag reflex. Why had the medical gene completely skipped her genetic code? Back in high school psychology class, she had been forced to watch a recording of a birth. Mrs. Mattson had said it would be magical and beautiful. The teacher was either a liar, or she was nuts. The birth was bloody and grotesque. The mom was sweaty and screaming in pain. Everly had closed her eyes through most of it and promised herself to adopt if she ever got baby fever.

"Nadia will be giving birth at home. She's opted for a water birth. All natural."

Oy.

"The baby could decide to come any day, although her mid-wife, Estafani, said she isn't dilating yet, but she is starting to efface." Whatever that meant. Probably better off not knowing. "Will you be in the area the next few weeks?"

"I will." Aside from celebrating Christmas with her family. She would pray the baby would come early.

"How wonderful! I'll let Nadia know."

So, this was happening. "I'll need Nadia's contact information. Her phone number and address." She would also like to speak with Nadia to be sure the new mom was on board with the plan to have a photographer snapping pictures of her pushing out a baby. "I like to meet with my clients before the photo shoot. Discuss expectations and go over what kind of pictures they'd like. Black and white versus color, for example."

Yvette rattled off Nadia's information. An inkling of hope that Nadia indeed would not allow a photographer during the actual birth gave Everly courage to commit to this job. She would call the mother-to-be tomorrow after sleeping on it and getting accustomed to the idea of watching a woman split open to produce a gooey, wailing human being.

She spent the rest of the evening studying professional photography of births. The pictures were surprisingly tasteful. Honestly, she was moved by the precious reactions of mothers meeting their babies for the first time, their faces glowing with wonder and love despite the gruesome pain they had endured moments earlier—nothing short of miraculous. The humility of the fathers, standing by, doing what little they could to ease the pain of their wives during labor. His hand on her lower back. The worry lines creasing his forehead. Moisture gathering in his eyes as he gazed at his wife. And then, tears raining down his cheeks as he cut the umbilical cord and looked into the face of his child. Everly realized there were tears in her own eyes.

Not that she felt inspired to birth a child anytime soon.

But she felt honored by the invitation to witness such an intimate, miraculous event.

CHAPTER 3

The cursor hovered over the send button as Ian skimmed his résumé one last time. No red lines squiggled under misspelled words. The "work experience" section boasted a rather impressive list of bullet points. The document was ready.

His office door blasted open after a swift knock, and his boss breezed in. Kevin Green was always in a rush and always sweaty, his comb over perpetually out of place. Ian minimized the document. "Would you like to join us at the diner for lunch?" Kevin asked, adjusting his tie. Kevin refused to dress in business casual attire although he allowed the rest of the office staff to do so.

"No, thank you. I brought a sandwich."

With a nod, Kevin left and closed the door with a whoosh that sent loose papers on Ian's desk sailing to the floor.

Leaning back in his swivel chair, Ian contemplated the repercussions of accepting a position across the country. His career in computer science would be advanced, and he'd earn a higher salary. The location of San Francisco would be interesting and was likely to lend to job advancements. The pros list was extensive.

However, the short list of cons possibly outweighed the positives, comprised of merely one powerful word—Mom. She'd be destroyed over her one and only son leaving her. He rubbed the back of his neck. Mom was precisely the reason he felt an itch to leave Diamond, although he loved and appreciated her. She had done an excellent job raising him, as he'd told her many times over the years. She and Dad had done such a good job, in fact, he was fully capable of doing his own laundry, buying his own groceries, and cleaning his own house. Yet she continued to coddle him. The hovering was suffocating. He craved independence and privacy.

Even his dating life was affected by her helicopter parenting. Yvette Knight was known in town as a social butterfly, an admirable trait. She struck up conversation with anyone she rubbed elbows with, and people adored her. The downside was every woman he had dated in Diamond, although not an exceptional number, already knew his mother. Oftentimes, the date was set up by his mother. Too soon in the relationship, he and his date would be sitting down to family dinners at his parents' house, and his mom would be quizzing her on how many children she wanted and if she planned to raise said children in Diamond, emphasizing her desire to visit her grandchildren—often. Ian expected his dates to run away, scared off by the overbearing future mother-in-law. Oddly, the women expressed delight at earning her respect and seemed eager to settle down and start popping out those babies. *Ian* was the one running.

He'd prefer to meet a woman organically, take his time getting to know her, and introduce her to family once things were serious. Like normal people do.

He clicked send.

Over lunch, he caught up on personal messages and scrolled through his social media accounts. He came across a meme of himself—the notorious picture Everly had snapped like shameless paparazzi—with a staggering number of views and comments. The words "Hot, Single, Hockey Hunk in your area. Click now." flashing over his head. A gleam on his teeth and a sparkle in his eye had been photoshopped in. One of the guys on the team must have done this. He couldn't help but laugh.

On second thought, was Everly responsible for the meme? Maybe she was determined to post this picture everywhere she could think of. Rub it in his face. The newspaper was one thing. Social media was another. The meme suddenly lost its humor.

Everly may have lost possession of the rink the other night, but she'd won the battle overall. Apparently, she was not done fighting.

Everly ran downstairs the second she heard the roar of the delivery truck idling behind her building. Diamond might be a charming town, but that didn't mean all the townspeople were charming or even trustworthy. She wanted her camera equipment hand-delivered.

Unboxing the goodies in her apartment, she felt like a little girl on Christmas morning. Of course, these packages weren't gifts. She had paid for them with hard-earned money, which made the unwrapping extra rewarding. She was so excited about assembling the accessories she almost didn't hear the knock on her door.

"Who's there?" she called out, gently setting the diffuser on the coffee table. She waded through boxes, packing peanuts, and bubble wrap on her way to the door.

"It's Jade."

Everly swung the door open to find her friend holding two mugs, one topped with whipped cream and candy cane sprinkles. "Peppermint Mocha!" She accepted the cup and took a delicious sip. "Mm. Dark chocolate and oat milk. You know me too well."

"A good way to celebrate your big delivery and giant leap toward entrepreneurship." She made a "cheers" motion with her cup, then took a drink. Her olive skin was flushed, and her Lakeview Brew T-shirt was dotted with moisture and hung askew at her waist. Signs of a busy day at the coffee shop. Still, Jade took a break to come say hi. Such a sweetheart.

"Thank you. I'm so excited. This caffeine is going to make me even more hyper. Come look at this stuff."

Jade stepped in as far as she could with all the mess. "Wow, Everly. Where are you going to store all this?" Her brown eyes widened as she scanned the cramped space. She grasped a strand of ebony hair that had escaped the bun perched on top of her head and twirled it between her slender fingers—something Everly knew her to do when stressed.

"It'll be fine after I clean up all the garbage." Everly set down her coffee and stacked a few boxes. "Better already."

Jade sat on the daybed and eyed the equipment. "I'm so happy for you. This is your big break, and you deserve it. You are way too talented to be an assistant, lugging around equipment and doing paperwork for Melody. I mean, look at these." Jade crossed the room and picked up a canvas print of Laura and Rob from a stack leaning against the wall. "I can make out individual strands of her curly hair. Incredible. And the couple looks so carefree. Blissful. In love. I don't know them, yet, looking at this picture, I feel happy for them."

"You got the blissfully in love part right. This couple knows no boundary with public displays of affection. They're cute, though."

"What is this?" Jade set down the canvas and picked up the one behind it. "I didn't know you'd been taking photographs of professional athletes."

"Hardly. That's the guy I told you about. Ian Knight."

"Oh, yeah." Jade gawked at the picture, her mouth agape.

"Don't drool on my print. I'm planning to hang that up in my very own studio one day."

"This is the picture Levi helped you get in the *Diamond Daily*?"

"That's the one."

"Is he single?"

"The hockey player? No idea. But you have a boyfriend. Remember Drake? The refined gentleman you've been seeing?"

Jade rolled her eyes. "I was asking for *you*. He's cute. Ruggedly handsome."

She had noticed but wasn't ready to admit it. "You think so?"

"Undeniably." She set down the canvas. "It's his sister who's having the baby?"

"Yep. Nadia."

"Nadia Hamilton? Yvette's daughter?" As a coffee shop owner, Jade knew all the caffeine addicts in town.

"Yes. You know her?"

Jade nodded. "Nadia is super sweet. Makes sense she'd deliver at home. She's really into homeopathic stuff. She's a big tea drinker."

"Jade, can I be honest with you?"

"Is something wrong?" Jade sat on the daybed next to her.

"Look at all this stuff." Everly swept her hand over the equipment, fresh out of the boxes. "Check out these receipts." She held up a pile of little white papers inked with great big numbers. "Am I in over my head? Not just the expense. My first gig is a live birth. How am I supposed to be professional and composed in the same room as a woman giving birth?" She stuffed her face into a throw pillow and let out a whimper of despair.

"At least you can hide your grossed-out facial expressions behind the camera."

Good point. "I mean, did you ever freak out when you were starting your business?"

"All the time. I still do. We have a slow weekend, and I worry we won't make enough money to pay the bills. We have a busy weekend, and I worry we'll run out of products before the next delivery. Owning your business is a lot of pressure, but if it's your dream—like opening Lakeview Brew was mine—and you are committed to making it succeed, it will be worth it. The joy will outweigh every ounce of worry and every penny spent."

Everly committed Jade's words to heart. Jade had set an example of success. She had been around Everly's age when she'd started her business just a few years earlier.

"I mean it when I say you are talented, Everly. I one-hundred-percent believe you will be successful." Everly knew her friend meant every word.

Jade returned to Lakeview Brew, leaving Everly alone with her thoughts—her excitement and anxieties about her business venture. Better to prepare instead of agonizing. She was lugging broken down cardboard boxes to the recycling bin outside when her phone buzzed in her pocket. With her hands full, answering a phone call wasn't an option. The caller would have to leave a voicemail.

Once back in her loft, she finished tidying up, designating the front closet to photography equipment, piling coats and shoes in the entry area until she purchased coat and shoe racks. Staring at the heap of displaced outerwear, she decided to order those racks online immediately. Her apartment needed a cheerful vibe at Christmastime. Not chaotic.

When she opened her phone, she was reminded of the missed call. She listened to the voicemail—Melody's voice killing any remnant of cheer. "I don't appreciate you taking advantage of my altered health status to swoop in and steal my clients." Melody made a growling sound. "Laura and Rob fired me." *Oh, no.* "They hired a different photographer. I assumed they were unhappy I sent my assistant to their appointment, which was understandable, so I offered to retake their photos. For free. Laura finally blurted out she wanted to hire *you* personally as their wedding photographer. Are you competing with me now?" Everly could picture Melody's angry face. The flared nostrils and squinty eyes. Melody was the type of person you wanted on your good side. She was smart, confident, and would go to bat for you. As long as you didn't cross her. "Call me."

Everly needed to set the record straight. No, she was not competing with her. If she went out on her own, she would move away from Diamond, but she wasn't ready to take that step. She dialed Melody's number.

"Hi, Everly." Sounded like she'd cooled down a bit.

"Melody, I never meant to take business from you. Laura and Rob were so pleased with their engagement photos they asked me to photograph the wedding. I told them I'd be your assistant."

"Really? Because Laura said you told them you'd be honored to."

"Oh. I guess I did. I mean … I meant I'd love to, but I couldn't. Or I'd have to talk it over with you."

"This thing with Laura and Rob was the last straw. First, there was this hockey photo showing up all around town that I knew nothing about. I'm guessing you used my camera for that shot?"

"Well … yes." Everly's legs felt like noodles. She sat on her bed. "I didn't plan to. I was waiting for the clients to show up. I actually thought Ian was Rob."

"Ian Knight. You bring up my next point. Rumor has it you are photographing the Knight girl's delivery. Are you planning to use my equipment for that too?"

"No. Melody, I didn't ask for the job. They asked me to do it."

"And you said yes instead of signing them on as Melody's Portrait Studio clients."

"Yes."

"You can try to compete with me, but remember I've been doing this for ten years here in Diamond. I have established, loyal clientele. I photograph all the school pictures in the county, including most senior class pictures. I photograph all the families for the church directories ..." Melody droned on and on about all the pictures she took of everyone in town, and it was everything Everly could do not to burst into tears. She already knew she could never compete with Melody, and she didn't want to try. "... I'll no longer be needing your assistance at the studio. I'm off the painkillers. I'll take it from here. Thanks for your help during my recovery." The line went dead.

Everly shimmied between the covers of her bed and cried herself to sleep.

CHAPTER 4

On Christmas Eve morning, Jade treated Everly and Levi to coffee and Swedish pancakes topped with lingonberry sauce. A fabulously delicious way to start the special day. Jade's loft, like Levi's, was more than double the size of Everly's studio. Jade's decorating style was eclectic in a way that made sense when arranged together. The brick walls had spotlights shining on local artwork pieces. Beautiful rugs covered the wood flooring, defining small spaces—the entryway, a reading nook, and the living area. Of course, she had the same gorgeous view of Lake Diamond, now covered in snow and dotted with ice fishing houses.

Everly didn't dare make the two-hour drive home to be with family at Christmas and risk missing Nadia's labor. This job was paramount to launching her business, and sadly, to making ends meet. Her next booking wasn't until Valentine's Day when Laura and Rob would tie the knot. She tucked the idea in her pocket of asking Jade if she needed help at Lakeview Brew. For now, her savings was enough to keep her afloat.

Levi dabbed the corners of his mouth with his napkin. "I have a gift for each of you." He reached into a brown bag.

Jade laughed. "I hope you have my new subscription to *Diamond Daily* in that bag."

"You spoiled the surprise," Levi teased back. "Of course, I renewed each of your subscriptions. I sleep better at night knowing at least two citizens of Diamond read my articles." He set two wrapped boxes on the table. "But I got you something more tangible to go along with your subscription renewal."

Everly and Jade each unwrapped identical miniature succulent plants. "Thank you, Levi," Everly said. "This is my first plant."

"Your first one?" Levi asked. "It's good to practice taking care of something. If you keep this alive, someday you can get a pet."

"I don't know if I want a pet."

"Okay, then a baby."

"Whoa. Slow down," Everly said. "A baby is way different than a plant. And I really don't know if I want one of those. At least not yet. I need a man first. I always thought a man was the starting point, not a plant."

Jade got a sly look on her face. "How about Mr. Hockey Player Man?"

Levi nudged Everly. "The guy you asked me to put in the paper?"

Everly felt her face flush. Her fair skin kept no secrets. "There's nothing going on with Ian. He's cute, but he's also a bully."

Jade eyed Everly skeptically. "You said he apologized."

"He did."

"Did you accept his apology?" Jade asked.

She had to think about that. "Not verbally." She would accept his apology next time she saw him. Holding a grudge was not her style. The score had already been evened out by the raving reviews of his picture in the newspaper and his landing her a job. "Moving on ..." She set gift bags in front of each of her friends. "Merry Christmas!"

They opened their gift of handknit mittens. "My friend makes these and sells them online to people all over the country. I promise you'll love them. Hashtag mittens by Amy. She made my cute beanie with the pompom I always get compliments on too." Jade and Levi tried them on, commenting on how soft and warm they felt. Next, they each unwrapped a framed photo of the building they lived in that Everly had taken last fall. Burnt orange and yellow leaves rained down like confetti, carpeting the sidewalk in brilliant golden hues. Each business showcased arrangements of autumn flowers outside their store fronts. The scene had screamed to be photographed. Everly already had her identical print hanging on her wall.

"This is definitely going up in the café. No way will I hide it in my apartment for only me to enjoy."

"Thank you, Everly," Levi said. "I will selfishly hang it in my loft and feel no regret over keeping it to myself. I know just the place."

"My turn," Jade said. She gave Lakeview Brew gift cards and hoodies sporting the coffee shop's logo.

"Ladies, I wish you both a very merry Christmas." Levi gathered the wrapping paper littering the table and floor. "Let me help you clean up, and then I need to catch my flight home."

Hugs and well wishes were exchanged, and soon Everly found herself alone in her apartment. She slipped into her cozy new sweatshirt and placed her succulent on the coffee table where it could keep her company. This would be her first Christmas alone. In years past, her family attended the Christmas Eve church service where they listened to the pastor read the Christmas story from the Bible. Then attendees circled around the perimeter of the sanctuary, each holding a flaming candle, to sing Christmas carols. After church, her immediate family—and sometimes a grandparent or two—congregated at her parents' house to exchange presents, drink eggnog, and devour trays of frosted sugar cookies. This year, Everly had shipped her gifts to her parents' house, and family had done the same for her. The wrapped boxes sat decoratively under her tree. Didn't seem as fun to open them alone. Although ... she could celebrate with her family over a video call tonight—a suitable alternative. She texted her family the idea, and they made a plan to call after church.

What to do in the meantime? Lounging around, even watching a classic Christmas movie, lacked appeal on what was one of the most special days of the year. Snowflakes descended from the sky like fluffy goose feathers, covering Lake Diamond in a billowy blanket of white. Playing in the snow—now that was a fun Christmas activity, even if she had to do it by herself. She dug snowshoes from a closet, geared up in warm layers, and headed outside to trek around the lake.

Sweat beaded on her forehead by the time she made it outside.

"Everly?"

She turned to the male voice coming from the Lakeview Brew entrance. "Ian." Sheesh, he was looking dapper. If she thought he'd been handsome with the rugged look, this clean-cut look suited him just as well. His face was freshly shaved, and he looked like he'd gotten a haircut. Actually, this was perhaps the first time she'd seen him without a hat. His short, sandy blond hair was styled and held in place by a bit of gel she guessed as a light breeze passed through it, ruffling the strands but not mussing it. A gray sweater and black jeans were visible under his wool coat. This hockey player cleaned up nice. A waft of woodsy aftershave or cologne drifted her way. She inhaled deeply, enjoying the masculine scent as it mingled with the fresh winter air—until realizing she was sniffing him like a crazy person. She wondered if she had rubbed shoulders with him previously in this small town. How had she not taken notice?

"Do you live up there?" He squinted into the falling snow, looking up at Everly's loft window.

"Yes."

He nodded approvingly. "Merry Christmas."

"Merry Christmas. You look spiffy. Are you headed to a Christmas party?" Did she just say *spiffy*? Who says that? The awkward compliment would betray her attraction to him if sniffing him hadn't already given it away.

"Yep. Headed to my parents' house. Don't tell anyone, but I stopped here to pick up a Lakeview Brew gift card for my brother-in-law. I couldn't think of what to get the guy, and time is running out."

"You can't go wrong with coffee. Especially from this place."

"My thoughts exactly, but I'm not even sure he drinks the stuff." He stepped aside for people to enter the café.

"Ask Nadia."

"I can't. She'll know I waited till the last minute to buy him something." Snow gathered on his shoulders and hair. The tips of his ears and end of his nose were reddening from the chilly air. She motioned for them to walk to his SUV parked by the curb.

"Men are hard to buy for. What did you ask for this Christmas?"

"I couldn't think of anything."

"The trouble with you men is you buy everything you want, and the items on your wish list are too expensive. My Dad said he needs a new snowblower, and he'd like an electric bike. Not that he expected me to buy either of those items. My brother only had snowboard boots on his Christmas list, which my parents got him. So, I gave him a virtual gift card to a ski resort."

Ian unlocked his car and started it with the remote starter. "And for your dad?"

"A Vikings football sweatshirt. Even though he has a closet full of Vikings clothing."

"Maybe you should've gone for a Minnesota Wild hockey sweatshirt." He sipped his coffee.

31

"I'll remember for next year. You can get one for your brother-in-law too."

"Good idea." He climbed into his vehicle. "Have fun snowshoeing."

"Have fun at your party. Let me know what you get for presents."

Watching him drive off to be with family while she trekked around the lake by herself was a little sad. At least she had some plans today—breakfast with friends and a video call with family. Christmas Day, she'd be completely alone, and businesses would be closed. She would be alone with her succulent.

CHAPTER 5

One and a half laps around the lake, Everly was sweating through a layer of clothing, yet her toes were numb from the cold and her cheeks stung from the brisk air. She jabbed her poles into the deepening snow, trudging across the frozen lake. The mesmerizing beauty of the winter wonderland had lost a touch of appeal. Now the only view she wanted to take in was the four walls of her shower. Or the inside of her refrigerator.

At least she didn't feel alone out here. Lots of people had strapped on their snowshoes to walk around the lake, and the ice-skating rink was bustling. The atmosphere buzzed with excitement.

A man was running toward her, waving his arms like there was some sort of emergency. She hoped no one fell through the ice or something. Was she on thin ice? Wait, was that Ian? Sure enough, she recognized the wool coat, and then he called her name. She waved back to let him know she was heading over. Maybe Nadia finally went into labor. An ember of fear flickered in her heart. Did something happen to the baby? She picked up the pace, her legs burning from the effort, as she closed the gap between her and Ian. "Is everything okay?" she called out as she climbed the embankment of the lakeshore. She bent over, catching her breath.

"Nadia's water broke."

Hardly an emergency.

"Fantastic! Why didn't you call me?"

"I did. You didn't answer."

Everly checked her pockets. "I guess I left my phone at home."

"You knew she could go into labor at any minute."

"I didn't mean to, and I don't appreciate being yelled at. I'm not going home for Christmas because I'm waiting for this baby. I'm out here trying to pass the time and scrounge a bit of cheer. Besides, it's only been, like, two hours since I last talked to you."

"I get it. Sorry I snapped at you. Things are tense with Nadia." Everly noticed the crease between Ian's eyebrows. "My mom wants her to deliver at the hospital because of some article she read online about infection with water births after the mother's water breaks. Nadia and the midwife insist the information isn't true, and my brother-in-law, Garrett, wants to go to the hospital if it's safer."

"Oy. Sounds messy." She unbuckled her snowshoes and walked with Ian across Lakeview Drive to her apartment building. Ian's SUV was parked outside of it. "If it were me, I wouldn't want a photographer added to the mix." Why did she say that when she needed this job like a snowman needs snow? "Not that I mind being there. I'll do my best to stay out of the way. The photos will be a treasure."

Ian laughed and patted her shoulder. "Don't worry. They want you there no matter how tense things get.

"Are you going to be there?" For some reason, she wanted him there for a sense of security, but maybe it was weird for a brother to witness his sister giving birth.

"I'd be content waiting to meet my niece until after she's all cleaned up and dressed in one of the millions of pink sleepers my mother bought her. But they want me there in case of emergency. To drive people to the hospital or do whatever needs doing. Fetch hot water and towels. That's a thing, right?"

Everly shrugged. "Beats me."

"I'll mostly be keeping my dad company in a separate room of the house."

Everly unlocked the tenant entrance door and invited Ian to follow her up to her loft. "Give me two minutes to change clothes. Then I'll need you to help me carry a couple things out to my car." She scurried into her bedroom, flinging off her coat, hat, mittens, and boots along the way.

"I'll drive you," she heard him say from behind the closed door. "My mother just texted. The contractions started, but Nadia is only dilated two centimeters."

"What does that mean?" she yelled, pulling a sweater over her head.

"I'll ask."

Once dressed in clean, dry clothes, Everly raced into the bathroom to wash her face, smear deodorant under her arms, and run a brush through her hair. She emerged from the bathroom to find Ian holding the 24 by 36-inch canvas print of himself, inspecting it with a cocky grin on his face.

"Excuse me. Don't touch my stuff." She took the print from him and leaned it back against the wall. Her issue was less with him touching her things and more about him seeing she'd blown up a giant picture of him.

"I'd sensed an attraction, but this is more like obsession."

She punched his arm—hard, but playfully. "Before you let your head get any bigger, you should know I'm proud of the skillful, artistic quality of the photograph. I'm not obsessed with you."

He was laughing—so heartily that tears gathered in the corners of his eyes.

"I'm proud of this shot. The lighting was perfection. See the lens flare from the floodlight?" She stood back, admiring her work. "I'm going to hang it up at my own studio someday."

"Hey," he said, furrowing his brow. "Did you post that meme?"

"What meme?"

"The one everyone is—" Ian's phone dinged. He read the text out loud. "It will probably be a few hours until the baby is born. Still, don't dilly dally."

"A few hours?" Her stomach was growling. She grabbed a handbag and threw in an apple, a banana, a bag of cashews, and a water bottle. "Now for the camera equipment." She loaded up both their arms. "Let's do this."

"I ordered pizza and wings from Marinara," Ian's dad said from his recliner. "It'll be ready in forty minutes. To think, all the food we prepared for Christmas Eve dinner is sitting in our fridge back at home."

"You ordered the pizza for delivery, I hope," Ian said. "Mom will freak out if anyone leaves to pick up pizza."

Dad looked guilty as a teenager caught texting at the dinner table. "Son, I've been married to your mother over thirty years. Of course, I ordered it for delivery, but let me just call to be sure." He winked, then changed his order to delivery.

Everly wandered into the living room. Her camera dangled from her hand at her side. She plopped onto the opposite end of the couch from him and blew wisps of hair off her forehead.

"How's it going in there?" Ian asked.

"She still has three centimeters to go." Everly put her feet up on the ottoman.

Ian had learned the goal was ten centimeters. Apparently, they were in for a long night. It was already eight o'clock. "Dad ordered pizza."

Everly's eyes brightened. "Sounds amazing. I'm famished."

Ian liked the way Everly fit in so naturally with his family. Even at such an intimate time as his sister having a baby, it felt as if Everly belonged there. He had to remind himself she was practically a stranger and that she wasn't too fond of him. She was there on business.

Ian, on the other hand, was growing fonder of her by the minute. Not only was she pretty—shiny, honey-blonde hair his fingers itched to explore, mesmerizing amber eyes that peered at him from under long lashes, a body that curved in all the right places and moved in a graceful yet swift and productive way—she was also kind, almost to a fault. Ian was figuring out when she came across as brash, she was merely fighting to stand her ground, compensating for feeling overwhelmed and overpowered. Her nature was to be generous and put others first.

"So, Everly," Dad said. "How long have you lived in Diamond?"

"About three years. I grew up a couple hours north of here, got a Bachelor of Fine Arts in photography in Chicago, and moved to Diamond to get experience at Melody's Portrait Studio." She looked at the floor and shook her head. "Somehow I got stuck. I'd planned to go back to school for my masters after a year or two. Not sure if I'm interested in continuing my education anymore. Now my goal is to open my own studio. I would also like to travel. Maybe do travel blogging and photography." She shrugged. "Whatever I do, I won't be in Diamond much longer. I don't work for Melody anymore."

Disappointment jolted Ian. "What? Why? You're moving?" He realized his reaction was over-the-top, considering he barely knew Everly.

At first, she looked caught off guard by all the questions, but then she smiled. "I love Diamond, but there is only room for one photographer in a town this size."

He couldn't argue.

"Good for you, Everly," Dad said. "You'll make it just fine on your own. So, are you married or have kids?"

"Dad," Ian said. "Stop interrogating her. She came out here for some peace and quiet." They all looked toward the bedroom door where moans and screams transpired from.

"It's fine," Everly said. "No significant other. No kids."

Ian was secretly grateful for his dad's probing questions. He was even more grateful for Everly's answers. She was available.

"This is the first birth I've ever attended." She scrunched her nose and shivered.

Ian hadn't thought about the fact Everly could be uncomfortable witnessing his sister give birth. He just thought of it as girl stuff. She actually looked a bit pale. "Can I get you a sparkling water or a Coke?"

"A sparkling water would be fantastic."

Ian went to the kitchen. "Sure, son. I'll have a Coke. Thanks for asking," his dad called.

Oops. "Sure thing, Dad."

In the kitchen, Ian checked his phone notifications. There was an email about the job out in California. He read the first line.

Congratulations ...

He went to the living room and doled out drinks, mulling over the option of accepting the job. The work seemed to be exactly what he was looking for, and the pay was more than he had been hoping for. The stumbling block was disappointing family—especially Mom—by moving so far away.

"Thanks, Ian." Everly took her drink and returned to the labor suite.

"You okay, son? Why the hefty sigh?"

He sat on the couch. "I didn't realize I'd ..." *Why not run it by Dad first?* "I got a job offer in San Francisco. Just read the email."

"That's great, son. Why so glum about it?" Dad looked perplexed.

"It's all the way across the country."

"California is beautiful. Of course it's crowded, and your commute would likely be much longer than it is here in Diamond. You don't have to accept the offer if you'd rather not move out there."

"I *do* want to move out there." He filled his dad in on the specifics of the job. "The work practically seems tailor-made to suit my abilities. It's just ... I dread breaking the news to Mom."

"Is that the hold-up, son?" Dad bellowed a hearty laugh, then leaned forward and slapped a hand on Ian's knee. "Your mother will be thrilled."

"She will?"

"The woman has been stressing out, wondering how she'll have time to help Nadia with the baby and still keep your fridge stocked and your house cleaned."

"Are you serious?"

Dad nodded. "I've been telling her you're a grown man, perfectly capable of caring for yourself. She thought you'd feel bad if she stopped doting on you. And she's afraid you'll starve. Says you never cook for yourself."

"Because I don't have to. I can hardly eat all the food Mom makes me before it goes bad."

"Son, Mom will be proud of you."

What a relief. Truth be told, now there was another lady he didn't want to move away from—the cute photographer. They had started out on the wrong foot, but now he was gaga-eyed over her.

Nadia began pushing shortly after midnight. If Everly had thought the labor looked unbearable, this part was worse. She found herself Lamaze breathing along with

Nadia, reminding herself it would be over soon, and it would all be worth it. She'd earn a paycheck and more photos to add to her portfolio. Just a few more pushes.

"The head is crowning," Yvette said. "Your daughter is almost here."

Everly sat on the edge of the bed with her camera poised at Nadia in the blow-up pool. Her fingers ached from holding the camera so many hours. She had captured tender moments between husband and wife and mother and daughter in addition to great shots of Ian and his dad pacing the hallways, praying, listening at the closed door, and devouring pizza. But this was the moment she had been waiting to memorialize. The baby's entrance into the world, breathing her first breath, being held by her parents for the first time.

The mid-wife, a woman named Estafani who had reportedly assisted with three hundred and sixty-two births in her career, reached into the bath water. "The head is out," she said. "The shoulder is stuck." Concern tinged her voice. Nadia screamed at an ear-piercing, other-worldly decibel, and pushed.

Click, click, click, click. Everly snapped a series of pictures.

"There she is," Yvette said, removing her glasses to wipe tears from her face. "My granddaughter."

Everly moved into position to view the baby being lifted from the water. Estafani laid the tiny human on Nadia's chest. *Click, click, click, click.* Then Estafani showed Nadia's husband how to cut the cord. *Click, click, click.* A few precious moments later, Yvette wrapped the baby in a blanket. The birth was just as beautiful as everyone had made it out to be. Everly was blessed to have played a part.

Estafani hunched over the side of the tub. "Nadia, I need you to push one more time."

What was happening? Were there twins? Everly angled her camera and held her breath as Nadia pushed. How exciting! Surprise twins!

"Almost there," Estafani said as Nadia tucked her chin to her chest and pushed. "Perfect. You did it." Estafani heaved a thing that was definitely not a baby into a bowl. "All done. The placenta is out."

Everly's stomach spun itself into a knot, and she grew lightheaded. She turned away and blinked her eyes, struggling to focus. Voices in the room became muffled. Everly heard someone say, "The photographer's going down."

Everly woke, drenched in perspiration and suffering a throbbing left shoulder. A cool, wet washcloth draped across her forehead. "Are you okay?" Everly pried her eyes open to see Ian's face, creased in worry, hovering over her. The baby was crying somewhere behind her.

"I think so. What happened?" Everly pulled herself to a sitting position and leaned back against the foot of Nadia's bed.

"You fainted. Sit here a minute. I'll get you a ginger ale."

She wouldn't be going anywhere even if she wanted to—which she did. Wetness seeped into her pant legs from the pool her feet were abutting. *Eew.* That water was nasty, and now it was soaking into her pants. Thank goodness her camera was dry and intact, hanging from her neck.

Ian walked in, crouched next to her, and handed her a can. "How're you feeling?"

She took a sip of the cold pop. "Embarrassed."

He smiled and blotted her temple with the wet cloth. "Trust me. If I'd have been in here, I wouldn't have lasted as long as you did." He looked her up and down—surely not a pretty sight. "Do you need to get checked out at the hospital?"

"No. I'll be fine in a minute."

Estafani stepped over her legs and made a frustrated grunt. "Ian, please help her out of here. I need to stitch Nadia up."

Everly's stomach rolled. "Please, Ian. Get me out of here." He grinned, clearly empathizing.

She tried to stand up but was too weak. Ian wrapped her arm around his shoulder and helped her up. Her body pressed into his side as he practically dragged her. Once outside the room, he swooped her into his arms and carried her to the couch. Maybe she'd misjudged this guy the night out at the rink. He wasn't such a bully after all.

He sat on the ottoman, facing her. "Thanks for giving me an excuse to leave the room. I prefer to wait until everyone is cleaned up and ... stitched up." He scrunched his nose and stuck out his tongue.

She took a drink of ginger ale. "Did you meet her yet? Your niece?"

"I saw her. She's ... you know ... all pink and wrinkly. But I'm sure she'll get cute." He smiled, revealing an adorable, subtle dimple in his right cheek.

"Yeah, all newborns look the same. Don't tell your family I said that."

He locked his closed lips with an invisible key. "I agree one hundred percent. I don't buy into the 'Oh, look, she has her father's eyes and her great-grandmother's nose business.' They just look like babies."

Everly laughed. "It's true." She pressed the pop can to her forehead to ease a headache.

Ian studied her seriously for a moment. "Do you think you'll ever have kids?"

"Ha! After witnessing that? No way." He looked disappointed by her answer. "I'm kidding. I think I'll want to be a mom someday. I'm sure the whole grotesque birth thing is different when it's your own baby. Do you think opting for a c-section is possible?"

Ian shrugged his shoulders. "No idea. But I would take that option too if I were a woman."

"Your turn. Do you want kids?"

He didn't hesitate. "Absolutely. At least a couple. Someday."

"You'll make a good dad."

"Really? What makes you say so?"

She thought of him offering her sparkling water earlier, carrying her to the couch, keeping his dad company all day while his sister gave birth. Subtle gestures, revealing his soft heart. "You're attentive. Caring. Empathetic."

"Wow. Not sure how you came to such a conclusion by my saying babies are pink and wrinkly, but I'll take it as a compliment."

"You should."

Their eyes held for a moment. Even his brown eyes were compassionate. The way he looked at her made her feel secure and special. He was giving her undivided attention as if there wasn't a newborn waiting to meet him or a family wanting to include him in their joy.

"Your color is returning." With his fingertips, he combed hair out of her eyes and tucked it behind her ear. She shivered.

"I'm better now. You can go in and meet your niece. You don't need to babysit me."

"I'm giving them a chance to bond. I'll hold her when they all conk out for the night."

"Your mom and sister must hate me." The weight of her mishap hit her like a wrecking ball slamming into a building. "I missed out on capturing some of those first moments after the baby was born. I passed out at the very moment they hired me for."

"Trust me, there will be a plenty of pictures. Everyone but Nadia and Estafani had their phones out."

"Even so, I should get in there now. You too. You need to meet your niece."

Nadia was snuggled under the bed covers, cradling a swaddled infant in the crook of her arm. The baby was looking around, taking in the view of the outside world. She made sweet little noises, turning Everly's heart to mush. *Click, click, click.*

Ian sat next to his sister. "Good work, Nadia." He stroked the newborn's cheek. "I'm your Uncle Ian." He looked at her adoringly. "What's your name?"

"Holly," Nadia said. "She needed a Christmas name, of course."

Ian nodded in approval. "She looks like a Holly." *Ha!* This coming from the man who said all babies look alike. He turned to Everly and winked, acknowledging his fib. She winked back and resisted declaring the baby had his eyes. He returned his attention back to the cooing little bundle. "It's nice to finally meet you, Holly. You get to share a birthday with Jesus." He kissed her forehead. Despite the facetious comments, the man was obviously smitten with his little niece. "Merry Christmas, little one."

The strangest vision filled Everly's mind. A vision of Everly in Nadia's place. Ian kissing her and his newborn.

Maybe she had hit her head and needed to get checked out at the hospital after all.

CHAPTER 6

At three o'clock in the morning, Ian chauffeured Everly to her apartment and helped haul photography equipment back up while she jumped in the shower, unable to stand the ickiness of damp labor-water pants a moment longer. She emerged from the bathroom feeling fresh and energized despite the late night—make that early morning—hour. Ian was sitting at the kitchen table. "Ian, I thought you would've left."

"I didn't want to leave without knowing you were okay. You could've gotten a mild concussion when you fainted. Sometimes symptoms show up later."

She ran her fingers over her scalp. No pain. "I didn't bump my head." She sat across from him at the table. "It was sweet of you to stay."

He nodded. The poor guy had bags under his eyes, but he didn't seem anxious to get home.

"Would you like something to eat or drink?"

"Yeah, sounds good."

Everly opened the fridge. At Christmastime, there were always plenty of goodies to choose from. "I've got apple pie, the Swedish meatballs and mashed potatoes I'd planned ahead to bring to my parents' house, apple cider, fudge—"

"I'll take a slice of apple pie. Did you make it?"

"As a matter of fact, I did." She dished up two slices of pie and warmed them in the microwave. "The crusts are store bought, but the rest is homemade." She plopped a dollop of whip cream on each slice. "What would you like to drink?"

"Milk, if you've got it." She poured him a glass and made herself a cup of instant decaf coffee. Jade would be appalled. Ian brought the plates to the table and Everly carried the beverages. "Do you know where you're moving to?" he asked.

Moving. Leaving Diamond. An idea she wasn't yet accustomed to. "Not yet. I didn't exactly choose to stop working for Melody. She fired me because she thinks I've been stealing her clients—like you and your sister."

He put his fork down, mid-way to his mouth. "That's not true."

"Honestly, this is the push I needed to start my own business. I got the experience I came here for. I'm as ready as I'll ever be. But now ... let's just say, fainting on the job wasn't a big confidence builder." She stuffed a forkful of pie in her mouth.

"Someday you'll look back and laugh." He chuckled. The melodious sound hushed her anxieties.

"Too early for me to see the humor."

He gulped milk, leaving behind half a milk mustache. Because it was so cute; she didn't tell him. "Since we're being honest," he said. "I have news for you." He heaved a massive sigh.

Oh no. "You're married?"

"Nope. Never been." He studied the poinsettia on the countertop a moment before continuing. "I was offered a job in San Francisco."

Whoa. Thousands of miles away. Just when she was warming up to him. "That's ... amazing. I've always wanted to visit San Francisco."

He licked the milk from his top lip. "Come to San Francisco." He looked as shocked hearing the words come from his mouth as she was. "I mean, since you plan to move anyway, and you love experiencing new places. We can both get a fresh start out there and have a … friend to explore the city with."

"You're suggesting I move out there?" She would be suspicious he was a creepy abductor type if she hadn't observed him with his family and been on the receiving end of his compassion.

"Why not? We'd get our own places, of course."

She was too shocked to respond. He could not be serious.

He slit the air with a wave of his hand, nixing his suggestion. "It's a crazy idea. It … it just sprang to mind."

"Yeah. It *is* crazy." So why was she considering it? "San Francisco," she said pensively, picturing the city—the Golden Gate Bridge, the steep hills, the cable cars—and imagining herself there. "Isn't it expensive out there?"

"That's what I've heard. Let's look it up." They poured over her laptop for a couple hours. Soon they had a list of possible housing opportunities at least equaling the space of her studio in Diamond, though they costed significantly more. Professional photographers in the area charged twice the amount per sitting fee as Melody's Portrait Studio. The numbers equaled out enough. "What do you think?"

Hmm. Could she see herself as a Californian? Adapt to crowded cities and bustling traffic? Swap lake life for ocean views? Not a bad compromise. Long snowy winters for occasional mountain flurries? Yep. "I could become a Cali-girl."

His eyebrows lifted. "Really?"

"Don't look so surprised. This was your crazy idea." But it felt right. After being complacent in her job far too long, this kind of change would be good for her. And if Ian got on her nerves, the city was big enough it'd be easy to avoid him. If he turned out to be a psycho stalker or something, she could pick up and move on to her next destination.

God, is this your plan for me? Until the Almighty blocked this path, she would assume he had paved it for her.

Everly was actually considering the move to California! Okay, so Ian had sensed a mutual attraction, but he'd feared it was wishful thinking. The enlarged print of his mug, staring at him from across the room indicated she wasn't overly disgusted by him. Yet recommending she move across country with him had been a long shot. The idea had flown from his mouth before he'd given it a second thought. They were both overtired. Maybe they would come to their senses after some rest. Or not. They had barely just met, yet his fondness for her increased by the hour. Felt like a love-at-first-sight situation. Not that he'd verbalize the "L" word at this point. The unfortunate possibility remained she thought of him only in a platonic way. Like a bonehead, he had been the one to use the "friend" word earlier. He'd been kicking himself ever since.

"Everly, I don't know how serious you are about moving to California, but I really would like seeing a familiar face out there."

"Trust me. I'm more shocked than you are that I'm considering it." She gnawed at her bottom lip, mulling over the idea. "What've I got to lose? The city of San Francisco lends beautiful backdrops for photos. I'm all in." She squealed and clapped her hands.

At her declaration, he suddenly felt awake and alert as if he'd drank half a pot of coffee. His mind buzzed with planning and anticipation. "In that case, I'll accept my job offer." Everything seemed to be falling into place. So much so, Ian was sure God had orchestrated the events.

Everly jumped out of her chair and began pacing erratically. "This is so exciting! We definitely need to get together out there. It's such a big city. I'll get culture shock after living in Diamond."

"We can sightsee and explore restaurants together."

"I'd like that."

He wanted to express his desire to be more than her travel buddy. "You know, there are restaurants here in Minnesota I'd like to try too." He cleared his throat. "Everly, would you like to go out to dinner with me?"

Stopping in her tracks, she clasped her hands under her chin and smiled. "I'd love to."

Awesome. Ian was as giddy as he was in eighth grade when the cute girl in science class agreed to be his date to the homecoming dance.

"Oh, my goodness. I never opened my Christmas presents. I was planning to unwrap them last night with my family over a video call." She looked longingly at the packages under her tree.

"Would you like to open them now?"

"You read my mind." She flew over to the tree, kneeling in front of it. "Come on over." She reached for a box and began ripping the paper.

He sat beside her, mesmerized by her excitement. "Is it your family tradition to open gifts on Christmas Eve?"

"Yes." Most of her focus was on the box she held. She reached in and pulled out a beaded necklace that shimmered in the lights of the tree. "Would you fasten it for me?" She turned her back to him and lifted her hair off her neck. His fingers grazed her silky skin, momentarily fumbling the tiny clasp. "This necklace was designed and crafted by women rescued from human trafficking. My mom knows I only wear jewelry from this company." She faced him so that their knees were touching. "Look how pretty it is."

The necklace was pretty, but he couldn't take his eyes off Everly. Her eyes sparkled as much as the jewelry. He was speechless.

"Aw." She touched his arm. "I wish I had a present for you, Ian. I'm sure it's a bummer watching someone else have all the fun."

He wouldn't tell her just how much he was enjoying watching her. "I'm living vicariously through you. Besides, my family opens gifts Christmas morning. I'll have my turn."

"That makes me feel better." She unwrapped a Starbucks gift card from her brother and shook her head, giggling. "I love Henri, but he's bad at buying me gifts. He knows I'm loyal to Lakeview Brew."

"Save the Starbucks card for San Francisco."

"Good idea." She sighed, peering over her shoulder at a plant on her coffee table. "I'm going to miss Jade and Lakeview Brew. And Levi."

"We'll stop by Lakeview Brew when we come back to Minnesota for visits."

She smiled and looked up at him from under hooded eyelids. "I like how you said 'we'."

He leaned forward, placing his hands on her knees, wanting to kiss her more than he'd ever wanted to kiss a woman. "There's a gift I'd like to give you."

She leaned in, her face inches from his. "They say the best gifts are free." The tip of her tongue swept over her bottom lip, anticipating his kiss, he guessed.

"Really? Like what?" Why not have a little fun? Heighten her suspense. Though by delaying the kiss, he was torturing himself as well.

"Like God sending his Son to be our Savior. To save us by grace." He'd met his match in game-playing. "A superbly awesome, free gift."

He fell back in a fit of laughter. "I can't compete with that kind of gift."

"I'll settle for ... a kiss."

After composing himself, he lifted his hand to the nape of her neck and pulled her to him. Her lips were softer than he'd imagined and tasted of apple. When they separated, her eyes remained closed. He took advantage of the opportunity to shamelessly admire her beautiful face.

"San Francisco will be fun," she said.

"I agree." He kissed her again.

He restrained himself from making out with her long enough to allow her to unwrap the remaining presents. They'd have plenty of time together both here in Diamond and later in California.

EPILOGUE

"Place your seats in the upright position, and prepare for takeoff."

Ian clasped Everly's hand and kissed her knuckles. "Time for our adventure to begin."

Everly squeezed his fingers. "Goodbye, negative twenty-degree days."

"Goodbye, mosquitos."

Leaving frigid winters and pesky mosquitos behind in Minnesota was nice, but saying goodbye to the beautiful state she called home stirred an air of melancholy. Better to refocus on the journey ahead. "Hello, ocean." She couldn't wait to fill her portfolio with pictures of ocean waves colliding with craggy rocks and the sun setting over the seemingly infinite distant horizon.

"Hello, wineries."

"Good one. I second that." The airplane began taxiing down the runway. Ian leaned over her, peering out her window at the snowy night resembling the day they'd met. "I'm glad we met out at the rink that night."

"I second *that*." He leaned back in his seat and laughed. "I'd figured you were from the newspaper. I thought it must be a slow news week, so you'd settled for taking random pictures around town."

"Funny your picture landed in the newspaper after all." So much had happened between them since that night. She remembered seeing his brown eyes for the very first time and thinking his supposed fiancée was a lucky lady. Turned out, Everly was the lucky gal who'd get to gaze into those soulful eyes and be wrapped in those strong arms.

He must've been entertaining nostalgic thoughts as well, because he was staring at her adoringly, making her feel warm all over. "And to think you were in Diamond all that time," he said. "Three years."

"Somehow, we weren't bumping into each other naturally, so God decided to smash us together, whether we liked it or not."

"Smash us together." He chuckled. "I like that." He wrapped his muscular arms around her shoulders and squeezed her tight as the airplane lifted into the air. The armrest jutted into her ribs, and her lungs were getting squished.

She put her hand on his chest and pushed him away, gasping for air dramatically. "I didn't mean literally smashed together."

He sat back in his seat. "I've been meaning to ask you ... since it turns out I'm a good guy after all, can you please take down that meme from social media?"

"Are you implying *I* posted that? You think I would defile my work of art?"

"If it was at my expense, yeah. You weren't so fond of me at the time."

"Turns out I'm not as evil as you think."

"And you were fonder of me than I think?" He nudged her elbow.

"I wouldn't say that. You and your whole team steamrolled me. I was there first." Feelings of anger rose up in her chest all over again. She felt her neck and cheeks flush.

"You swear it wasn't you?"

"Cross my heart. But good luck getting it off the internet. The thing went viral."

"No kidding." He cringed.

"Take it as a compliment. You're famous. Single women's dream man."

He shook his head. "I prefer anonymity. Good thing I'm getting a fresh start in a new city."

A teenaged girl in the seat next to Ian looked him up and down. Apparently, she'd been eavesdropping. "Hey, you're the hockey player. I knew you looked familiar." She reached in her bag and pulled out her phone. "Can I get a selfie with you?" She snapped a shot before Ian had time to answer. "My friends are *not* going to believe this." She began showing a side-by-side of Ian's picture and the meme to nearby passengers.

Everly could not stop laughing no matter how hard she tried. So much for anonymity. "Sorry, everyone," she announced, struggling to rein in her laughter. "He's no longer single."

"This lady took the picture," Ian said, pointing enthusiastically at Everly. Passengers turned their phones on her, falling for Ian's plan of involving her in his misery. He patted her knee. "I didn't want these lovely people to miss a photo op with such talent." He formed a syrupy, mischievous smile.

"I'll have to add the meme to my portfolio."

"Nah. You already have a stunning portfolio, and it's about to get even better with the backdrop of the Golden Gate Bridge." He swept those alluring brown eyes over her face, landing on her mouth.

She leaned in. "I can't wait for you to be the subject of more of my photos."

His lips finally pressed hers in a spellbinding kiss. Cheers went up from the passengers around them. Still lip locked, she peeked one eye open, noting their kiss was becoming a part of many other portfolios. So be it. The people needed to know this hot hockey hunk was no longer single.

ABOUT STACY BOATMAN

Stacy Boatman, author of *What Love Looks Like: A Lake Diamond Romance* and a contributor to *Chicken Soup for the Soul: Miracles & Divine Intervention: 101 stories of Faith and Hope*, is a pediatric nurse in Saint Paul, Minnesota, where she lives with her husband, four children, and Labradoodle. An outdoor girl, she loves kayaking, downhill skiing, and running at sunset under a cotton candy-colored sky. Reading and writing preferably take place on her front porch—a cup of coffee within reach. Visit her at stacyboatman.com; Facebook: Stacy Boatman; Instagram: stacyboatmanbooks

ALMOST CHRISTMAS AGAIN

Jessie Mattis

CHAPTER 1

Grace slammed her laptop shut and let out a low growl of frustration. Never mind that she was a seventh-grade science teacher with a terrible boss, measly pay, and a pile of unrealistic expectations slapped on her plate, or that she now lived in Cleveland, Ohio, hours away from most of her family and friends in Pennsylvania. Most of her adult life had consisted of one disappointment after another, and here was yet another thing to add to the list.

Marcus Brown was getting married.

Not only was the former love-of-her-life getting married, but he was marrying Denise Thacker of all people. The very same Denise who had flaunted her parents' money in every possible way during high school and made it clear that she could have any man she wanted upon graduating college. She had made Grace miserable most of her teen years. Grace couldn't believe Denise had gotten her claws into Marcus, for as long as they both shall live.

She knew she shouldn't be this upset. After all, she was the one who broke it off with Marcus three years ago. It was her own fault she'd wasted several good years waiting for him to come around. She had looked the other way far too long as Marcus made offhand comments about Christians, laughing at them, and calling them delusional. When she'd called him out on it, he assured her he didn't mean *her*, just the other Bible-thumpers. She didn't regret her decision to end things and wished she'd done so sooner.

The holdup had been that every other thing about Marcus was just about perfect—he was handsome, caring of the less-fortunate, fun, intelligent ... other than not following God, the only thing missing, which she supposed didn't *really* matter on a large scale, was her dream of being with a man who was musical. With all of these desirable qualities, part of her held on to the hope that she and Marcus would get married and live happily ever after, but in her heart of hearts she knew that would never be the case.

When she broke up with him, he left her with the parting words, "You're so ... *responsible*." As if responsibility were a bad thing. The words had haunted her many times over the last three years.

There was no question that she didn't truly want Marcus back—she knew they would never work out. She just didn't want Denise to have him, flaunting him like a piece of her mother's jewelry. Yep, this news stung. Another growl escaped her lips, and she was glad to have her own apartment without having to explain herself to roommates.

Her eye caught sight of the small, fake table-top Christmas tree standing upright on an end table, and she felt even more depressed. Almost Christmas again, and nothing in her life had changed since last year at this time.

Grace attempted reason. She knew God had bigger plans. She just couldn't make any sense of those bigger plans, and nothing seemed to be lining up according to her plans. She was tired. *Not my will, but yours,* she silently prayed in a feeble, last-ditch effort, hoping her heart would believe her words.

She picked up her phone and scrolled through contacts until she found Joelle, her best friend from college. They hadn't seen each other since graduation nearly ten years ago when Joelle had moved to Colorado, but they spoke a few times a year, and always picked right back up where they had left off. She had a few local friends, but Joelle always seemed to understand on a deeper level than most. Grace tapped her name to place the call and waited.

"Hello?" Joelle's voice rang through the line.

"Marcus is getting married." No other information was necessary. Joelle would understand.

"Oh, Grace, I'm so sorry! Are you okay?"

"I guess."

"It's Denise, isn't it?" Joelle did get it, as Grace had known she would.

"Yes. Tell me I'm not crazy for leaving him, Joelle. I had good reasons, right?"

"You're absolutely not crazy. You need someone who loves God as much as you do, not someone who secretly thinks you're a wacko for your faith. Things would not have gone well if you'd stayed together. I'm sorry, Grace. I know it's hard."

"Thanks."

"You know what you need?" asked Joelle.

"A husband, family, and job I don't hate?"

"Well, besides all that."

"What?"

"You need to get away. You need to get out of Cleveland for a few days and separate yourself from everything."

That sounded amazing. If only it were possible. "I wish I could, but I don't have the money for something like that. At least Christmas break is almost here, and I won't have to go to work for a couple weeks. The kids are mostly great, but the principal is a monster to work for. Anyway, I have that to look forward to."

"Come here. Stay with me. I have a gazillion frequent flyer miles I've saved up from work, so all you'll need to pay for is a rental car and meals, and you'd have to pay for meals in Cleveland anyway."

"Colorado high country? In December? Thanks, but I can't risk getting snowed in at your place right before Christmas." Her mouth watered and her heart warmed just thinking of her mom's traditional Christmas Italian beef and all the homey traditions and decorations that awaited her on Christmas Day at her parents' house.

"Actually, I was just checking out the forecast this morning, and it's looking unseasonably warm. And for a tourist town, we don't get a lot of traffic in December. It'll be great—come on!"

Grace wasn't sure what to say. She didn't want to impose or make her friend go to all this trouble. On the other hand, the offer did sound like exactly what she needed right now. "Joelle, you can't be serious, making an offer like this."

"I'm as serious as Denise is about marrying Marcus."

"But you'd have to work all week, and I don't want to be in the way." Grace was sure Joelle would see the error of her offer and retract it once she pointed out the facts.

"I have vacation days to burn, and it's the end of the year. I may have to run to the office a time or two, but I should be able to make it work. Can you come next week?"

Grace did some quick calculations. It was the Monday of her last week before Christmas break. Next week would be the week before Christmas, so she would get home in enough time to visit her family in Pennsylvania for Christmas as always. Why not? She never did anything spur of the moment, and she felt new life rushing into her at just the thought.

"Okay, Joelle. If you're sure you're sure, then I'm in." She gave a little squeal, this time of excitement rather than frustration. "And thanks. I think this is exactly what I need."

"Oh, wait!" said Joelle. "I forgot—my brother Bennett is coming for most of next week too. Shoot. He won't mind if you're there, but if you want to reschedule, we can look at the week after Christmas."

Grace remembered Joelle's older brother, Bennett. She had met him years ago when she and Joelle were in college. She didn't know much about him other than he'd gotten married eight or nine years ago. She really wanted this trip to happen as soon as possible and supposed there was no harm in Bennett being there since he was spoken for and all. There would be no pressure, and she could still have a week away from Cleveland in the beautiful Colorado Rockies. Clear her mind. Press the reset button on life.

"It'll be fine. Let's do it. Get me out of Cleveland, Joelle."

CHAPTER 2

The plane jostled to a stop at Denver International Airport, and in an hour Grace had retrieved her suitcase and obtained her reserved rental car—a Jeep Wrangler. She smiled. How very *Colorado*. She was thankful her flight landed early that Sunday afternoon so she wouldn't be making her hour-and-a-half drive up the mountain in the dark.

She loved driving and looked forward to the scenic trip. Cleveland had gorgeous Lake Erie, but that was nothing compared to the Rockies. Her heart grew lighter as she watched Denver fade into the rearview mirror, buildings and cars being replaced with mountain roads and wildlife.

With a cleansing exhale, she turned up John Denver on the radio for a few songs before switching to James Taylor's Christmas album. Both were so soothing against the backdrop of the snowcapped mountains in the distance, she felt like all her problems in Cleveland were a million miles away. Their voices made life feel simple.

Two mountain goat sightings later, Grace double-checked the address on her phone's navigation and pulled up along the curb of a yellow duplex situated on the outskirts of the small mountain town. She shifted to *park* as the left front door opened and Joelle came running outside.

"You're really here!" Joelle said, throwing her arms around Grace.

Grace hugged her back. "I can't believe it! How has it been ten years since we've seen each other?"

"Seems like just yesterday we were flirting with all the cute guys at the Student Union, claiming to be studying. Now you're a teacher and I'm a marketing consultant—it's like we're actual grown-ups or something!" Joelle laughed, and Grace joined in.

Grace grew serious as she stared at her longtime friend. "Thanks again for all of this. You have no idea how much I needed a change of scenery."

Joelle smiled. "Anytime, my friend. Come on—let's get you settled!"

The front door of the duplex led to the small entryway off the living room where they removed their shoes and hung up their coats. Joelle carried Grace's bag inside and up the stairs to the right, leading the way into a small, pale-blue room. Grace observed the sprinkling of tasteful Christmas decorations placed precisely throughout the house and felt a sudden excitement for the normalcy of Christmas at her parents' house next week.

"You'll stay in here. My room is just down the hall next to the bathroom. Bennett is arriving tomorrow, but I already told him he gets the couch." Joelle laughed. "He didn't mind."

Grace felt guilty for displacing her friend's brother. "I feel bad. I really don't mind taking the couch, you know."

"Nah, he understood."

"I didn't even ask before, but what is Bennett coming to town for?" asked Grace.

"He loves all the snow sports and fresh air up here. He sort of made it a tradition in recent years to come here before Christmas to take advantage of all that outdoorsy kind of stuff. And visit me, of course." She grinned. "He's a high school teacher, so his Christmas break is the same as yours."

"Oh, nice—he's a teacher too? Where does he live again?" asked Grace.

"New York."

Grace had always thought New York City would be an interesting place to visit but couldn't imagine actually living among all the nonstop hubbub. She thought she remembered Bennett's wife was named Sarah and wondered how Sarah felt about her husband's yearly trip. They must have an arrangement. She had heard of couples taking separate trips in order to retain a little bit of their independence. Anyway, it was no concern of hers. She had enough on her mind.

Joelle dropped Grace's purple suitcase on the floor next to the full-size bed. "Bennett probably won't be around all that much. He always keeps pretty busy while he's here."

"Okay. So, what are you and I going to do this week? It's only Sunday night and we have until Saturday!"

"Well, I'll have to go into the office for a few hours on Thursday morning, but other than that I should be free. And there are lots of options! The temperature is supposed to be in the forties all week, so we could do the normal things like hiking or boating. And the resort has a winter festival going on this week that we should definitely check out. I mean, I go basically every year, but since you're here, we *have* to go." Joelle grinned. "It's really not even an option to miss."

Grace laughed. "Is that so? What sort of things go on at this winter festival?"

"What *doesn't* go on at the winter festival?" Joelle laughed again. "This is a tourist town, and December is one of the few months there aren't swarms of tourists as far as the eye can see, so the locals go a little crazy and do all the fun stuff they can while they have the space. Let's see, last year there was disco snow tubing, an ice-skating show, an epic s'mores bar, dogsledding, zip-lining ... oh, and tons of food."

Grace's head began to spin at the thought of all these activities. Everything sounded fun, but she didn't have the first clue how to stand up on skis, let alone go disco snow tubing. She laughed to herself. This was her chance to relax a little and escape the predictability of her Cleveland life—take life by the horns. She was determined to step out of her comfort zone. "You'll have to teach me how to do all those things. Well, besides the s'mores bar. I think I can handle that one." Grace's eyes crinkled into laughter. "But anyway, I'm game."

Joelle rubbed her hands together. "I'm so excited you're here! Let's order a pizza. I'm sure you're exhausted after a day of traveling. We can have a relaxed evening and then start the fun first thing tomorrow. Bennett will be here after lunch."

CHAPTER 3

Grace stumbled downstairs and made a beeline for the half-full coffee pot.

"Morning, sunshine." Joelle smiled at her from the kitchen table where she sat with her laptop open.

"Morning," Grace answered back as she poured a large mug mostly full.

"Creamer's in the fridge."

"Thanks." She found the peppermint mocha creamer and poured in a generous amount, then took the seat across from Joelle.

Joelle quickly finished typing something up and closed her laptop. "Just returning some work emails. Emails have no sense of the word *vacation*, and I don't want to go back to an overflowing inbox next week."

Grace nodded, still waiting for the coffee to kick in and help her eyelids stay open.

"I hope you don't mind, but I don't really cook." Joelle looked at her with an apologetic squint. "I'm more of a take-out person."

Grace shrugged. "Doesn't bother me. I'm tired of cooking. Eating out all week sounds perfect."

"Great. I know a perfect diner with great breakfast choices. Want to go?"

"Yep. Just give me twenty minutes."

A half-hour later, Joelle pulled her white Chevy Tahoe into the parking lot of a small diner that looked to Grace like every other diner she'd ever seen—a little run down, once painted white, but now greyish and peeling, with a flashing neon *open* sign in the window. It was hard to imagine the breakfast food here wouldn't be swimming in grease.

They walked inside, and Grace was astonished to find clusters of people standing inside the entrance and sitting on soft benches with peeling red vinyl, waiting for tables—at nine-thirty on a Monday no less.

Joelle laughed when she saw Grace's furrowed eyebrows. "You should read the online reviews. This place is a hidden gem. But you pretty much have to call ahead anywhere in this small town. Even when it's not tourist season, there are plenty of people visiting and clogging up the restaurants."

The busy hostess put Joelle's name on a list and told them their wait should be no more than twenty minutes, so they huddled to one side of the door to kill time. Grace asked Joelle all about life as a big shot consulting professional, silently thanking God it wasn't her profession.

Joelle asked Grace all about life as a teacher, and she was able to share a few stories of her unpredictable students that made Joelle laugh out loud, including the one about Nathan P. locking the girls into the bathroom during a restroom break. Grace could still hear the bone-rattling, echoing screams of the junior high girls from inside the cement bathroom while they waited for a janitor to unlock the main door.

"Your life doesn't sound so bad to me," said Joelle. "At least you have a bunch of kids who love you."

"True. I guess I've just always thought by now I'd have a husband and kids of my own to love me. There's not a single eligible bachelor in the greater Cleveland area." Grace sighed before determining to shift the mood. "But now's not the time for a pity party. I'm in the Rocky Mountains, for goodness sake!"

Joelle's attention wasn't diverted so easily. Grace knew Joelle had no interest in marriage or a family herself right now, but she apparently thought it was fun to dream with Grace. She leaned her elbow on the wall with her head leaning onto her fist. "Let's see. He's got to be smart, loving, kind, and handsome."

Grace picked it up from there. "And he's got to love Jesus and make me laugh. No budging on those two."

Joelle nodded as the hostess called them to a small booth against a window looking out across the parking lot and handed them two menus.

"Your server will be with you soon. Enjoy your meal," said the hostess before returning to her station.

Grace's stomach wasn't really in the mood for diner food, and she was starting to question Joelle's usually exquisite taste. She opened her menu, and her eyes widened as she scanned the options—fried egg and cranberry feta breakfast salad. Berry quinoa salad with mint. Smoked salmon breakfast tacos. Roasted tomato caprese frittata.

A small box on the side of the menu listed traditional breakfast fare, but Grace felt like she was in breakfast heaven just imagining the featured dishes. She glanced up at Joelle who was watching her with a smile.

"Surprise," she said. "And the head chef is a friend of mine. His name is Ethan, and he makes the best breakfast salads you'll ever find. Each one is seriously like a work of art."

Grace wasn't sure she had ever even heard of breakfast salads until this morning, but she was excited to try one. The waitress returned, and Grace ordered the berry quinoa salad while Joelle ordered the breakfast tacos. "With extra sour cream, please," Joelle added, before the waitress took off.

Grace stared across the table at her friend. "Is this how all of Colorado is? Full of hidden, magical places like this?"

Joelle chuckled and shrugged. "More or less."

Ten minutes later, Grace watched a tall, muscular man with a bandana wrapped across his curly blond hair turn their way from the kitchen, balancing two dishes piled high with food. He placed their plates in front of them and greeted Joelle immediately.

"How've you been, Joelle? It's been a while since I've seen you inside this place!"

"I do a lot of pick-up orders on my way to the office these days. But I'm doing well, thanks. How are you, Ethan?"

He gave a few bobs of his head in an affirmative nod. "Can't complain. Who's your friend?" He smiled and stuck out his hand toward Grace. "I'm Ethan. I work in the kitchen."

Grace smiled shyly back at him as she took in his tousled, casual look. It worked for him.

Joelle spoke up before Grace could answer. "He *runs* the kitchen, more like."

Ethan shrugged while Grace found her voice.

"It's nice to meet you, Ethan. I'm Grace, a long-time friend of Joelle's."

"Well, any friend of Joelle is a friend of mine." Ethan did a little bow in Grace's direction.

She laughed. "Thank you. And by the way, this salad looks incredible. I've seriously never been this excited for breakfast before." Her eyes sparkled.

Ethan laughed. "Well, I personally created each dish on the menu, so I hope it doesn't disappoint. But if it does, we have a money-back guarantee. Love it or leave with the same amount of money you came with." He winked.

Grace's heart pounded a little harder than before.

"I'll leave you ladies to your breakfast. Good to see you, Joelle. And nice to meet you, Grace. Enjoy your food." He smiled and disappeared into the kitchen.

Joelle's eyebrows raised as she stared down her nose at Grace.

"What?" Grace decided to play innocent.

"Do I detect a bit of a flush in your cheeks?"

"Of course not."

"But Ethan is pretty good-looking, right? And nice?"

"Sure, but I'm not dating anyone who's not a Christian, remember. I'm sure there are tons of perfectly nice guys out there, but I've learned from experience I'll only be disappointed if I wade into those waters again."

Joelle's eyes turned to crescent moons as she smiled. "He plays drums for the local nondenominational church."

Grace slapped her hand to her face as her grin spread. "Of course he does. And I didn't even mention to you my perfect man must be musical too."

Joelle raised her eyebrows up and down a couple times as she laughed out loud. "Now let's eat up. I wanted to run by a couple shops with you and do lunch at this cute little café downtown before Bennett gets here.

Grace nodded and stuck a forkful of berry quinoa salad into her mouth, where it melted into pure bliss. She couldn't believe Ethan created this magical breakfast dish. She could get used to life in the mountains.

CHAPTER 4

After a busy morning, Grace was glad to be back at the duplex with her feet up. She and Joelle had enjoyed a morning of browsing some shops, enjoying a light lunch, and sipping coffee inside a cute coffee shop. The pine walls and the moose head above the door, which was decorated with a large Christmas wreath hung over one antler, had felt like tourist bait, but the coffee was good, and the people were friendly. Colorado was a whole different world from Ohio, and Grace was glad. She scrolled through TV channels and landed on a home decorating network, which she watched mindlessly as Joelle sat in the kitchen catching up on more work emails.

Grace looked up when she heard the scraping of a kitchen chair being pushed back across the laminate flooring.

"Bennett's here!" called Joelle, rushing to the front door.

Grace stood, not quite sure where to go since the couch was to be Bennett's home base. She watched Joelle pull the door open and hug her brother, who entered with a big smile and a brown duffel bag. His eyes met hers, and he placed his bag on the floor near the door before approaching with an outstretched hand.

"You must be Grace. I'm Bennett. I think we met once years ago, didn't we? It's nice to see you again." He wore a half-smile.

"Yes. It's nice to see you again too." Grace smiled and shook his hand as she took in his broad frame and made note of his piercing, copper-colored eyes that perfectly accompanied his short reddish-brown hair. A light dusting of freckles lay across his nose and cheeks, and the faint lines around his eyes proved that laughter was a regular part of his life. Her eyes found his plain gold wedding band. Why were all the good men taken? If she had a man like Bennett, she wouldn't want separate vacations. When—if—she got married, she and her husband would take all their fun trips together.

She folded her fingers together in front of her stomach. "Joelle insisted I take the guest room, but I hate to make you take the couch. Why don't I gather my things, and I'll move out here? You're her brother. You should have the spare room."

Bennett raised his hand in protest. "No, ma'am, I'll be just fine on the couch. I want you to take the room."

Joelle gave Grace an *I-told-you-so* look. "See? He insisted when I told him you were coming."

Grace threw up her hands. "Well, if you're both sure. Thank you."

Joelle plopped onto the couch, and Grace sank into a deep armchair. "What are you hoping to do this week, Bennett?"

He sat next to his sister. "I'm definitely going to get some mountain biking in. And being the week before Christmas, I assume there will be some Christmas events downtown, yes?" He looked at Joelle in question.

"Yep, lots of fun stuff going on this week," she confirmed.

Bennett glanced at the sparsely decorated room. "And, of course, we'll need to get you a Christmas tree."

Joelle waved him off. "Christmas trees are more trouble than they're worth. Real ones make a mess of the carpet, and fake ones require storage space I just don't have. Thanks anyway, but I'll be fine."

Bennett looked at Grace. "Have you ever heard of a proper American Christmas without a Christmas tree?"

"Why, no, as a matter of fact I haven't." Grace smiled as she watched Joelle shake her head.

Joelle pointed her head toward the ceiling in an exaggerated eye-roll. "Fine," she said, drawing out the word for emphasis. "I'll get a tree this year. A small one, though."

Grace clapped her hands. "Oh, that will be so much fun!"

Bennett smiled quietly at his success. Grace watched him discreetly. She knew he was two years older than his sister, and therefore her, but something about the way he carried himself made him seem even older. Wiser than most guys his age, maybe.

Joelle stood. "Well, what does everyone want to do this afternoon?"

"I don't want to interrupt your girls' week. I was thinking I might explore the area this afternoon and map out my week. You gals don't have to worry about including me. Except for the tree—I definitely want in on getting the Christmas tree." Bennett smiled.

Grace ignored the twinge of disappointment that he wouldn't be joining them in activities for the week. He was married, and of course, there were unspoken boundaries around married men.

Grace spoke up in answer to Joelle's question. "I don't care what we do this afternoon, just as long as we go back to that diner for breakfast. There are so many incredible dishes I need to try before I leave." She wouldn't mind getting another glimpse of Ethan and his blond curls again. She was on vacation, after all, and didn't want to leave any stones unturned.

Joelle eyed her knowingly. "Definitely back to the diner for breakfast."

CHAPTER 5

"I want to see at least one big wild animal while I'm here." Grace stared seriously at Joelle, who sat across from her in the booth at the steakhouse they'd chosen for dinner. "I saw mountain goats way out in the distance on the drive up, but I want to see a moose. Or a bear. Something I would never see in Ohio."

Joelle laughed. "Then let's go hiking tomorrow. We can make a day of it and then go get a Christmas tree with Bennett afterward. I normally wouldn't suggest hiking here in December, but it's been a surprisingly mild winter so far. We should take advantage of it while we can."

"Perfect!" Grace wiped barbeque sauce from the corner of her mouth. "A day of Colorado-style nature sounds amazing."

Grace took care of the bill, and before long they pulled up to Joelle's duplex. Bennett's rental truck was already parked alongside the curb. Grace and Joelle walked inside, and he lifted an arm in greeting from his place on the couch, where his eyes were glued to a survival show playing on the TV.

Joelle sat next to Bennett, and Grace took her now-usual place in the chair.

"How was your afternoon exploring?" asked Joelle.

Bennett looked up. "Oh, it was good, thanks. There are some great mountain biking trails just a few miles down the road. I think I'll rent a bike and hit those tomorrow. And I'll definitely get some snowboarding in before I leave."

"You should be worn out after a day of traveling and running around the mountains," said Joelle.

Bennett nodded, still watching the screen.

"Would you be up for getting the Christmas tree tomorrow? Maybe around four?" asked Joelle.

"For sure. What are you girls going to do tomorrow? More shopping?"

Grace grimaced at his assumption. "Actually, we're planning on doing some hiking. My new hiking boots don't have many miles on them yet, which I'm looking to remedy. And hopefully, we'll see a moose or a bear or something more interesting than white-tailed deer."

Bennett's attention suddenly left the TV. He turned to Grace with raised eyebrows. "Oh, really? I didn't peg you for an outdoorsy sort of girl."

At Grace's indignant expression, he stumbled on his words. "Sorry, I didn't mean anything by it. I just meant ... oh, never mind. No digging myself out of this hole."

Grace laughed while he fumbled for words. "No offense taken. But yes, I am an outdoorsy sort of girl, believe it or not."

"One who's not afraid to encounter a bear? Or even worse, a territorial moose?" He looked at her with an incredulous grin as if he didn't believe she knew what she was saying.

"Correct. I know how to handle myself."

Bennett gave a nod that appeared to be laced with admiration as he fingered his wedding ring.

Joelle broke into the conversation. "Bennett, do you want to join Grace and me in the morning for breakfast before we go our separate ways? We're going to that little diner on the edge of town. You and I went there for breakfast last year when you visited, remember?"

"Thanks, but no thanks. You'd just try to convince me to order a breakfast salad again." He spoke the word *salad* as if he'd just tasted something bitter. "I'll eat a salad any day of the week alongside a juicy steak, but salads should stay where they belong—as a side dish in the evening." His eyes twinkled. He seemed to be annoying his sister on purpose.

Grace laughed.

Joelle rolled her eyes at her brother and stood. "I'm sorry, Grace, but I really need to check in about some work stuff." She scrunched her forehead in apology. "Late night ice cream meet-up in the kitchen in a couple hours? I've got cookie dough."

Grace slapped her hand onto the arm rest of her chair and stared at Joelle. "Do you know who you're talking to? Cookie dough ice cream has been my favorite ever since you introduced me to it in college. You have exactly two hours before I leave you in email land and eat it all alone."

Joelle laughed and took her laptop to her room. Grace was suddenly very aware of being alone with Bennett. She was just about to excuse herself and hunt down a book to read in her room when Bennett spoke up.

"I don't mean to take over the living room. A new episode of this survival show is just starting if you want to stay. Looks like a marathon, actually." He looked up from the TV and grinned. "You never know—some of these skills might come in handy on your hike tomorrow."

If he had been anyone else, Grace would have pelted him with a throw pillow from her spot in the chair, but she wanted to avoid even toeing the line of flirting. Instead, she laughed and reminded him that the same might be said about him and his upcoming mountain biking excursion, which he quickly denied with a laugh.

Grace leaned her head into her hand, elbow perched on the armrest. "If you're sure I'm not in the way, I might stay and watch for a while—this stuff is interesting, isn't it?"

"Sure is."

She hoisted herself from the deep chair. "I'm going to grab something to drink. Do you want anything while I'm up?"

He hesitated, then glanced her way with a friendly smile. "I wouldn't mind an unsweet tea if she has any. Otherwise, water would be great. No ice. Thanks."

"No problem." She walked toward the kitchen in slight disbelief at his request. She hadn't spoken the words aloud, but those were her exact choices too—right down to the *no ice* in her second-place choice of water.

She had to get Bennett and his mesmerizing eyes off her mind immediately. Noticing a married man in that way made her feel like a horrible person. Instead, she veered her thoughts toward Ethan and his rugged mop of blond hair and began planning her breakfast order for the next morning. Hopefully, Ethan would personally deliver it to their table again. Maybe he'd even see her hiking boots and appreciate her for the outdoorsy person she was.

CHAPTER 6

"It's forty-five degrees out, and I'm sweating under my ski coat!" Grace peeled off her outer layer as she and Joelle walked into the duplex after a long day exploring. "My new hiking boots finally got a workout, but I can't believe we didn't see any interesting animals. I mean, honestly."

Joelle laughed. "Sorry, Grace. I don't understand it, either. Normally we would have seen all sorts of creatures out there. Surely you'll see something before you have to fly home in a few days."

"I'm beginning to think all this Colorado wildlife is just a myth," Grace pouted.

"Oh, come on, you can't be bummed. We're about to go get a Christmas tree, remember? The one you and Bennett forced me into? You should be happy!"

"You're right. Just let me shower real quick. I can't believe how sweaty I got."

"Okay, but we're going back into the forest, remember, so don't get too gussied up. Bennett will be back in about an hour and then we'll go." Joelle placed her purse in its spot by the microwave and immediately picked it up again. "Oh! I meant to get a Christmas tree permit while we were out! I'm going to have to run to the hardware store—they sell them there. I won't be gone long." She trotted for the door as Grace gave a wave and headed upstairs.

A hot, relaxing shower was just what Grace needed after a day of disappointment. Sure, the hike through the Rockies was gorgeous and invigorating, but she was disappointed they hadn't seen much wildlife—the one thing she was hoping for. And breakfast at the diner had been delicious, of course, but Ethan had been stuck in the kitchen, so all they got from him was a quick wave from a distance. Not exactly the romantic interaction she'd mapped out in her head last night. Things could obviously be worse, but they could certainly be better—the story of her life, it seemed.

Grace finished her shower, dressed, dried her hair, and bounded back downstairs upon hearing Joelle in the kitchen.

She stopped short when she entered and found Bennett just sitting down with a cup of Greek yogurt. "Oh, hey!" she said. "Sorry, I thought you were Joelle."

He raised his spoon in greeting as he swallowed. "Sorry, just me. We share DNA, but not quite to that extreme."

Grace chuckled and poured herself a cup of water from the Brita pitcher. Feeling awkward, she leaned against the counter on the opposite side of the small room. "How was your day mountain biking?"

"Excellent, thanks. The rental bike was way better quality than my own back home, so I'm not even sore. So far, that is." He took another large spoonful of yogurt. "I stopped at a small lake for a drink—thanks to my new filter straw I'd been wanting to try—and just sat for a while. I'm not kidding—in ten minutes of sitting quietly I saw a mama black bear and her twin cubs from across the lake, a moose, which was a little too close for comfort to tell you the truth, and a small herd of elk. It was pretty awesome. God's creation never ceases to amaze me."

Grace just stared. Why hadn't she and Joelle thought to stop and simply sit quietly instead of hiking on their merry way all day long? They had been careful not to be loud, but clearly their approach hadn't worked.

Bennett's eyebrows raised at her silence. "How was your hike? See anything interesting?"

"The hike was nice. No interesting wildlife, though. Sounds like everything was flocking your direction instead," she joked.

"Bummer," he said. "But there's always tonight."

"Yes, there's always tonight."

The front door opened, and Joelle walked inside waving a piece of paper. "We won't get very far trying to cut down a tree in the Arapaho Forest without a permit," she said. "Can't believe I nearly forgot." She looked at her watch. "It's almost four. Who wants to go chop down a tree and then order in Chinese food?"

Grace raised her hand. "I'm always up for Chinese."

"Same," said Bennett.

"Okay then, let's go. Bennett, can we take your truck? Easier to haul a tree in the bed of a truck than strap the thing to the top of my Tahoe." Joelle gazed at her brother with pleading eyes.

He smirked. "With or without the puppy dog eyes, it's not a problem," he said. "Do you have a handsaw, or do we need to go back to the hardware store?"

"As a matter of fact, I have one in the attic. Only used once, so it should be nice and sharp." Joelle laughed as she went to retrieve the saw.

Fifteen minutes later they pulled into a small parking area of the district in which their permit allowed them to search. Bennett killed the engine, and the cozy sound of Nat King Cole singing The Christmas Song disappeared too quickly. Grace eyed the sky and saw the sun lowering into the tree line. "Um, is it getting dark already?"

Joelle squinted toward the sun. "Yep. I wasn't thinking. We should have come earlier." She shrugged. "We still have time, though. I'm not in search of a perfect tree or anything."

Bennett led the way. "Then let's get going."

Most of the trees were far too large, so options were limited. They walked about half a mile into the forest before Joelle stopped.

"How about this one?" asked Joelle, stopping and gesturing toward a tree like Vanna White.

Grace wrinkled her nose. "It's more of a Christmas bush than a Christmas tree."

"Agreed," said Bennett. "This is not the tree for you, Sis."

Joelle threw up her hands. "Fine."

A sudden high-pitched scream pierced the otherwise silent evening, and Grace turned to look, her heart pounding. A protruding tree root caught the toe of her shoe, and she felt herself falling. She hit the ground hard, forcing the wind out of her lungs. As her breath returned, she looked around in every direction from her place on the ground, trying to identify the location of the wildcat.

Grace watched as Bennett quickly pulled a whistle to his mouth from where it hung inside his coat. He blew sharp blasts on the whistle, clapping his hands in short, loud claps, sounding almost like gunshot.

Bennett let the whistle drop from his mouth and turned to Joelle. "Raise your arms and make yourself look big," he said in a low, steady voice. He kept up the slow, loud clapping and glanced at Grace. "Are you hurt?"

She realized her ankle was throbbing terribly and groaned inwardly. Just what she needed—to become easy prey. "My ankle," she said through a grimace. "But I'll be okay."

Bennett backed up close to where she lay, nodded, and paused to listen. "Mountain lion," he explained. "I think it's gone. They don't like noise. Or humans."

Trembling, Joelle lowered her arms, eyes wide. "Thanks, Bennett. I'm so glad you're here. We should go home and make sure Grace's ankle is okay."

"It hurts, but I'll be okay. I'd hate to go through all this and wind up with no Christmas tree," said Grace. She clenched her teeth as her ankle throbbed.

Bennett looked at Joelle and shrugged, then leaned an arm down to pull Grace up into standing. "Up to you, Joelle."

Bennett placed an arm around Grace's mid-back to steady her and kept it there for support. She tried not to notice his warm, spicy scent.

Joelle gave a single nod. "Then I'm making an executive decision. We're chopping down this tree right here and then going home."

Joelle put her arm around Grace for support while Bennett settled down at the base of the small round tree with the saw. "One Christmas bush, coming right up," he said. "And then you can drag the tree back to the truck, Joelle, while I carry Grace piggy-back. Gotta keep her off that ankle."

Grace raised her eyebrows at that but was grateful for Bennett taking care of things since her twisted ankle had ruined their plans. She wished more men were so gentlemanly.

CHAPTER 7

"Should we go to the ER?" Joelle grabbed a throw pillow and stuffed it between Grace's elevated ankle and the coffee table.

"I'm no doctor," said Bennett, coming in from the kitchen with an ice pack, "and it's up to Grace, of course, but it looks to me like a pretty mild sprain. I think she'll be back to normal in a week or so." He placed a dish towel over Grace's ankle and situated the ice across it. "Fifteen minutes on, forty-five minutes off, by the way."

"Thanks, you guys," said Grace. "I think Bennett's right. I'd rather not worry about medical bills if all they're going to tell me is to stay off it, ice it, and elevate. Google can tell me that much for free. And anyway, it doesn't seem as bad as I initially feared."

Joelle shrugged. "Whatever you think is best—it's your ankle. You should probably plan on resting it most of tomorrow, though."

Grace's shoulders slumped. "I just hate to miss out on the fun. The festival starts tomorrow, right?"

"Technically," said Joelle. "But nobody really goes in the middle of the week. The good stuff starts Thursday evening. Maybe if you rest all morning, you'll be able to get out for a little while in the afternoon."

"Definitely. Okay, are you guys going to decorate this Christmas bush or what?" Grace smiled. "I'll sit here and tell you when you've missed a spot."

Bennett laughed. "Oh, great. Just what I was hoping for."

Joelle grabbed Bennett's arm. "Bennett. Do you remember Great Grandma Edna's eggnog recipe?"

"Sure I do. I make it every year, and it's pretty simple." He eyed her suspiciously. "Why do you ask?"

"I was just thinking that eggnog might help Grace feel better, not to mention make all this decorating a little more Christmassy. Don't you think?" She batted her eyes at her older brother.

Bennett rolled his eyes and laughed. "Oh, fine. Just give me twenty minutes. But only to help Grace feel better. I'm already pretty exhausted from saving your hide from a cougar."

Smiling, Joelle gave her brother a shove, sending him stumbling a few steps backward. "Sure. For Grace, then."

Grace's eyebrows raised. How had she been dragged into this sibling squabble?

Bennett turned to Grace with a grin. "I guess you got to see that wild animal like you were dreaming of, huh?"

She tilted her head in thought. "Actually, no. I definitely heard a wildcat scream, but I never saw it." She sighed quietly to herself. Wasn't that just the way life went?

Bennett retreated to the kitchen while Grace and Joelle chatted on the couch and breathed in the strong scent of pine from the fresh-cut tree, which sat bare in a tree-stand in the corner. Exactly twenty minutes later, Bennett returned with two warm mugs of thick white liquid, sprinkled lightly with what smelled like nutmeg and cinnamon.

He handed the mugs to the girls. "Go ahead. Try it."

Grace had never tasted homemade eggnog. Her family usually bought one carton from the store during the holidays, but she had never really cared for the stuff. She glanced at Bennett and then at Joelle, nervous to taste their great-grandmother's recipe and offend them if she didn't like it. She'd just have to fib. She moved the mug to her lips and sipped.

Her jaw nearly dropped. "You guys, this is actually *good!*"

Bennett grinned. "I'll try not to take offense at that statement."

"No, really, I've never liked eggnog before, but this—this tastes just like melted vanilla ice cream." She smiled and took a bigger sip. "I'm going to need this recipe for next year."

Bennett and Joelle beamed. "Gladly," said Joelle.

"Now can we get this Christmas bush decorated, please?" asked Bennett after returning from the kitchen with his own full mug.

Joelle pulled out a large box of new-looking ornaments and garland. "I haven't used these more than a time or two. There should be plenty."

The ibuprofen had kicked in so that Grace hardly noticed her sore ankle, still elevated on the coffee table. She wrapped her hands tightly around her warm mug and sighed contentedly. Who would have thought a couple weeks ago that she would be spending the week before Christmas in Colorado with her old roommate and her brother?

Everything felt so homey and cozy in this moment. She was thankful she had decided to get out of Cleveland to clear her head. She hadn't felt this at peace in a long time, and Marcus and Denise were blessedly distant memories. Now if only she could cross paths with Ethan at the festival ... then things would be just about perfect.

Bennett plopped onto the couch right next to her, and she sat a little straighter in surprise. She could smell his spicy aftershave, which lingered on his skin even now, into the evening.

"What do you think, Miss Grace?" he asked, leaning his head toward hers with his eyes on the tree.

"It looks great," she said.

He put his arm around her and gave her shoulder a squeeze before pulling his arm back and standing. He absently gave his wedding ring a little twist on his finger.

Her heart pounded, and she felt a little sick. She had been using a good amount of effort to keep her thoughts off Bennett, but this gesture, alongside his tantalizing scent, made her heart thud inside her chest beyond her control.

He looked into her eyes with what appeared to be genuine concern. "How is your ankle feeling? Can I get you anything?"

Why did he have to be so considerate? Even if she had needed something, she wouldn't have allowed herself to ask Bennett. "I'm doing fine, thanks. I'll probably head up to bed a little early."

He nodded.

"Let me help you up the stairs," offered Joelle.

"I don't mind helping you up," said Bennett.

Grace's eyes widened. Obviously, Bennett was the strongest choice, but she quickly spoke up, "Joelle can help me, but thank you, Bennett. Have a good night."

"You too."

Grace somehow pulled her pajamas on, brushed her teeth, and crawled into bed, raising her ankle on a couple spare pillows. What on earth was going on with Bennett? If he were any other guy, she would think he was flirting. Surely Bennett wouldn't do something like that. Not to her. Not to his wife.

CHAPTER 8

Grace opened her eyes and stretched. Her ankle throbbed as yesterday came flashing back to her. The cougar. Her sprained ankle ... Bennett and all his helpfulness. Ugh.

Why did he have to be so great? Well, she supposed he wasn't all that great if he *had* been flirting with her last night. She had to stop thinking about him. The first order of business was seeing how bad her ankle was today.

She slowly stood and attempted to bear weight on her sore ankle, which hurt some, but held. She sighed with relief, knowing the sprain was definitely minor, although her ankle did appear a tad swollen still, and she knew a doctor would tell her to stay off it, probably for the entire week. She would try to stay off it that day, but staying put for the rest of the week just wasn't an option.

Joelle and Bennett kindly volunteered to stay home with her for the morning. They all agreed to stay in pajamas and play board games, giving Grace a chance to prop up her foot and further evaluate Bennett's behavior toward her. The classic Christmas station they listened to made everything festive and cozy, and by lunchtime she decided Bennett hadn't been treating her any differently than he treated Joelle, and she was satisfied that last night had been all in her mind. She relaxed, loving how Bennett kept them laughing off and on all morning even while he beat them at most of the games.

After a quick lunch of sandwiches and chips, Bennett left to go skiing while Joelle and Grace piled blankets onto the couch. They turned on the TV, retrieved an ice pack for Grace's ankle, and lost themselves in Christmas movies and hot chocolate for the entire afternoon. Bennett returned at seven with two large pizzas to share and settled in for the grand finale of the movie marathon— White Christmas. They all agreed that White Christmas was a must-watch movie every single Christmas season.

Full of laughter, friendship, and excitement from simply being in the mountains, Grace fell asleep peacefully as soon as she snuggled into bed.

She woke up and blinked at the clock, which read nine o'clock. The winter festival activities officially kicked off yesterday, though the opening show wasn't until that evening.

Grace remembered Joelle saying she would have to go to the office that morning, maybe until lunchtime, but Grace couldn't stand the thought of sitting around all morning, especially after such a long day of doing nothing yesterday. Her ankle still throbbed some, but all she needed was a couple ibuprofen and she'd be all right. Thankfully, her left ankle was the injured one, so driving would be no problem.

Pushing her weight onto the handrail along the stairs, she made her way down the stairs and into the kitchen for pain medicine and coffee. She stopped abruptly upon seeing Bennett at the table with a cup of coffee and his worn-looking Bible spread open before him. Were there really still guys in the world who started their day with the Bible? The sight alone gave her hope for her future husband. Attraction to Bennett came like a wave, and she mentally scolded herself. *Not my will, but yours, Lord*, she prayed.

Feeling like an intruder, she quietly turned for the living room.

"You don't have to go," said Bennett, eyes still on the open page.

She paused for a second, not sure what to do, then he gently shut his Bible and looked up. His face was peaceful, and his eyes alive.

"I was just finishing up a chapter," he said. "Want to have a seat? I can get you some coffee if you'd like."

She slid into a chair, propping her bad ankle on the empty chair across the table. "Thanks. I guess I would take some coffee, if it's not too much trouble."

"None at all." He filled a mug. "Cream or sugar?"

"Cream, please."

He brought her the creamer and a spoon. "I'll let you do the honors. I don't want to over or under cream it for you." He smiled.

She smiled back. "Thanks." His eyes were speckled with gold. She turned her gaze toward her coffee as she stirred. She wondered if Ethan would visit the festival after breakfast hours were over at the diner.

"Joelle is at work, but I can take you out for breakfast if you'd like," Bennett offered casually.

"Oh, no thanks. I'll just have a bagel here." She couldn't eat out with a married man by herself. Why was he acting like it was no big deal? He had been married at least eight years. Did he and his wife really have that level of trust?

"Okay, then," he said. "When you're finished, do you want to head out to the festival? I wonder if the s'mores bar will be open. I could use a mid-morning snack." He grinned. "If nothing else, it's a beautiful day to sit and see the sights, even if we do have to bundle up."

Grace wasn't sure what to do. She had been planning on heading to the festival by herself, but she didn't want to be rude. And it *was* a very public event. Nobody would think anything of it to see them walking around together as friends. Although, it would certainly put her in an awkward situation if she *did* run into Ethan like she hoped. She supposed that couldn't be helped at this point. She didn't want to offend her friend's brother.

"Sure, I was thinking of heading out there this morning anyway. After my ibuprofen kicks in, that is." She opened the small pill bottle she had left in the middle of the table last night, popped the top, and swallowed two little round pills, washing them down with a swig of coffee.

"How bad is your ankle today?"

"Not terrible. I'll stop and rest here and there, but I think I can manage."

"If you say so. But speak up if the walking gets to be too much for you." Bennett gave her a look which almost seemed filled with fatherly concern. No one except her parents had been terribly concerned about her well-being in a long time. It felt nice.

Forty-five minutes later, Bennett pulled his truck into a spot in the large resort parking lot. People bustled everywhere, and Grace saw skiers and snowboarders sliding down the slopes in the distance, behind the rows of activity booths. She guessed she wouldn't be participating in any of the fun athletic activities. So much for taking life by the horns.

Moving quickly, and somewhat awkwardly, she pulled herself out of the truck and onto the pavement before Bennett could get around the truck and attempt to help, which she was certain he would do. For a New York City man, he sure was full of manners—an anomaly in a world where well-meaning men were often shut down in their chivalrous attempts. Normally, she would be pleased by the gesture of an opened door, but now her guard was firmly up.

Bennett seemed to sense she didn't want help, so he walked slowly beside her, matching her pace as she limped with each step, having refused to purchase crutches as an aid. Keeping her eyes low, she caught sight of his hands swinging at his sides.

His wedding band was nowhere to be seen.

She felt her face flush. What was going on? Did the ring slip off and get lost? Unlikely. Did he remove it on purpose? If so, why? What was he trying to pull?

They had hardly completed their slow walk across the large parking lot before Grace realized what a mistake she'd made. Out with a married man. On a sprained ankle, no less. She either had to power through and hobble along independently or submit to her throbbing ankle and let Bennett assist her, leaning on him like a crutch. Suddenly she felt disgusted with both Bennett and herself.

"Will you help me get to the nearest bench, please?" she asked in a quiet voice, surrendering to her ankle's needs.

"Of course."

She grasped Bennett's shoulder and used him like a crutch, willing herself to ignore the scent of his aftershave and the way his cheekbones curved sharply to the bottom of his barely curved nose.

They found a vacant bench and sat. She stuffed her cold hands into her coat pockets and stretched her leg along the rest of the bench, hoping some of the throbbing would subside.

She wasn't in the mood for playing games. Bennett hadn't so much as mentioned his wife since he arrived, and suddenly it angered her. On Sarah's behalf as well as her own.

"So," she said flatly. "What about your wife?"

A shadow quickly covered his once-sparkling eyes. "Sarah?"

"Yes, Sarah," she almost sneered. *Who else?*

"Are you being serious right now?" he asked. His eyebrows furrowed into a V-shape.

"Of course, I'm being serious. You haven't mentioned her once since you arrived. Tell me this—where did your wedding ring go? You've been wearing it since you got here—until today. Did it fall off? Or get lost?" Her accusation was thick, and she wasn't ready to back down. Sarah deserved better than this.

Bennett's forehead creased, and suddenly he looked worn. "And just what exactly are you trying to imply?" He glanced up at an approaching shadow behind Grace and spoke again before she could answer. "Joelle. Good, you got off early. You can take things from here. I'm going snowboarding. Alone." He stormed toward his truck without a single glance backward.

Joelle took his place on the bench and stared at Grace, clearly concerned. "What's going on, Grace? What just happened? I haven't seen my brother this upset since ..."

"Since what?" Grace snapped. She wasn't in the mood to care about Bennett's emotions.

"Since Sarah died."

Grace's jaw dropped, and she covered her gaping mouth with both hands as her heart sank past her toes. Her heart pounded in her throat.

What had she done?

CHAPTER 9

Grace slowly pulled her hands away from her mouth. Her jaw still hung slack at what had just transpired. "What ... did you just say." It wasn't a question, but a plea from the depths of her heart.

Joelle nodded slowly. "Sarah died three years ago. Cancer. She was sick for three years—half of their marriage—before she died." Joelle's eyes were as big as frisbees. "I thought you knew. How could you not have known?"

Grace's head turned back and forth slowly, mechanically. She felt stunned. "Nobody told me," she whispered. "I had no idea."

"Good morning, ladies! Is this seat taken?"

Grace's eyes shot up at the loud, husky voice and found Ethan grinning down at them. He sat next to Joelle before they could say a word. He looked at Grace. "It's Grace, isn't it? Did you hurt your ankle?"

Grace stared at Joelle, begging her with her eyes to get them out of this situation. Her frustration silently flowed out to God. *Are you serious, God? Now?*

"Hey, Ethan!" said Joelle, plastering on a fake smile. "It's so good to see you. Grace has a bit of a sprain, and we were just heading back home for her to rest. But hopefully we'll see you around soon!"

Grace rose to her good foot and gave a partially fake apologetic smile. "Bye, Ethan."

"I hope your ankle feels better soon," he said.

"Thanks."

Ethan disappeared into the crowd as Joelle helped Grace across the expansive parking lot to the Chevy Tahoe, which was still warm.

Back at the duplex, they made some hot tea and talked for hours with plenty of tears and lengthy silences mingled into the conversation. Grace hadn't realized how little she knew about Bennett, and even Joelle. Though she and Joelle had always picked right back up and continued their friendship whenever they spoke, they hadn't always gone back to fill in the information gaps. She knew that now.

Their spotty communication was why she was ignorant of Bennett's widower status and probably caused him more pain than she could ever know. She felt awful. If only he would finish snowboarding and come back to the duplex already. She needed him to understand. She needed to apologize.

Joelle looked at the clock. Two o'clock. They had entirely skipped over lunch, but neither seemed to care. "He'll probably still be a while. If I know him, he'll go until his legs are spaghetti and he literally can't stand up," she said. "Why don't you go elevate your leg and take a nap? It'll help the time pass, and I'm sure your ankle could use it."

Grace agreed. "That sounds nice."

"Need help upstairs?"

"I can do it. Thanks," said Grace.

"Oh, and Grace?"

"Yes?" She turned at the bottom of the stairs to face Joelle.

"Bennett hasn't dated anyone since Sarah passed. It's kind of a big deal if he was showing an interest in you. Just be gentle with him, okay?"

"Of course." Grace hobbled up the stairs, her mind spinning. She needed a nap to stop the mental barrage and had no trouble drifting off.

Grace opened her eyes and found the clock. Her mind felt like only a few seconds had passed since she'd lain down, but really two hours had passed. Thankfully her ankle wasn't still throbbing.

Grace sat up in bed as she heard the front door open and close. Voices wafted up the stairs, through the hallway and into her cracked-open door. She didn't mean to eavesdrop, but Joelle and Bennett were making no effort to keep their voices down.

She winced as Bennett gave Joelle his side of the story and felt ashamed of how she had snapped at him so harshly.

Grace strained to hear as she imagined him sitting at the kitchen table with tears in his eyes, the pain of losing his wife freshly awakened. Joelle comforted him in low tones.

After letting Bennett process his side of things, Joelle spoke up. "She didn't know, you know. About Sarah. She thought you were still married all along. In a way, you might appreciate her zeal—after all, she thought she was defending Sarah."

Thank you, Joelle, Grace thought, wishing she could send the message through telepathy. What a true friend she had in Joelle, even when she was probably going through her own pain, being reminded of her beloved deceased sister-in-law.

Silence followed Joelle's words to Bennett.

Grace heard a guttural sound come from Bennett, somewhere between a growl and a heavy sigh. What did that mean?

More silence.

Grace heard the coffee pot begin to brew.

"Joelle," Bennett finally said in a voice that sounded older than his age. "What do you think of Grace?"

"Would I have been friends with her for over a decade if I didn't think she was great?"

More silence.

Grace sucked in a breath as her heart sped. She bit her bottom lip as she lay frozen in place. Now what?

Now she had to go downstairs and face whatever came, though that was the last thing she wanted to do. *Not my will, but yours, Lord ... and please give me strength.*

Grace's feet shuffled as she entered the kitchen.

"Hey, there," Joelle greeted her. "How was your nap? How's your ankle?"

"Fine, thank you. And it's better than this morning, at least." Grace eyed Bennett who was staring into his coffee mug as if studying for a test.

"Coffee?" asked Joelle.

"Yes, please. But I can get it."

"It's no trouble. Just have a seat."

Grace sat across and diagonal from Bennett—the farthest she could get and still be at the same table. He didn't even glance up.

Joelle stirred some creamer into a mug of fresh coffee and placed it in front of Grace. "Here you go. Excuse me for a few minutes, but I have a couple phone calls to make."

Grace stared at Joelle in horror, silently pleading with her to stay.

Joelle gave a gentle nod as if to say, "You can do it." She grabbed her phone from the countertop and headed for her room.

Grace had no choice. She knew they needed to talk. Her jaw clenched, and she wished Bennett would speak first.

CHAPTER 10

Grace took a long sip of coffee and a deep breath. "How was snowboarding?" She hoped her voice didn't sound as shaky as it felt.

"Good." He twirled the spoon in his coffee, never taking his eyes off the mug.

Well, small talk was getting her nowhere. Grace decided to jump in with both feet. Get the conversation over with. "I'm really sorry, Bennett. I had no idea about Sarah, honest. And when I saw you suddenly weren't wearing your wedding ring ..." She trailed off, not sure where to go from there.

Bennett nodded. Finally, some sort of response.

He paused before speaking. "I understand ... now, that is, after speaking with Joelle. And I'm sorry too," he said. "I shouldn't have assumed you knew about Sarah. But since I did think you knew, I thought you were implying that I was dishonoring her memory and the relationship we once had by taking off my wedding ring three years after the fact."

Grace gasped. "Oh no, I didn't mean that at all!"

"I know that. Now." Bennett's eyes finally met hers. She was once again mesmerized by the unique color and flecks of gold that swam in his eyes. "I've worn this ring every day for most of three years. This is the first day I've taken it off in public, so I was already a little on edge—on the inside at least."

Grace nodded. She couldn't even begin to imagine the mental process he had been going through, working up to the point where he could remove the ring—the symbol of his dedication to the woman he had loved with all his heart.

Bennett cocked his head and squinted toward her. "Do you know why I took off the ring today?"

Grace's heart began to thud, though she wasn't sure why. "No. Why?"

"Remember this morning in the kitchen?" he asked.

She nodded.

"I'd just been having a conversation with God. I felt for the first time like he was releasing me from my covenant with Sarah ... allowing me to pursue a fresh start. I didn't use to believe I could ever find another girl I'd want to care for like I did my Sarah."

"Oh?" She bit her tongue, trying to let him do the talking.

He nodded, his eyes boring holes into hers. "Until I met you."

Her mouth went dry as her eyes grew wide and millions of different thoughts pounded through her brain.

"There's no pressure here, Grace. I'm not saying the Lord told me we would be together or anything like that. I don't want to scare you off. It's just that—I finally feel free to choose."

She slowly blew out an exhale. She'd spent so long trying not to focus on Bennett romantically that the freedom to now consider him made her unsure. Was this okay? Was it right? Her mind flashed replays of all the instances over the past few days when she had longed for a man with Bennett's qualities.

"I don't know if I could ever measure up to Sarah, Bennett," she heard herself say, before she even realized that concern was on her mind.

He nodded. "I can understand that worry. But believe me when I say this. I know you're not Sarah. I don't expect you to be Sarah. In fact, I don't *want* you to be just like Sarah. She was the only Sarah that I wanted, but the Lord saw fit to take her home, and now ... here we are. This—you and me—would be something entirely new."

Bennett looked away as if suddenly hearing his own words and assuming they would fall on deaf ears. His usual self-assuredness evaporated, and he looked small. Helpless.

"I know this is a lot to think about," he mumbled. "And I know this is all coming from left field to you right now. But you really don't need to spare my feelings, so please—just tell me what's on your mind."

Grace closed her eyes. This is exactly what her heart had been wanting ... being denied ... since Bennett walked in the door on Monday, just three days ago. Her heart had led her astray before and caused years of heartache and regret. She knew this wasn't a decision she could make soundly of her own accord. *Not my will but yours, oh Lord,* she begged. *Show me what to do, God. Please.*

With eyes still closed, a simple image flashed through her mind of her and Bennett on the couch, laughing and holding hands. She felt peace deep in her soul and had the strong sense that God was smiling. Approving. Blessing.

Grace opened her eyes, thankful for such an immediate answer to prayer, knowing that God didn't always speak so clearly and quickly.

Bennett sat across from her as if made from stone, waiting patiently.

She opened her mouth. "Forgive me, but I've spent the past several days seeing you as forbidden fruit." She gave a low laugh. "It's going to take a bit of a mental adjustment, but ... " She reached across the table and took his warm, rough hand in hers. She gave it a tender squeeze before pulling her hand back to her lap. "I'd love to give us a try."

A shy smile warmed her face as a broad grin stretched across his.

Grace couldn't believe the change from a couple hours ago, when she thought she had ruined everything, to now where the future seemed to teem with life and possibilities—with hope. Her small smile broadened to match Bennett's.

They both glanced up as Joelle walked in from around the doorway, arms folded across her chest, nodding in satisfaction.

Bennett shook his head. "I should've known you'd be spying the whole time. Phone calls, my foot." His grin stayed put. "Some sister."

Joelle shrugged. "As the sister, it's my job to do what needs to be done to make sure you're on the right track." She looked at Grace and winked. "And as the friend, it's my job to keep you away from cute guys like Ethan when you're so clearly meant to be with my brother. You're both welcome, by the way."

Grace chuckled. She couldn't get mad at her for eavesdropping. After all, hadn't she just overhead a conversation between Bennett and Joelle not long ago?

Joelle clapped her hands together in excitement. "Who wants to head back to the festival for some dinner and disco snow tubing?"

Bennett spoke up. "I don't think Grace should be snow tubing on that ankle of hers."

"She wouldn't be on her feet, Bennett. It's tubing, not skiing," said Joelle. "And besides, last I knew, her ankle was feeling a lot better."

"I guess so. And there is a lift to the top," added Bennett, reconsidering.

Grace sat silently, amused at the conversation about her flying through the room. Finally, Bennett and Joelle looked at her for input.

"Do they have double tubes?" she asked.

"I think so," said Bennett.

"Then I want to give it a try. My ankle really is feeling a lot better, and I'm sure everything will be just fine, with you next to me."

Bennett's eyes sparkled. "You've got it. I'll do my best to steer, and I'll be right beside you if you fall."

Grace's heart pounded in sheer joy and anticipation. "That sounds just perfect."

Joelle gave a satisfactory nod. "Awesome. Dinner first, disco snow tubing second, s'mores bar third. Sound like a plan?"

"Sounds incredible," said Grace, eyes glued to Bennett's. She didn't care a bit about her ankle. She couldn't wait to spend time with Bennett now that keeping her distance wasn't a requirement.

CHAPTER 11

Double snow tubing was exhilarating, and the flashing red and green colored disco lights against the night sky made for a festive and exciting slide down the smallest mountain run. Two turns were enough for Grace before deciding the responsible thing to do was to rest her ankle.

Bennett helped her to a bench near the s'mores bar and rubbed his hand across her back, sending warm shivers down her spine. "I appreciate a girl who's responsible and not reckless in the name of fun. There are too many girls in the world who aren't."

Grace's breath caught in her lungs as Marcus' words from years ago rang back through her mind. *You're so ... responsible.* He had nearly spat out that last word.

"Thank you, Bennett. That means more to me than you realize." Her heart warmed as she embraced who God made her to be more fully than she had in a long time. She reached up to pull her black knit hat down over her ears to shield the cold.

Joelle brought over Styrofoam cups of hot chocolate and passed them out.

"Thank you!" Grace took a long drink and let her insides warm.

"Are you doing okay, Grace? A couple friends from work are here, and I thought I might do some more snow tubing with them. But only if you don't mind."

Grace and Bennett both grinned up at Joelle. "I'll be fine with Bennett, but thanks for checking. Maybe the three of us could watch a late movie or something when we get back to the duplex," said Grace.

"Perfect." Joelle pulled her gloves back on. "Have fun, you guys!"

"You too!" called Bennett as Joelle trotted off.

Bennett turned to Grace. "You stay here, and I'll fix you the best s'more you ever had in your life."

"How can I say no to that?" Grace laughed. "But I always thought s'mores were a fall tradition. I wonder why they chose them for a Christmas festival."

"Good question. Either way, I'm not complaining." Bennett shrugged.

A moment later Bennett returned with two full plates and a stack of napkins. "Mystery solved," he said.

"What?"

"I know now how they make s'mores a Christmas treat—red and green marshmallows, red and green sprinkles, and red and green M&Ms. Just look at these and tell me they're not Christmassy." His head bobbed back as he laughed at the festive mountains of sugar on their plates.

They ate their s'mores in silence as they people-watched, then washed them down with cold hot chocolate. Grace could barely swallow the last of the sugary snack and looked forward to a bottle of water sometime in the near future.

"That was so good, I hardly care that I haven't seen any impressive wildlife yet." Grace smiled as she wiped her mouth.

Bennett chuckled. "You're the only person I know who comes to Colorado high country and can't find any wildlife." He paused. "I can't believe we only have two more days together."

"I know." Grace spoke quietly. She'd already thought of all this on the drive to the festival. To finally find the one who, so far, seemed to be her perfect match, and then to have to go back to their separate homes made her heart feel like it was being squeezed in a vise.

"I want to be honest with you, Grace. I wouldn't be willing to do the long-distance thing with anyone I couldn't imagine a future with. For you, I'm more than willing. For some reason, I feel like we've been friends forever. But the ball is in your court."

"I feel the same way, Bennett. I only want to date someone I can see possibly settling down with in the future. There's no pressure, of course, but I would love to see where this goes."

Bennett exhaled like he'd been holding his breath, and his smile grew bigger than Grace had ever seen it.

The prospect of a promising new relationship was exciting, but Grace worried a little about the distance. And part of her wondered how she would ultimately get along with someone from New York City. She was a small-town girl at heart. "Bennett?"

"Yes?"

"Do you really think we'll be okay? A seven-and-a-half-hour drive between us is a lot."

Bennett's eyebrows pinched. "Seven and a half? You live in Cleveland, right?"

"Yes."

"The drive isn't that long. It's …" He took out his phone and tapped a few buttons. "… just over two hours."

"That's impossible! Cleveland to New York City is way longer than two hours," Grace pushed back, confused.

Bennett stared at her through examining eyes and laughed. "Uh, Grace?"

She tilted her head, still attempting mental calculations.

"I don't live in the city. I live in Fredonia with less than fifteen thousand people. On the far west side of New York State."

Grace's eyes grew large, and she gave an uncharacteristic shout, ignoring the faces that turned her way. "What?

That's fantastic! Two hours—even three hours—is totally doable for weekend visits!"

"Absolutely. Whatever made you think I lived in the city?"

"Um ... I have no idea. All I knew was that you lived in New York. I guess I just assumed. Oops." She gave him a sheepish look.

Bennett shook his head and laughed. "Well, you're not the first one to make that mistake. Pretty much anyone outside New York State thinks the whole place is just one big city."

"Sorry about that. But you have no idea how glad I am."

"Oh, yes, I do. Because I'm that glad too." Bennett took off a glove, then took her hand and tugged off her glove. He laced his thick, warm fingers through hers. "This is the first hand I've held since Sarah's."

Grace winced. "Oh?" She suddenly felt self-conscious and hoped she wasn't falling short in comparison.

Bennett nodded. "To be honest, I was a little worried it would bother me on some level—emotionally, you know?"

"And?"

He squeezed her hand a little tighter. "It's definitely strange—new, I mean. In a good way."

She raised her eyebrows, amused yet understanding.

"Anyway," he said, "I think our hands are a perfect fit. And just so you know, I really am finally ready to start something new. I promise not to compare you to someone you could and should never be."

"Thank you, Bennett. I'm glad to know." Her fingers stroked his. She felt thick callouses on his fingertips and looked at him with questioning eyes.

He seemed to read her mind. "Oh, yeah. I play guitar. I actually lead worship at my church. Sorry if my fingers feel rough."

Grace sat, stunned. "You're a worship leader at your church?" She shook her head and leaned back against the bench. "Pinch me."

He laughed. "Why, exactly?"

"Bennett, you have checked every box on the imaginary boyfriend list I've had since I was young—except, I thought, being musical. You being a worship leader is the icing on the cake." She smiled and leaned into him.

"Wow, is that so?" said Bennett. "Well, I'm afraid I look better on paper than I will in real life." She could tell he wasn't joking.

Grace shook her head. "I don't expect perfection, Bennett, and I hope you don't either. I just want to take it a day at a time and see where God leads us."

"Excellent. Me too." He glanced at his phone to check the time. "Hey, they're going to light the massive Christmas tree in five minutes! Want to head over so we can get a good view? I doubt it's any Times Square, but I'll bet the tree is impressive anyhow."

A feeling Grace hadn't felt in far too many years surged through her. The Christmas Feeling—the overwhelming feeling of joy, thankfulness, and hope that made her heart pound in anticipation of whatever was next to come. "Let's do it."

Bennett suddenly froze and pointed about twenty yards away into the shadows.

Grace's eyes focused on a large animal, sauntering through the outskirts of the festival, unconcerned by all the commotion. "A moose!"

"Look at that. You finally got to see some Colorado wildlife." He grinned.

Grace's eyes shone with delight. "I guess dreams really do come true."

Bennett stood and turned so his back was facing her. "Hop on."

"Hop on?"

"You know, piggy-back style," he said. "I want to do all I can to let that ankle heal so we can fully enjoy the last two days we have together here in Colorado!"

Grace's laugh rang out like Christmas bells across the expansive festival grounds. "Whatever you say!" She had never experienced a relationship with someone so thoughtful. She climbed on with a smile that spread from one of her stocking cap's earflaps to the other. "Thanks, Bennett!" she said. *And thank you, Jesus.*

Grace wrapped her arms securely around Bennett's neck as he took off across the grounds. "Thy will be done," she whispered so quietly only she and God could hear.

ABOUT JESSIE MATTIS

Jessie Mattis is a Jesus-loving wife, homeschooling mom, and award-winning author of *Power Up*. She hopes to inspire readers to embrace the adventure of holding tight to Jesus through the difficult times as well as the good.

Jessie lives in Bloomington, Indiana, with her husband, Chip, and their three amazing kids. Road trips, reading, and laughing with family and friends are some of her favorite things, and a mug of black coffee is never far from reach.

Connect with her online at jessiemattis.com or on social media—she would love to hear from you!

THE LOST BOX

A HAMILTON HARBOR CHRISTMAS

Sally Jo Pitts

CHAPTER ONE

The Christmas train clicked a lazy cadence, winding its way through the wooded countryside to the Davenport Christmas Tree Farm. Maury Sinclair had returned to the Florida Panhandle from Los Angeles to visit her parents, who had recently moved from Tallahassee to Hamilton Harbor.

She stood beside her mother in the open-air observation car. Maury lifted her jacket collar against the chill and enjoyed breathing in the refreshing air. In LA, the air burned her eyes and tasted of diesel fuel, although the locals claimed their air had 'substance.'

"Look, you can just see the roof of the Honey Ridge Children's Home," her mother said.

Maury nodded. "The location of my college theatrical production." The home's directors and the children at Honey Ridge had assisted with her college drama assignment to write, produce, and direct a play three years ago.

"The play was outstanding, and the young police officer who volunteered was so attentive and enthusiastic. What was his name?"

"Tony Duncan."

"Tony. Yes. Have you kept in touch?"

The question hurt, though her mother had no clue. When she journeyed to LA for an audition, Tony had said,

"Write me when you get the part. Texts won't cut it." He held up his phone. "I have service issues and police regs. Long story. Just write, so I'll have your autograph when you make it big."

The role she read for went to a belly dancer instructor, but she sent Tony her contact information anyhow. He never got in touch. She had misread his thoughtfulness as attraction for her. If she hoped to become an actress, she needed to improve her ability to sense feelings and emotions.

"No, we haven't kept in touch. Besides, I've had no time for relationships, long distance or otherwise. I've been busy trying to be successful in the entertainment industry and make GG proud."

As a child, GG and GG Mama were the names Maury had given her great-grandparents, both now eighty-nine. GG Mama had a few acting roles in traveling theater when she was in her twenties. But GG was an actor of some notoriety, playing supporting roles on and off Broadway in the 1960s and 70s.

"You have made your great-grandfather proud by pursuing a career in theater."

"Pursuit isn't the same as attaining a movie role. I don't want to disappoint him."

"You did very well working with the children in the play production at Honey Ridge. Since you've been teaching children in the after-school drama program in California, why not move here and take a similar job?"

Maury elbowed her mom and smiled. "I wondered how long it would take for you to make your 'move back home' pitch."

"Seriously, you should think about it. Your dad's job sends us out of town on occasion. You could house sit while we're away, rent free, and avoid paying the outlandish LA rent."

Rent free had a nice ring. She had to hold down two jobs to keep a roof over her head in the city of actors' dreams.

She'd agreed to handle after school tutoring sessions on top of her teacher's aide job and to work back-to-back weekends waitressing for the entire month of January in order to return to Florida for Christmas.

Arriving at the tree farm, the train's bell clanged, and brakes squealed against the metal tracks. On the boardwalk at the tiny depot, a sign displayed sixteen days until Christmas. A troubadour played "O Christmas Tree" on guitar, spectators cheered, and workers in red and green knit caps waved.

"What a joyous greeting," Maury's mother said, and accepted the offered hand of the conductor to descend the steps from the train.

Maury followed. "I smell cinnamon roll and coffee temptation coming from that Davenport Snack Wagon."

Maury's mother waggled her finger at her daughter. "You may only succumb to temptation after finding the perfect tree for GG."

"But of course." Maury stepped next to a sign with instructions on obtaining a Christmas tree. She tilted her head and spoke in a deep baritone imitation of her great-grandfather. "The Christmas tree is to represent life, not the facsimile thereof. It must be fragrant, flawless, full, and above all—fresh." She finished her recitation with a twirling twist of her hand.

Her mother chuckled. "There is no question you inherited the family trait for drama."

After twenty minutes of wandering through the rows of junipers and pines looking for a Christmas tree meeting her great-grandfather's standards, Maury spotted a tree two rows over. "Mom. I think I see the perfect tree."

Beelining toward the tree, Maury caught the toe of her shoe on something hard.

"Watch out!"

She pitched forward and hit the ground. "Oomph," Maury grunted. The heels of her hands broke her graceless fall.

She saw pant legs and shoelaces running toward her. *Whump.*

Pine branches grazed Maury's shoulder as a tree hit the ground beside her.

A hand touched her arm.

"Ma'am, are you okay? I didn't see anyone around when I was cutting. I am so sorry."

Maury pulled herself up to a kneeling position. "My fault. I charged over here without looking." Her hands stung as she dusted them together, then brushed gritty sand and bits of sticky pine sap from her clothing. She smelled like a Christmas tree and dirt. "I'm okay. Just skinned hands."

"Maury?" her rescuer asked.

The sun's glare impeded Maury's sight. She held up her hand to block the rays. Tony. The man who never responded to her letter.

CHAPTER TWO

The girl with the honey-colored hair peeking from under her knit cap blinked up at him. "Hello, Tony."

"Maury, it *is* you." *Maury Sinclair. What were the odds?* "Again, I'm sorry the tree nearly fell on you." He offered his hand and pulled her up.

"No worries. Injured pride only."

Her iridescent blue eyes connected with his.

"Good to see you. It's been a long time." He made the statement general, but he knew exactly how long the time had been. The soon approaching December 28th would mark three years since she won the opportunity for a screen test in Los Angeles. He had waved goodbye expecting to hear from her but never did.

"Looks like we are destined to meet amongst Christmas trees," she said.

"Yes, it does." Years ago, when he had helped her with her play production, they had tromped through the woods with the children from Honey Ridge to find a tree. Her quick smile and ability to joke with the children had made her an instant success.

Tony reached up and extracted a small pinecone stuck in Maury's hair, and she graced him with her quirky smile.

Maury's mother joined them. "Maury, what happened. Did you fall?"

During Maury's play production, Tony had been impressed by the support Maury received from her mother and father, especially when his own parents had never encouraged him in anything.

"I got excited when I saw a tree GG might like. Careless me, I tripped on a stump and took a dive." Maury gestured toward Tony. "Mom, you remember Tony Duncan who helped me with the play at the children's home? He just saved me from getting smushed." She twisted her mouth into a cute grimace.

"Well, for goodness' sakes," Maury's mother gently squeezed his hands. "Are you still a Hamilton Harbor policeman?"

Tony smiled. "I am. Four years now."

"Maury and I were just talking about you."

He wrinkled his brow and looked at Maury.

"The train passed by the children's home," Maury said. "It brought back memories of the Christmas play."

"Ah, I see."

"Mom and Dad just moved to Meadow Lakes in Hamilton Harbor."

"Nice area. I know it well."

"We like it so far. We're at 400 Wildflower Circle. Stop by. I mean if that's something you're allowed to do."

"Checking on people goes with the territory." But stopping by with Maury there might be awkward since he had thought she would contact him but didn't. "I'll come by when things slow down after Christmas."

"Good. Maury, you spotted a perfect tree? Where is it?"

Maury pointed to a tree in the next row. "See what you think. I don't know about the other side."

Her mother went to inspect the tree.

"So," he shoved his hands in his pockets, "home for Christmas?"

She nodded. "I wanted to see Mom and Dad's new home. Grandma Carol is coming from Tallahassee, and my great-grandparents are flying down from New York. GG, that's what I call my great-grandfather, is the reason for the perfect tree search. Number one, the tree must be live. He says artificial trees have contributed to artificial sentiments and people just going through the motions at Christmas time."

"He makes a good point, and it's nice you want to please him."

Maury's mother emerged from the other side of the tree grinning. "I think this tree is the one." She flipped up her thumb.

"Would you like me to cut it for you?"

"Sure," Maury's mother said.

Maury sent her a cautionary frown.

Her mother added, "But you're busy with your own tree, and we don't want to detain you,"

Did 'not detaining' mean he should be on his way? Or did she really not want to encroach on his time? Maury's smile and surprise at seeing him had seemed genuine. "I'm picking out a tree for the church, but I'm in no rush."

"In that case, thank you. We accept the help," Maury said.

Tony stretched a piece of plastic provided by the tree farm on the ground and slipped beneath the tree. "If you push away from the cut while I'm sawing—"

"It will make the cutting easier." She finished his sentence for him.

"You remembered." *Tree cutting, she recalled but didn't remember to write? Or was not writing intentional?*

He started cutting and the pine needles on the rough branches whacked his ear. The pine scent grew stronger, and with each pass of the saw grinding at the tree trunk, Tony recalled their final conversation.

"Tony," Maury had squealed and wrapped her arms around his neck. "My acting coach entered my head shot and video footage in a contest. I won a trip to Los Angeles and a screen test. You're the first one I've told."

"Congratulations. When do you leave?"

"After Christmas."

All the air emptied from his lungs, and he found it hard to breathe. "Oh, wow. So soon. I'd hoped to take you to see the Christmas boat parade and lights in Hamilton Harbor."

"Maybe next year?"

But next year didn't materialize. He had asked her to let him hear from her, but Maury never contacted him. Out of sight, out of mind?

"The tree's leaning," Maury said, bringing him back to the present.

"Look around you for anyone who might be in the way, then let it drop."

"Coast is clear," she called out and the tree toppled.

Tony made the last few cuts to free the tree completely, then Maury helped him lift it onto their wagon.

"Tony, is this the tree for the church?" Seven-year-old Richie wearing a red worker vest walked up.

"No. I was helping these ladies. The church tree is on the ground over there." He pointed. "Maury and Mrs. Sinclair, meet my little brother with the Big Brother program, Richie Davenport."

"Davenport of Davenport Plantation?" Maury's mother asked.

Richie grinned and nodded.

"Richie's parents are Clifton and Emme Davenport, part owners in the family plantation. Richie has been learning the cut-your-own tree part of the business and knows more about these trees than I could begin to tell you."

Maury's face brightened. "Richie, you may not remember, but you helped me keep everyone's names straight at the children's home a few years ago."

Richie frowned.

Tony placed his hands on Richie's shoulders and spoke to him. "This lady put on a Christmas play. You would have only been four."

"I don't remember," he said to Maury, "but I can help you with Christmas trees now."

"What do we do with this tree already loaded on the wagon?" Maury's mother asked.

"I can pull the wagon to the barn for you," Richie said. "The tree is put on a shaker to make sure it's varmint free, then wrapped and labeled. Did you come on the train?"

"We did."

"Your tree will be loaded on a flatbed car for the return trip. Would you like to see how the train turns around?" Richie asked.

Maury's mom looked up at Tony. "He does know his stuff. I certainly would like to see the train turn around."

"Richie, go ahead and take their tree to the barn. I'll load this tree and follow you."

Richie left with Maury's mother.

"My turn to help you," Maury said. "Is this an imperfect tree?"

"How did you guess?"

"Because I've never forgotten how you looked for a tree with a flaw. I believe you said the original children's home director started the tradition?"

"One Christmas when I lived at the home, he brought in a crooked tree unable to stand straight with a huge gap in the branches. He said, 'This tree represents your imperfect lives, misshapen by troubles. And you have a choice. You can dwell on the flaws or make corrections by adding positives.'"

"Where's the flaw on this tree?"

"Help me lift it on the wagon and I'll show you." They lifted the tree and turned it over while loading it, exposing a big bare spot.

Maury's eyes lit up. "The concept has stuck with me. Adjustments made to the imperfections in the tree become blessings to our misshapen lives." She ran her hand over the pine needles surrounding the void in the branches. "I love the message. Since I've been in California, I look for a scrawny tree and cover the flaw with a replica of a positive occurrence I experienced during the year."

She'd taken up the tradition in California? Interesting. "So, how are things going for you out there?"

She huffed a sigh. "I've gathered plenty of experience in the imperfect category. No movie contracts. I seem to meet the criteria of what they are *not* looking for rather than the other way around. I hold down two jobs to pay the rent—waitress and teacher's aide." She held up her index finger. "However, if you look really fast, you'll see me closing a car door in a Ford commercial, and you can catch sight of my profile while riding horseback in a real estate ad. I filled in the imperfect gap on my scraggy Christmas tree last year with transcripts of two drama therapy classes I managed to squeeze in."

"Sounds like you stay busy," Tony said.

"I do. How about you?"

"I've settled into the Hamilton Harbor community and still volunteer at the children's home. It has its ups and downs but nothing like the fast pace in LA."

"In many ways, I envy you."

The wagon he pulled rumbled lazily on the path to the barn while they talked. Conversation came easily. Maury had made no excuses about not writing. He assumed she'd wanted to cut her past ties and move forward. But talking to her was enjoyable. Should he risk asking to see her while she was home? What was the harm? She might say no, and the rejection would not be pleasant. But not hearing from her still caused an ache anyhow.

Tony took a deep breath. "How would you like to go on a Festival of Lights walk this Thursday evening? There are over 500,000 lights on a trail along a bay cove in Hamilton Harbor. It's part of a new event I've been helping plan."

She looked up at him, her brows knit together. "It sounds wonderful, but I'm afraid I can't with my grandparents coming. I shouldn't leave them."

"Bring them along."

"I'd like nothing better, but it's not that easy. GG can't handle a lot of walking, and they may be from New York, but GG Mama, my great-grandmother, says they stay out of the cold especially at night because it takes so long for them to warm back up."

Was she using the grandparents as an excuse to not go with him, or should he come up with a solution? If he was reading her expression right, she seemed genuinely concerned. Face it, he had longed to see Maury again. Why pass up the chance?

"I learned a lesson from a girl name Maury Sinclair a few years ago. She said if there is a need to fill, all you do is look for ways to fill it and pick one."

She sputtered and wrinkled her nose. "Oh, is that all," she said, with a sarcastic lilt. "Did I really speak those words?"

He grinned and nodded.

"Sounds like something a naïve, 'wanna be' actress who was trying to be writer, producer, and director of a play might say. One thing I've learned in LA is the reason for the long list of credits on the screen at the end of a movie." She made a rolling gesture with her hand. "There might be one way selected to fill a need, but it may take a multitude of people, bells, and whistles to make it happen."

As if on cue, the engine rolled in from the opposite direction. Steam-generated smoke puffed from the smokestack while the engineer waved and clanged the bell. The flatbed cars were ready to be loaded with the passenger's wrapped and tagged trees.

Mrs. Sinclair with Richie joined them. "Our tree is being loaded now. Richie is an excellent host. Watching the train turn around was amazing. The train makes a huge three-point turn on a track shaped in a Y."

Tony's spirit was boosted with the puff of the train, the heady aroma of cut trees, and the strumming troubadour singing, "It's Beginning to Look a Lot Like Christmas." He turned to Maury. "Your slogan about filling a need is not so naïve. If a train can make a three-point turn, there's a way for your grandparents to go on the Christmas lights walk.

CHAPTER THREE

Maury's mother pulled into a parking place at Hamilton Harbor's Feldman Square.

"What a lovely place tucked off Main Street," GG Mama said from the back seat. "These old homes remind me of Academy Street Historic District in Poughkeepsie."

Maury, stuffed between her great grandparents, wiggled forward on the seat. "Tony said he'd meet us here at five o'clock. He arranged an early tour but wouldn't tell me exactly what he had worked out."

"Here only a few days and already we have the law after us, Mama." GG reached over Maury to pat his wife's knee. She cut her eyes toward Maury. "GG, the jokester."

Maury's mother peered into her rearview mirror and grinned. "I see," she said. "Look to your right."

Tony pulled a six-seater electric cart decorated with twinkling Christmas lights beside her mother's car. Tony assisted everyone out of the car, and Maury introduced her great-grandparents, Gerard and Victoria Lansing. "Aka GG and GG Mama, and this is my grandma from Tallahassee, Carol Humphries."

"Welcome to the Festival of Lights at Feldman." Tony said.

Vendors and people with craft booths were busy preparing for the evening's event. Maury breathed in mixed smells of smoky roasted corn on the cob and yeasty funnel cake dough.

GG sniffed the air. "Is this trickery?" As long as she could remember, GG had spoken in perfect, stage worthy diction. "I smell Italian sausage."

"You have a good nose. The sausage vendor is a crowd pleaser. We're set for an early tour of the Christmas lights before the trail opens to walkers at six o'clock. Our mode of transportation is equipped with blankets, battery-operated heaters, and an enclosure with transparent windows to ward off the cold." Tony pulled back the flap and helped everyone in.

Maury slid onto the front seat next to Tony. "I'm impressed."

A smile spread across his face. "I looked for ways to fill the need and picked one."

Taking in the glint in his eye, she warmed inside. "Where did you get the cart?"

"County fairgrounds. I work security for the fair when it's in town. The fairgrounds director was happy to loan the cart for the festival."

For a man who didn't bother to answer her letter or attempt to stay in touch, he'd put in a lot of effort to make her family welcome. Or was this normal Hamilton Harbor southern hospitality?

"Young man," GG said, "you have made us feel like royalty."

"It is my pleasure to welcome you to our little coastal town. I'll fill you in on some of the history then we'll head to the trail."

"Good," Maury's mom said. "Since we just moved here, all this is new to me."

Tony gave a brief history of the Hamilton and Feldman founders and backed the cart from the parking space. "My goal is for you to sit back, relax and enjoy the sights."

"I can take direction. Press on," GG said.

Maury relaxed.

Circling the square, Tony explained who occupied the house originally and the current owners. "All of the homes are combined residences and businesses now, including a combination maternity home and restaurant, interior designers, a florist, home restoration, private investigations, and the historical society."

"Restoring the houses and giving them a dual purpose is an awesome idea," Maury said.

"No question the restoration has revived the downtown area. Tonight is the official opening of the festival at the park. Saturday, Main Street will be blocked off for Christmas Magic on Main with special displays and events. The trail we will be going on leads from Feldman Square and meanders behind the homes in a cove on Harbor Bay."

At the trailhead, they entered into a world of peaceful repose through a tunnel created with strings of blue and white lights. Soft background music played "O Come all Ye Faithful." The homes sat on a bluff with sloping backyards on the left. To the right, bordering the bay, was a natural wooded area of oak trees and palmettos all highlighted in strings of lights.

Maury spoke softly, feeling almost a sense of reverence. "Amazing how lights lift and dazzle the spirit. This is beautiful, Tony."

"The project took months of planning and hours of preparation and needs to be shared."

Tony had also put a lot of time and energy into her play project three years ago. Service was his gift as evidenced by keeping her family warm so they could enjoy seeing the lights on this cold night. Too bad his service trait didn't include keeping in touch.

"We've entered an enchanted forest," GG Mama said.

"Well put." GG made an approving tap of his cane to the floorboard. "It is a production artist's dream."

Tony traveled slowly along the path of Christmas inspired scenes tucked along the wooded trail. Soft lights entwined sprawling branches of oak trees above them and lights on the palm trees swaying at the water's edge, shimmered on the bay.

With every turn of the cart, the winding trail took them deeper into a world of lights and Maury into deeper appreciation of the man sitting beside her. She glanced at him now and again, taking in his strong, clean-cut features. When they reached the end of the trail, a display released a puff of snow and "White Christmas" played.

"We don't have snow-making machines in Poughkeepsie," GG Mama said.

"Ours is manufactured by God," GG proclaimed with melodramatic flourish. "But I grant, it is cold down here in the South. Thank you, young man, for warming us inside and out."

"You are welcome," Tony said. The cart rattled across a bridge on the road that circled back to Feldman Park. "You should return in the fall for the Pumpkin Walk. The trail is filled with candlelit jack-o-lanterns carved by townspeople."

"Sounds lovely. We'll plan on it," Maury's mother said.

"Last stop is the historical society that will give you more of an appreciation of Hamilton Harbor." Tony stopped the cart and took care helping everyone out. "This house first served as a school in the early 1900s and the society has a display of Christmas traditions and decorations inside."

"I await with bated breath," GG said.

Tony looked at Maury. "Good, I think?"

Maury giggled. "Shakespeare."

Inside, they were met by a short, slender lady with gray, tight-permed hair. Her eyes took in each person as Tony made introductions, but her smile seemed forced.

"Welcome. Won't you please enjoy our Christmas display?" She motioned for the group to enter the exhibit room but tapped Tony on the shoulder and remained in the hall with clutched hands.

Maury hung back with Tony.

"Francine, you seem nervous. What's wrong?"

She gestured to the small office across the hall, and they followed her.

"I just talked to Pastor Creighton." She held her hand to her throat and stopped to catch her breath. "Loretta Huggins and all the Christmas play participants are in North Carolina caught in a snowstorm."

"Are they in danger?"

"No. They found a motel, which was difficult since all travelers were having to stop. But the axle broke on the trailer hauling all the equipment and props. They won't make it back to present the Christmas play on Saturday, which will ruin our plans for the opening of Magic on Main Street."

"The group's being held up is a shame, but we have the solution right here."

Francine's brow furrowed.

Tony nodded toward Maury. "Maury is a Christmas play expert."

With bony fingers, Francine took Maury's hands in a firm grasp. The woman's expression spoke of hearing sensational news, while Maury's stomach knotted.

"Oh, how wonderful. Please, we need your help. The tickets are sold out." Francine blinked back moisture from pale blue eyes magnified with wire rimmed glasses. How could Maury turn her down?

CHAPTER FOUR

Tony pulled into the brick drive of Maury's parents' house. A silver tinsel garland looped along the porch railing sparkled in the afternoon sun. He'd spent a restless night and miserable morning worrying about offering Maury's services without discussing it with her first. He was off work through the weekend. The least he could do was help her with the production he'd volunteered her for.

Tony was ready to go to the front door when Maury came out and hurried to the passenger side of his truck. With her golden hair pulled into a ponytail and a jacket slung over her arm, she looked the part of Christmas cheer in a red sweater emblazoned with HO HO HO. He circled the truck to open her door.

"You could have unlocked the passenger door," she said.

"Is that the way it's done in California?"

"Well ... no, it's ... I appreciate your picking me up but we're working on a project. It's not like this is a date."

Perhaps the answer to his question of why he hadn't heard from her was wrapped up in the one statement. This was a project not a date. Maybe Tony had misinterpreted the time they'd spent together working on the play three years ago. To her it had been a work project, nothing more.

"I feel the need to at least open your door as a courtesy, since I got you into this misadventure or whatever you might call it."

"GG has declared the necessity of the play 'a fortuitous happenstance.'" She stepped away from the door and made a palm-up gesture. "If you insist." Her eyes shone bright with amusement.

He opened her door and offered her his hand. She accepted. The touch of her hand and spring of her ponytail was delightful and entertaining.

He circled back around the truck and slid onto the driver's seat. "I must apologize for roping you into this job and taking you away from your family."

"Far from it. The family is excited. You know the storyline of the Christmas play I wrote. GG has agreed to play the grandpa which makes him happy. And GG Mama says she is secretly happy he'll be out of the house. 'Your GG has a bad habit of devouring Christmas cookies before we can get them decorated,'" Maury mimicked, imitating her GG Mama's voice.

Tony gave Maury a sideways glance. "Sugar cookies without the frosting? Maybe he's trying to shave off calories."

She chuckled. "No, I think it's called impatience."

Her fresh fragrance and the spirited sound of her voice sent feelings to his heart he wished he didn't have. "Your great-grandfather taking part in the play is wonderful. I spoke to Jill at the children's home last night. She said the boxes of Christmas play props are still stacked in the attic and the children are enthused about acting in the play."

"Jack and Jill are still the directors at the home?"

"Yes. Except Jack is working out of town right now."

"Jack and Jill. So cute. And hard to forget, not only their names but what they do. Taking in all those children is amazing."

"I agree. Jill said she'd drive over from Honey Town after the children came home from school and loaded the boxes on the van."

"Good. I've been replaying what I could remember of the lines in my head and picturing the set up all night."

Cranking the truck, Tony backed from the drive. "We should have time for you to meet the pastor and see the facility before Jill arrives."

"How many children are at the home now?"

"Eleven. Seven boys and four girls. Ages ranging from six to fifteen."

"I'll try to give each one a speaking part."

"Is that every actor's goal? A speaking part?"

"Pretty much. Having lines to speak is a benchmark. I auditioned last week for a speaking part. Not many words but it did require speaking with great emotion."

"Try it out on me."

"Really? It's kind of loud."

He nodded.

"Okay." She tossed her head back and shouted, 'The last one who went in there never came out!" Then she let out a horrifying shriek, jolting enough to motivate a sloth to swift action.

"Good grief." Tony shook his head and tapped his right ear. "People are going to think I'm kidnapping you."

"Sorry." She grinned. "But I warned you. I practiced the line a jillion times, putting the inflection on each word until I hit on the one I gave you."

"You nailed the emotion part. I felt anguish and fear rolled into one. What is the movie about?"

"A monster that apparently lives in a hole underground. Not exactly the kind of movie to contribute value to mankind, but I gave it a try."

"You have an agent?"

"Sort of. Donovan told me about this audition and arranged for the commercials I've been in. He works on commission but has only earned enough from my talents to feed his cat for a day, assuming the cat only eats one small-portioned meal."

"You mentioned being a teacher's aide. You work with children?"

"Elementary school age in an after-school drama program designed to occupy latchkey kids who would otherwise be unsupervised and possibly getting into trouble."

"Then you know how different children can be. One of the boys from the home, Sawyer, will definitely not be clamoring for a speaking part."

"Shy?"

"Umm. Yes, and maybe more than that. He's pretty stingy with his words. He will talk to Richie when we visit the home, but he clams up in new, unfamiliar situations."

"I'm glad you told me. I've dealt with a youngster like him. I'll try not to make him feel uncomfortable, and I do have some tricks I've used."

"Great. Here we are, New Hope Church."

Maury craned her neck, reading the marquee from the truck window. "The church is in an old movie theater?"

He thrust the truck gear into park. "Complete with amphitheater seating and a stage."

"You have my drama passion drooling."

She stepped out of the truck before he could open the door for her, but he made it to the glass front door, opening it first.

"You make me feel special."

Had she become unaccustomed to common courtesies? Maybe she still didn't want things to appear like a date. "Anyone who pitches in to produce a play on short notice *is* special."

Inside the vestibule, Maury twirled about, taking in the restored theater with maroon and gold carpet, a gilded staircase, and crystal beaded chandelier. "Wow. It's like the elaborate theaters of old."

"This theater has been a part of downtown since the early 1900s." He pointed. "What do you think of the tree that almost fell on you at the Christmas tree farm?"

She stepped over and took a closer look. "The imperfect tree looks and smells perfect."

"Children in Sunday school classes made the decorations."

Maury examined a snowflake ornament made from a paper plate and read the writing on it. "'God made everything.' I remember making snowflakes with my mom as a little girl."

Her voice was tender. He smiled inside thinking of her talent to convey a range of emotion from a horrified scream to a soft utterance. "Let's speak to the pastor. He's expecting us."

The pastor's office was at the end of the Sunday school room hallway. He knocked on the pastor's door. The door opened and Pastor Creighton peered down at them with kind eyes. He stood a good six inches taller than Tony's six feet, putting him a foot taller than Maury who tilted her head back to see Pastor's face as he introduced her.

"Please come in." He stepped back and motioned to empty chairs.

"Any update from the group stranded in North Carolina?" Tony asked.

"I spoke to Loretta. The snowplows are clearing the roads for travel. The problem is having to wait on a part to be delivered for the trailer. In the meantime, she and two others have developed bad colds. She sounds exhausted, and Maury, she asked if there was any way you could handle the play next week as well. But I certainly understand if you can't."

"Loretta must be bushed to make that request," Tony said. "She loves putting on the play." Tony turned to Maury. "We appreciate your stepping up tomorrow, but we don't want to impose on your time for the shows next week."

"I'm willing. We need to pray everything comes together," Maury said.

"Yes, let's do that right now."

The three stayed seated, joined hands, and Pastor Creighton prayed.

"Father God, you are to be glorified in this season. I join my prayer with these two who have graciously offered their time and talents. Guide their efforts to produce a play to honor Jesus's name. Lend your insight to Maury and Tony as they work together and bless the children who have agreed to participate."

A knock came to the partially open door. "We're here from the children's home." Jill peeked around the door.

Pastor raised his hands. "Amen and praise the Lord for answered prayer."

"Jill, welcome." Tony stood and opened the door wider.

"Hi, y'all. Maury, good to see you. I was so excited when Tony said you were back and will be working with the children again on your play."

"I'm looking forward to it."

"I'm parked out front. Where do you want the prop boxes unloaded?" Jill asked the pastor.

"Pull in the alley behind the building. We'll meet you at the back door."

Tony followed the pastor and Maury down the side aisle in the darkened theater to the loading doors at the rear of the stage. Outside, the children hopped out of the van in what seemed an unending stream, while Jill opened the rear doors of the van. The alleyway created a wind tunnel, pummeling them with a cold blast of winter air.

Pastor Creighton wheeled out a hand truck. "Use this for offloading."

The children laughed and chattered while helping with the boxes, except for Sawyer who was silent.

With some boxes carried and some wheeled in on the hand truck, pastor hurried everyone inside and closed the door. "The theater is hard to heat, so I like to keep as much warm air in as possible."

"Where would you like everyone?" Jill asked Maury.

"Front row seats please."

"I've placed large letter nametags on the front of each child." Jill began ushering the children down the stage stairs. When all were seated Maury took command. She was at home in the theatrical world. Tony stood off to one side.

"Hello everyone. I'm Maury Sinclair. Please call me Maury. We have been asked to perform a very important task. To put on a Christmas play," She threw up her hands in emphasis, "with one day's practice."

She proceeded to make an impromptu performance of her own.

She walked stage left and stopped. "There were Christmas play participants anxious to return to their home church where people were counting on them to perform for the Christmas Magic on Main Street event. But," she strode to center stage, "a massive blast of cold weather ensued. The storm dumped oodles of snow," she wiggled her fingers and raised her arms up and down, "blocking their way. The trailer holding their play props and equipment collapsed."

Maury plunked on the floor. The children giggled. "People in Hamiton Harbor were distraught over the bad news. What would they do? They had planned for months. Tickets for the play were sold out." She stood and paced. "They stewed and fretted." She pressed the back of her hand against her forehead and drug her feet. "Then someone," she poked her finger at Tony, "remembered a play the children at Honey Ridge Children's Home presented a few years ago. The director happened to be in town." She poked herself in the chest and feigned almost toppling over. "A concerned Hamilton Harbor citizen asked, 'Do you think you could convince the children to save Magic on Main Street?'"

Maury lifted her shoulders. "I don't know but I'll ask. How about it kids? Are you up to the challenge?"

"Yes!" they yelled.

"Are you sure?" she said, hands on hips.

"Yes!" they shouted louder.

A grin spread over Maury's face. "Then we'll get to work. Be ready to take instruction."

The children cheered. Maury's enthusiasm was contagious.

"Count on me for sound and stage lights," Pastor said. "Anything else you need from me?"

"Would you have a rocking chair and floor lamp?" Maury asked.

"In the nursery."

Maury jumped into her directing role and sent two volunteers to retrieve the chair and lamp. Turning to Tony, she asked, "Could you find the box with scripts?" Then she turned back to the pastor and continued talking music and lighting.

There were six large boxes. Contents were labeled but hard to read. Jill came on stage to help.

"I'll open the boxes. You look inside." Tony used his pocketknife to slit through tape used to secure the boxes. "Jill, Maury was asked to present the play not only tomorrow but for the shows scheduled next week. Do you think you can do it?"

"If Maury's willing. The children are out of school. Becoming actors could be just the ticket to keep them occupied. Send me the show dates and times."

"Terrific." Tony opened the last box and papers peeked out. He lifted a script for Maury to see.

"Hallelujah." Maury walked over and peered in the box. "Good, there are multiple script copies, and the cue cards are in here."

"Do you want me to pass out the scripts?" Jill asked.

"In a moment. Tony, we've taken a lot of your time. With the script copies and everyone here. You can go. Don't you have work obligations?"

"I'm off work the next couple of days. I can stay ... unless you don't want me to."

Jill gave him a swift, smarting jab to the ribs.

"Tony could unpack these boxes," Jill said. "We'll need his help."

"If you're sure, Tony. I don't want to take advantage of your kindness."

"Are you kidding? He is happy to be a part of this." Jill said, giving him a pat on the shoulder. "Aren't you?" She pressed her finger hard into his back. If he didn't respond in the affirmative, he might have a permanent indention.

Maury gave him an inquiring look. Was she testing his desire to stay, or did she really not care one way or another? He'd go for the former. Smiling, he said, "I'm sure."

Jill released the pressure on his back.

CHAPTER FIVE

Maury puffed out unexpected tension. Tony didn't take her up on the offer to leave, but at the same time, she didn't want him to miss work or only stay because he felt duty bound. After all she was a 'duty assignment' when they first met three years ago.

Outside the Honey Ridge Children's Home, she had been struggling to lift out a box of props wedged in the trunk of her Ford Fiesta. A car pulled in beside her and a tall, nice looking man carrying a gift basket and accompanied by a young boy, walked over.

"Are you the Christmas play lady?" the man asked.

"Maybe. At least I hope so. How did you know?"

"You're my duty assignment. Let me help with the box. Richie, hold this, please."

He handed the basket to the little boy and pulled the box from her car as if it contained nothing but air.

"Duty assignment?"

He tucked the box under one nicely muscled arm and flashed a 'together' sign, joining his index and middle fingers. "My boss and your professor are tight. I do as I'm directed."

His brown eyes twinkled, tipping off a kind heart that sent a spark to her own.

Maury had enjoyed working with Tony who became her instant hero but the connection she thought they shared must have been more on her side. Which made the overtures by Jill to put them together embarrassing. She didn't want to put Tony in an awkward position or make too much of his kindness.

"Go ahead and hand out scripts, Jill, and I'll assign parts."

"Do you have a job for me?" Tony asked.

Maury looked at the lines for the grandpa on the script. "A very important job. Could you pick up GG and bring him here?"

"I'd be glad to."

"Mind if I use your pen?"

He unclipped the pen from his shirt pocket and handed it her.

She wrote on the top of the script. "This is his cell phone number. He's expecting a call."

She handed him his pen and the script. "GG said he would be ready whenever we needed him. I expect he'll read over the script on your way back. He's a quick study."

"I don't doubt that about your great-grandfather. I'll call him now."

The glint in Tony's brown eyes gave her heartstrings a tug. As Tony left with the script, Pastor returned with the lamp and the two volunteers carrying the rocking chair. Maury directed their placement.

Jill came back on stage. "Just so you know, Sawyer, on the end, is phobic about speaking in groups and new situations."

"Selective mutism?"

"Yes. You've heard of it?"

"I worked alongside a child with the same diagnosis in California. Tony gave me a heads up."

"That Tony, quite a guy, don't you think?"

"I do, but we have a play to concentrate on."

"No problem." Jill winked.

Maury didn't question her competence in making the play happen. But Jill's matchmaking efforts were setting her on edge. A lot was riding on the success of this play. She didn't want to disappoint Francine, the pastor, the children, Tony, or this little town that had worked hard planning the Main Street celebration.

She pulled the cue cards from the box and handed them to Jill. "The cue cards are numbered. Write the names of the children on the cards as I assign the parts. Pastor, please unpack the boxes and set out the props."

"Everyone." She waited for talking and shoe shuffling to subside. "This play is about a grandfather who has his grandchildren gathered at his feet and he poses the question, 'What makes Christmas?' You," she pointed along the row, "will be the grandchildren, and each of you will give an answer. There is a prop for each answer. When it's your turn, you speak your response, pick up the item matching your answer, and take it to Grandpa, who will be sitting in the rocking chair. Set the item down at his feet."

"For simplicity, I am going to assign parts in the order you are sitting. Pastor, as I assign parts, will you hold up the item they will mention?"

He gave a thumbs up.

Down the line she read the names, and Pastor located and held up the props. Barry—table-top Christmas tree, Debbie—string of lights, Sammie—large star, Steve—Christmas cookie poster, Jason—angel, Meagan—wrapped gift boxes, Joey—Santa mask, Ethan—mistletoe, Lisle—music note poster. All was going well until she called out Janine's name and Christmas cards.

"I don't see any cards," Pastor said.

"There should be some giant-sized Christmas cards."

He shrugged. "I don't see any, but I have some in my office we can use. There is a Santa mask and a Santa suit. Which should Joey use?"

"The mask." Maury had forgotten. The Santa suit went with the mistletoe. The line for Ethan to speak was, 'Mistletoe and Mommy kissing Santa Claus makes Christmas.' Three years ago, Jack, in a Santa suit, and Jill were spotlighted kissing. She could change Ethan's line to just say 'mistletoe makes Christmas.'

"Lisle, when you say, 'Christmas songs make Christmas and my favorite is "Away in a Manger,"' Grandpa will give his summation. All the items point to the manger and baby Jesus as what makes Christmas."

She turned to Pastor Creighton. "At that point, you spotlight the baby in the manger, turn on the music and everyone sings "Away in a Manger.""

"I'll have the song ready to play," Pastor said.

"Most of the children learned to sing the song before they could read." Jill said. "We'll practice on the way home."

Sawyer sat at the end of the row, attentive but silent. The key to working with a youngster who became severely anxious and unable to speak was to offer patience and reassurance, not pressure. "Jill, hand me the cue cards, please."

Maury descended the stairs. "Sawyer, I'd like for you to be the prompter, which is the person who supplies lines an actor may forget during the performance. When it's time for each person to speak, hold up their card. Let me show you."

Maury walked down the steps leading into the orchestra pit and went to the conductor's podium. She placed the cue cards on the music stand and held up the first card facing the stage. "The speaker can look at the card for help in case they forget what to say. Are you okay with the job?"

Sawyer dipped his head down and up, stiffly.

Maury turned to the rest of the children. "Does everyone understand? If any of you have trouble remembering your lines, Sawyer will be holding up your lines."

"I hope my cue cards are among them." The powerful, deep-toned voice electrified the room, and all heads turned to see GG walking beside Tony down center aisle.

"Children meet Gerard Lansing, the man who will play the part of Grandpa," Maury said as she climbed the steps out of the orchestra pit.

A hush remained over the group watching GG use his cane to step onto the stage and sit in the rocking chair with the authority of Basil Rathbone. Maury had always identified her great-grandfather with the classic actor who had played Sherlock Holmes in the 1940s. GG rested his hands atop his cane, his back erect.

Patting Sawyer's shoulder, Maury said, "When you hold up the cards, you will make everyone feel comfortable."

Sawyer made eye contact and smiled. Progress.

Maury followed Tony onto the stage. "Okay, everyone, let's get ready to answer the question, what makes Christmas?"

"Wait," Jill said. "We have two more parts to assign." She held up the Santa suit jacket and the mistletoe and walked behind Tony. "Kids, who should play Santa who kisses Mommy underneath the mistletoe?"

"Tony!" the children shouted.

"And who should play Mommy kissing Santa?" GG bellowed in his deep voice, and his eyes swept to Maury.

"Maury!" came the children's enthusiastic answer.

Maury felt her face flush.

"It's Christmas, and some sacrifices have to be made," Tony said.

"Sacrifice?" Maury faked a scowl at Tony.

"Yeah, but I don't think you're gonna hate it," Ethan said.

"Good one." Joey high fived Ethan.

Tony grinned. "All for a good cause, right kids?"

The children giggled.

Maury's control was slipping. And she needed to rein in the adults first. "Jill, direct the children to the stage.

Tony, help seat the children near GG's rocking chair, allowing space for them to move and place their props at his feet."

Play practice proceeded smoothly until Ethan stood and said the 'Mommy kissing Santa Claus under the mistletoe' line. All eyes turned to Tony standing beside a prop box. Jill dangled the mistletoe over his head.

Ethan pointed to the cue card Sawyer held up. "It says on that card that I point to Mommy kissing Santa."

All eyes turned to Maury. She pushed back her inner feeling of embarrassment. She was an actress after all. What kind of actress was she if she couldn't handle a kissing scene? She responded in director mode and walked to center stage. "For this scene, Pastor, the mistletoe should be hung from the beam behind the center stage curtain which will be closed and then opened after Ethan's line. Tony, you will stand here in the Santa suit. I will be here." She pointed to the floor.

"So, kiss already," Ethan said.

Tony stood facing her. He was a good six inches taller. She raised on tiptoe and pecked a kiss on the side of his mouth.

"Aw, that was no kiss. You missed," Ethan said, slapping the side of his leg, and he slumped back to his spot on the stage. "You two need to practice."

Muffled laughter trickled among the children.

Her insides burning, Maury avoided looking at Tony. "Let's carry on with the rest of the speakers, please."

Each child read his or her lines, then GG gave his concluding eloquent oration.

"Where's the manger and baby Jesus I'm supposed to spotlight?" Pastor asked.

Embarrassment vanished and a flush of adrenaline hit Maury. No manger? No baby? The whole point of the play. "Jill, could another box be in the van?"

"No. But maybe we missed a box in the attic."

"Pastor Creighton, do you know of anyone who might have a manger large enough to spotlight on stage?"

His brows creased. "Our manger scene is ceramic and too small but there was a life size nativity at the Feldman House last year. Your best bet will be to talk to the Hens and Roosters at the downtown bistro. They should be gathered about now for their afternoon coffee and tea break."

"Hens and roosters?" Maury looked at Tony, who spoke up.

"Hens and Roosters are the names given a group of retirees who keep tabs on Hamilton Harbor and gather every morning and afternoon at the Harbor Town Bagel Bistro. Pastor is right. They will know if there's a suitable manger around."

Jill glanced at her watch. "We need to get back to the home. I'll check for the missing box, but you better locate a manger just in case. When do you want us here tomorrow?"

"Curtain is 6:30. Can you be here at 5:00 for a quick rehearsal? Have the children wear something colorful."

"Will do. And seriously, you two need to practice your part. Jack and I made that kiss way more believable three years ago." She wiggled her brows. "Let's go kids." Jill herded them out the backstage door.

GG approached. "She's right. You have a scene to work on and a manger to find. Preacher Creighton is headed to Meadow Lakes, and I'm hitching a ride."

"See you here tomorrow," Pastor said. "You two tend to business." He winked, offering his elbow to GG.

Maury and Tony were left staring after them.

CHAPTER SIX

Tony helped Maury into her puffy jacket before stepping onto the sidewalk outside the church. The sun hung low over the bay waters at the end of Main Street, casting a warm glow on the downtown buildings. Dark came early in the days before Christmas. Tony shoved his hands in his jacket pockets. "Okay to walk? The bistro is only a block away."

"March might be a better word."

He looked at Maury with her arms crossed. "Right. We were given marching orders."

"You realize the orders about the mistletoe practice wouldn't have been made a big deal if you hadn't made the crack about sacrifice."

His stomach clenched then relaxed when he saw the twinkle in her eye. "Correct me if I'm wrong. You're the actress. Kissing in a play is really no big deal, right? I mean it's acting."

"Hey, I did my part. I kissed you."

A seagull screeched overhead.

"But is that the way Mommy would have kissed Santa Claus?"

"Make fun." She nudged him with her elbow. "The production being for a good cause I won't argue with, especially if the play contributes to the spirit of Christmas in town."

"You're right, and you work well with the children. Giving Sawyer the cue card job was genius."

"A child like Sawyer needs patience. Coaxing can turn him away."

Unlike Sawyer, talk was coming easy to them. Tony enjoyed her company. At the antique shop ahead, the owner was on a ladder struggling with a Main Street Magic banner.

Tony hurried to him. "Mr. Hinkledorf, let me help you."

"Thank you, Tony."

Steadying the ladder, Tony handed him the end of the dangling sign.

The shop owner secured the banner. Hopping off the last rung, he said, "You're the best. I take back every time I ever said, 'Where's a cop when you need him.'" He chuckled and shook Tony's hand.

"Mr. Hinkledorf, this is Maury Sinclair, working on the Christmas play for the Main Street event tomorrow night."

He touched the brim of his flat cap, "Pleased to meet you."

"We're looking for a life-size manger. Do you happen to have one?" Tony asked.

"No. But check with Olivia." He nodded his head across the street.

Olivia Appleberry, seated at an outdoor bistro table with one of her bichons, waved and called across the street.

"Your banner looks good, Mr. Hinkledorf. Frank hung one at the furniture store earlier today."

"Good. We want Main Street to look glorious," he called back to her then slapped Tony on the back. "Good luck you two on your mission. And thank you, ma'am, for taking on the play."

Across the street, Tony made introductions to Olivia and pointed to the dog with the powder-puff coat. "Is this Corky?"

"Yes. Frank has Fritz at the store. Ever since Corky and Fritz wreaked havoc at the bistro's grand opening, I don't allow them here at the same time." She shook her finger, and Corky peered at her with black eyes and waggled his white fluffy tail. "Claudia has worked wonders with the boys, but I still don't trust the two of them here. I'm meeting Claudia for a coffee. Will you join us?"

"Thank you, but we are on a search for a life-size manger. Do you know of one?"

"We have a manger in the store window I'd be happy to loan you, but it's not very big. The regulars are gathered inside—they may know of one."

Tony opened the bistro door for Maury. The entry bell jingled. The afternoon tea and coffee klatch was under way. All talking stopped, and the men and women stared at Tony and Maury.

Tony, hand on Maury's waist said, "Everyone, I'd like to introduce Maury Sinclair, working to save the day since Loretta and the cast for the Christmas play are snowed in."

Dave Burbank at the rooster table stood and tipped his head toward Maury. "Howdy, Maury. Thank you for stepping up. I'm Dave." He pointed to himself. "This here is Lake Spencer and Grady Miller. We're all retired law enforcement." He hiked his thumb over his shoulder. "And those cackling women are the hens." He turned toward the ladies. "You want me to introduce you?"

"Thank you, no." Francine stood. "You can sit down. I've met Maury, and I'm the one who asked her to help. We have two sets of sisters. Mellie Tidwell and Margaret Meadows and Marigold and Petunia Hamilton."

"We appreciate your coming to our aid," Marigold said, and the others nodded.

Maury smiled. "Nice to meet all of you."

"Where's Elaine?" Tony asked, when the two-way door to the kitchen whooshed open.

"Elaine is right here."

Elaine Robinson held a tray of bagels, filling the room with yeasty fresh baked smells. She stayed busy in the bistro but always managed to look perky with her pixie haircut and quick smile.

"This must be *the* Maury I've heard so much about. You are just in time to try my latest Christmas experiment, cranberry walnut bagels."

"We love her experiment days," Dave said.

"Grab napkins, Tony, and serve our newcomer first."

Tony complied, took two bagels, and handed one to Maury.

Maury took a bite. "Mmm, very good."

"Thanks." Elaine beamed.

Tony bit into his sweet and nutty bagel. "These will be a hit for the Christmas season."

"I hope you're right. Pass these out, will you?" Elaine handed Dave the tray and motioned to Tony and Maury to sit at the counter. "I'm making coffees for Olivia and Claudia outside. Coffee or tea for you?"

"I'd love a mocha," Maury said.

Tony ordered a black coffee.

Elaine busied herself at the coffee machines. "How is the play coming along?"

"Actually, we've hit a snag, and that's why we're here." Tony swiveled around on the stool for everyone to hear him. "The play is progressing, but we ran into a problem and hope you can help."

"We'll do our best," Lake said.

"We need a life-size manger."

Lake grimaced. "I loaned my nativity materials to a church in Melrose Beach."

"We have a manger in the display window at the florist shop," Mellie said, "but it would be too small."

"The historical society has one of those life-sized nativities in a lighted frame," Francine said. "Will that work?"

"No. It should be a manger made of wood, so it can be spotlighted on stage."

The bell over the bistro entry door tinkled.

"Bells are ringing. It's that time of year." Izzie Ketterling sang as she entered.

The local interior designer wore jeans tucked into knee-high boots, a bright red sweater with matching knit cap, and dangling earrings that brushed her shoulders.

"Elaine, your dinging entry bell rings in Christmas cheer." She exaggerated drawing in every delicious smell in the room with one breath.

Elaine placed their coffees on the counter. "Sounds reasonable. Try my new Christmas bagel creation."

While Elaine went to deliver coffees outside, Dave held out the tray to Izzie. She took one and walked to the counter. "Hi, Tony. Is this our Christmas play producer?"

Maury gave Tony a puzzled look.

He shrugged. "Small town. Maury meet interior designer Izzie Ketterling, who is marrying interior designer Reed Harrison, when?"

"Valentine's Day and don't forget it." She took a bite of bagel. "Yummy," she said, then turned to Maury. "You need a life-size manger, right?"

Maury wrinkled her forehead.

"Don't freak. I'm not clairvoyant. Small town, like Tony said. Pastor Creighton called me. You need a manger kind of like this?" Izzie held up a dangling earring replica of a wooden manger for Tony and Maury to inspect.

"Yes, only a hundred times larger," Tony said.

Maury examined the earring. "You made these?"

Izzie nodded. "Out of chop sticks. I thought about using Popsicle sticks but I was afraid of too much drag on the earlobes."

"Ideas where we can find a manger?" Tony asked.

"I've been thinking on it. I talked to Claudia outside. Pete is our go-to builder, and Reed is good at construction too, but they are both out of town. Claudia offered the use of Pete's workshop and tools, but he just gave away his scrap wood."

"I have a wood pallet left from a load of sod," Lake said.

Grady set down his coffee mug. "I know how to use a skill saw."

The bistro was suddenly abuzz with ideas and offers of help. Tony's heart filled with gratitude. But the greatest thrill was the glow of wonder lighting Maury's eyes.

CHAPTER SEVEN

On stage, an involuntary shiver ran through Maury, and she rubbed her shaky hands together.

"Nervous?" GG asked.

"No. Well, maybe ... I don't know."

"If you weren't nervous and didn't have butterflies the size of Atlas moths, you'd be losing your acting zeal."

"Do you have butterflies, GG?"

"I do. Mine are of the regal Monarch variety."

Maury snickered. "You always could make me laugh."

"It is the best medicine for opening night jitters."

"Anxious anticipation might be a better description of what I am feeling. What time is it?"

"A minute later than it was when you last asked."

"I'll check the backstage door just in case it's locked."

"Right." A grin crossed his face. "I'll be right here."

GG had taken his place in the rocking chair. Opening night jitters wasn't really Maury's problem, not after last night's events, and she sensed GG knew it too. She had never experienced the coming together of community as she had last night. The wood pallet had been pulled apart and cut according to Izzie's earring pattern. Inside the workshop behind the Hamilton House, the men conferred, sawed, hammered, and sanded. Elaine furnished sandwiches and coffee. Mellie and Francine brought thermos bottles of hot chocolate. Margaret baked a batch of chocolate chip cookies. Emme Davenport furnished straw from the florist shop. Petunia and Marigold supplied a life-size baby and a hand-knitted baby blanket used in parenting classes from the maternity home.

In a little over two hours, a manger worthy of the spotlight had been completed and loaded on Tony's truck. Tony and Maury walked arm in arm one block from the workshop to a dock on Harbor Bayou.

"What an incredible experience." Maury said. "I've never seen a community come together the way you all did tonight."

"What Hamilton Harbor can't offer in big city extras, it makes up for in congeniality and caring support."

The outdoor lighting cast wavy lines of shimmery white across the dark water. Maury had hugged her arms against the chilly air.

"Cold?"

"A little."

Tony removed his jacket, wrapping it about her shoulders.

"Now you'll be cold."

"North Florida cold snaps are invigorating. Frigid evenings are especially useful for keeping me awake on boring patrol nights."

"Do uneventful nights happen often?"

"Depends. When the weather is really cold, people stay inside. But sometimes, I get more calls from people being shut up and getting on one another's nerves. Too much togetherness."

"Love hurts?"

He shrugged. "It can."

Small boats tied to another dock, bobbed in the restless water. Then he added, "Externally and internally."

Maury knew about internal hurt—like the ache she felt from misreading Tony when she had assumed he'd wanted to keep in touch. "Coming together to build the manger showed the opposite of love hurting."

They were silent a moment listening to the water lapping against the dock pilings, stirring the scent of salt encrusted ropes wound on cleats.

Tony turned to her. The soft glow of the moon highlighted his face. "We still have another task. Our play critics say we need to practice the mistletoe kiss and make it more believable. As director and actor, what do you suggest?"

She gave a slight smile, but inside, this task was way more appealing than she was showing. "First, study technique. Jack and Jill handled the mistletoe kissing in the first production. Envisioning is a method used by actors to activate the motor pathways as if actually performing the action."

"Actors reduce kissing to scientific textbook technique?"

"Mental practice can be powerful."

"Okay." Tony faced her, stood straight, arms at his sides and closed his eyes. "I am visualizing the two of us close together ... mistletoe dangles above us ... we gaze at the mistletoe ... our heads lower ... eyes meet ... we're drawn closer ..."

Maury leaned into his description.

"... The force becomes unrelenting. My arms encircle your shoulders. Your lips, ever closer, irresistible ..."

His eyes popped open.

Maury startled.

"How am I doing?"

His description had her motor pathways stirred up. "Very good."

"Now what?"

"Turn your mental instructions into actions."

He stepped close, wrapped his arms about her in a very nice embrace, leaned down, and gently touched his lips to hers. His hands caressed her shoulders. His shirt carried the faint wood scent of sawdust from the manger project. Then he deepened the kiss, sending tingles all through her. He tasted of hot chocolate ...

"Maury."

Maury snapped back to real time. Pastor Creighton motioned for her to join him at the sound and lighting control booth.

"Do you want the white or blue spotlight on the manger?" He demonstrated both. "And shouldn't the mistletoe scene be spotlighted?" He tilted his head to one side. "I believe the script calls for it."

Another matchmaker. She was not exactly opposed to the idea after their practice last night, and the scene should be spotlighted to make it effective. Her phone vibrated and she checked the screen. Her agent. "I'd better take this. Spotlight both with the white light. Excuse me."

Maury went to the vestibule breathing in the fresh pine scent from the imperfect Christmas tree.

"Donovan, hello."

"Maury, babe. Good news from the audition. They've offered you a part."

Her heart jumped. "The part that I auditioned for?"

"Well, no. They really liked your scream. They want you to play the part of the girl who is bludgeoned with a knife."

The thrill of his call faded.

"I know it's not the part you wanted, but you'd be on the credits with a well-known actor, on a big budget film, with a chance to get noticed by a highly respected director."

"Oh, wow. When does filming begin?"

"Monday."

"As in *this* Monday? The week before Christmas?"

"The park they are using for the night scenes can only be reserved that week."

"But I'm helping with a Christmas play here that runs all next week."

"Sacrifices, sweet, the name of the game. Text me when your flight is to arrive."

"Yes, of course."

She ended the conversation, stunned. She stared at the imperfect tree with popcorn and paper chains camouflaging the gap in the branches. When she turned, she came face to face with Tony.

She held up her phone. "My agent says I was offered a movie part."

"Congratulations." He sent a smile that wavered. "Looks like this is a repeat of three years ago when you were awarded the screen test opportunity. But shouldn't you be jumping around? Did I hear you say filming starts on Monday?"

"Yes, but I—"

He held up his hand. "Don't worry about us."

"I don't want to disappoint the children. I'd planned to help with the shows scheduled next week."

"They'll be disappointed," Tony said, "but you have given them excellent instructions. They'll understand."

Did last night mean nothing? Just a mental exercise? Call her silly, but she was hurt that he didn't seem to care. If this was like three years ago, she had her answer as to why she never heard from him. 'Out of sight, out of mind' could be his motto.

"You've gotta do what you've gotta do." He turned away then back again. "I came to tell you the children are here. They're waiting to start the dress rehearsal. Show starts for real in an hour. I have to put on a Santa suit."

Go or stay, do what you gotta do? She might as well leave and at least make her GG happy that she was following in his theatrical footsteps. But happy was not how she'd describe her feelings. Maury hurried down the aisle toward the stage where the children were taking their places in front of GG's rocking chair.

Sawyer scrambled down the stage stairs when he saw Maury and actually ran up to her.

"Sawyer, hello. You're looking spry today."

He uttered the first words she'd heard come from his mouth. "The missing box. I know where it is."

"Really, where?"

"Out back."

"Can you show me?"

He nodded, took her hand, and led her to the backstage door. GG, Tony, and Pastor were deep in conversation. Jill looked up, puzzled.

"Have the children take their places and practice their speaking parts with each other," Maury said to Jill. "I'll be right back."

Outside, Sawyer rushed to the railing of the backstairs landing. Because of the sloping property, the back of the buildings on Main Street were about eight feet off the ground, necessitating a flight of stairs going down to the alley. Sawyer leaned against the railing and pointed down. Wedged between a dumpster on the alley level and the side of the cement stairs was the missing box.

"The box must have fallen off the hand truck as everyone was hurrying to get in out of the cold yesterday. Thank you for showing me." She gave him a shoulder hug. His smile warmed her more than the agent's call. "You have been a great help. Are you ready for your prompter job?"

"Yes, ma'am."

Maury opened the door for him. Tony and GG were on the other side.

"We were just going to check on you," Tony said.

Sawyer stepped to one side and stared at his feet. She would not make him uncomfortable by announcing his good deed. "Sawyer. Go ahead and make sure the cue cards are in order."

He nodded and left.

"Everything okay?" Tony asked.

"More than okay. He talked to me and showed me the missing box." She wiggled her finger for Tony and GG to follow. At the rail, she pointed down. "Hidden in plain sight."

"Leave it to a child to find," GG said.

"What's amazing is you made him feel comfortable enough to tell you." Tony's eyes spoke a sincerity unlike the congratulations he gave her earlier. "I'll retrieve the box," he said, and went down the steps.

"Tony says you have some news." GG said.

"I was offered a part in a movie."

"The result of your audition?"

"Yes, but not the part I auditioned for. They like my scream."

GG pressed his lips together and nodded. "Your agent encouraged you to take the part to get your foot in the door?"

"He did."

"Which is sometimes good advice. When do they want you?"

"Monday."

"Hmm. And that would mean leaving when you've agreed to direct the shows scheduled next week."

"Yes, so—"

"You're not sure leaving is the right thing to do. What did you tell the agent?"

"I didn't really say, but he asked me to text my flight information. I'm not sure what to do. I know you have big ideas for me, and I've always loved acting and drama. The opportunity might be beneficial."

"My dear, acting encompasses a vast array of opportunities. Remember this. What is perfect for me may not be perfect for you."

She thought of GG's perfect tree compared to Tony's imperfect one.

GG rested his hand on her shoulders. "Not everyone fits the same mold or there would be only one actor and one play. How dull. But this is a decision you must make."

"How did you get so smart?"

"By living eighty-nine years. Now, my dear, I have a role to play, and you have a directing job to do."

GG stepped back inside, and Maury turned her attention back to Tony. He'd angled his upper body behind the dumpster, straining to reach the box.

"Do you need help?" she called to him.

"Just longer arms. Do you want to use the manger in this box?"

"No way. Not after the love that went into the one made last night. But I would like to have the large Christmas cards that should be in the box."

"I'll look around for something to push it out. You better get back inside."

She left him struggling to reach the box and returned backstage to deal with her own struggle. Which way should she turn?

CHAPTER EIGHT

Tony managed to tip the box slightly, making it flip further from his reach, but the different position revealed the handwritten label identifying the contents.

WHAT MAKES CHRISTMAS—MANGER/BABY JESUS.

"Truth, hidden behind a dumpster," he muttered.

The box out of reach wasn't the only concern weighing on him. Maury might be leaving. Rediscovering her had sparked new life into his spirit. Last night, he'd felt a connection to her. And it was not just a mental exercise. No acting necessary. Had she felt it too? But get real. A movie opportunity was the reason she went to California. Her last venture to LA in search of stardom led to three years with no word. If she did accept the part, would she step from his life for good?

He'd better stick to the task at hand. Time was running out. He located a metal post from a discarded shelving unit left behind the business next door, which gave his arm a three-foot extension.

Success. The box moved and he was able to push it far enough to one side and lift it out of the narrow space.

Backstage, he set the box down and opened it. The large Christmas cards were tucked in a bag. The children were all on stage and he heard Maury giving final instructions.

"Good job, everyone. Remember when you go up to Grandpa, speak and hold your Christmas item toward the audience."

Jill was observing in the wing, and he waved her over. "Tell Janine that Maury said to use these cards as her prop in place of the smaller ones."

"Will do. You better hurry and put on your Santa suit. Pastor Creighton has the spotlight set for the center stage curtain and made certain the mistletoe was secured overhead. Did you practice like I told you?"

"You want me to kiss and tell?"

She chuckled and took the bag.

Tony located the Santa suit and went to the men's dressing room. He pulled on the Santa pants made with fur-topped boots attached and strapped on the stomach padding. The arms of the fur trimmed red jacket hung below his fingertips. He rolled up the sleeves and was fastening the Velcro belt when a knock came to the door.

"Tony, you've got mail."

Jill's voice.

He opened the door. "Are the kids sending me their lists already?"

"Good idea, but no. Janine handed this to me. A letter addressed to you was mixed in with the cards. I thought you might want to see it right away. Hurry with that beard. Show time in ten minutes. Maury said to meet her at center stage."

She left him holding the unopened letter. He flipped it over. The envelope was addressed to him in care of the Honey Ridge Children's Home. The return address read: Maureen Sinclair, 2042 Sunset Avenue Apt. 2B, Los Angeles, CA. The postmark was from three years ago. He turned the letter over and broke the seal. His fingers trembled as he pulled out a letter.

Dear Tony,

I made an A on the 'What Makes Christmas' production. I am indebted to you for your help.

Your dedication to the children's home and encouragement to me as I worked with the youngsters was a genuine joy.

You said to write when I got that movie part, but since that is such a long shot, I took a chance in writing you anyhow.

Thank you again for your kind words and assurance that I'd be successful in whatever I choose to do. Those words will keep me going on this journey—destination unknown.

I hope to hear from you soon.

Maury

XOXO

Hope to hear from you. She must have thought I didn't care enough to respond.

He shoved the letter underneath the wide Santa belt. Putting on the Santa wig and beard, he added the cap and opened the door.

Maury stood behind the center stage curtain with the mistletoe dangling above her. She motioned to him.

On the other side of the curtain, Tony heard GG's eloquent voice asking the question, 'What makes Christmas?'—starting the play.

"You make an adorable Santa," she said in a low voice and patted his fake tummy.

"Santa just received a gift."

"The box behind the dumpster?"

He pulled the letter from his belt and handed it to her. "This was inside the box."

Her eyebrows furrowed. "My letter?" Then her eyes met his in realization. "You thought I never wrote to you."

He nodded. "And you thought I never answered."

"Any chance I can cash in on the Xs and Os on the bottom of your letter?"

Maury tugged the furry mustache and beard from his chin and their lips met, just as the curtains parted center stage.

"Grandpa," Ethan said, "what makes Christmas is mistletoe and Mommy kissing Santa Claus."

Bathed in the spotlight, Tony played his part with no hesitation. The children giggled, and GG said, "Love for one another is a joyous part of the season that points us to what makes Christmas."

The curtain closed and the play dialogue blurred into the background.

Tony pulled off the cap and beard and fanned his face with the letter.

"I don't think we'll have any complaints about an unbelievable kiss," Maury said.

Tony held up the letter. "I have the blessing to fill the gap in this year's imperfect Christmas tree."

"My blessing is three-fold—reconnecting with you, this town, and Sawyer talking to me."

Tony took Maury's hand and they walked to the side wing to watch the end of the play.

Lisle on stage said, "Christmas songs make Christmas. 'Away in a Manger' is my favorite."

The spotlight lit up the manger, and the music began to play.

"The sweet sound of the children singing is far preferable to me screaming in a movie."

"Does that mean you'll stay?"

She nodded and her eyes sparkled.

The soft music swelled as the audience joined in singing.

The lost box held the answer to the question of what makes Christmas—the baby in the manger—and answered why Tony never heard from Maury.

Tony gave Maury's arm a gentle squeeze. A smile graced her lips, then they joined the others singing about the little Lord Jesus asleep on the hay.

ABOUT SALLY JO PITTS

Sally Jo Pitts brings a career as a private investigator, high school guidance counselor, and teacher of family and consumer sciences to the fiction page. Tapping into her real-world experiences, she writes what she likes to read—faith-based stories, steeped in the mysteries of life's relationships. She is author of the Hamilton Harbor Legacy romance series and the Seasons of Mystery series. You can connect with her at www.SallyJopitts.com

THE LIGHT AT ST. SILVAN'S

Murray Pura

CHAPTER 1

LEAVING AND BECOMING

Not that she did not wish to have friends--she loved to be around people. Not that she wanted to keep all her thoughts to herself—sharing her feelings with others, and listening to others share theirs with her, was an important part of her days and weeks. No, but just to be alone, by the sea, in the light, was a time to discover who she was, to know her soul in all its depth and intricacy and mystery. By the sea was a place to dream, to pray, to worship, perhaps even to dance where no one was watching except the gulls that swooped across a sky of blue or gray or gold. Here was a place only God knew, and here was where she came to know God.

> A strange admission, Sara King thought to herself. After all, she had been raised Amish, baptized Amish, married Amish. She was an Amish woman. Sometimes she felt she was more Amish than she was American.

Where ocean met sky did not seem real. There was so much of everything—air, wind, water, space—it was as if all of heaven was over her head and in front of her eyes. Trying to take it in, she felt she had to become a new person because what she used to be could not hope to contain the half of what rushed over her senses. She reached out with her hands to hold it, but it slipped through her fingers and into her heart, all of it. She became the sea. She became the air and the sky, became the long stretch of shore and all its sand and rocks. When a wave broke into a spray of light, it was her.

It had never been easy. No matter what the tourists thought about the Amish--theirs was not life under a lilac bloom. Amish life was not the way so many of those who wrote Amish stories said it was--one long romance with God, and with farming, horses, and the land under beautiful sunny skies. One long romance with your man. The life could be so wonderful, yes. But that way of life could be hard. Hard as hidden boulders striking a plow.

"I am being born," she whispered. But there was no pain. Not for her, not for her mother and not for anyone else. There was only the release, the freedom, a delight that carried a child's innocence and a young girl's wonder at seeing beauty for the first time.

There had been one son. Sara was unable to conceive after that. Doctors were no help. Her husband blamed her. Why did he marry her? Why could she not give them a family like the Millers or Bylers or Hostetlers? When the boy had been killed in a farming accident at eight, her husband could not forgive God. Nor could he forgive himself. He could never forgive himself. Many tried to help. She could not deny that. So many in the Amish church tried to help them in their dark and terrible grief. But he took his life with rope in the barn. While she was in the house preparing their lunch. It was a cloudless April day. She thought of it as a perfect day, though her heart remained dark with the loss of her boy the month before. Perhaps the best day since the accident. She looked out the kitchen window at the farmyard while she peeled carrots. The barn was green and huge and silent, and her husband did not respond when she opened the window and called him to the table.

The light cut through mist and darkness and warned sailors about the rocks at St. Silvan's. It also guided them to port and to safety, no matter what sort of problems they were dealing with in their ships or what sort of storms they were attempting to weather. She often wished, as she stood on the upper deck of the lighthouse and watched its beam stretch over the waters, that the light could do the same for her. At such times she began to pray, and the prayer was nothing like church prayers at all. They came up from deep within her and were often as wild and rugged as the Atlantic itself. But they were her words, and they were from her heart, and somehow, she was aware God knew that and loved her for them. That love burned through any night that had descended on her and any storm or cloud that shrouded her soul.

Sara King never thought of herself as someone who might run. But her husband's suicide, falling so closely after her son's death, after a marriage of bitter words from a man who could not accept her or love her as she was, caused everything to collapse. A year after the loss of her son and her husband, she left. She gave the farm to the bishop in a legal document he would not receive until after she was gone. Friends who had helped her work the farm that lonely year would take care of things while she was away. She told them it was only for a few days. She had taken the train and the bus and finally an Uber. Then several ferries including one that only sailed on Fridays until July and August when it made the trip once a day. Her bid on an old abandoned lightkeepers' cottage on St. Silvan's had been accepted. A realtor met her on the mainland in Gloucester. They did the paperwork and Sara was handed the keys.

"It's fine for summer," the realtor told her. "Of course, it's winterized too. Keepers lived there year-round. But it will need a bit of TLC."

"Thank you," Sara responded. "I'll take care of that."

"Oh, are you handy?"

"I am, yes."

"Are you a carpenter?"

"I am a farmer. One who didn't stay in the kitchen or laundry room."

"Will your family be joining you on St. Silvan's?"

"No, they will not."

Sara had boarded the first train dressed Amish but changed into jeans and a blue chamois shirt in a restroom in the car, tying her sand-colored hair back with a blue bandana. She took her battered navy backpack onto the ferries along with a sky-blue mountain bike she bought in Gloucester. A man on the first ferry told her everything matched her eyes. She surprised herself by her reply. "My eyes aren't yellow like my hair."

The smell of the sea overpowered her and broke through all her fear and doubt about what she was doing. The tar of the wharves, the gray planks, the roll of the ferries, the spray, the gulls—all were part of a magic kingdom that promised far more than what she had left behind. Yet she sang an Amish hymn to herself as the ferry approached the wharf at St. Silvan's. And said a prayer in High German out loud when she unlocked the door to her cottage and stepped inside after a ten-minute bike ride. Peace. An overwhelming sense of peace.

"Lived in but lived in well," she said, after one long glance.

She knew keepers and their families had lived in the cottage since 1705, and that the house had been improved upon a dozen times to add plumbing and wiring and new roofs. But because most of it was stone, it had withstood the test of time and storm without sinking. Furniture from the 1700s and 1800s had been removed to a museum in Gloucester. The description of the property had said most of what remained was from the 1930s and '40s, though the large oak desk was from 1912. She sat in one of the solid wooden chairs. There had been one room, then two, then three. When the light was automated in the 1970s, the government had turned the house into a writers' retreat—the only stipulations being occupants could stay no longer than three years, they had to write about the sea, and they had to have published something beforehand, however small or light.

After forty-five years, the government wanted the old cottage off their hands and listed it with the Gloucester realtor. Since the lightkeeper's house was a heritage property, all sorts of do's and don'ts were involved, which was enough to scare off any number of potential buyers. On top of that, no more than two people could be in residence. There had to be a family connection to the sea through fishing or the Coast Guard or the Navy. There had to be a writer of fiction, preferably sea fiction, somewhere in the lineage. The successful buyer had to agree to write a weekly blog about the island that was upbeat and positive. Finally, they had to learn enough about the lighthouse that they could step in for a tourist guide if the need arose. Sara had no idea how many others met all the eccentric terms, but she did, and she was accepted.

The cottage could have been expensive and should have been more than she could afford. But a nest egg had been saved for her by an aunt who wasn't Amish. Sara had been certain she would never use it. When she did, the guilt almost paralyzed her the moment she made the bank transfer at the realtor's office. But the nest egg was little enough, truly. She would do good with it. And she was no longer Amish.

"Look at you." Sara got up from the chair, went over and stared at her face in the mirror in the cottage's bathroom. "Such blue eyes and dark eyebrows. Blonde hair and black eyebrows—how is that possible? Not that you were ever vain about it. But still."

She read her German Bible for half an hour that first afternoon. Prayed. Then went outside the red wooden door that had a weather-stained brass knocker of an anchor she admired a moment. The museum had not removed it despite fear of theft or vandalism. Something to do with a legend about good luck and God's blessing. She touched it, unsure. She walked around the stone cottage with its flower gardens and bright red window baskets. There was a sign on the cottage that named it Round Turn and Two Half Hitches. After that, she followed the worn flagstone path to the lighthouse which was two hundred yards away—locked. Only the crew who came and went and maintained the automated light had the key.

That didn't matter. There was a metal ladder, well-riveted from what she could see, that ran up one side of the lighthouse to the lantern deck. Signs warned people off and threatened prosecution. But since the end of the ladder was at least twenty feet off the ground, it would take an athlete to jump and grasp the bottom rung. Or there would need to be something or someone for a person to stand on. That night, she made a running jump and caught the end of the ladder on her second try. She hadn't expected to miss her first try. Jumping games like this had been common in the barns of the Amish when she was young. And she was still young. Only twenty-eight. She scaled the lighthouse and stood on the lantern deck while the powerful electric light blazed over her shoulder and out across the dark ocean.

"There be coastline here," she murmured. "There be rocks. There be dragons."

She stayed a long time watching the blackness. Now and then the lights of a vessel moved past from north to south or south to north. It was a warm April night without much of a breeze. Still, as midnight came and went, she hugged her jeans jacket closer to her body. Time for bed.

> She missed the lowing of cattle and swirling fireflies and the clip-clop of Morgans pulling buggies home for the night. Though at one in the morning, everything would be as quiet there as it was on St Silvan's. Except she could hear the waves. Ocean swells thumping into the rocks. Just before a sleep of deep greens and blues, like the song she shouldn't have heard as a teen put it. The sound of water lapping against a sandy beach made its way through the dark and the noise of the surf pounding the rocks offshore.

Who are you now, Sara King? What is your name? Tell us. Tell the seven seas.

CHAPTER 2

SARA NOT SARA

I wasn't able to stop myself from rising early any more than I could stop the sun from doing it.

I made myself coffee from the beans and hand-grinder I had brought with me. My navy backpack had more tools than clothing. I'd left all my dresses and shoes behind, including the ones on the train. Jeans and shirts and hiking boots were good enough. After a quick shower that was colder than I liked, I went outside to water the flowers and window baskets with the hose. I saw there had been a vegetable patch once, maybe for strawberries too, and thought about purchasing seed packets in the village. A white pickup was parked by the lighthouse, so I decided to go down and take a look. There was no one around but the door to the light was open.

I waited, biting into an apple I'd brought along from a fruit basket. Someone had been kind enough to stock a few items in the fridge and cupboards too. I suspected the realtor. Surprisingly, she had bought items I could make use of––corn meal, oatmeal, whole milk and butter from a local dairy, apples, pears, carrots with their tops still on, and some decent flour. I had to remember to thank her. I was halfway through my apple, a green one, before a young man and a young woman in bright blue overalls came down the inside staircase and emerged into the morning. Both of them seemed a little taken aback. I responded to that with one of my best smiles.

"Hello," I said. "I'm Lyyndenna Patrick."

The woman, about twenty, looking to me like a college student hired on for the summer just as English neighbors did in Pennsylvania, finally smiled a bit. "Hey. We're just making sure the light is a hundred percent."

"All's well?"

"It is. Are you a tourist? I don't think they start doing island tours till after July 4th."

"No. I live here. At least, I live here now. I'm in the cottage."

She was a redhead with the freckles and jade eyes. The jade eyes widened considerably and took in all kinds of morning sunlight. "You bought it? You're Sara King? I thought she was an old widow." Then she went crimson. "I'm sorry. What a thoughtless thing to say."

I wasn't bothered by her comment. What stung was my boy Daniel's death. That was what hurt the most. Not so much the loss of Jacob, my husband, to be honest.

"No, it's all right," I told her. "I guess I look old to you."

She shook her head. "That's the thing. You absolutely don't. You look amazing. It's like you're a Harvard fourth year or something. You're totally young and pretty."

Now I was crimson. I knew I was. It felt like I could fry an egg on my forehead. "Thank you. You're too kind, really."

"It's the truth. I'm Kara Wingate."

"And you can call me Lyyndenna."

"I thought the woman buying the cottage was someone called Sara King."

"Yes. That's me. The old me, I guess. The old me from a million years ago and a million miles away. Please call me Lyyn. Or Denna. Or the whole name at once. But never Sara."

"So, you're not Sara."

"I am. I was. But now I'm Lyyndenna Patrick. Which isn't much of a stretch really. Patrick is a family name. Back to Revolutionary days."

"I like Lyyndenna."

"And I like Kara."

The young man with her, sporting a full-blown black beard, carefully trimmed, nodded his head at me. "Lyyndenna Patrick. Good name. I'm Tyler. Tyler Franklin. Welcome to St. Silvan's. You really need to come down to Breakers some evening. That's where everyone gets together. Even if you don't drink. That way you'll get to know the islanders before all the tourists show up."

"Hi, Tyler. So, how many tourists are going to show up?"

"Thousands. We have some pretty nice beaches here and some great hotels and restaurants. Even in the winter we get people from Boston and Cambridge and Salem. Of course, they'd need to stay a week because the ferry is only a Friday ferry then."

"And you both live here?"

They nodded.

"Except sometimes, I go to be with my parents on Scrimshaw," Kara added. "It's a small island just south of us in Massachusetts Bay. Maybe eighty people on it. Dad just comes and gets me in our boat."

"Spoiled," teased Tyler.

She stuck out her tongue. "Jealous."

"You get so many storms on Scrimshaw. And so many sharks."

"We get some of the nicest weather, and you know it."

I jumped in. "I read that about eight hundred live on St. Silvan's?"

Kara gave Tyler a fierce green-eyed look before turning to me. "That's about right. I'd say closer to a thousand now. Some take their own boats back and forth. In the winter, they'll work from offices in their homes if they can. What do you do, Lyyndenna?"

"Well. Right now, it's going to be writing."

"Really? Like with Harlequin or something like that?"

"Something like that."

"Wow. Good luck. What a perfect place to write, hey?"

I smiled. "I agree."

"There's another writer," Tyler spoke up. "Hawthorne. His place is a couple of miles from the cottage here. Old like yours but a bit fancier. It used to be owned by a sea captain in the 1800s. It's kind of an old, dark, rambling house."

Kara grinned, her eyes coming even more alive. "It's fascinating. And he's not the only one, right? Isn't there a group?"

"An artists' group. Yeah. Like I said, you really need to show up at Breakers, Lyyndenna. You passed it coming up from the wharf. It's made of all that cool driftwood and the planking from a tall ship. Old man o' war. It busted up at the lighthouse two hundred years ago. I forget who retrieved it for the tavern."

"Todd Smiths. Remember?"

"Oh, yeah. Todd."

I felt drained after they left. I hadn't expected to talk so much, so soon. Why had I been going nonstop? Why did I have to act like I was some NYC writer when all I was going to do was produce a weekly blog? Why did I even bring up my name change? Now it would be all over the island. The old widow Sara King is really the young widow Lyyndenna Patrick. God help me.

"Be quiet, Lyyndenna," I murmured. "You need to talk much, much less. This needs to be a quiet place. Prayer, mediation, your German Bible, gathering wild flowers and driftwood. Why talk at all?"

I made my way from the lighthouse along a path through tall sand dunes that were half grass and came to one of the beaches. White—like beaches I'd seen the one time we'd visited the Amish community in Sarasota, Florida. Once I got closer,

I realized the white came from seashells the ocean swept against the southeastern shore. From my map of St. Silvan's, I remembered there was a beach called White Shell. This must be it. The beach spread for several hundred yards before it changed into a light-colored sand for a few hundred more. I bent down and put my hand to the shells. Some were crushed but most were only broken in half or badly chipped. They felt smooth against my palm. I tugged off my boots and socks and went barefoot. It felt fine, it felt good. I walked awhile, enjoying the sensation. Somewhere sometime, I'd heard a line from a poem—nor can feet feel, being shod. I'd been barefoot a lot as a girl. Time to go back there.

The day was not hot, the day was not cold. When I reached the sand, I paid more attention to several families flying kites with their children. The kites were all colors and all shapes. They swooped and spun and darted into the sun. I couldn't see the lines that held them to earth, so they appeared to be more independent than they were. I craved that independence. From my past. From the deaths of my husband and son. From the years of my husband's cutting words. From the manner in which my faith had been lived out under the Amish ordnungs.

Does God really care if I pin up my hair? Or wear a prayer Kapp? That my clothing has no buttons? That my dresses are long and dark? Does it matter to God whether the men have mustaches or not? That they have beards that must not be trimmed? Is it a matter of life or death that Martin Luther's Bible be used, that we only sing hymns in German, that Pennsylvania Dutch be the language we speak among ourselves? Does God say no cars or trucks? Does God say no airplanes? Does God say no electricity? Or do men say all of that? I don't mind leaving those rules behind. It is the friendships I miss. The faces that wrinkle with smiles. The honest laughter. The many kindnesses. Working together with the other women at a quilt, or at baking five hundred loaves of bread, or at preparing all the food for a wedding. I miss someone taking my hand and praying for me. Like the kites, I am free to roam. But only so far. They are tethered to their lines and to the hands that hold them. Just as I am tethered to the lines of my past and my faith and to the many hands that hold those. Lines that can be as taut as steel cable and hold just as firmly.

A kite broke free and sailed out over the ocean.

"Yet even the strongest line might not hold forever," I whispered.

A boy ran along the sand calling out to the green kite.

A bishop from another county had visited our church once.

His message had been unusual.

"Sometimes some of us leave the Amish path. It may only be for a while. It may be forever. It may be a mistake. It may be the Father's will. Despite what others may say or not say, you must answer to God for your decision, you alone. Listen to the advice of your church. Then pray and make up your own mind before the Lord. Only take this with you if you must go—-simplicity. Ours is a simple life and a simple faith. Do not lose the simple ways. Or if you lost them before you left, go out there and find them again and bring them back to us."

I was not surprised the sea and its shoreline brought so much into my head. I had always longed for what the English called blue water, but rarely had I been able to go to it. The farm kept me landlocked. Had I stood by the ocean more than five times? How often had my Daniel seen it? Once, twice? So that it should stir the blood and free up my thoughts—-I had expected that. I had wanted that. It's why I'd fled to St. Silvan's to begin with and not into the deserts of New Mexico or Arizona. Saltwater that stretched out far beyond what my eyes could penetrate. A sky that poured into the sea so there was no way of knowing where one began or the other stopped. I'd wanted infinity. That's why I went to the sea to discover what was unknown.

I was just thinking about using a gas stove for the first time that evening when the brass knocker sounded. It actually had a deep bell-like ring to it, making me think it might be hollow. I opened the red door, pushing my loose hair back from my face. It was Kara. Bubbling.

"Hey, I want to take you to Breakers, my treat," she said, everything about her a bright smile. "They have the best halibut and chips. I'll introduce you to everyone you need to meet."

I knew protest would be in vain, but I tried anyways. "Kara. That's so sweet of you. But honestly, I don't have anything to wear. And my hair's a mess. So, I'll say no‑‑"

She cut me off with a laugh. "Oh, Denna, believe me, you are perfect just as you are. You couldn't be more perfect. You mustn't change a thing. It's Saturday night at Breakers on St. Silvan's, and you absolutely look the part."

CHAPTER 3

BREAKERS

I was in the sort of fix Grandpa King used to call a perpedoodle, making up his own Pennsylvania Dutch word. On the one hand, I just wanted to be left alone with the sea and sky and God. On the other, I did want to make some friends and I didn't want to wait till the island was overrun by tourists. So, I climbed into Kara's green-like-her-eyes Jeep Rubicon and went hurtling down the road to the village, Kara talking like she drove, fast and nonstop. I wasn't at all ready for the interior of Breakers. A dory hung from the ceiling, anchors and nets and harpoons from the walls, empty barrels and kegs were our seats and tables, ship's brass lanterns our lighting. I wasn't quite ready for the crew seated around the barrels Kara steered me towards either. Her friends and Tyler and his buddies, about ten altogether and none of them older than twenty-two. It wasn't just that I was a widow with a name change that was widely known. That I was Amish was apparently island news too, and all of them wanted to know about the farming, life without electricity, the Morgans, and the buggies and the commitment to nonviolence. I was surprised I did not mind sharing the Amish ways with them as I was still very upside-down about what I'd done. However, talking about why I'd left was another matter.

"So, I have just lost my son and my husband," I told them, sipping my Pepsi and picking at my halibut and chips. "Both were ... farming accidents. Both a year ago. In March and April. I needed to get away. That's all. No, no, don't think the Amish community was insensitive or unsupportive. I just couldn't be there anymore. I needed a completely different place. I'd always dreamed of the sea, of being by the sea. So here I am."

"But why St. Silvan's?" asked Tyler, one arm around his tall, dark-haired girlfriend.

"Because of the cottage. I saw the advertisement in our paper in Pennsylvania for the lightkeeper's house so I wrote the people in Boston."

"There were a lot of questions they put to you, weren't there?"

"Yes, there were."

"And you have a naval person in your family?"

"Yes. Coast Guard. An uncle. All the way back to the 1930s."

"What about the writer?" This from Kara.

"Serenity Grace Greenwood. Popular in her day but overshadowed by Louisa May Alcott. Who she met."

"Like Little Women Alcott?"

"The same."

"Wow. So, you write like them? Like Alcott and Greenwood?"

Right then and there, as I sprinkled more malt vinegar on my chips, I decided to give up the ship. "Oh, I need to explain about all that. I did write stories as a girl, and they were smiled upon. But when I wrote stories as a teen, writing was frowned upon. So, I gave it up."

"But—" from one of Kara's friends.

"I'll be writing a weekly blog. I'm supposed to be getting a new iPad for that from Boston. I pray that may lead to something more. Something like Alcott or Greenwood. I have no idea. It may have been bred right out of me by the ordnungs."

"What are those?" the friend asked me.

"Rules. Laws. Policies. How the Amish organize and govern themselves."

"Which doesn't include painting The Last Supper or writing books or playing the violin." said Kara.

"No. It doesn't."

"Is that another reason you left? So that you could try and be a writer like your relative?"

I shrugged. "Who can say what God has planned? If my son or husband were still alive, I wouldn't be here."

"Or what the universe has planned," said Tyler.

"As you wish," I replied, popping a chip in my mouth.

"Hey." Kara sat up in her chair. "There's Hawthorne. And Sydney Ryder. And Scott Munro. They're in that artists' group I was telling you about, Denna. I invited them here to meet you. Come on. They're sitting down at another table."

"You mean another barrel."

"Hurry. Grab your plate and your Pepsi. I'll introduce you."

"I'm good where I am, Kara. I don't want to intrude on them."

"How can you be intruding on them when the reason they're at Breakers tonight is to see you?"

"I'm a blogger. An amateur blogger. Not even that."

"Wait till I tell them about Serenity Grace Greenwood and Louisa May Alcott."

"Kara, Kara, please don't."

I took the three writers in, and they were a quick blur of faces. Honestly, later on I couldn't recall the details, exactly how they looked, exactly how they dressed. I remember one of them saying I looked like an islander. Kara told me on the drive home that was because I was tanned, my hair was streaked, my denim shirt and blue jeans were faded, and I had the jeans rolled just above the ankles.

"I bought the shirt and jeans at a secondhand store," I told her. "All my English clothes are second hand. My tan? Well, it is a farmer's tan, what else? And the sun streaks my hair, not a hair salon."

"Well, Denna," Karla said as she drove, "I suppose it will embarrass you for me to say this. But it all comes together extremely well. You're truly a beautiful woman."

I lowered my head and felt the burning on my cheeks. "I'd rather you didn't say things like that, Kara."

"It's true."

"I … I am not used to compliments of that sort. They make me uncomfortable."

"Surely men have—"

"No. It is not the Amish way."

"When you were dating—"

"We do not date. There is only the courting. All right, yes, yes, Jacob said sweet things to me in those days. But such words quickly dried up."

"Why?"

"You will have to ask him."

"I can't ask him."

"And I can't speak for him."

Sydney wanted to know about Serenity Greenwood. Apparently, her works were experiencing something of a resurgence. She had a new paperback of my ancestor's novel Three Shorelines and wanted me to sign it. They used SG Greenwood for her name. I knew the book, I knew all of Serenity's books, even though I wasn't supposed to. For the longest time, I wouldn't sign. But Sydney, a firecracker of a brunette, wore me down. I finally took the pen from her hand. To me, it was just a simple signature. To her, it was something fashioned in gold. She showed it around the table and Hawthorne and Munro praised the curves of the letters and the broad loops of the capitals.

If I had been honest with them and Kara, which I was not, I'd have told them when I was a teen, and thought the bishop might let me become a writer, I'd practiced my autograph over and over again. I'd been caught and scolded for this and told to develop a signature that was plain. I'd thought my author signature was plain. So, I'd created something that made mama and papa happy. Which also meant not using my pen name of Lyyndenna Patrick, Patrick being my mother's maiden name as she was a convert to the Amish faith.

That night, I went down to the beach in the April dark. The crests of the waves gleamed. I began pitching pebbles into the surf. I was wondering if I'd fled the Amish because I couldn't stay where my son and husband had died or because I'd been restricted from being a writer and a thinker. Hawthorne had said Greenwood was superior to Alcott but had never received the breaks or reviews she deserved. Munro had agreed and quoted a line from Greenwood's August: The light never got through. Not through the windows. Not through the doorways. Not through her gray eyes and into her mind. The years had smudged her and put a thick streak of charcoal over everything that had life. She did not know how to kindle another fire.

"Brilliant!" he'd exclaimed. "You can't imagine how I'm looking forward to your writing, Ms. Patrick."

"It's blogging, sir, only blogging," I'd protested.

"I'm sure you've written something."

"I haven't."

A lie. I had. Munro seemed to be able to pluck that information right out of my brain. I had started the book at thirteen, hidden it at fourteen, thought about destroying it at fifteen, then resumed writing it at sixteen. Every now and then I had snuck it out and worked on it, right through my twenties, my marriage and motherhood. I'd brought it with me.

Munro the Magi. Yet all I could recall of him that night was his New England accent and that he wore glasses.

And that he looked like pictures I'd seen of Stephen King. Hawthorne? I couldn't recall Hawthorne at all. But the lighting had been dim and the ship's lantern flickering.

Except. His hands resting on the table. Large. Rugged. Brown with sun and weather. Fingertips stained. From pushing tobacco into the bowl of a pipe, I suspected. Exactly like Grandfather Patrick's hands. Just younger.

I found larger pebbles and threw them too. Then stones. I was fighting something but I did not know what. It was my young son, Daniel. How he would have loved to have been here throwing stones into the sea in the dark beside his mother. How he would have loved it. And my heart broke all over again.

CHAPTER 4

MOUNT SURIBACHI

May and June passed like the ocean passed by St. Silvan's—in a hurry. I fell into a routine of reading, and blogging, and watering flowers, and wandering beaches, and praying. On July 4th, the ferry began bringing hundreds of people to St. Silvan's. It ran four times a day, and a second ferry began sailing a week later. There were seventeen beaches on the island, and half of them had hotels right on the shoreline, far enough back to keep them free of high tide and storm surge. The Independence Day fireworks were set off at the rocks a good distance from the lighthouse. The crowds were kept well back as yellow and orange and blue burst over the sea—all new to me because I'd never attended any July 4th celebrations. And though I'd seen the fireworks from far away, I'd never seen them explode in front of my face.

The tours began then too. Guides took people inside the lighthouse between ten and four, and they walked around the cottage too though the guide kept them about a hundred feet away. I didn't know what to do with that. I wasn't the person to stand outside and grin and wave to hundreds of tourists. So, I hid indoors or made my escape between mobs to the library in the village or down to the White Shell. There were hundreds of tourists on the beach too but at least I was anonymous there as I rolled my jeans up and waded in the sea.

I desperately wanted to swim, but I had no suit, and the ones I saw for sale in the village, I found immodest. Kara to the rescue. It seemed she and her girlfriends were always at my side. They wanted to teach me to drive. They wanted to find me summer dresses I could live with—long ones with lots and lots of color. They chose the ball caps and sandals and the simple island jewelry of wood and bamboo I could actually say yes to. I was Amish Not Amish and trying to find my way in my new life and my new world.

The suit they picked out was a one-piece Speedo, modest enough except it was far too snug. The girls complained and remonstrated with me but I was unmoved. I purchased one in black two sizes too large. It drooped a bit, and that was what I wanted.

"Oh, Denna," Kara moaned. "It's summer and you have a perfect figure."

"I want to go in the water," I snipped back, "not parade myself down a runway."

"Well, you definitely could parade yourself down a runway, Mrs. Patrick," said her friend Jazz.

"Lyyndenna, please. Or Denna. So, becoming a supermodel is not what God and I had in mind."

Kara put her hands on her hips. "I thought you weren't Amish anymore."

"I'm not. But there is still some Amish I want to keep in Lyyndenna Patrick."

"How much?"

"Enough yeast to make the dough rise properly."

"What?"

"Just let's go swimming. All of us. I'll pretend to be your mother, ha-ha. Take me to your favorite beach."

"Our mother?" snorted Jazz. "They'll believe one of us is your mother before they'll believe you're ours."

I had quite a time with the girls that summer. In truth, I did need swimming lessons as well as driving lessons. They took care of both. I suppose I could tell a thousand stories about learning to drive Kara's Jeep Rubicon. What a trusting soul she was. I almost went off the wharf twice and off cliffs into the sea more than I want to say. Though the time that made Kara and Jazz laugh the hardest (the cliff times were screams) was when I panicked and hauled back on the steering wheel like a pair of reins to make the jeep stop. It didn't work, and we bounced off the curb. The times we didn't go over the cliffs, Jazz said made her believe in an Amish God. The time I pulled back on the reins, she said made her believe in a God who enjoyed a good laugh.

The beach? Well, what can I say about swimming and the beach? I didn't mind drowning and tried it several times. It's not as if I hadn't swum in ponds and creeks and lakes. But ocean swells were something else. I had to use stronger strokes, and kick harder, and hold my breath longer as I learned the crawl and the butterfly from Issime. She was a champion swimmer at Boston University and waitressing at Breakers for July and August. She had me using weights at the village gym, the Shoals, to put muscle on my arms and back and shoulders. So, by Labor Day, I was swimming better than I had my entire life. I surprised myself.

I surprised myself by buying a new Speedo too. The droopy one drooped too much. The undertow kept pulling it off. Not that anyone ever saw my Speedo struggles underwater. I was quite the aquatic gymnast, ha-ha. The girls were there to clap when I tried on a suit that fit like it should. But I now had the problem of swimming in a Speedo that fit like it should.

I was reminded of my girlfriend Lydia Zook who was always getting in trouble at sixteen for what the bishop called her "rock and roll dresses". It's just that she wore dresses that were slender and hugged her figure a bit. Which her mother never seemed to notice. Now I had a swimsuit the undertow couldn't touch but which made me look like Lydia in a rock and roll Speedo. My solution to the problem was to run out of the water at full tilt and dive into the biggest beach towel I'd been able to buy. Wrapped up in that, I looked like a pile of laundry. The girls harassed me about being a prude, but I didn't care. I had no desire to be St. Silvan's new center of attention. I just wanted to swim, lie on the sand, look for seashells and live a simple, unobstructed, unnoticed life. Amish Not Amish.

So, by the end of July, I had a license and had been blessed by a local on the island who wanted to sell me his Willys Jeep from 1945. He had kept it in beautiful condition since he'd acquired it in Arizona in 2010 and had fought a winning battle against our saltwater climate. He also offered to be my mechanic as long as I owned the Willys which I accepted. Mike was sixty-two and a Vietnam vet. He and his wife, Amy, became my dear friends. As did the jeep which he'd nicknamed Bachi because it had actually been on Iwo Jima during the battle in 1945. (Mount Suribachi was where the Marines had raised the flag in the iconic photograph everyone knew about including my "no war" Amish church.)

Not that I knew anything about that except for the famous photograph. Mike had to explain Iwo Jima to me. There were three bullet holes just by the spare tire at the back of the Willys. "Nambu machine gun," he'd told me. I'd nodded. Of course. A Nambu machine gun. "They have to stay." I nodded again. Where would I take them?

"And it has to keep its sand camo. Ok?" It did have a paint job that reminded me of the color of light brown sand. I nodded a third time. "And it has to remain stock." Mike had a lot of faith in me if he thought I could customize a motor vehicle and give it chrome wheels and bumpers.

"Definitely, it will." I'd begun to pick up on the girl talk.

It was a standard. Kara's Rubicon had been a standard too. Just an easier kind of standard. It took a while. I popped and stalled and backfired my way around the island before I finally got the hang of it, but I was determined not to disappoint Mike. Why had he sold me his vintage jeep which had only ten thousand miles on it? He liked my online blog which also got printed in the island weekly, Spindrift. I honestly don't know why anyone liked my blog. But he did. Especially the one about an Amish woman who'd only driven Morgan horses learning to drive a Jeep Rubicon off a cliff. So now Bachi and I were partners.

Mike wasn't the only one who liked the blog. I began getting all kinds of good feedback. So much so that papers in Boston picked it up. It was God. What else could it be? My editor at Spindrift was ecstatic and offered me a salary.

A salary! The whole blog idea had just been a requirement for being allowed to purchase the cottage. There hadn't been any income attached to the deal whatsoever. I'd been living off what was left of the nest egg, which I hoped I could stretch over two years before it was exhausted. Now Fwanya, from Namibia, was talking about five hundred dollars a week but he wanted two blogs, one on Monday as well as Friday.

"Of course, I said yes," I told Mike and Amy at Inked, a coffeehouse in the village. "But. It's happening so fast. I'm farther away than I wanted to be this soon."

"Farther away from what?" Amy asked.

"From where I came from. From the Amish. From my past."

"How long has it been?"

"Over three months."

"You've told us you still believe in God, isn't that so?"

"Yes, yes, nothing about that has changed. I'm just

trying to find a different way to live and express my beliefs."

"Then perhaps things are moving along as they should, Lyyndenna. It's still about faith for you, isn't it?"

"Of course. Yes."

"Then keep going that way."

"I will. I have to. I just don't always know what to hold onto from my past and what to let go. And I don't understand why my blogs should matter to so many people."

Mike smiled at me. "It's not just that you wrote a blog about learning to drive that amused me. We both like the way you mix your Amish memories and beliefs with discovering the island and Massachusetts Bay. It's an intriguing blend."

"Thank you, but to me it's a confusing blend. It's so difficult to work through what I've walked away from and what I'm walking into. I'm sorry that struggle is so apparent in what I write."

"How could it not be when you're so open? It doesn't make you odd or unpleasant to read. Lyyndenna, we are all struggling in one way or another. The blog is popular because you are a good writer, and you are an honest to God human being."

I hoped I was being honest to God. I felt like Sara King less and less every day. Yet I didn't feel farther from God or farther from my own soul. Just farther from what I used to be. Even though much of that still lived in me.

I had pored over the book I'd been writing since I was a teen, sure I'd be asked to share something with the artists' group besides my blogs. Which everybody could read anyway. I'd found out they didn't meet from May to September, so I began picking away at my book in August. I made changes and added new parts to the story. I didn't use my iPad. Just pen and paper. It was all pen and paper. Three notebooks so far. I was surprised by how autobiographical the book was. I thought there must be something wrong about that. But my pen and my mind kept writing that way. In a biography of SG Greenwood, there was a quote from her that helped. "All good fiction is, in one fashion or another, a matter of autobiography, of telling your own story through fictitious personalities and fictitious events. That's what gives it its reality and its power."

So, I carried on, sometimes thinking I knew what I was doing with my life and my writing and sometimes not. I drove Bachi everywhere, I walked everywhere, I cycled everywhere on my blue mountain bike, I laughed with Kara and the girls (who began including older siblings and friends twenty-five to twenty-eight for my benefit). I wrote everywhere too, in my head and in the notebooks. I visited all seventeen beaches and swam at each one. I got into beachcombing. I prayed at the seaside, and I prayed in the moonlight, and I prayed watching the phosphorescence burn bright in the ocean. By September, I can't say I felt complete. I can't say I felt incomplete. I mourned my husband, but I cannot say I missed him. However, I mourned my son and wept over him every day.

In Amish romances, a man would have come into my story to save me. A knight in shining armor. I didn't want a knight in shining armor. I didn't want to be saved by a man. My life wasn't Amish fiction. I wanted to be saved by a God. One true, loving, kind-hearted God.

So, when Mark Hawthorne tried to be that Amish fiction savior, I wrote him out of the story. Or tried to.

CHAPTER 5

THE GOD GAME

The artists' group was not just a writers' group.

There were painters, and sculptors, and actors, and musicians, and dancers, and poets and essayists. There were all kinds of artists of different races and different faiths. It was bewildering. I'd go away from the weekly get-togethers with my head in a spin. Yet I couldn't deny the meetings stimulated and inspired me too. They made me want to write and write in a way that was honest to God, not sugar-coated and glossed over and fuzzy-wuzzy. Not a rose garden without thorns. I'd never been able to talk about my secret book with anyone before, let alone as freely as this.

There were three basic rules. No politics, no religion (including the atheists who liked to say they weren't religious and then go on to tell everyone what they believed), no cruel feedback. Unless politics and religion were part of a character's story. I listened for the first two months and said very little. Finally, one Saturday morning before the end of October (we always went from nine to twelve and then had lunch together at Breakers), I had been asked to be prepared to share from my WIP (work in progress). About two dozen of us were seated in a circle in a large study room at the library.

I thought I'd be far more nervous than I was. I suppose if I'd had to read from my notebooks in June or July or even

September, I'd have been stuttering. However, I was in a different state of mind altogether. I felt like I was dreaming my reading to them. I read for half an hour. I was calling the book Harvest that Saturday morning. I told them I might call it something else by Saturday night.

There was this one thought that ate into Becca. If God was a father, was he anything like her father? Gracious and patient and kind? Well, how could God be? God was spirit. In the Bible, he roared and thundered and slaughtered Israel's enemies and broke people's hearts. Jesus was a better idea. Her father and Jesus were more like one another. Jesus was the father figure she wanted in her head and her soul. He was the one that said to love all her enemies. The other said to kill them.

And there was the suffering. Her two children dead as stones. Where was the love of God when they gasped for life after a truck smashed into their buggy? Where was the God who intervened and saved? She could never voice these thoughts aloud. But she thought about them in the long fields and in the barn with the horses. She thought about them before she fell asleep. Becca wondered if she would ever stop going over them. She wished she would. She prayed she would. It felt as if all the person she was and could be had been locked in chains and could neither grow nor be free until she resolved the issue of God and where God's love was or wasn't. The rain, at least, still fell, and the sun, at least, still rose, and the land, thank God, still turned every shade of green.

"How old were you when you wrote this?" It was a man named Erikk, who made sculptures with metal. "Didn't you say you've been working on this since you were thirteen?"

"I have," I told him and the circle. "I was about twenty-one here. I'd been married for three years and a mother for two."

"There's some lovely prose when you talk about rainfall and sunshine," said Munro. "It's poetic, and it works well with the heavier thoughts."

"Thank you."

"Let's hear something from later on in the manuscript. Let's see how Becca and your style grow together. Does this theistic issue continue to dominate?"

"I suppose we'll see."

It did. It does. Jazz was, not surprisingly when you combined her beauty with her energy and athletic ability, a dancer and part of the group. She made sure she sat with me at lunch. She wanted to talk about the part I'd read where Becca thinks she might be falling in love and is afraid. We actually took it to the beach, went for a swim, and then I dived under my gigantic towel before I froze. The Atlantic was an ice bucket in late October. Nevertheless, I would go on to swim at least once a week every month of the year. That's how crazy the sea air made me.

Jazz took off at one point to meet up with some friends at Inked but I stayed on at Northwest. I lay on my back and stared up at an impossibly blue sky that beat like a heart. I liked Northwest because it faced towards Gloucester and the shoreline so it was sheltered from the wind. I'd dressed under the towel and felt warm as a waffle. Not toast. A waffle. My son Daniel's expression. No, remembering did not make me cry this time. I smiled at the sky and one high white cloud.

I breathed in a scent of vanilla and tobacco. There might have been a hint of cherry. I recognized pipe tobacco because of Grandfather Patrick's smoking habits. I sat up and looked around but the smoker wasn't obvious. They should have been because the beach was half empty. What breeze there was came out of the south, so I walked that way, off to the left if you were facing Gloucester and the mainland. I still didn't see anyone.

"Your writing actually reminds me more of Virginia Woolf. With a dash of Melville. You're a thinker. A philosopher. It's not just about a narrative with you."

The smoker was behind a large boulder covered in seaweed.

"Mr. Hawthorne," I said.

"What surprises me is there is no bitterness. Angst but no bitterness."

I came around the boulder. Dark hair and dark eyes. Skin still dark from his summer tan. Khaki shirt and pants. A pipe I knew was called a freehand, looking as if it had been carved from a tree trunk. He had just successfully blown a smoke ring.

"I'm not bitter," I replied.

"But like Becca you felt you had to move on."

"There were too many associations with the deaths of my son and husband."

"And?"

"I needed to write freely. I realize that now. Without censure or condemnation. It's how I am working everything through."

"About God and suffering?"

"The love of God, God's absence, death, faith, loss of faith, all of that and more."

"I'm thirty-eight now. Exactly ten years older than you. In my twenties, I was a minister. Even while I was giving messages and trying to help others, I had questions no one could help me with. Finally, I had to move on from that. At least until I had figured things out."

"What things?"

"Well, some of the same questions you have."

"And?"

"I wrote my first novel. Break Break Break. From Tennyson's sea poem. Do you know Tennyson?"

"No."

"Yet you've read lots of other books an Amish woman wouldn't normally have access to."

"I felt compelled to use the library in our town."

"Openly?"

"Quietly."

"Have you read my novel?"

"No, I'm sorry, I haven't."

"It was on the New York Times bestseller list for three months."

"Lots of books are on that list, sir. Many of them are poorly written. You get on that list for selling a lot. Not necessarily because you're good."

"You're blunt."

"One of my virtues."

"Good is a matter of opinion, Mrs. Patrick."

"I'm not Mrs. Patrick. Lyyndenna, please."

"And I'm not a sir. Not with only ten years between us."

I smiled. "Fair enough."

"So, you haven't read my book?"

"Mr. Hawthorne, I didn't know you existed till a few months ago."

"Hmm." He blew out a cloud of creamy white smoke. "Perhaps one day."

"Perhaps."

I sat down on the sand facing him.

"One thing that happened for me, Lyyndenna, was reading the Bible and realizing it said I could also learn about God from the things God had made. It's in Romans."

"I know. The first chapter."

"Then I read in Matthew where Jesus changed the Bible. You know. You have heard it said but I say?"

"Ja. Of course." Grrrr. I annoyed myself whenever I slipped into German or Pennsylvania Dutch. "You have heard it said, love your neighbor and hate your enemy but I say to you, love your enemy."

Hawthorne went on. "So, for me, that changed a great deal in my brain. And in my heart. That is a very sweeping statement. It changes the Bible. All those nasty verses about killing Israel's enemies with vengeance no longer apply. They are not right. They are not true. That is not who God is. Jesus altered the whole picture. He set things straight. God is not slaughter and bloodshed. God is love your enemy. God is pray for those who persecute you. God is don't resist the evil person. God is turn the other cheek. Do you agree?"

Right from the beginning, Mark Hawthorne could be so convincing. And interesting. And, unfortunately, attractive. Him and his rugged, handsome face and his flashing eyes. Ugh. Flashing eyes. I'd already put him in a romance.

"I don't know," I responded. "That's a lot to change with just a few words."

"To me, it's simple. Jesus says that verse is wrong, and he changes it. The verse has universal application. You can't have God telling you to wipe out your enemies, even the infants, say that's God, then say love your enemies is God too. God is one or the other. I decided to go with the change Jesus instituted. God is love, not hate. Simple. Are you opposed to simple? Perhaps Lyyndenna Patrick prefers layered, complex, and complicated?"

He made me laugh and I didn't want to laugh. I didn't want to react to him in any positive way at all. I was totally frustrated with myself. "Simple is good if simple is true."

"You have left the Amish behind. Have you left Jesus behind?"

"No. And I haven't left the Amish behind either. Just parts."

"So, Jesus still matters to you?"

"Ja. Na sicher."

"What he says makes all the difference to you?"

"Ja. Yes. Of course."

"That is what he said. What will you do about it? Hmm?"
I didn't respond.

He got to his feet and knocked his pipe against his palm to remove the ashes, then slipped it into his pants pocket. "Would you like to walk the beach a bit, Lyyndenna?"

No, as a matter of fact, I would not. I am perfectly fine here on this island without you intruding. But, I liked his voice, and I liked listening to what he had to say. So off we went. Grrrr.

"Would you like to play a game?" he asked.

A game? "No, thank you."

"From that verse in the Bible. In Romans. We can know what God is like by looking at the things God has made."

"How does that become a game?"

"What does the sea make you think of? Quickly. Don't overthink it."

"Why ... power."

"God's power?"

"Nature's power, God's power, yes."

"What about the sky?"

"The sky? Heaven. Peace. When it's a blue sky."

"Wind?" he asked.

I thought as fast as I could. "Wind? A strong wind?"

"Yes. A strong wind."

"God is spirit."

"Fire."

"God is intense."

"A breeze."

"God is gentle."

"Sand."

"God is infinite. His ways are infinite and past counting."

He kept coming at me. "Sun."

I had no intention of losing the game. "God is warm.

"What else?" he prodded.

"God is light."

"What else?"

"God is clarity."

"Stars."

"God is light in darkness."

"What else?"

"God is beauty."

"That piece of driftwood there."

"Just a minute." I seized his arm without thinking and then swiftly drew back, horrified at what I'd done. "Uh ... it's your turn. Not mine. Driftwood yourself."

"God takes what is lost and turns it into something marvelous. God restores."

"Salt air," I put to him.

"God is bracing," he responded. "God is invigorating."

"Seashells."

"Eternity. God is eternal, and we are eternal with God. Death cannot change that."

"Seagulls."

He laughed. "God soars."

I wish he hadn't laughed. A peculiar tingling silvered through my body. No, no, no.

"Uh. Thank you very much, Mr. Hawthorne. I must get going. And ... and ... we probably shouldn't meet like this again."

"Why not? It was a chance encounter."

"Nevertheless, Saturday mornings are sufficient."

"But, Lyyndenna, we're having an amazing time."

"Yes, yes, we are. Too amazing. I'm not used to social interactions with men. It's awkward. It's uncomfortable."

"You're not uncomfortable."

"I don't even know you."

"Well, how else do we fix that except by chatting?"

"I don't want to chat. I don't want to fix it. I'm a widow. I just want to leave."

"But, Lyyndenna."

"I have to leave. God knows I have to leave."

And I fled.

I ran all the way back to where I'd parked my jeep.

I was breathing so hard I waited five minutes to start the engine.

What a mess.

CHAPTER 6

SOMETHING RICH AND STRANGE

I am not an unburdening person.

But I wound up unburdening myself to Kara.

I did not want anything to do with men romantically. Saturday morning and Breakers was enough. It was casual but professional. Whatever that meant. I did not want to be dated as the English dated. I for sure did not want to be courted the way we Amish courted.

"What do you want from men?" Kara asked me.

"Nothing!" I snapped. "I don't want anything from men. Except to leave me alone."

"Were things so bad with your late hubs?"

"What?"

"Your husband. Were things so bad?"

"No, no, they were fine. Oh, what a lie. He was very harsh with me. Very unkind. Thank God, I had Daniel at nineteen so I could pour my affection into him. And receive his in return."

"Don't you think the way your husband treated you has something to do with the way you're feeling about Mark now?"

"I don't feel anything for Mark."

"I mean the way you don't want to feel."

"I don't know. I definitely don't want another Jacob. And I definitely don't want another man. I don't want anyone."

"Well, I doubt he'll talk to you again except about writing. Not after you ran from him and left him standing there like a duh."

Hawthorne didn't talk to me. I'd had my hour and wouldn't have another till the new year. When I interacted with others in the group, he listened but never jumped in. He let others do that. He'd only speak up after I'd had my say about someone's art and water had passed under the bridge. At lunch, he sat with Sydney and Munro. And that's the way it went for three Saturdays. Hawthorne wasn't rude, and he didn't snub me. He just made sure he gave me my space. As Jazz put it.

It was what I wanted. I felt good. I blogged, prayed, walked the beaches, collected driftwood to place around the cottage, spoke to tourists now and then, drove Bachi to the cliffs to admire the view, sang hymns in German there where no one could see or hear me, weathered the storms as November ended with a howl, sat in on the Saturday meetings and enjoyed the talks given by landscape painters and photographers, worked on my novel. I knew eventually I'd have to get it typed into Word, but for now I was content to scribble away in my notebooks and leave the book like that. Sometimes the skies were navy and indigo, other times the color of steel anchors. I wrote on and prayed on regardless.

I have tried to understand what happened at the end of November. The very last day. I deliberately drove to Northwest, did what my friends called the Iceberg—jumping in the cold ocean—dressed under my towel and went exploring. I thought my wandering was aimless. Till I smelled the pipe tobacco.

You might think I'm making it up and knew exactly where I was going. I had no idea. The cliché applied to me--my head was in the clouds. The clouds were grey as mud and my head was stuck in them. The moment I took in the scent of tobacco, I started to go back. I thought that's what I wanted—to turn around and go back. Instead, I went towards the boulder and stepped in front of him.

"It's a bit like following the smell of cookie dough or baking bread," I told Hawthorne.

"This comes from a tobacconist in Boston. Pippin and Took is the shop. She calls the blend Sea Change."

"That's an odd name."

"It's from Shakespeare. 'Full fathom five thy father lies, of his bones are coral made, those are pearls that were his eyes, nothing of him that doth fade, but doth suffer a sea-change, into something rich and strange.'"

"So, the sea changes him into something rich and strange?"

"Or you. Or me. It can mean any big change, Lyyndenna. Like a caterpillar turning into a butterfly. Metamorphosis. Maybe the sea does it. Maybe a song. Maybe a book."

"Maybe God."

"Maybe God. But God usually uses something or someone."

I sat down on the sand and faced him like I had before. "I just want a friendship. Someone to talk with who understands what it means to write your life and feelings out in a book."

"Sydney or Munro could do that."

"No."

"Why Hawthorne?"

"I don't know."

"You don't need to worry about relationship or romance. I don't want a serious relationship ever again. And I don't believe in romance."

"Well, I feel the same way."

"Good. Then that's settled. The air is cleared. We can carry on with our sea change."

I smiled. I felt as light as air. "Into something rich and strange."

He fussed about a moment, relighting his freehand pipe. "Where are you with your epic?"

"My epic? Becca is working through her feelings about her Amish husband who was killed in a haying accident. It isn't feelings of love she's wrestling with. She feels guilty she is grateful he is not there to hurt her with his sharp tongue anymore."

"How sharp a tongue?"

"Carving knife sharp."

"Is she getting anywhere?"

"Not really. She is supposed to love her enemy. He acted like her enemy. She loved him when they were younger. Her love eroded over time as he became more and more strident with her. She doesn't know what she feels for him now that he's gone. When she was crying at his funeral, she was crying over what they'd lost, the years they'd lost, the kindness toward one another they'd lost. She doesn't know how to pray. The Bible is like a dead stick when she tries to read it."

"We should walk, Lyyndenna." Hawthorne kept smoking as we roamed the beach under a sky as gray as the sides of a warship. "What is it Becca wishes to achieve?"

"She? Or the author?"

"She."

"She would like to be reconciled to her husband. She would like to recover the love they lost for each other. Even in death, she wants this more than anything else."

"What about the children she lost?"

"She did not lose them. The love was always there. She is confident she will see them again, and the reunion will be beautiful. Although she cries over them, all her memories are wonderful. It isn't that way with her husband. There are good memories from their first few years together. But they are buried by the pain."

"Because they weren't able to have more children?"

"Yes."

"He blamed her?"

"Yes. Constantly."

"Can she forgive him?"

"She wants to. Very much."

"What does the island offer that your Amish do not?"

"I can write a book about my struggle. There is no shame in that."

He took his pipe out of his mouth and tapped it against his palm before slipping it into his pocket. "We have some potters in our group. Pottery can be made in two ways. Where each piece looks virtually the same depending on the theme—cups are identical, saucers, vases, pitchers. Or where pieces, even of the same theme, do not replicate one another—each cup is unique, each bowl, each vase. The first approach is manufacturing. The second is art—especially when the potter is not exactly sure what she will get when she removes each piece from the kiln."

"All right. You're going to tell me it's the same way with books."

"Yes. Fiction can be manufactured just like pottery. Books can look the same when it comes to the covers. They can sound the same when you open them up and begin to read. The characters can resemble the characters in other books. Plots can be the plots you've experienced a thousand times. Many people like this sort of repetition in their fiction. They like it in their religion, and they like it in their life. It makes them feel comfortable and secure and that there will be no unpleasant surprises. It may not be true to life, but they don't want true to life. Just peace and quiet. The books are manufactured to give them the same experience over and over again. Just like getting the same sort of cup, the same sort of painting, the same sort of clothes. I pass no judgment. It is what people choose, and we all benefit from manufacturing. But when it comes to fiction, and you are trying to be honest to God in what you write, and you are not exactly sure what your book will be like once you work through the process and remove it from the kiln, that is art. The book will be unique. It will not be like another, though it may share certain qualities. It will be one of a kind in every way including the cover and the ending. Art not only surprises the audience. It surprises its creator. It surprises the writer and painter and photographer. You don't know how things will end for Becca, do you?"

"No. And I don't know how things will end for me."

It began to snow.

He looked up. "Snow is better than rain sometimes."

"When it's gentle, yes."

CHAPTER 7

AMISH FICTION

I wanted it to be real. I wanted it to be real for Becca, and I wanted it to be real for me. I remembered standing by an open door at one of the library rooms in Pennsylvania and listening to a chat with two Amish romance authors— one a woman, the other a man. What struck me was how real the Amish characters in their books had become to the people in the audience. They acted as if the fictional lovers were real. I thought they were crazy, the way they went on. Why did she do that? Why didn't he say he loved her? How come she's so reluctant to get close to him or go to a hymn sing in his company? I could not take it seriously. The English and their butter churn fictions about Amish life and how we fall in love.

Now, I found out differently. Becca was real to me. She not only took on a life of her own as I wrote her story. She took on a mind of her own. She did things I didn't plan. She said things that weren't in the script in my head. Sometimes, I knew exactly what she was going to say. Other times, I had no idea what was going to come out of her mouth. I wanted to understand suffering and how to comprehend it in the light of God's love and mercy. She had other ideas. Becca wanted to find true love again.

She felt she'd had it once, for one or two years, before her husband began to speak harshly to her and avoid her. After waiting what she considered was a reasonable amount of time after his death (six months), she decided to pray about a second husband. The man who seemed kindest was not Amish. However, she was determined he would become Amish.

It started when she was running for her buggy in a sudden thunderstorm in town. The buggy was three long blocks away, and she knew she was going to get soaked. Then she slipped and fell, causing her to cry out as her hip slammed into the pavement. The bishop and his son were suddenly there, helping Becca to her feet and guiding her along the sidewalk to the buggy. Still, the rain was pelting down. Then it stopped. Only because a man was holding a large umbrella over the three of them. He held it over them until they had climbed into their buggy. Of course, he himself was drenched. The bishop shook his hand warmly. Becca did not look up but she memorized every detail of his face and smile regardless. She wondered if he would have come to her rescue if she had been by herself. She decided, yes, he would have held the umbrella over her head all the way to the buggy.

So, that was the man she began to pray about—handsome, polite, gallant. She asked God if she might see him again. Her request appeared to be granted. The next five times she went into town, she spotted him each time. Once, Becca was in the company of the bishop and his wife, and the bishop waved him over. He introduced his wife and Becca. This time she smiled and did not drop her eyes. Oh, he was beautiful. Such a pleasant spirit. Samuel. She thanked him for his rescue. As the four of them chatted, he mentioned he was a member of the Episcopalian church. Becca thought, Well, Lord, soon enough Samuel will convert, and then he will be a member of the Amish church. A moment later, the bishop invited him to attend their church picnic the following Saturday and he accepted.

ME: Oh, Becca, for heaven's sakes!

BECCA: Vas? What is the problem?

ME: Life is not that neat and tidy.

BECCA: Sometimes it is.

ME: I suppose you will make sure you are at the bishop's picnic table, ja?

BECCA: So? Why not? Wouldn't you?

ME: No, I would not be that forward.

BECCA: Forward? How is that forward? The bishop will invite me to sit with them, and I will accept. You are far worse than me.

ME: I am? I? How?

BECCA: Oh, my goodness, here is a boulder. Oh, my goodness, someone is sitting with his back against it gazing out to sea. Oh, my goodness, it's Mark Hawthorne, the kind and handsome writer. Who would have guessed?

ME: I had no idea who it was the first time.

BECCA: What about the second, third, and fourth time? Etc., etc.

ME: I can't believe I'm arguing with a fictitious character.

BECCA: I am not a fictitious character.

ME: Yes, you are. I made you up.

BECCA: You did not. I was already there. You just made use of me.

ME: I made use of you? To do what?

BECCA: To try and figure out your life. I'm you.

ME: You are not me. You are just an idea.

BECCA: I am very much you. I'm just way ahead of you. I know I want to get married again. I know who I want to get married to. I've given my future to God. I've given my past to God. I've given my pain and suffering and confusion to God.

ME: I'm there too.

BECCA: No, you are not, Sara or Lyyndenna or whatever your name is today. We're not even in the same county on all this.

ME: Hey. I decide what you say and do. I'm the writer.

BECCA: No, you don't. I'm the character and I tell your head what I'm supposed to say and do. You're just an innocent bystander.

ME: I'm involved.

BECCA: Your buggy is far, far behind mine and I'm pretty sure your Morgan has thrown a shoe.

It was insane. Who was writing my book *Harvest*? Me or my fictitious Becca? In a roundabout way, I brought it up with Hawthorne. He had a good laugh over that.

"Every writer talks or mutters or complains or pleads with their characters," he said. "Readers do the same thing. It's inescapable. Imagination can give the breath of life to anything and make it three dimensional."

"What if you have an argument with your character and lose the argument?"

"From the moment you wrote your first page as a thirteen year old girl, any plans you had for how your story was supposed to work went out the window. The same is true every time you sit down to create. The process and your mind and your fiction takes over. You race to keep up. Sometimes your plot is extraneous to what's really going on in the story and between the people who are in it."

"So, who's writing who?"

"You're just one of many authors, Lyyndenna, and not always the dominant one."

Well, all right, fine. In a second conversation, Becca pointed out that while I was still tumbling with pain and suffering and a good God, she had embraced that dark side of life. Jesus had legitimized it with his own suffering. So had all the people in the Bible. And there weren't two Gods, one in the Old and one in the New. There was only the one. Jesus was the face of God in the whole Bible from Genesis to Revelation. You have heard it said but I say. He was the Living Word. He was it. His words finalized everything.

ME: So, you believe all Hawthorne's gobbledygook?

BECCA: I wouldn't call it gobbledygook. He's just trying to figure it all out. Most people are complacent and swallow whatever they're fed. Ja? So, my Bishop Mueller believes the same thing as your Hawthorne.

ME: He is not my Hawthorne.

BECCA: Jesus is the face of grace, the face of love, the face of the Father, the face of God.

ME: And he is not your Bishop Mueller. I invented him.

BECCA: (laughing) You don't invent anyone. You are just a writer. Not God Almighty. Bishop Mueller was given to you and me. You just wrote him down.

ME: Never mind. Is it true you have forgiven your dead husband?

BECCA: I have.

ME: So easy, hmm? So simple?

BECCA: The problem was not simple, but the solution was. What about you?

ME: I'll get there when I get there.

BECCA: I thought you liked simplicity?

ME: I do like simplicity. I like sincerity just as much.

BECCA: Oh, I'm sincere all right. I just decided I'd never get an apology from a dead man. But I might finally get some love from a live one.

ME: Really.

BECCA: Your buggy is stuck. Your wheel is in a rut. Maybe it's broken. All I know is, you're not going anywhere.

ME: Oh, what do you know? You're a work of fiction.

BECCA: If I'm a work of fiction, then so are you. I came out of your head.

ME: I thought you were already there, and I just made use of you.

BECCA: I was already there. But you're the one thinking up my story. Or trying to. You're still getting a lot of it wrong, and I have to correct you in your sleep. Or even when your eyes are wide open.

ME: Imagine it however you like. You are not my story anymore. Our stories are completely different.

BECCA: They aren't. I told you. I'm just well ahead of you, that's all. I can forgive. I can accept suffering and the loss of my girls. You can't accept loss, and you can't forgive. Because of that, you can't see the love of God. It's hidden.

ME: I wish you would please stop talking. Just stop. I'm trying to write.

Becca had a wonderful picnic. Samuel was a charming guest, in the best sense of that word, making magic and drawing people out of their woes, making the whole table smile and relax. Becca had made up her mind she was going to chat with Samuel as long as possible. She sat across from him and kept him engaged for the better part of three hours. The next day Bishop Mueller dropped by to tell her Samuel had been to see him.

"He is interested in our faith," the bishop explained. "I promised to meet with him once a week and answer all his questions."

Her blue eyes sparked. "Why, that's wonderful. Isn't it?"

"Ja ja, sure, sure. It's wonderful if he's sincere."

"Why wouldn't he be sincere?"

"Because he likes you very much. And why not? You are sunlight, thanks be to God. But I mustn't judge. I mustn't jump to conclusions. He could be sincere about you and our faith both. You pray. I'll pray. We'll find out."

"Amen."

"Amen."

Becca was so excited she wanted to dance. But the Amish do not dance. Yet David had danced. And she'd decided Jesus would have danced at the wedding feast at

Cana. So, in her kitchen, all alone, she danced after the bishop had brought her his good news. She danced until she dropped into a chair, exhausted and laughing.

"Praise God!" she sang out loud.

"Do we write the stories or do the stories write us?" Lyyndenna asked Hawthorne during a snowstorm walk the third day in December.

He managed to keep his pipe lit and puffed a few times. "You know how they say. Everybody has a story. Or as Anna Deavere Smith puts it, 'each person has a literature inside them.'"

"What does that mean?"

"It means you don't just have a story or write a story or have a story writing you. You are it. You're the story. All that you are. That's the book. That's the work of art."

CHAPTER 8

CAPPUCCINOS

Kara and Tyler and a work crew wrapped bulbs around the lighthouse. They had to keep them white so as not to confuse shipping. The mayor and council spared no expense. The tall column blazed like the star of Bethlehem once the sun was down. Kara said the mayor would like permission to light up the cottage as well. I told her to go ahead. Christmas lights were something I never had with the Amish. I was also asked to join a caroling group that dressed up as if it were 1890 on the island, and I said yes to that too. Caroling was something else I was never able to enjoy in Pennsylvania.

"So, what did you enjoy when you were Amish?" Hawthorne asked me over cappuccinos at Inked.

"Oh, well," I replied, "I guess I still am Amish in so many ways. I like the quiet way of doing things. I like the German. I know many find it a harsh language, but I don't. I like the plain and simple way of living a life. We go at a horse's walking pace so much of the time. I like the emphasis on prayer. I like the emphasis on kindness and forgiveness. There is so much centered around God's love. So much centered around Christ's compassion and giving his life so we could have a good life to live. And, you know, I adore the horses. Not just the Morgans that drive the buggies. I loved watching the Percheron plow the fields and bring in the hay or the harvest."

"Would you go back?"

"I've thought about it, of course. A part of me expects the bishop and elders to show up here one day and coax me to return to Pennsylvania. Would I be persuaded? Maybe yes, maybe no."

"So, then, explain to me what hold the island has on you."

"The island? I suppose, well, the ways are simple here too. It's easy to find quiet spots and solitude. Easy to pray and think. And I can drive a jeep here, beachcomb here, look out over the wide rolling sea. In Pennsylvania, it's waves of grass—here it's waves of blue water and whitecaps. I like the people. I like the food. I like my cottage and my privacy. Hmm, and it matters a lot to me that I am free to write."

He paused to sip from a ceramic mug with his name on it. "And your novel is going how?"

I had to roll my eyes. "Ha. Well, I thought it was about me finding my way. But my Becca is finding her own way without me. She has no plans to leave the Amish behind, she has forgiven her dead husband, she's met someone she likes, and the love of God dazzles her."

"Isn't her story your story?"

"Do I look like a work of Amish fiction?"

"Well, Lyyndenna, the best fiction is autobiographical."

"Who said that?"

"I did. And many others."

"Is it true? But I've been self-absorbed. Forgive me. How is work on your own novel going? Do you have a title?"

"Titles come and go, though they can help you focus on the main theme of the book. Today, it's *Gale*. Last week, it was *Storm Surge*. Tomorrow, it will probably be *High Tide*. I could also go with *Paean*."

"That's a big switch. Paean to what?"

"The lonely sea and sky."

"So, is that what the book's about?"

"It's about a person reaching out for a rediscovered life living by the sea."

"Hey. That's what I'm writing about."

"I thought Becca was on the farm in Pennsylvania."

"She is. Her author and creator is here by the ocean trying to make sense of everything."

Hawthorne smiled that good smile he had. "Then I guess we're on the same page."

"Well. I think others have been there before."

"In one sense. It's a familiar theme. But that doesn't mean each story will be the same. It can be manufactured. Or it can be unique."

I paused a moment. Then blundered ahead. "I hesitate to ask this but is there ... is there romance in your story?"

"Why do you hesitate to ask it?"

"Because you said you didn't like romance. And because ..."

"You don't want to go there with me."

"Something like that. I'm sorry."

"Nothing to be sorry about. We both agreed on friendship and not a seashell more. As a matter of fact, Lukas is content with waves and sand and bowls of clam chowder. His last book was a thriller about the Navy Seals, and he doesn't want to write thrillers anymore. Even though that genre has made him a pile of money."

"So, then ..."

"So, then, he wants to write stories about transitions and transformations. People going into tunnels and emerging into the light."

"Metamorphosis stories?" I asked.

He drained his cappuccino. "Sure. Chrysalis."

"And no romance? Ever?"

"So far nothing like that. Why? What does it matter?"

"It's just that for Becca, I see that romance is a big part of her healing. She wouldn't be so far ahead of me except for recovering God's love and recovering man's love."

"Does a man love her?"

"No. And she doesn't love him. But it's leaning that way."

"Does it bother you?"

"A little. My main character is far more content than I am."

"Just remember that romance doesn't have to be slick and cheesy. It can be honest and true. Just because publishers might use it to bait readers doesn't mean the real thing isn't out there."

"Out there like the sea wind?"

"Out there like the seagulls crying."

I tinkled my glass of water with a spoon. "I want to hear something from Paean."

That smile. "I don't have it with me, and there's nothing on my phone."

"I'm sure you have something memorized."

"Are you?"

"I am."

He plunged right in.

> It got to the point that any wave that touched the island touched him. Any breeze, any stiff wind, any gale. Every gull that perched, every ship that docked, every shell cast upon the sand. Whenever a big roller shook the black rocks, making them run with water like a beard, he felt the blow in his body. Soon he could not distinguish between the island and his own skin and body.

I honestly had nothing to say to except a pathetic "good work." It was more than good work. Hawthorne deserved accolades. I wanted to write like that. But how?

236

CHRISTMAS FROM THE HEART

I decided to snub Becca and her romance and focus more on Christmas and the wild winter sea like Hawthorne was obviously doing with his novel. The village was festooned with all sorts of wreaths shaped like anchors, waves, gulls, and ships of every shape. The older section, which had buildings and streets from the 1700s, was literally dancing in holly with its bright red berries every time the wind gusted. Which also set silver bells tinkling and ringing that were hidden among the spiky green leaves.

The tall ship Paul Revere docked at our wharf for a week, its rigging flying the colorful signal flags the Navy relied on in times past, at night the same rigging streaming with Christmas lights of every color, some of them flashing and winking. Men and women in naval attire from the War of 1812 (a war even I knew New Englanders hadn't approved of and wouldn't participate in) formed up on the main deck every night, regardless of snow or cold or cutting winds, and belted out a mix of sea shanties and carols. I couldn't get enough of "Haul Away Joe" followed by "Joy to the World" and didn't miss a night. I bundled up in an old pea coat I'd found at Davy Jones with all its vintage clothing and marvelous antiques. The coat was two sizes too big, and I loved it that way.

I did my own caroling too as I'd promised I would. The outfit they gave me, replica of a winter coat, skirt, and bonnet from the 1860s, in forest green, wasn't too big or too small but, like the porridge I'd heard about as a child, just right. Of course, I was used to singing without musical accompaniment, so caroling outdoors with just our voices was pure joy for me. It not only took me back to Pennsylvania, it took me back into a great warmth of the heart. We did this three times a week for most of December, and it never got old. Good things never get old.

But, from time to time, I had to leave the carols and wreaths and tall ship and roast chestnut vendors behind because I needed to go to sea again. Outside of my iceberg dips, I hadn't sat and gazed at the blue waters for some time. Waters, to be honest, which were sometimes steel gray or a kind of chilly raw green. The sea wind nipped and bit and cold spray chilled my face, but I embraced it all.

I was never a tropical girl. Our one visit to Florida was long enough at two weeks. I liked the Pennsylvania snowfalls and the sleet of New England. I wanted to be able to wear boots and sweaters and heavy warm jackets. I was a North Country Woman. Like Kara and Jazz and Isieese and their friends.

There was one small beach which wasn't even listed with the other seventeen. It was only fifty yards long and sandless. I discovered it, you could say, by accident. I heard a long sharp rattling sound, like hundreds of marbles rolling over one another, and found a stretch of smooth stones, stones that fit nicely in my palm. Every time a wave came, it pushed the stones up. Every time a wave fell back, it drew the stones with it and created the smooth rattling sound. It wasn't irritating or unpleasant. It relaxed me. It soothed. As I had so many times on the island, I imagined Daniel beside me, and I knew how much he would like the round rolling stones carried back and forth by the sea.

It was only natural I should feel the sting. A mother doesn't expect to lose her son. Outgrow him. Outlive him. You should be towering over me at sixteen. Picking me up in your arms as if I were no heavier than a vase of roses. Making me laugh. Bringing home girlfriends I don't think are right for you. Giving me grandchildren that exhaust me with joy. Now it's a cold darkness.

But not for you. Not for Becca's two girls. You're in light. You're with a God of love. I have to trust something, and I trust that. I'll live and die with that.

Jacob. We had love once. We lost that love. You never lost God's. Everything I see in nature, in the sea, in the Bible tells me what is lost, God recovers. You too. Never in my Amish life have I believed that unbaptized infants go to a hell. It is not the Amish way to baptize infants or teach such a horror. Never have I believed that to take your own life is stronger than the mercy of God, the love of God, the strength of Jesus. You live. I should like to have been reconciled with you here. This is the best I can do. From here by the stones, I forgive you.

God. It's bitter for me some days. I'm not sure of myself. I'm lonely. I'm wind and rain and ice. I could not do this if you were not someone who knew pain. If you were above it all, my story would be impossible. Becca could not have mercy on her husband or be reconciled to the loss of her daughters. She could not love a man again. And if she can't, I can't. You are a man of sorrows and acquainted with grief. Isn't that how the English Bible puts it? That's my hope. That you have suffered like we have suffered. And know us. And carry us. That's my only hope.

The waves were still there when I fell asleep in my cottage, Round Turn and Two Half Hitches. The stones rolled up and rolled down and provided a rhythm for my dreams. When I woke up I felt different. I picked up my mobile which I was beginning to use more and more. I texted Hawthorne. It was five o'clock.

ME: Are you up?

HAWTHORNE: I've been writing since four. Good morning.

ME: Can we walk and talk?

HAWTHORNE: When? Where?

ME: Once the sun's up. At White Shell.

HAWTHORNE: Just like that?

ME: Yes.

HAWTHORNE: What's so important?

ME: I don't know.

HAWTHORNE: Can't it wait?

ME: No, it can't.

CHAPTER 9

I'M NOT HERE

Poor Hawthorne.

The sea wind reminded me of a hammer and anvil. It struck and sparked. A hard-blown spray coated our jeans and jackets and faces. Yet it seemed like I just had to talk to him by the open ocean in a cold gray dawn. Nothing else would do.

"Well, this is bracing," Hawthorne laughed. "You've really become an island gal, haven't you?"

I hadn't expected him to be that warm and forgiving about being dragged away from his cozy house and his writing. "I wanted to tell you in person."

"Tell me what?"

"I've made peace with the loss of my son. With my dead husband. With a God who has the face of a dead Jew. A Jew who isn't dead but knows what it means to bleed."

"That sounds like a lot."

"I guess it is a lot. Except, it's not complete."

"What do you mean?"

"I'm still angry about my life. Hurt. Disappointed with God. I feel like this island still isn't far enough away from my past. I need to get on a boat and go farther."

"Really?"

"Yes. Really. Maybe I need an island off the coast of Africa. Or off the coast of Vietnam. Or maybe I need another planet."

"So, you've accepted but haven't accepted?"

"I'm not sure how that works but yes. I'm content in my discontent. Or I'm discontent with my content."

"Now is the winter of our discontent made glorious summer."

"Who are you quoting now? I wish I did feel like glorious summer inside. I did for a while. I thought I'd resolved all this at Rattling Stones Beach. Honestly, I felt different inside. But I wake up, and I still don't understand the reason for putting people through suffering, especially suffering they had no part in causing. I don't understand why some women have experienced nothing like what I have, while others are exactly where I am--they feel like a sword has pierced their hearts. I don't like God's selective interventions--some are spared, some aren't, some are healed, others aren't, some are lifted out of darkness and many, too many, are left there. I hate to say it, but I feel like throwing a brick through God's front window."

Hawthorne could light his pipe under the most adverse conditions. He took his time doing just that, his back to the sea wind and to me. Then he blew white smoke that was immediately caught and carried away.

"You are a woman who not only values faith but clings to it. Yet faith does not mean you see everything and comprehend everything. It's very much a trust thing. You won't get all your answers here, Lyyndenna. You can't get all your answers here. You have to carry everything that's unresolved, believing there's more to it and that somehow the agony is a fit. That there's a purpose. That God isn't indifferent or malicious or void of love or powerless to make things right. Faith is about the invisible and the not yet and the incomprehensible. You know the prayer of the man with a desperately ill son in the Bible? 'I believe, help my unbelief?' It sounds like that's where you are. Not a bad place to be. Considering the outcome he enjoyed."

I was in a mood despite all his strong words. "I've never enjoyed that kind of outcome."

"No one can say what the outcome will be. It's the faith route, Lyyndenna. It's unseen."

For a flash of a moment, I thought he was going to put his arm around me as a fierce gust rocked us both. To my surprise, he didn't. To my greater surprise, I realized I wished he had. Inwardly, I kind of cringed. Now what was happening in my head?

I begged off going for breakfast at Breakers and drove to the cottage. I was about to burn my since-I-was-thirteen manuscript in the wood stove in the front room. Then I decided to retain it as an historical artifact and locked the notebooks in a drawer of the 1912 desk I wrote at. The desk Sydney Ryder called The Titanic. Because that was the year the ocean liner sank.

I immediately began a new manuscript. Typing it on my iPad rather than scribbling with a pen. I wrote the title, *I'm Not Here*, and the first sentences--

> I'm not writing a novel. The novel is writing me. I have no narrative in mind. But a narrative is happening just the same. I am writing about what someone else is writing about me. I'm keeping track of the storyline. That's all I am doing. Running to catch up. I have no real idea of the plot or it's denouement. I'm just going to tell you about what I feel, what I think, what I pray, what I see and what I don't see. Scrapping *Harvest*. Becca has it all together anyway and doesn't need my meddling.

To begin again. *I'm Not Here*. Under the pen name of Lyyndenna Patrick.

> At dawn, she went to the sea and told a friend about her struggles with loss and suffering and God and realized, like a breaker crashing completely open on the rocks, she didn't want

him as a friend anymore. She wanted something more. It was an overwhelming thought she was by no means ready to receive. She denied it. Said no to breakfast with him and raced home in her jeep, driving sloppily, skidding on icy patches despite the winter tires. Without removing her pea coat or brushing off the snow, she sat down at her iPad and stared at the screen. Nothing came. She never had writer's block, but nothing came. Finally, she typed out two sentences. "It's not just the man. No woman is an island either, John Donne."

Which was the first thing I said to Kara after driving far too quickly to her condo in the village. "No woman is an island. I can't be that anymore. Don't ask me how I know about John Donne."

Kara stared. "What's going on? You look like you came in with the tide."

"I'll explain. But don't you—?"

"I have today and tomorrow off." Kara peeled off my pea coat, hung it, took my hand and tugged me onto a glassed-in balcony where it was warm as summer. "Sit. Exhale. I'll be back with coffees and some cinnamon rolls."

She had a perfect view of the harbor. The tall ship Paul Revere was at one side of the wharf, and people were standing in a long line ready to board and view it. Revere wouldn't weigh anchor for another two days. The wind was still up but not as raw, the sun was over the cloud bank, the bright signal flags snapped against the blue. I felt my body uncoiling. But I was still determined to say everything I felt I needed to say.

Kara shared the place with Jazz and Issime. Jazz was assistant manager at Breakers, and Issime was back from Boston U for Christmas break. Both were asleep.

These Compass Rose units were new and pricey. Kara's parents had bought her condo for her, and she shared it with her friends who chipped in for utilities. I liked Jazz and Issime, but I was glad they were still in their rooms and under the blankets.

Kara was in her Snoopy pajamas. She came with the coffee and rolls. Swept a tangle of red hair back from her forehead and plopped in a big, fat, comfy chair facing me.

"What's the drama?" she asked.

I wrapped my fingers tightly around the coffee mug she'd given me. I liked the heat. But I didn't say anything.

She swept her hair back again. "No woman is an island. So, is that what you feel like you've been?"

"Yes."

"You have a lot of friends now. Me and the gals. The artists' group. Don't you and Hawthorne have a good friendship?"

"No. Yes. But no. No."

"What?"

"He's been so good to talk to. He's such a good listener."

"Totally. He's the nicest guy."

"I have to let him go. But how do I avoid him when we're both living on a small island?"

Kara stopped sipping from her mug and put it down on a round coffee table. "I must have missed something. Why are we letting him go?"

"He's too nice."

"Too nice?"

I blew out a lungful of air I'd been holding in. Time to stop shaflooting around. A word my mother had made up. "I want him to hold me in his arms."

This information stopped Kara cold. I got the big eyes, green eyes stare. "You do?"

I nodded once and held my coffee close enough to my mouth to cover most of my face. "Very much. Too very much."

"Umm. I guess I'm having trouble seeing the problem here, Denna. A nice guy. A nice woman. God or fate or the universe brings them together to give them some happiness. And the issue is—?"

"I'm a widow."

"So? Widows find new relationships all the time."

"It's only been eighteen months."

"How long do you want it to be?"

"Two years. Three years."

"What? Who told you that? The Amish?"

"No. Amish widows may remarry sooner than that."

"The Bible?"

"No."

"So, who?"

"Me."

"So, Sara King is alive and well and punishing herself. Why?"

"I'm not punishing myself."

"Do Amish widows take three years to remarry?"

"Not if God brings a good man to them."

"So, hasn't God brought a good man to you?"

I closed my eyes. "What am I supposed to do? Approach him? Women don't do that."

"It's the 21st century, girl. A woman can do whatever she wants."

"It's too bold. It's awkward. It's uncomfortable. And I have no idea about dating. No Amish do."

Kara bit into a roll and chewed a moment. "Do you want him or not?"

"I ... I would like to see if we could draw closer, yes."

"So, talk to him about it."

"I can't. It's too ..."

"Weird?"

"All right. Ja. It's too weird."

"It's only weird in your head. He'll be perfectly fine talking about it."

"No, he won't. He said he didn't want anything to do with romance. Friendship was all he was interested in."

"Yes, well, I'm sure he said that because he knew that's where you were in your thinking, and he didn't want to scare you away. Any man would be a fool not to take you up on an offer to explore the possibility of a romantic relationship."

"It's not what he wants."

"Why don't you ask him if that's what he wants today? Now? This Christmas?"

"How do I do that? I can't do that. I have no idea how to say I want him to hold me in his arms."

"Mark, I really want you to hold me in your arms." Jazz had showed up. "It's easy. Only eleven words. You don't even need German or Pennsylvania Dutch."

I made a face. "Easy for beautiful you, Jazz."

"Ha. Which should make it even easier for far more beautiful you, Lyyndenna."

I shook my head. "It cannot happen. It simply cannot."

Kara raised those dark, dark eyebrows of hers at Jazz. "Better get Issime in on this. We're going to need all the help we can get."

CHAPTER 10

WE ARE AND WE ARE NOT

She spent the morning with the girls. It was all about dating and relationships and being real and being herself. In their words. She went away bewildered. And completely uncertain about the role she was supposed to play. Among the Amish it was easy to court and be courted. Everyone knew what they were supposed to do. Out beyond the Amish farms and communities? Everything was out the window. There was no one way of doing anything. Let alone courting. Or dating. Or relationships. Or romance.

Romance. Was that truly what she wanted? She realized she had to be the one to broach the subject with Hawthorne. She had, in Issime's words, dumped him at least twice, "... leaving the sad dude on the beach with his hands in his pockets, the wind in his face, and his heart in his boots. No way in the universe is the guy going to bring up a romantic relationship with you. I don't care how uncomfortable you are, Denna. If you really want something to happen with this guy you're going to have to do the heavy lifting."

She brooded about this. Decided she either had to spill all to Hawthorne or forget about him forever and find another island. Like Martha's Vineyard, ha-ha. It had three.

She bit her lip and texted him a week before Christmas.

SHE: Hawthorne?

HE: 'Lo!

SHE: Can we get together?

HE: I just saw you Saturday at the group.

SHE: Ok, yes, I know, I mean another kind of get-together.

HE: A beach get-together.

SHE: Yes. That.

HE: Which beach? What time?

SHE: Northwest? In half an hour?

HE: I'll be there.

She waited the whole half-hour and a bit longer. Almost didn't leave the cottage. Then hurled herself into Bachi and drove to the beach. Her fingertips felt as cold as snow and her heart as rigid as cast iron. She took her time walking to the boulder covered in seaweed. Hawthorne was actually sitting on it.

"Hey." My new way of talking I'd picked up from Kara and the crew.

Hawthorne turned around and smiled. He was wearing an old army jacket in OD, olive drab. The sight of women and men in jackets like his was not uncommon on the island.

"Hey," he responded.

"Are you warm enough in that?"

"I am. It's got sheepskin lining."

"Would you like to walk?"

We headed along the beach. It was cold and quiet and still. Not yet lunch. He started chatting about Christmas Eve so I knew I had to jump in or that's all we'd end up talking about.

"Hawthorne," I interrupted.

I think my tone was a bit strident. He stopped walking and looked at me. "What is it? What's the matter?"

All my careful plans about when I would say what, in a perfectly choreographed progression, flew away with the December wind. I had to give him the opportunity to say what he truly felt, and I didn't want to lose my nerve. I looked up at him, and I know very well I was looking at him differently than I ever had. Not that I thought about it at the moment.

"Is it difficult for you to spend time with me?" I asked.

Which was not what I intended to say. My brain and my tongue were clumsy. And now it was out there and up to him to deal with. I only regretted it sounded confrontational. But better that than nothing.

Hawthorne was perplexed. "Why ... what makes you say that? Have I given you cause to say that? I'm truly sorry if I have, Denna. You're a delight to be with."

"Truly?"

"Of course. Yes. Truly. What makes you think otherwise?"

"Nothing makes me think otherwise, Hawthorne. I just want to know if ... if you think well enough of me to take our friendship further."

"Further?"

This was getting more difficult instead of easier. Do I have to spell everything out? "You once told me you didn't want romance. Ever. With anyone. Do you still feel that way?"

I could see he was staggered. "Romance?"

Oh, Hawthorne! I am terrible at this. But so are you. Are you going to keep on repeating back to me everything I say? "Yes, romance, Hawthorne. Like in your novels. Like in your characters' lives. Is romance completely out for you? Do you ever, would you ever, do you think it would be something special ... if ..." I prayed and took the plunge. I might as well get it out and over with. He could call me crazy and we'd go back to our lives and iPads and loneliness. "If we had a romance of our own? A real genuine honest to God romance that was more than skin deep?"

Okay. Done.

I was still looking up at him as the wind picked up, and pieces of snow caught in our hair and melted against our faces.

So, I don't know what I expected, but I should have expected more from a writer because that's what I got.

"You have the bluest eyes." His voice had dropped almost to a whisper. But I heard him. "I've never given myself permission to really look at them until now. But you have the bluest eyes."

I liked the warm feeling his words gave me. Thank the Lord God he felt something for Lyyndenna Patrick. How much? Who knew? For that matter, how much did I feel for him? But no one other than my mother had ever drawn attention to the vivid color of my eyes. They simply were not plain. For years I had hated their brilliance and felt they made me mawkish and ugly. Now I was having a new sensation altogether. Hawthorne was gazing so deeply into my eyes I felt his look penetrated to the red marrow of my bones. There was an immediate rush of pure happiness that made me almost cry.

So long. It had been so long since I mattered to anyone. So long since a man I liked had liked me back. I sank my head upon his chest. I didn't even think about it. It was either that or sit down. I didn't consider it bold or presumptuous. It was simply the most natural thing to do. Jazz had said, "Go with simple and uncomplicated. Go with natural and uncontrived. But go." The great gift came seconds after I closed my eyes over his heart. His arms slowly and carefully wrapped themselves around me, as if I were fragile, as if I might say no. If he only knew.

His great kindness was in those arms. His friendship. It was the thing I wanted most. I placed a mittened hand on his coat and chest. I was in seventh heaven. I didn't say it out loud but I wanted to be held a little tighter. Just a little tighter. As if he were listening, bit by bit his arms put more strength around me like a band of copper. I snuggled. I burrowed. My cheeks shone with the quiet crying from my eyes. I felt safe. So safe. So wanted. I felt his lips gently press against my forehead. The wind struck and struck, but I didn't care. I didn't want to go anywhere. I understood nothing except that right now was the place I most needed to be.

It felt strange, strange, but the best kind of strange, a strange that did not paralyze, a strange that beckoned and enticed and exhilarated. If you thought I was going to pull back and run again, you had no idea of how his spirit drew me in and held me. His arms were wonderful but had little to do with my staying in his embrace. It was all that I felt far past his skin and muscles and bones. Far past his heart. The essence of who and what he was held me. The Amish would call that his soul.

At some point, we walked again. It snowed, it stopped, it snowed, it stopped. "Be a little presumptuous," Kara had advised, "but be presumptuous gently and a little secretly." My plans now were even simpler than they had been when I first showed up on the beach. I went with the flow of the tide. The tide within. I took his hand. I leaned my head against his shoulder. It made walking more awkward. I didn't care. It felt spiritual. It felt right.

I prayed to God he would not kiss me. I did not want that. It would break something. Everything was so fragile right now. We needed time to grow into something more. He must have felt the same way because the only kisses he ever gave me were on top of my blue knit beanie. I could feel those from far away, and I liked them very much. I suppose the biggest realization was that I liked him very much too. More than I thought I had. A seven, the way Issime put it, was actually an eight and hovering at nine.

"No, it's not a nine," I told her that evening at their condo in the Compass Rose building. "But definitely a solid eight."

Issime smiled. "Definite?"

"Definite."

"What's next?"

"Another long walk and then dinner at Bowline on a Bight."

"Ooooo," they all went at once.

"Fancy." Kara.

"Posh." Issime.

"He does like you," laughed Jazz. "All along he's had this secret crush he didn't dare talk about. Now he can cut loose ha-ha-ha."

"Ha-ha-ha yourself," I fired back. "I'm sure he's nowhere as interested in me as you think he is."

Which I didn't think was true and certainly hoped wasn't true but I'd learned to have the last word with that crew whenever possible.

Hawthorne understood I was still Amish enough not to enjoy posh. The truth was that Bowline on a Bight wasn't posh at all. It was old (I think 1745), brick, splendid with antiques, and the food was excellent. A little more than chowder and sourdough but, to be honest, the meal wasn't the highlight of the evening. It was a calm night, and Hawthorne drove us away from the village in his pickup so we could watch the Christmas stars glittering over a flat black sea. Then he took me to a church away and gone I didn't even know about, a simple white wooden church with a simple white steeple. It was locked, but he had a key.

"How did you get that?" I asked him.

"Well, the long story is my novel Walking on Water."

"I'd like to know right now. So, what's the synopsis?"

"I can do better than a synopsis. I can give you the two sentence blurb. Mark Hawthorne used to pastor here many moons ago. When I returned to be Joe Writer on St. Silvan's, they gave me a key, so I could pray here whenever I wanted."

"Now I want to read the novel."

"It's at the public library in Gloucester. You can have it sent here to ours and snag it."

"You were a pastor here. I'm amazed." I tried to read the sign in the dark. "What church is this?"

"St. Mark's."

"How appropriate."

"I thought so."

He guided me inside and flicked a light switch. Electricity at the snap of a finger was still something I was getting used to. I rarely used it at the cottage. The church was small, lined with enough wooden pews for fifty or sixty, had a sturdy pulpit carved like a wave, and stained glass windows lit from beneath that were fragments of blue. I adored the blue. Which I knew he knew. I sat down by one of the windows. Closed my eyes. Let my mind drift. Deep greens and blues, just like that song again.

"You're not going to fall asleep on me, are you?" Hawthorne teased.

I smiled, leaving my eyes shut. "I'm mediating. Just waiting for the service to start."

"It started the moment you walked in the door."

"Then I'm waiting for the message."

"The message? I don't do that anymore."

Be bold when it suits, the girls had coaxed. Boldness was in my nature. I was able to admit that eight months after leaving the farm. But not when it came to men. About whom I knew nothing. Nevertheless. "You'll do it for me."

I couldn't believe I actually said that.

Truthfully, I thought my feigned self-confidence was going to fall flat on its face.

I could feel the heat in my cheeks.

Then he began to speak.

I can't describe the storm of emotions that set off in me.

He really was going to do it for me.

I wasn't used to that from anyone.

Let alone a man I'd come to admire.

Still, I did not open my eyes.

"This chapel was built for fishermen and whalers and their families in 1699," he said. "Of course, it's been repaired and refurbished over the years, but it's still substantially the same chapel set on the same foundation. There was a garrison here once too, but its barracks and brick buildings were destroyed during the course of the Revolution. It changed hands many times so far as denominations go—Methodist, Calvinist, Baptist, Episcopalian. Now it's considered interdenominational. Various members of the congregation, women or men, speak on Sunday evenings when they gather."

I didn't respond.

So, he picked up where he'd left off. "I suppose you want me to say something spiritual and not just recite a history of St. Mark's. So, then it's this—we're all rebuilt and restored and renewed over a lifetime. There's fire and theft and storm and destruction. But we're built on the foundation we had from the beginning. Our body and our soul. Foundations are improved upon and strengthened. But it's still us with different windows and roofs and doors. In one sense, we are always ourselves from day one. In another sense, we aren't because we are constantly in flux and constantly changing. We are old, and we are new. We're ourselves, and we're different selves. We're still us, and we're altered versions of us at the same time. We are, and we are not. God help us."

I was thinking of Daniel and Jacob. I was thinking of the Pennsylvania I left behind. I was thinking of how good life had been during my twenties, and I was thinking of how hard and painful it had been too.

God help us? Yes, sometimes God's presence and blessing were obvious. Other times God was nowhere to be seen, felt, or heard. What did it mean to live and love by faith? To never see the unseen but still trust it? To never hear the unheard but still hear it? Did it mean to walk through the valley of death over and over again but fear no evil regardless of a constant shadow or grief or threat? What if there was no healing, never any healing, what if Jesus did not come by? Was my foundation truly still there being restored and rebuilt? Or was I a wreck built on sand and sinking, sinking, sinking ...

My tears were streaming down my face. I could not help it. I kept swiping at my cheeks with my hands, but it did not help. I could not stop the pain and bewilderment and loss.

"Denna," came his soft troubled voice. "Lyyndenna."

"Don't talk," I told him as I sobbed and choked. "There's nothing to say. Just hold me, Mark. Just hold me. Please."

I wept into his arms and chest and could not be consoled.

CHAPTER 11

BEAUTIFUL

So, if my story were one of the Hallmark Christmas movies the girls got me to watch, my life would have been put in order and healed by God and romance on Christmas Eve. If it were one of the Amish fictions so many read and enjoy, the result would have been something along the same lines. I know because I've read the Amish love stories. Three of them.

Few Amish read such books. Few English who read such books become Amish. It is a pleasant entertainment to them and, I pray, a spiritual encouragement. I do not begrudge them their innocent pleasures. But real Amish life is both beautiful and difficult, light and shadow, sweet and sour. It is a different path and for some the best path. But no path on earth is free of stones and stubble any more than any bed of roses is free of thorns or every green forest, lovely as it may seem, is absent of poison oak. Yes, I know a number of the Amish romances are honest about that. God bless them.

Still, according to a typical Hallmark or romance storyline, Amish or not, Hawthorne and I should have kissed under the English mistletoe about the same time as everything dawned on me, and I understood exactly what God was doing and had been doing all along. Any bitterness or resentment would have been washed away.

Or if not then, I would have been granted an extraordinary spiritual resolve to get me through and keep me going. I suppose if you wanted to stick to that script then Hawthorne was my miracle.

But he wasn't really. He was simply a good man who did not have all the answers or the keys to all the doors. He was my rock, for sure, as much as any human could be, but he wasn't God or the universe or the road through the valley of the shadow of death. We had to walk that together. Everyone has their own wounds and they seek their own healings. Including Mark Hawthorne. So that's what happened Christmas Eve and Christmas Day. That's what happened New Year's Eve and New Year's Day. Beginnings. Not endings and resolutions.

Besides. The whole week was a blizzard. In the books, the skies would have been crystal clear Christmas Eve. Or, if we did get snowed in, we'd finally be stuck together and kiss. Instead we met in the storm New Year's Eve and walked by a raging sea, tightly holding hands as the wind beat and battered us.

"Would you return to Pennsylvania?" Hawthorne asked me, holding his head close to mine, so I'd hear him despite the howl.

"I might." I was just being honest. I wasn't trying to hurt him.

"Would you take up the Amish ways again? Pin up your hair? Wear the long dresses?"

"I might."

"So ..."

"So, no, I can't tell you what will happen next year. And you can't tell me. But I'm also being honest if I tell you I might stay on this island with you for the rest of my life."

"You might?"

He looked so hopeful. Like a puppy. I laughed and patted his cheek. "You're too sweet for me. Ja, I might.

Just as you might return to Pennsylvania and convert. So much is possible. But I confess. The crooked places in my head and heart need to be made straight and the rough places plain before I'm going anywhere. Whether that's a geographical location or a relationship."

"What about us then, Lyyndenna?"

"Us? This is us now. Life isn't a movie or a storybook, is it? Things don't come to completion in one reading or in two hours. We have a lot to talk about, don't we? It will take time. But please don't look so worried. I'm ready to take the time. And I want to be with you, Mark. Take a moment to look at what my eyes are saying. I want to be with you."

He stared past my frozen eyelashes and laughed. "They certainly are saying something nice to me."

"Good. I'm glad you're picking up on what Jazz would call my vibes, ha-ha. Are you picking up on anything else?"

A fierce blast tore my knit beanie from my head and sent it spinning off into the sleet and dark. I squealed as the storm grabbed a hold of my hair and played with it, streaming it behind me like the mane of a palomino mare. I could almost hear the wind laugh in a silly, happy, boyish way. I could certainly hear Mark Hawthorne's laugh. It was the same kind.

"Yes, I'm picking up on something else." He was smiling, trying to catch my hair for me while it ran and looped through his hands like a golden rope. "You're beautiful, Lyyndenna. The most beautiful woman I've ever seen. You're more beautiful than the ocean. You're more beautiful than a dream."

ABOUT MURRAY PURA

Murray Pura has over twenty-four novels to his credit and, in addition, has published dozens of short stories, novellas, and poems along with numerous books of nonfiction. He has worked with Baker, Barbour, Zondervan, Harvest House, MillerWords, HarperCollins, Harlequin, Harper One, and Elk Lake Publishing. His fiction has won or been short listed for a number of literary prizes. Pura has lived in the UK, the Middle East, the USA and Canada. He now makes his home in the Rocky Mountains of Alberta.

A BABY IN THE BARN

PeggySue Wells

CHAPTER 1

Glancing at the time, Larkin Hammond knew she would land in plenty of time to sweep her husband away from the office to their surprise date. Feeling the commercial airplane begin its descent to the San Francisco Airport, she gave her empty cup to the patrolling Flight attendant, and slid sketches and purchase receipts into her briefcase.

The August trip to San Diego had been productive and she felt eager to show her husband the sensational pieces she'd selected for their showroom. Hammond Interiors catered to wealthy homeowners in the San Francisco Bay Area, blending the customer's unique personality with an efficient layout.

For the final minutes of the flight, she opened email on her phone, already envisioning an evening with her husband at a candlelit table featuring entrees prepared by her favorite chef.

"Hey, Mom, loved seeing you this weekend. Can't wait for your next buying trip so we can go shopping again."

Larkin smiled at the message from Jillian. An unexpected pregnancy brought Larkin home to raise their daughter, and once Jillian launched, Larkin returned to the store. This buying trip had been the best of both worlds. Larkin shopped favorite suppliers for the latest designs and spent the weekend with Jillian, a marine biologist at Scripps Institution of Oceanography.

Today, Monday, Larkin had checked in early at the airport. "Is there a seat available on an earlier flight?"

The airline representative had studied her computer screen, and when she arched a perfectly shaped eyebrow, Larkin knew the answer was yes. Now, she scanned her inbox and opened a message from a law firm.

> As per his last will and testament, your father left the Old Traction Barn to you. Following months of legal requirements, the title search and other details are complete. As the representing firm, we would like to finalize the transfer of ownership as soon as you can make arrangements to travel to Indiana.

With the customary roar of the powerful engines, the plane dropped easily onto the tarmac and taxied to the terminal. Larkin made a mental note to follow-up regarding the quirky inheritance as she disembarked. Pulling her wheeled case behind, she threaded her way through the familiar passageways. Ducking into a restroom, she freshened her make-up, reapplying smudgy eyeliner and rose-tinted lipstick. Expertly, she tucked the front of her shoulder length hair into a clip, pulling loose several strands to fall whimsically around her face. Last, she applied her husband's favorite perfume from an airport-approved sample size before tossing her makeup case back into her oversized designer purse.

Outside the airport, the air felt thick with exhaust from airport shuttles and city buses. She hailed a taxi. Smelling of cigarette smoke, the driver nodded when she gave the address. She settled back in her seat and used her cellphone to make dinner reservations for two.

The taxi efficiently deposited her at the stylish front of Hammond Interiors. Larkin pushed open the front door and inhaled the fragrance of new furniture and polishing oils.

One of the designers came forward. "Welcome home, Mrs. Hammond. May I take your case for you?"

"Thank you." She surveyed the welcoming showroom as she followed Charlie to the offices. An instrumental soundtrack, mixed with water sounds, played in the background.

Approaching her husband's office, her heartbeat quickened. Surprising him now was part of the evening she had anticipated all weekend. But, the room was empty. A quick search of the other offices produced the same results.

"Hey, Charlie," Larkin found the designer in the showroom, "where's the boss?"

A quiet and steady family man, Charlie avoided conflict like a toothache. "Oh." Charlie appeared to consider. "He had a meeting with legal."

"Legal?" Larkin took mental inventory but couldn't recall any reason to consult with their attorney.

"Something about tightening the wording on our design contracts."

"I see." Grabbing her purse, she turned toward the door.

"I can call him for you," Charlie offered.

"No, I'll pick him up at their office."

Charlie cleared his throat. "They were meeting at the Hyatt."

"Perfect. There is a guest chef, and I made dinner reservations for tonight." She called over her shoulder, "See you tomorrow."

A second taxi took her to the Hyatt. The open interior sparkled with light that reflected off polished surfaces. Larkin made her way to the comfortable yet formal seating clusters where businesspeople typically met. Her husband wasn't there, so she sat down.

Maybe this was silly. The whole idea of surprising him with her early return and a romantic evening was becoming cumbersome. She fingered her cell phone. She could call him. It would eliminate the surprise element, but at least she wouldn't be chasing him across the city. No doubt he would still be surprised by her early arrival. Even when she had completed a buying trip ahead of schedule, it had never occurred to her in the past to request an earlier flight.

Larkin pressed speed dial for her husband's number. At the bar a short way from where she sat, she heard the notes to the song she and her husband danced to at their wedding reception. Glancing toward the sound, Larkin saw her husband perched on a stool next to an attorney their office kept on retainer.

There he is. She hit the end button and began walking in his direction even as he picked up the phone from where it lay on the table. But rather than answer, Larkin saw him hit the end button, set the phone back down and lean close to the attorney. Very close.

Confused, Larkin slowed her steps, and then stopped. There were people all around, but now she was only aware of two. To be that close, he should be leaning over paperwork, but there was nothing on the small round table where they sat but two empty drink glasses. Laughing, she ran a brightly polished fingernail suggestively down his cheek. When he said something close to her ear, the young woman nodded. As the two got up, the woman's purse dropped, and several items spilled out. She knelt to pick them up, revealing mile long legs under a short skirt, a view Larkin could see her husband taking in as he reached for a tube of lipstick that rolled away.

Larkin felt her own legs begin to tremble.

Squatting next to the attorney, Larkin's husband placed the lipstick in her palm and his lips on hers. Though brief, the moment was so intimate that Larkin felt like an intruder. Tears filled her eyes, and she bit her lip to hold back the sob that threatened to burst from her heart.

Feeling colorless, lifeless, invisible, she followed at a distance on leaden legs as the couple left their table. In seconds, the two were inside an elevator, the doors closed, and Larkin's husband took another woman into his arms on their way up to a hotel room. From below, with tears streaming down her cheeks, Larkin watched through the elevator's glass walls.

CHAPTER 2

While the taxi sped through traffic, Larkin made a quick phone call to a company that delivered for Holland Interiors. Next, she wrote a list.

At her home address, she handed the list and a company check to the muscled men from the delivery company. "Pack these items and place them in storage. Have these things out of the house before 7:00 o'clock tonight, and I'll double the amount."

The fellows grinned. "Count on it."

Checking the time, Larkin sent her husband a text telling him she made reservations for dinner at 7:00 o'clock. She would meet him at the restaurant. Calculating the time, she filled a suitcase with personal effects, jewelry, important papers, and cash she kept in a safe just in case.

Satisfied that the packers were well on their way to completing her list, she gave them the second promised check with instructions where to store her things, and to keep the information private.

"I understand." The young man was the son of the storage company's owners. He soberly held out his hand. "Call me when I can do anything to help."

"Thank you." She accepted his handshake. "I'll take you up on that."

Larkin gave the house a final glance. She wheeled her suitcase to the taxi driver, who had waited at the curb as instructed.

At Holland Interiors, it was nearly closing time. Larkin held her phone to her ear as if on a call, avoiding eye contact with staff. She grabbed empty boxes from recent shipments, and behind the closed door of her office, quickly packed personal items. When everyone had gone for the evening, the driver, who she had again asked to wait, loaded the boxes into the taxi.

"Where to?" The taxi driver looked at her from the rearview mirror.

Good question. Her cell phone dinged with a text. The message was from her husband. A single question mark. It was 7:30 p.m. and he waited for her to join him at the restaurant. The reservation had given her just enough time to clear her office. Now what? Should she confront him now or later?

Seeing her reflection in the rearview mirror, clearly the day had held enough excitement. She needed time to gather her thoughts and respond rather than react.

Another text came in. *Where are you?*

The exact question she planned to ask him when she had telephoned at the Hyatt.

"Where to?" The driver repeated his question.

She fought the temptation to let her emotions dictate her actions. An email from the moving and storage company provided the code to access her things, and she gave the location to the driver. As the taxi wound through the streets, Larkin recalled Charlie's stiffness when he told her where to find her husband. Like a knife to her gut, she relived the scene where her husband kissed another woman in a way he had not kissed her in a long time. She swore. Apparently, Larkin had been the only one in their immediate circle unaware of the affair.

Being alone tonight would not be smart. Neither would she go to a friend's house. She didn't want expressions of pity. She didn't want to feel naïve in front of friends, who would realize she had been the only one unaware for who knows how long.

Feeling humiliated and stupid, she scrolled through her email for ideas and saw again the message from the law office. "Perfect timing."

She needed to think, to respond wisely. At the storage place, she added the boxes from her office. Quickly, she packed two large suitcases and got back into the waiting taxi.

"Where to?

WHERE ARE YOU? Another text from her husband. No phone call to say, "Hey, are you all right?"

She turned off her phone. "The airport."

CHAPTER 3

Leaving the Midwest airport in a rental car, Larkin found comfort in the consistent miles of corn, soy, and wheat fields. Soon, John Deere tractors gave way to horse-drawn plows cultivating clean fields skirting white farmhouses and barns, large kitchen gardens neatly edged with flowers, and handmade clothes drying on outdoor lines. She passed an occasional buggy pulled by a trotting bay horse, as well as a number of bonneted girls and shaggy-headed boys astride bicycles.

At Troyer Elevator, Caleb Troyer handed her an oversized envelope the law firm had left for her.

At her destination, Larkin parked and read the information about her inheritance. The Old Traction Barn once served trains, then housed a grammar school, and was converted into apartments before being abandoned. The traction barn looked as deflated and worn as Larkin felt.

Fishing a key from the envelope, she let herself inside and took an extensive interior tour of the historic structure. Back outside, she circled the property and found a fairly new barn equipped with three stalls, working lights, and a water spigot. In fact, the barn was in better shape than the larger building.

Her exploration complete, Larkin returned inside the Old Traction Barn. Using the facilities, she felt relieved to find the law firm had kept the utilities in operation. Alone in an unfamiliar town and feeling like an alien in a foreign country, Larkin stood in the silent, dusty heirloom amidst piles of forgotten furniture, stacks of aged household items, discarded clothing, dusty books, and pieces of unneeded construction.

What good is this old building? What good is a middle-aged woman with one previous owner?

"Looks like we both need a future." Resting her hands on her hips, she regarded the large structure with an artist's eye. "Let's help one another. I'll fix you up. Then, you sell for a tidy sum which will fund my future."

The next day, Larkin sent a text to let her daughter. "I'm in Indiana for a while, updating a piece of my father's property."

Considering the list she had made of the improvements needed to make the Traction Barn sellable, she placed orders with suppliers. Caleb Troyer provided the name of a respected contractor in the area, and Larkin walked the property with the contractor, weighing options to refurbish the structure economically.

The next several days felt like Christmas as Larkin's orders arrived. She came to know the UPS driver on a first name basis and formulated plans for where she would craft her new life as a single woman. San Francisco was an obvious choice since she had connections there, but the city by the Bay had a small-town atmosphere, and she didn't relish competing against herself. After all, so much of Holland Interiors reflected her business plan and design skills. Traveling in similar circles with her ex would prove awkward at least, and most likely result in hostility. Too exhausting. In San Diego, she could be near Jillian.

Then Troyer's Elevator declined her credit card as did her most used supplier. The credit card company said the card had been cancelled. An online check of her bank accounts showed a zero balance. She telephoned her attorney.

"The news isn't good." Her attorney explained her finances and possessions in San Francisco were frozen, and Larkin recalled that Holland Interiors had hired a bright and quick-thinking legal firm. The same attorney who was her husband's girlfriend.

Larkin hung up and fought an overpowering urge to weep. The situation was terribly unfair. Bypassing the Kleenex, she swore and began to clean. The sooner she got the Traction Barn ready for sale, the sooner Larkin could move on and build a life for herself.

For three days, Larkin worked through her frustration by sorting and cleaning. She made lists of what she had. A shopping list of supplies to make improvements. Piles of recyclables, piles of donations, and piles she didn't know what to do with. When she felt like screaming and breaking someone's neck, she channeled the hurt and anger into productive effort. When sleep eluded her and her mind went back to California, she rolled up her sleeves and tackled the next project.

Saturday afternoon, she answered a knock to find Jillian on her doorstep.

"How are you, Mama?"

Larkin brushed away happy tears, and the two embraced for a long time.

Jillian took her by the shoulders. "Really. How are you?"

Larkin waved a hand to indicate the Old Traction Barn. "Like this place, I've seen better days."

"Give me the twenty-five-cent tour."

After seeing everything, Jillian put on the kettle. Over cups of strong black tea laced with honey and cream, her daughter asked questions ranging from who Larkin had met in the community, to her split of the interior design business. They created a timeline for making the Traction Barn marketable and Larkin's move to Southern California.

With a sigh, she poured them both a second cup of tea and buttered two slices of sourdough bread she'd brought from California. "Remember when I was a kid and you read all those books aloud to me?"

Larkin smiled. Reading aloud had been something Larkin began when Jillian was a baby. After Jillian learned to read, they read to one another until Jillian went to college.

Her daughter swept her arm to include their surroundings. "This feels like being the Boxcar Children. For now, you need to make this collection of things serviceable to generate income."

Larkin nodded. "Leverage what you have in your hand."

"The apartment can become a bed and breakfast." Jillian began a list. "And the front room can be an interior design showroom."

"With what stock? I don't have the finances to purchase inventory."

"Not the way you did in San Francisco. But different clientele would be interested in shabby chic." Her daughter tapped the tabletop. "This place is already a showroom for that style."

The multitude of items that populated the Old Traction Barn had been a mess to clean around. Now she considered the bounty with fresh eyes.

"Good," Jillian enthused. "Let's see what we can accomplish in the week I'm here."

She shook her head. "Don't spend your hard-earned vacation on a mission trip to bail your mother."

Jillian stood and tied an apron around her waist. "This is not charity. This is a new beginning. My mother told me to embrace them with arms wide."

CHAPTER 4

They made a trip to the elevator where Larkin frugally spent some of her cash on key items that would provide the most return for the investment in terms of sellable inventory.

At the counter, in boots and jeans, a man talked with the owner. "I need a sack of horse grain, a salt block, a bale of alfalfa, and a place to house a pregnant mare."

Caleb Troyer tipped his chin to the trailer parked outside. "A patient of yours, Doc?"

"Worse, she doesn't have a home."

"She'll keep just fine in your vet clinic." Caleb hitched a suspender. "Seems the best place to birth a baby."

The vet shook his head. "There's no room in my inn. I'm full up with patients that need to be there, and with winter weather setting in and predators, I can't leave her in the pasture."

Jillian stepped closer. "We—I mean she—" she indicated Larkin "has a barn."

Immediately both men focused on Larkin. "That's not entirely true," Larkin stammered.

Her daughter went on. "You have a barn."

"And I'm not the person to care for a horse."

The vet shouldered the 50-pound sack of grain. "Come on and meet her."

Jillian linked her arm through her mother's and steered her outdoors. Parked near a grassy patch, a white horse trailer was hitched to a matching pickup. Green letters on the side read, Midwest Veterinary. The vet opened the horse trailer door and led a brown and white paint down the ramp.

The mare knickered softly and touched her nose to the man's knee. "Okay, girl." He reached into his pocket, removed the wrapper, and offered her a candy cane.

"She's just like Mary." Jillian stoked the soft-eyed mare's neck. "She needs a place to have her baby."

"I can't keep a goldfish alive." Larkin shook her head. "You had pets only when you were old enough to care for them."

"She's an easy keeper," the man said. "I can show you what she needs."

Glancing from the vet to her daughter, she could see this had quickly become two against one. "I'm not in a place to take on an added expense." Now this was embarrassing.

The vet's shoulders sagged. "I understand."

Jillian appeared deep in thought. "Business 101. You and your horse need a barn. She has a barn and would benefit from income."

His eyes brightened. "Where is your barn?"

Larkin hooked a thumb in the direction they had come. "The Old Traction Barn."

"Ah, I thought I saw lights when I drove past recently." He considered. "How about I pay you room and board to keep her until something else can be arranged."

"But I don't know the first thing—"

"I'll set her up, leave instructions, and check in between my rounds."

Before Larkin could protest, Jillian held out her hand. "Deal."

With a grin, he accepted the handshake. "Done."

Back at the barn, the vet expertly maneuvered the horse trailer near the doors and parked.

"What have you gotten me into," Larkin murmured as they watched him unload the wide-girthed horse.

"Just let her eat grass." He handed the lead rope to Larkin, and he and Jillian set about hauling feed and bedding into the barn.

Larkin and the mare studied one another. She patted the broad forehead of this large animal who smelled of peppermint.

"The inn is ready." Jillian looked positively beaming.

Indoors, fresh shavings filled the stall, and a grain bucket hung next to a salt block. The mare took a long drink, and water dripped from her lips as she investigated her new surroundings.

Opening the grain sack, he showed them how much to feed morning and night. Larkin served the evening's meal, and the horse eagerly tucked into the mix that smelled of rich molasses. With a pocketknife, he cut the bailing twine on the alfalfa and peeled off a couple flakes. "Open the rear door each morning and she will go out in the corral as she wants. Close her indoors when you feed in the evening."

"When will she have the baby?" Larkin fought back panic.

"Probably at night when she is safe indoors."

"Soon?"

He looked her over. "I think it will be a while yet."

Having finished her grain, the horse went into the corral. Outside, Larkin, Jillian, and the vet leaned on the railing. The corral was overgrown, which seemed just fine to the new resident.

From his wallet, the vet peeled off four hundred-dollar bills and handed them to Larkin. "This is the going rate for board, and I'll provide feed and bedding."

"What about a contract?" In California, Larkin did everything with a contract.

His eyebrows went up. "Well, if that makes you feel better. Otherwise, I'll be stopping in regularly, and," he checked the date on his watch, "pay by this day each month."

"Hopefully, you will find her a real home before next month."

He surveyed the yard. "Where will you put your garden?"

"Why would I have a garden?"

"Why not? Just let me know where you want me to dump your steady supply of fertilizer."

Before Larkin could think of a reply, his phone rang, and he walked away to answer.

Jillian grinned. "Your first B&B customer."

"This isn't how I thought it would look." Larkin sighed. "Nothing in my life right now is how I thought it would look."

Jillian threw out her arms. "Except me. I turned out okay."

Larkin put an arm around her daughter's shoulders. "You turned out better than I'd imagined."

The vet returned with a box of mini candy canes. "Gotta go for a farm call." He handed the box to Jillian. "You'll need these, she's pretty fond of them."

Jillian took the box. "What's her name?"

"Didn't come with one, so you can name her." He was nearly to his truck when he turned back and held out his hand to Larkin. She took in his graying temples, the smiles lines by his eyes. Honest eyes.

"By the way, I'm Tobias."

CHAPTER 5

With sandpaper, stripper, and paint from the Troyer's Elevator, Larkin and Jillian stripped and refinished furniture. Once there was a respectable amount of inventory, they worked on creating a showroom in the broad first room. Lunch breaks, the two fed the eager mare apples and candy canes. Each morning and evening, they went to the barn and followed the instructions Tobias left for the care of the horse.

With Jillian there, the week flew by. Larkin's heartbreak took a backseat to joy in her daughter's presence and their shared goal to create a future.

"We're going to church," Jillian announced Saturday night as she fed the mare.

Broom in hand, Larkin swept cobwebs from the rafters. "Why?"

"Church is a good place to meet people. I'll feel better leaving in the afternoon if you have connections."

Dread. Larkin didn't want to face people just yet. Maybe ever. Didn't want anyone to see the shame she felt after being rejected by her husband. Betrayed by her work associate. She beat dust from the corners.

Jillian took her by the arm and led Larkin to the stall. She put a soft-bristled brush in her hand. "Time to tell me what's on your mind."

Running the brush along the horse's back, Larkin didn't want to open that Pandora's box.

With a comb, Jillian smoothed the mane on the opposite side of the mare who contentedly munched grain from her bucket. "If I were you," Jillian began, "I think I'd feel like I needed a redo like the furniture we've been fixing."

Tears stung Larkin's eyes.

"I might feel like this mare who is about to give birth and needs a home and someone to care for her."

A sob. "And you have to leave too."

"I'm returning to work. That's not leaving." Jillian came around to look into her mother's eyes. "I know at this moment they feel the same, but this is living life. Not another rejection."

Backs against the wall, the two sat in the stall as Larkin's tears continued to fall. The horse finished her grain and nosed through the alfalfa, coming up with a mouthful of dry green leaves.

"Like all of us," Jillian put an alfalfa stem in her mouth, "you have now. This place, which feels kinda like a foreign country emotionally and physically, is your steppingstone to the life you will build in San Diego. Tomorrow, we'll go to church and meet people in the community. You can carry in the pain and feelings of abandonment like pulling suitcases behind you. Or ditch those and walk in as someone in the process of becoming."

She sniffed. "Becoming what?"

"Not 'what,' but who." Jillian indicated the mare. "Speaking of who, what should we name the horse?"

Larkin shrugged.

"Just like Mary, she needs a place to have her baby." Jillian thought for a moment. "Noel is Latin for 'to be born.'"

"Noel it is."

While in California, Larkin had not heard of a Mennonite church. Or Brotherhood or Wesleyan. They chose the Mennonite and took seats toward the rear as the service began. Larkin focused on the message and the people around her, reminding herself she had checked the painful baggage at the door.

The pastor spoke to the congregation. "No matter what choices you've made, or the choices others have made that impacted you, your relationship with Jesus is yours if you choose to accept. Once our salvation is settled, our eternity is settled. For those of us who have had little to depend on, this is the ultimate security."

The pastor went on. "Accepting God's grace and unconditional love is the best decision we can make with only upsides and no downsides. The process is simple. You can pray, 'God, thank you for sending Jesus Christ to die on the cross for me. Forgive me. Be my Lord and Savior.' Done. Secure. For eternity."

Prayer time felt like balm for her aching soul. During corporate prayer, people talked to God about world affairs, national concerns, and local requests. Midwest Veterinary had a full house of patients and a pregnant horse that needed a home. Larkin felt relieved to know Tobias was serious about finding a real home for the horse. And there were prayers for a safe delivery for a family anticipating the birth of their baby.

When the service concluded, the music director announced rehearsals for the traditional Christmas pageant. "We'll use real animals. Those who want to participate or contribute to the staging, please raise your hand. We'll build staging in October, rehearse through November for the live performances the first weekend in December."

As people of all ages volunteered, the music director wrote their names on her clipboard.

Jillian nudged her. "Raise your hand. Get involved."

Larkin shook her head. "Not my style."

"You have a new style, remember?"

Across the aisle, they heard Tobias's familiar voice. "I'll supply the hay for the stable, as usual."

"See," Jillian spoke in a stage whisper. "Even he is participating. It's called community."

"There will be something for me," Larkin said. "But not the yearly play where the children are dressed in bed sheets and their fathers' oversized bathrobes, and solemnly sing *Silent Night*."

After lunch, Jillian loaded her suitcase into her rental car. "I stuffed all your baggage in here when you weren't looking." She patted the case. "In a couple hours, the case and I will be aboard the six-hour flight to Southern California."

"You are not supposed to carry my—"

Jillian laughed. "Nope, just taking the stuff far away so you are free to get this place sellable and join me in sunny California. We have a timeline, remember? Let me know when I can throw the whole caboodle in the ocean once and for all."

Through tears, Larkin hugged her daughter. "See you later." It was their familiar parting. They had agreed when Jillian began kindergarten that goodbye was not for them. Always see you later.

Three toots of the horn, *I love you,* and Jillian was gone.

Alone again. Except for a knicker from the corral. Answering the invitation, Larkin fed the mare candy canes, soothed by the velvety lips that swept the candy from her hand. Watching the horse neatly crop the grass in the fenced pasture, she felt tempted to drop into the pit of despair but refused to dishonor Jillian's visit in that way. She must move forward.

That night, Larkin couldn't sleep, but she could exhaust herself on furniture projects. She hauled a baby cradle from an upstairs apartment to the area she and Jillian had established as a studio. Sanding the wood, a knock at the door so startled her, she dropped the sander. She glanced at the time. Two twenty in the morning. Through the window, she saw a car parked in the drive.

She opened the door.

A woman stood on the porch. "I saw lights."

"Are you all right?" Larkin guessed the visitor to be in her late twenties, not much older than Jillian.

"I'm on my way home, but your light made me think I'm not the only one not sleeping at this hour." She held out her hand. "I'm Anna Miller, the local midwife."

"Would you like tea?"

She sighed. "That would be heavenly."

While Larkin prepared tea, Anna took in the beginnings of the showroom and the pieces on display. "You have an artist's eye."

With steeping tea, honey, and cream prepared, Larkin came into the room to invite Anna to the table. In the studio, looking stricken, Anna ran gentle fingers along the cradle. Suddenly, Larkin realized all the things in The Old Traction Barn had a story. Each item had belonged to someone before.

"Tea is ready if you are." Larkin waved her to the table.

Anna took the seat where Jillian sat earlier that day. When she made no move to fix her cup, Larkin poured tea and added honey and cream the way she liked her own. Anna smiled her thanks and sipped. She was halfway through her cup when Larkin noticed color coming into her guest's cheeks.

"Are you hungry?"

"No, thank you." Anna nodded towards the showroom. "You are giving the furniture new value."

"Shabby chic is what my daughter calls it."

"What brings you to our town?"

"I inherited the place and came to see what I owned." Larkin rested her chin on hand. "And you can't sleep tonight."

Anna shook her head.

Larkin refilled their cups. "I have an Indiana hutch that needs paint if you're interested."

When the sun came up, Larkin surveyed their work. Two could definitely make faster progress than she did on her own. "Wanna meet someone?"

Armed with carrots from the fridge, the two went to the barn where the mare knickered eagerly to know breakfast was minutes away.

Truck tires crunched the gravel drive and parked. Tobias came in. "Party in the barn." Hands on hips, he took in their paint-stained hands and messy hair. "Maybe more like an afterparty."

Anna tipped her head. "I know that unshaved look. You've been up all night too."

"Guilty as charged. Babysitting a quadruped." He took the stethoscope from around his neck and listened to the mare's belly. "I passed your car, Anna, parked at Jonas Troyer's."

The midwife looked away. "A baby boy."

Tobias settled the stethoscope behind his neck. "And?"

"Labor and delivery went well."

Larkin glanced from Tobias to Anna. Something was going on.

"And what else?" The vet looked concerned. "I've never seen you so shaken."

Anna swallowed. "I've never seen anything like this."

"Like what, Anna?" His voice was gentle, safe.

When she looked up, Anna's eyes were bright with tears. "The baby doesn't have feet. His legs stop just below the knees."

"That is hard, Anna." Tobias dropped onto a bale of alfalfa. "Really hard."

So hard that Anna had gravitated to Larkin's bright window like a moth to a porch light.

CHAPTER 6

September arrived, and Larkin planned a soft opening of her furniture showroom. The property could use sprucing, but for now she settled on a freshly painted front door and clean walkway. She wanted to generate foot traffic and enough sales to fund additional improvements, including hired help for the grand opening on Black Friday. Bountiful Christmas sales were the final step to make the Traction Barn attractive to a buyer. By Valentine's Day, she planned to be living in Southern California, working on her tan.

Early mornings and evenings, she fed Noel. Talking to a living creature proved therapeutic. Having something dependent on her was a deterrent from dropping completely into the pit of despair, sleeping for days, or eating herself stupid. Growing heavier, the mare seemed to welcome Larkin's company.

Anna continued to stop by when she wasn't busy with prenatal appointments or deliveries. Refurbishing furniture appeared medicinal to the young woman's spirit, and the two mostly worked in companionable silence. The midwife put a final color on the cradle, and though Larkin said she could have it, Anna insisted on paying, making the cradle Larkin's first sale. On Saturday, a tourist bus brought visitors to town to shop. Answering Larkin's hand painted *Welcome* sign, several women made purchases that the bus driver loaded into the luggage bin.

Closing the shop for the day, Larkin gratefully counted the day's income. In California, the legal process moved slowly. The divorce would finalize in February, six months and one day from filing, but not the property settlement. As long as the business remained in a legal tangle, her husband and his girlfriend benefitted.

October 1, Thanksgiving decor appeared throughout the downtown streets with the occasional Halloween ghost thrown in. Larkin often walked to the grocery, the elevator, and to the Mennonite church. Anchoring her days were the morning and evening barn chores. Tobias dropped by frequently as promised. He kept alfalfa bales neatly stacked, grain at the ready, and dumped the horse manure over a patch of ground he referred to as her garden. Larkin had no intention of being in Indiana in the spring to plant seeds.

One evening, Larkin came to the barn to find Tobias's truck parked outside. The overhead lights illuminated the vet, perched on the hay, smoking his pipe as he watched the mare eat her grain.

"Do you think she will deliver soon?"

He blew a ring of smoke. "Hard tellin' since I don't know when she conceived."

"Where did she come from?"

"Drought forced a farmer in another state to sell his livestock. A trader brought a handful of horses into the area, but the buyer refused to take the pregnant one. The trader took her to the auction where I vet out the livestock."

"And you left with a horse."

"The one person who bid was not anyone I wanted to have her." He checked his watch. "Staging and making wardrobe begins tonight. I have hay for the church Christmas pageant. Wanna ride along?"

Larkin's hand went to her hair. "I should—"

He stood. "You're dressed exactly right for delivering hay."

The church was a buzz of activity.

"Hammer or sequins?" Someone pressed a mug of hot chocolate into her hands. "If you want to hammer, they are building the little town of Bethlehem on that side. If you prefer to glue sparkles to angel wings, the costume creators are spread out on those tables."

Larkin had spent plenty of time with wood and construction recently, so she joined the group cutting burlap belts for shepherds, head coverings for townsfolk, and adding glitter to halos. Conversation covered last week's sermon, the upcoming quilt auction to fund disaster relief, and how nice it was to see the Old Traction Barn with lights on.

The next day, Anna brought back the cradle she had purchased. "I'm donating this to the quilt auction. Can you keep it here until then since I don't have room?"

"Of course." Larkin led her to the kitchen table. "I'll make tea."

Anna sat with her chin in her hand. Larkin made mugs of honey-sweetened tea and joined her guest at the table. "Tell me about it."

"I thought the cradle would be a nice gift."

"For Jonas's new baby."

She nodded. "There will always be a wall between us."

"You were there to deliver their baby."

Anna cupped her palms around the mug. "A blessing and a curse."

"How so?"

"My home was wildly un-nurturing for a child, but I spent a lot of time next door at the Troyer farm seeing what a family could be." She smiled. "When Mrs. Troyer went into labor with their youngest, the midwife let me help. The whole process was a wonder. I wanted to be a midwife."

Larkin waited.

"I could be Amish—or I could be a midwife."

"What about an Amish midwife?"

She shook her head. "The Amish don't do higher education, especially for women. I hoped they would make an exception for me when I could serve my community with medical skills. Amish friends use my skills but can't forgive me for leaving the faith."

"And being Amish was important because you were in love."

"Jonas and I planned to marry." Anna sighed. "When I went to California to train under a midwife, Jonas married someone else."

The same pain Larkin felt when she thought of her husband's betrayal pierced her heart. "Oh Anna, how do you cope with the hurt? Especially living in the same small community?"

She pressed her palms against her eyes. "I just do the next right thing."

"Jonas and his wife received your help as midwife but won't accept your gift for their baby." She recalled Anna's careful work on the cradle and swallowed against the lump in her throat. So many hard things for so many people. "The auction to benefit the disaster fund is a perfect place for your gift."

The night of the auction, Anna and Larkin hauled the cradle to the hall at the county fairgrounds. Scanning license plates in the parking lot, Larkin could see that people came from far and near for this event. Long rows of Amish buggies stood beside one another. Indoors smelled of pulled pork, cornbread, and homemade pies. The Mennonite pastor prayed for the meal, and people lined up to serve themselves on both sides of long tables heavy with food.

Larkin surveyed the scene, so vastly different from her life on the West Coast. The only comparison would be an occasional hoedown-themed event at a client's open house. But this place was real—from the pinned clothing of the Amish to the richly pieced quilts on display, from the autumn-colored leaves on the hardwoods to the horse she fed twice a day.

Following dinner, musicians took the stage. A fiddler, bass player, guitarist, and drummer were joined by a caller for square dance sets. In between, the group played songs for line dancing and an occasional slow dance. She followed Anna to learn a line dance, and though Larkin didn't know how to square dance, a group from church pulled her along through the pattern. She laughed until her face hurt, and the fun pacified her aching heart.

When a slow dance began, Larkin turned back to her seat, but Tobias caught her hand. "May I have this dance?"

She glanced at the others on the dance floor. "I don't know this one."

"It's easy." He placed a hand on her waist. "Two steps in this direction. One step back. Repeat."

She looked down to watch his feet.

"Forward, forward, back."

Their feet tangled, and they laughed.

"No, that's my part." Watching their feet, he rested his forehead against hers and guided with his words. "You follow, so you step back, back, forward."

Back, back, forward. Soon the movement felt familiar, and Tobias moved his hand to the small of her back. She met his eyes, and he easily led her around the dance floor. Passing the stage, he nodded at the fiddler who grinned back. The song lasted long enough for Larkin to shift from learning to dancing. Close to Tobias, she thought about his gentleness with the horse and with her—his intuitive questions that allowed Anna to talk.

"And now for the main event," the emcee announced as the music ended.

Tobias held her hand as they left the dance floor.

Those at Larkin's table made room for Tobias to join. He excused himself and brought back cups of apple cider while the emcee reminded everyone the auction's proceeds funded disaster relief. "When there are hurricanes, tornados, and earthquakes, Mennonites are not far behind."

The room quieted as the emcee opened the bidding. "Our first item is a beautiful baby cradle. Newlyweds and grandparents-in-waiting, wave your paddles high. Who will give me a starting bid?"

Anna and Larkin exchanged hopeful glances. The cradle was an exceptional decorator piece as well as functional. Next to her, Tobias dropped his drink. While others pressed napkins to the spill, the vet stared at the stage, his face ashen.

"Tobias?" Larkin put a hand on his arm. "Are you all right?"

He stirred, then looked around the hall. The spirited bidding eventually narrowed to two. Then one. Tobias raised his own paddle.

"If I'd known you wanted that, I would have given it to you," Larkin said.

He glanced at her questioningly. Then raised his paddle again. At last, the other determined buyer offered a large sum and Tobias did not counter.

"Sold!" The auctioneer appeared pleased with the amount the first item contributed to the disaster relief fund. "All for a good cause," he declared, and moved to the next item.

Tobias remained solemn and said goodnight early. Larkin continued to feel the assurance of his warm touch on her back. The comfort of his hand in hers.

CHAPTER 7

Larkin did not see Tobias the following week, though she knew he had been by to clean Noel's stall. Her divorce would be final as soon as the state's waiting period ended, and while she had no intention of seeking romance, she wanted connections in her new community. Had she somehow overstepped? Given a wrong impression?

Once again, she threw herself into her work.

Late Saturday night, Larkin glanced outside and saw lights. Wrapped in a coat, she walked to the barn. Tobias's truck was parked in his usual spot on the side away from the Traction Barn. Inside, she watched him brush the mare.

"Hey," she said.

He glanced up. "Hey back."

Country music played low from the radio. Larkin unwrapped a candy cane, noting Tobias had replenished the horse's feed. The mare eagerly accepted the treat, and Larkin combed tangles from the horse's mane. "Wanna talk about it?"

He pulled a pick from his back pocket and bent to clean a hoof. "Just surprised."

"More like rocked."

Tobias moved to another hoof. "Okay."

"That cradle is uniquely beautiful. Probably not another like it."

"Probably not."

Was this talking? Or was she poking outside her business?

When all four hooves were clean, Tobias returned the pick and began organizing the tack box.

Larkin turned to go. "Good night, Tobias."

She was almost to the door when he spoke. "The cradle was for my wife."

This is gonna be hard too. "What happened?"

Carefully, he cleaned each item in the tack box. "We were starting our family. Setting up a nursery. My practice was stable, and … "

"And everything felt right."

He nodded. "I ordered the cradle from a craftsman."

"That explains the artistry."

"She began feeling different, which we were confident meant she was pregnant." His voice caught. "Except she wasn't."

Larkin waited.

Done with the tack box, he absently took a stem from an alfalfa bale and ran it through his fingers. "The diagnosis was cancer. In about the same number of months it takes to grow a baby, the cancer took her life."

So hard. "I'm sorry, Tobias."

"Time doesn't heal wounds, but time teaches us to live with a gaping hole in our heart." He twisted the stem into a circle. "Seeing the cradle was just a surprise."

"How did the cradle come to be in the Old Traction Barn?"

He shrugged. "I asked the church ladies to place the nursery items where they would be used. They moved everything while I was working. I never asked, and they never volunteered."

"If I'd known you wanted it—"

"No." He drew in a deep breath. "It belongs where it will be used as intended."

She tried to follow the reasoning. "But you bid on it."

He gave a lopsided grin. "I know its value. I bid to drive up the price."

"All for a good cause."

They were quiet for a long time. Then, the song they had slow danced to a week ago played on the radio. Larkin took Tobias's hand, and they danced. This time, she rested her head on his shoulder where she could hear his heartbeat.

Monday morning, Larkin found a note on the mare's feed.

Tuesday is the first rehearsal. I'll be wrangling a sheep. Surely a sight not to be missed. If you want to come, the sheep and I will pick you up at 6:00 o'clock.

As promised, Tobias collected Larkin Tuesday evening. In the back of the truck, a wooden pen held four 4-H prime white lambs.

"I knew I had you at sheep," he said as he held her door.

She climbed into the pickup. "Because I am such an animal expert."

He climbed into the driver's seat. "You've certainly upped your skills from failing goldfish care to keeping a horse happy and healthy."

At the church, Tobias backed his truck to the stage door to limit the opportunity for a sheep to go anywhere but indoors. While Tobias wrangled sheep, parents wrangled baby angels and young shepherds. Larkin recognized Jonas dressed like Joseph, cradling his newborn while a costume designer fitted a blue head covering on his wife.

During a break in the rehearsal, two snack monitors distributed apples and popcorn while the kids listened to a Bible lesson. The director flicked the lights, and everyone returned to their places for the production.

As Larkin anticipated, a crowd of children rehearsed their roles while dressed in bed sheets and their fathers' oversized bathrobes. Tobias added straw to the manger scene and helped the shepherds guide a small lamb to the creche.

As the stage lights dimmed, Tobias joined her in a middle pew where Larkin watched the activity. "Surely the humble barn where Jesus was born was a quiet country setting where the hay smelled sweet and gentle doves in the rafters cooed a soothing lullaby."

He shrugged. "My experience with barns is that they are semi-organized chaos."

The music director approached after rehearsal. "Tobias, do you have other animals who play well with our sheep? The stable could use dimension."

Tobias considered. "I have a mare who would eat hay."

"I'd be grateful if you'd bring her."

When Tobias took Larkin home, they stopped first at the barn. The mare blinked against the barn lights, and knickered for a candy cane.

"Well, girl," Tobias said, "you're about to be a star."

For the second rehearsal, Tobias parked the truck and trailer at the Old Traction Barn's front door and knocked. "Wanna come along?"

Larkin fumbled for an excuse but came up empty.

"No pressure, but you might like to see the star practice her important and complicated part in the pageant." He held his hat near his mouth as if sharing a secret. "They don't let just anyone see behind the scenes, but the mare put in a good word for you."

Larkin grinned. "Let me freshen up."

Tobias checked his watch. "No time. She's gotta be on set."

She planted her hands on her hips.

"I know, a gentleman would give a lady opportunity to get ready." He held his hat over his heart. "I apologize. Please don't hold my lack of manners against the invitation."

"I'll come along." Larkin pulled on her coat. "For the horse."

Rehearsals were scheduled twice a week for the month of November.

"Why bring her each time?" After the second week, Larkin didn't see the point. "She knows her part. Munch hay, and eat candy canes the children give to her."

"She's learning to travel well and be comfortable with people."

As if on cue, a young boy in a shepherd costume shyly brought an apple. An alfalfa stem trailing from her lips, the horse smelled his hair which caused him to giggle. She took the apple into her mouth and bit, juice running down his palm. He squealed and wiped his hand down his costume. Larkin thought the smudge made the shepherd look more authentic.

Tobias handed a brush to the boy who tentatively smoothed the mare's forelock while she continued to chew the apple.

The director called for the merry band of shepherds to take their places.

Tobias watched the boy scamper to his place on the bustling set. "Her most important contribution is what she does for the rest of the cast."

CHAPTER 8

Jillian came for Thanksgiving weekend, and Larkin was overjoyed to see her daughter. For the holiday, the two attended the community meal. In Jillian's rented car, they drove to the square dance caller's oversized barn. Having given up chicken farming years earlier, he had converted the barn into an event center popular for weddings, family reunions, and community gatherings.

Jillian and Larkin contributed loaves of sourdough bread from California and mounds of butter from a local farmer, arranged on a large cutting board. After the meal, tables were pushed back and the fiddle band that played at the quilt auction played while the barn owner called the square dance. Jillian learned the patterns faster than her mother, and once again, Larkin felt her cheeks ache from laughing.

When the band switched to a slow song, Tobias appeared at Larkin's side. "They're playing our song."

She took his hand, and he held her close as they circled the dance floor. He was easy to be with.

On Black Friday, with Jillian's help, Larkin strategically held the official opening for the Old Traction Barn. Greenery and holly berries decorated the front door. Inside, Christmas music played, and shoppers were invited to a cup of Christmas tea while they browsed. To Larkin's delight, two tourist buses included the Old

Traction Barn on their route, and many people from the community stopped in.

The day's sales, coupled with the barn rent Tobias had paid for four months, looked good in her bank account. "I may make a go of this shabby chic style, after all."

"I knew it would work." Jillian grinned. "And you worked really hard over the past few months."

"Certainly better than wallowing in sorrow or bitterness as I figure out who I am now that I'm no longer Mrs."

"I'm proud of you, Mom. Despite limited time and finances, you gave yourself, this place, and these things a new beginning."

Larkin rested her hands on her hips. "There is still a trainload of work to do to make this place sellable."

"Good." Jillian tucked hair behind her ear. "I worry less if you are busy."

Saturday, Tobias took the mare to rehearsal. Larkin and Jillian rode along so Jillian could experience the pageant. The baby angels and young shepherds were enamored with the new baby who served as Jesus, but the horse was by far the favorite cast member. Noel gently accepted treats, leaned in to be brushed, and made the children squeal with laughter when she blew her nose to clear dust and alfalfa from her nostrils.

Saturday evening, Jillian and Larkin talked ideas for the shabby chic showroom while doing the barn chores. Tobias arrived with hot cocoas from the local diner.

Larkin counted the cups. "Four?"

"I spotted Anna's car early this morning at a house where a baby is due." He grabbed the pitchfork and wheelbarrow. "Guessing she will pass by on her way home tonight."

"And see our lights on."

As predicted, the midwife arrived. "Hey, Santa," Anna called to Tobias. "What's in the bed of your sleigh?"

He dumped a bag of shavings in the stall. "Come and see."

Outside, the women peered into the truck bed where a plump evergreen barely fit. "Seems the right size for The Traction Barn's front window," Tobias mused.

Jillian's eyebrows went up. "I think you're right."

"Only one way to find out."

The four of them centered the tree in the showroom window. Tobias moved the stands of twinkle lights from the banister to the tree and Larkin made popcorn to string into garlands. With red ribbon, Jillian and Anna tied wooden blocks and toy soldiers as ornaments on the branches, their conversation lively as they compared experiences as young professional women.

Though Jillian returned home on Sunday, the transition felt easier this time as Larkin focused on her timeline. She planned to list the Old Traction Barn for sale by January.

At last, the first weekend of December arrived. The pageant was scheduled for Friday night, Saturday night, and as Sunday morning's regular worship service. At the last minute, Tobias found a donkey to add to the live production.

On opening night, the church's staging was elaborate. The well-rehearsed singers took their place. The orchestra began on the downbeat. "Joy to the world," the audience joined their voices with the choir as the words appeared on the overhead. "Let men their sons employ."

Choreographed to mask the clamorous rearrangement of animals on stage, the pianist's solo was the only quiet part of the colorful extravaganza. The keyboard was unplugged. From behind the stage curtains, the audience heard Tobias smooching at the gray donkey whose reluctance to come on stage was only a shadow of his stronger reluctance to walk off.

The violinist's microphone was mute as the wise men bowed before the loudly wailing Christ child. Mary and Joseph did their best to appear holy while curious sheep nibbled their robes, burped, and chewed their malodorous cud.

Suddenly, a runaway sheep escaped his post and dashed about the little town of Bethlehem. So engrossed by the drama, the drummer forgot to drum. The music director looked up from conducting and blanched as the speeding sheep fairly leapt into her arms. The scene was bedlam.

"All we like sheep have wandered away," Tobias quoted as the crew met for post-production debrief.

Larkin ran fingers through Noel's mane, thankful that the expectant horse had peacefully stuck to her practiced role despite the lively and unscripted activities during the performance.

"What a disaster." From an over-the-counter bottle in her purse, the director shook two Excedrin into her palm and washed them down with a bottle of water.

"The newspaper reporter attended tonight's program." Jonas cradled his newborn son who had finally fallen asleep.

"Where did she sit?" The director closed her eyes against more bad news. "Was she in the back?"

"Front row." Tobias pointed. "Right in the center."

The director rested her forehead against her palm. "Of course. Where else would she be on this well-attended opening night?"

By the second performance, the "g" was added to sons on the overhead, the keyboard and violin found their plugs, and quality fencing had been installed for the roaming sheep.

The remainder of the Christmas performances played without a hitch, portraying the humble barn where Jesus was born as a quiet setting with sweet smelling hay and gentle doves in the rafters to sing a sweet lullaby. The crowning moment was the Nativity scene. Dressed in bed sheets and their fathers' oversized bathrobes, all the children solemnly sang *Silent Night*.

CHAPTER 9

Christmas or the birth of the foal? Larkin wondered which would be the next big event. The mare's taut belly rippled when the baby within jostled.

For several nights, Larkin checked Noel throughout the night, half anticipating the mare would be in labor.

"I brought you something." On her next visit, Anna held up what looked like a pair of walkie talkies. "Put this one near the stall and keep this one in the house. It's a baby monitor. You can hear what's happening in the barn and cut back on unnecessary trips in the cold."

Larkin listened to the baby monitor as if it were the radio. Surprisingly, the barn was far from quiet after she left. Birds in the rafters produced a cacophony of twittering and chirping. Industrious mice scampered and burrowed through hay, gleaning grain the horse generously spilled from her feed bucket. The horse clattered her bucket against the wooden beams and loudly chewed molasses-covered oats. After munching hay and slurping water, Noel rustled through shavings to bed down. Once asleep, she groaned while she napped. Several times, the horse passed gas so loud that Larkin was certain she was giving birth and dashed to the barn in the middle of the night.

"You sound tired," Jillian said over her weekly phone call.

"I am," Larkin stifled a yawn. "The baby will be born soon, and I'll feel better knowing mother and babe are fine."

The following evening, Tobias stopped at the barn as Larkin was feeding. The vet cleaned the stall, put down fresh bedding, and checked the mare.

He eyed Larkin. "You look more exhausted than the expectant mom."

"Nothing looks the way I thought it would."

He raised his eyebrows. "Nothing?"

"The barn is far from a quiet country setting where the hay smelled sweet and gentle doves in the rafters coo a soothing lullaby."

He smiled wryly. "Semi-organized chaos."

She nodded. "Several times the sounds were so loud, I dashed to the barn like Anna to a birth."

He thoughtfully chewed a stem of alfalfa. "I learned things rarely—maybe never—look the way I expect."

Larkin glanced around the barn. Certainly, she never thought she'd live in a Midwest Traction Barn, making regular treks across the yard to care for a pregnant mare and talk with a veterinarian. Her hands were flecked with paint from redoing furniture rather than ordering high-end decorator pieces. This looked completely different from her life in San Francisco.

"It's like the Old Traction Barn." Tobias gestured toward the historic building. "Designers crafted a blueprint for the building to serve a specific purpose. When the season for serving trains passed, the place was remodeled as a school, then apartments."

"Now an Airbnb, furniture store, and ..." She glanced at the stall. "... stable for a four-legged mother to have her baby."

"I've learned to let expectations go and look for what is. For what could be." He adjusted a heat lamp to radiate into the stall. "Life is sometimes harder and always deeper than this country boy can imagine. Even though these are events I would not have chosen, God molds my life. There's a relief in surrendering to the assurance that he knows where I fit in his story of hope and redemption."

Larkin's current circumstances were not anything she would have written on her own life script. She had interpreted this as proof that God didn't care and couldn't be trusted.

He shrugged. "The question is, can I be willing to go where he takes me?"

Their conversation lingered in Larkin's thoughts as she considered the Old Traction Barn and its contents with new vision. Like a character from *The Boxcar Children* storybooks she read to Jillian, Larkin viewed the strange pickin's in the Traction Barn no longer as what the thing had been, but as what each could be.

For window coverings, she threaded mismatched doilies onto curtain rods. An antique wooden toolbox became a coffee table. The carved wooden pew racks that once held church hymnals were repurposed to hold the TV remote and books. In the bathrooms, teacups housed cotton balls while a carved footboard served as a hallway shelf. Shoe forms mounted on the wall became hooks for coats or purses, wooden boxes doubled as kitchen shelves, and antique silverware stood in canning jars.

Featuring remodeled and repurposed decorator items, the Old Traction Barn became a unique shopping experience for visitors to her showroom. Word about the store spread, and people came to browse and shop.

Mid-December, Tobias freshened the stall as if preparing for Jesus to be born inside. "Usually, a horse shows signs of beginning labor by producing a waxy coating in preparation for nursing."

Larkin gave Noel a candy cane. "She's so large, she can't go much longer."

He crossed his arms and studied the mare. "I don't see anything to suggest the foal will be born tonight, but babies arrive in their own time."

CHAPTER 10

After weeks of false alarms, Larkin felt too sleep-deprived to tiptoe to the barn in the middle of the night. Early the next morning, she discovered a newborn in the stable.

Following months of waiting, the exquisite wonder of the new baby took Larkin's breath away.

Noel knickered as if saying, "Come and see."

Slow and quiet, she drew close. The black and white foal lay in the shavings, still wet. Brand new. Noel nuzzled the newborn who flicked small ears. Larkin felt a gentle hand on her back and Tobias winked, a finger pressed to his lips. His hand went to her waist, and she leaned into him as they stood at the stall and watched mother and babe.

With clumsy movement, the foal stood, legs splayed for balance. Tentatively, the little one began to nurse. Belly full, the foal toddled as if on stilts, learning to coordinate all four legs in the same direction.

The baby pooped, and Tobias squeezed her arm. "Both ends work. That's important."

Plopping back into the thick shavings, the exhausted foal napped. Noel looked tired too.

"Congratulations," Larkin ran a hand down the mare's neck. "You must be hungry."

Tobias gave the horse a generous amount of alfalfa and fresh water. Larkin added extra grain.

As Noel ate, Tobias checked mother and newborn. "Noel is the proud mother of a colt."

"Just like Mary," Larkin repeated what Jillian had said the day they first saw the horse. "She just needed a stable where she could have her baby."

He touched Larkin's nose. "For a reluctant innkeeper, you won her trust."

"What do you mean?"

"A mother is naturally protective of her newborn. Noel practically invited you to be part of these most vulnerable first hours."

"That's unusual?"

He adjusted his hat. "Nature is particularly inconvenient. I gotta defend myself sometimes when a new mom or foal needs a little assistance from their vet."

Larkin took several photos and texted them to Jillian. Her daughter telephoned right away. "Tell me everything."

Keeping her voice low, Larkin tried to describe the indescribable. Tobias gave a quick wave and left. Mother and daughter were still on the phone when he returned.

"Oh my," Larkin took in the packages he carried. "Tobias brought take-out from the diner."

"You ought to look into that," Jillian said, and Larkin could hear the smile in her daughter's voice. "Really, look into that."

"I'm sticking to the timeline." Larkin calculated the weeks. "In eight weeks, I'll see you in San Diego."

They ate the diner's lunch special and drank large cups of coffee, keeping near to watch the miniature nativity. At dinner, Anna brought take-out and apple cider. Temperatures dropped, and Tobias connected two more heat lamps and added a thick layer of shavings. Tobias and Anna talked about similarities in birth between humans and horses, and both agreed that Noel and her colt were sound.

The following day, Tobias placed a small halter on the colt. When the baby rested, he ran his hands over each leg and both ears. "This is called imprint training." He tapped the bottom of all four hooves. "Every day, get the baby accustomed to being handled."

On the third day, Tobias used the halter to lead the colt into the corral. Mother and baby stretched and trotted in the crisp air. Watching the colt explore his world reminded Larkin how new everything had felt when she first arrived.

As word got around town, friends and neighbors stopped by to see the baby and bring candy canes for Noel.

Monday, the newspaper reporter stopped in to see what was happening at the Old Traction Barn. As a young photographer took photos, Larkin dodged personal questions and focused on the renovation of the historical building and the furniture.

"I noticed you attended opening night," Larkin turned the conversation to the recent Christmas pageant. "The remainder of the performances played perfectly, but my favorite remains the opening night."

The reporter grinned. "Certainly the most entertaining."

"Let me show you something." Larkin led them to the barn which smelled richly of horses, pine shavings, and molasses. Golden straw dust danced like glitter in the air.

Seeing the place where she had spent so much time in recent weeks through the eyes of the newcomers, Larkin had a new appreciation of the attention Tobias paid to maintaining the space.

"Oh my!" Wonder showed on the reporter's face as she saw the mare and colt. The photographer stared, then remembered his camera.

"After having my own birth in the barn, that initial dramatization with the unscripted extra chaos seemed a sweet reenactment of what reality probably looked like for Mary and Joseph on that most important night." Larkin fed a candy cane to Noel. "That's why opening night stands as my all-time favorite pageant."

CHAPTER 11

Christmas Eve, Anna stopped by, her cheeks red from the cold. "Did you see the paper?"

Wrapping a purchase for a customer, Larkin looked up. "Thankfully, I've been too busy to read the paper." The truth was that living frugally did not include a subscription to the newspaper.

"Take a look." Anna snapped the rubber band and tucked the newspaper into the branches of the evergreen tree they had decorated with Jillian and Tobias. "See you at the candlelight service," she called as she left the shop.

At closing time, Larkin said goodbye to her last customer and turned the sign to closed. Weary, she felt pleased with the day's sales. Each lucrative day equaled a step closer to selling the dear old place and relocating near Jillian.

Her daughter arrived in time to share soup, sourdough bread, and tea before they went to church for the Christmas Eve service. Initially surprised, Larkin noted how natural it felt for Tobias to join them in their pew. They seemed to be side by side often when caring for Noel, at the quilt auction, and during pageant rehearsals. Happy to see Jillian, Anna took a seat next to her new friend.

An abbreviated cast from the Christmas Pageant, minus the animals, were center stage as the pastor spoke of the humble beginnings of the long-anticipated King of kings. "Because no one expected the Messiah to be born in a stable, many who would have been privileged to be there completely missed him. Herod, church leaders, and the mighty Roman occupiers didn't recognize their salvation. Some thirty-four years later, the chief priest, Pilate, and those who clamored for his crucifixion didn't recognize the unique packaging of their Savior. Christmas reminds us to see the world through God's eyes."

Larkin thought back to last year's holiday. Holland Interiors' decorated trees, designed dining experiences, and lit the homes and businesses of clients. This year, she and Jillian sat in a modest church, sandwiched between new friends in whom Larkin could find no guile. Tobias rested his arm along the back of the pew behind her.

After service, the veterinarian invited them to his house for games. Tobias and Anna taught them to play Dutch Blitz, a popular card game in the Midwest. Larkin and Jillian quickly became proficient, competition rose, and the group played round after round. It was late when Tobias walked them to their cars and said goodnight.

Christmas morning, Jillian's eyes sparkled to find four bulging stockings in the barn. "Anna or Tobias?"

"Santa, of course." Reading the names, there was one for her, one for Jillian, another for Noel, and a smaller one for the colt.

They opened the stall door to allow the horses access to the corral and topped off Noel's breakfast with extra candy canes.

After their own breakfast, Larkin and Jillian exchanged gifts and talked about the future. "I'll find a place in San Diego and tell the storage company to ship my belongings from San Francisco."

"When the Traction Barn sells, come live with me while you find your own place." Jillian surveyed the room.

"Although, there is something special about this place. I will miss it. And Noel and the colt. Anna. And Tobias."

There was a knock at the door, and Jillian answered. Tobias came in with a bouquet.

"That's a lot of roses," Jillian said.

"Today is December 25, and there are 25 roses." He brought them to Larkin. "For you. Merry Christmas."

Larkin put the velvet petals to her nose and smelled their fragrance. "Thank you, Tobias. They are beautiful."

"I read the article about you and the Traction Barn."

"Article?" Jillian looked from Tobias to Larkin.

"Oh my," Larkin nodded to the paper tucked among the branches. "Anna brought a copy of the newspaper and told me to look it over. I completely forgot."

Jillian opened the paper. The cover story featured the Old Traction Barn and a photo of Noel with her colt. Jillian began to read.

"Christmas Is Seeing What Can Be"

The article described the Old Traction Barn's new purpose as a showroom for repurposed décor.

> "Setting aside expectations and seeing possibilities is the theme of Larkin Holland's work. And, according to the decorator, that is the message of Christmas."

The story continued that Larkin had held to the traditional view of how the birth of Jesus had happened.

> "Then, I moved to the country, got my own barn, and had my own birth in the stable," Holland said. "This innkeeper found room in the Old Traction Barn's stable for the mother-to-be."

Jillian grinned. "With a little nudging from me."

"I went to the elevator for paint and came home with a horse." Larkin laughed.

"And a new friend." Jillian winked at Tobias. She read on.

"When Mary was due to deliver her firstborn, she and Joseph found the only semi-private setting in the little town of Bethlehem. The small town teemed with extended family members who crowded into the homes of relatives to be counted for the census."

Holland continued.

"Amidst unfamiliar noises, smells, and surroundings, Mary brought forth her first born child and laid the babe in the starlit manger. What an exquisite wonder to discover the newborn who made his entrance into our world and hearts by first appearing in the humble stable. But because the anticipated arrival of Christ didn't look the way people expected, many missed what could be."

Seeing potential in the building, Holland redesigned the historic Old Traction Barn into a home, attached Airbnb, and Furniture Showroom specializing in repurposed and shabby chic décor. Come and stay, come and shop, and if you like what you see, the lucrative business and property are for sale and ready for a new owner."

"Once you sell, what are your plans, if I may?" Tobias asked.

Larkin nodded. "Of course, you want to make arrangements for Noel and her baby."

Jillian's eyebrows shot up.

"The market is good," Larkin continued, "so I'm anticipating this will sell in January."

"Not the horses. I'll have room soon." Tobias sat forward, resting his elbows on his knees. "I want to know about you."

She shifted the bouquet, hearing the crackle of the floral paper. "I'll join my daughter in San Diego."

"Let me put those in water." Jillian took the bouquet, glancing from Larkin to Tobias. "I'll make tea too." She disappeared into the kitchen.

"Southern California is a long way from Indiana, but Jillian makes the trip easy enough."

Larkin shook her head. "I doubt I'll have reason to visit Indiana."

"As you told the reporter, Christmas is seeing what can be. Your words echoed what I've been surprised to be feeling since we met."

Larkin had kept her thoughts about Tobias tightly stuffed. She was raw and vulnerable, uninterested in a rebound relationship, and had no intention of being needy or misinterpreting a man's attentions. She had certainly misread her husband.

He lowered his voice. "I never expected the possibility of sharing life with someone again."

Looking into his eyes, she allowed herself to acknowledge feeling safe with him. The warmth when they held hands, the security of his hand on her waist as he guided their dance steps. The shared wonder as she leaned against him watching the colt's first hours. His integrity as he kept his word to oversee the care of Noel and her colt, do the barn chores, and paid the agreed upon board early.

She had observed his easy relationship with her and Jillian, his acceptance of community members, participation at church, and the empathetic way he talked with young Anna. The way her messy hair and paint-stained fingers were fine with him. The way he didn't demand anything from her, and she didn't feel the need to perform.

"How long have you felt this way?"

He looked sheepish. "A while, but I didn't let myself admit it."

"I may know something about that."

"Your words in the interview to look at what can be, helped me look at what is. And I don't want to miss what is here." Indicating the newspaper, he went on. "I understand you will sell and move to San Diego. Being here was temporary for you all along. If you don't mind, I'd like to visit when you are in Southern California. Maybe I can be a reason you visit Indiana."

"And while I'm still in Indiana?"

"You're a city girl. I want you to be sure about who you are getting under this hat." He removed his ball cap. "I care for the animals in the community, most are pertinent to their family's livelihood. Others are family members. Some are both. My uniform is jeans and boots."

She thought he looked good in his uniform. "Appears to be multi-purpose."

He took her hand. "As you know, life rarely, if ever, looks as we expect. But there are some things you can count on with this country boy. I'm not the kind to go behind your back."

She rested her forehead against his. "Thank you."

"If you're agreeable, I'd like to see what's possible." He paused. "You can think about it for as long as you need."

Larkin met his eyes. "Christmas is a time to see what can be."

Tobias cupped her chin and kissed her.

ABOUT THE AUTHOR

"Eminently quotable, PeggySue Wells is a tonic—warm like your favorite blanket, bracing like a stiff drink."

History buff and tropical island votary, PeggySue Wells parasails, skydives, snorkels, scuba dives, and has taken (but not passed) pilot training. Writing from 100-acre woods in Indiana, PeggySue Wells is the bestselling author of twenty-nine books, translated into eight languages, including The *What To Do* series, *The Slave Across the Street, Slavery in the Land of the Free, Bonding With Your Child Through Boundaries, Homeless for the Holidays, Chasing Sunrise,* and *The Ten Best Decisions A Single Mom Can Make.* A frequent radio and podcast guest, she is the founder of SingleMomCircle.com.

BITTERSWEET CHOCOLATE

Amos Wyse

CHAPTER 1

"Dad, why do we celebrate Christmas different from the English?" fifteen-year-old Jacob asked.

"Jacob, we do many things different from them, what has you asking?"

"But they have Santa Claus and elves and ..."

"And more presents than you?"

"Well ..."

"Christ himself got but three gifts, do you deserve more?"

Jacob sighed. "No, Dad."

"Good, now help me with this last batch of fudge, and then we can clean up and go home," Nathan Wyse said to his youngest son.

"Do you need a sampler for this batch?"

"You know we need to sample every batch. Are you volunteering again?" Nathan barely held back his laughter as his son repeated the actions of childhood with his own dad probably making up the job of taster for him.

Nathan checked on the thermometer as he stirred. "There we go, two-hundred-thirty-six degrees, perfect." The fudge was poured out into small pans to cool and be cut up for sale. The two made fast work of washing the pots and sanitizing the working surfaces.

"I suppose the fudge is cool enough for sampling now. Which one did you want to try?"

"Chocolate with walnuts, please."

"How did I know that?"

"I sometimes like the plain chocolate too."

"Well, you were extra helpful today—you can have a piece of both. Tomorrow, we will make chocolate caramels. We are almost out and that would not do this close to Christmas." There were but a few weeks left before Christmas, and Wyse Chocolates was a must for many of the local Amish and English. They would make three or four more batches of nearly everything they sold before New Year's and take a short break before Valentine's Day.

Tomorrow never came for Nathan Wyse. On the buggy ride home, they were hit by a driver with too much eggnog and too little attention to the road around him. Jacob was thrown clear and only suffered with a broken leg and bruised ribs.

CHAPTER 2

Jacob awoke from his recurring dream. Four years ago, and it still haunted him, the last time he and his father made candy together. At the tender age of nineteen, Jacob was now *the* Wyse at Wyse Chocolates. He looked over at his wind-up clock—four a.m. Close enough to time for him to get up, get breakfast and get to work. His mother had breakfast for him at four-thirty, and he was unlocking his front door at five a.m. November had come and brought cold winds. He shivered and made his way three blocks to downtown Barnsville. Another four hours would go by before he opened to the public, but the candies did not make themselves.

Today, he was making chocolate caramels. He wondered if that was why he had the dream again last night. He gathered up the ingredients, then looked at his father's old recipe card, grateful the recipes were written down.

The recipes all were written as if making them for home, the way the business started three generations ago. Today, they made the batches twenty times as large to hold up to the demand.

Jacob looked at the card:

    1 Cup Sugar
    1 Cup Light Corn Syrup
    3 Squares Baker's Chocolate
    1/4 tsp Salt
    1 1/2 Cups Heavy Cream

Jacob quickly did the math and combined the sugar, chocolate, salt, and, 2/3 of the cream over a low flame. He stirred constantly as the temperature on the candy thermometer slowly rose and the shop began to smell of warm sugar. The mix came to a controlled boil, and he watched over it until the temperature got up to 238 degrees, then he added the remainder of the cream to the mix, just as his father and grandfather had done before him. The mix came back to a boil, and Jacob watched closely until the temperature read 246. It was time to pour the caramels out into the buttered sheet pans to cool, stirring the pot until the last drop of caramel was poured out then smoothing the pans.

Some of these would get wrapped as is and others would get dipped in chocolate and put into sampler boxes. Jacob did a quick check and saw he had made five half-sheet pans of caramels—that would last him for at least a couple weeks. It was nearly time to open the doors and let his sister in. She would run the cash register while he continued to make candies. This was the time of year they stocked up on the usual favorites.

Jacob went to the door and looked. There was his sister, Emma, but with her was Twyla, a heavy-set girl he knew from church and had seen recently at singings.

"Emma, what is going on?"

"I found someone to work for us this holiday, and I wanted to give her some practice before it gets too crazy."

Jacob quickly ran the numbers in his head. He could afford to train Twyla for the few extra weeks, and to have someone up to speed on the second register they opened during the Christmas rush would be nice. "Sure," he finally said—long after the two girls had walked past him into the store.

"I remember coming here as a child. Your dad would hand out samples to the little kids. It was such a treat to get to come here."

"Well, if you can figure out how to run the register, you will be the one handing out samples this year."

"I will certainly try my best."

Emma joked, "You don't have to kiss up to him. He may run the place, but I hire the sales help. Feel free to kiss up to me as much as you wish."

The two girls laughed.

Emma did a quick how to on running the scales and using the charts to turn weight into cost. Twyla seemed to catch on quickly. At the end of the day, she had earned a "good job today" from Jacob—no small praise coming from him.

Within two weeks, Twyla was nearly as quick as Emma on the register and was substantially more friendly. She seemed to go out of her way to greet people as they entered the shop and to help them make their choices.

Emma found a keeper this year. Jacob watched from the glassed-off room where the candies were made. "Twyla, are you willing to get up early and earn some overtime? We are making peanut brittle tomorrow. I will need extra hands to help draw it out."

"Sure, I can always use a little more money coming into the holidays."

"Great, come in for seven a.m. We should be about ready to pull the brittle by then."

The next morning, Twyla got there an extra fifteen minutes early and watched as Jacob brought the sugar-filled mixture up to a hard crack stage, added the peanuts, then the soda to make it airy. He quickly poured the mix out onto the table and looked up.

"Okay, now comes the fun part. It is hot, but we have to pull it quickly. Here, like this," he said, demonstrating the way to lightly touch the mix with rubber gloved hands to thin and flatten the mix.

Emma joined in like the seasoned pro she was. Twyla was a bit hesitant, so Jacob went over behind her and showed her how to reach into the mass and pull the brittle out, "It is similar to a taffy pull, just warmer," he said, taking his arms from around her. "Your turn."

Twyla reached in, dug a bit too deep and quickly withdrew her hands. "Ooh that is hot! How can your fingers stand that?"

"Don't dig so deep. Just pull the surface," Emma explained. "Watch me for a minute, then do what I do." Emma quickly spread out pull after pull of the mix creating a thin layer at the center as she pulled the mass toward the edges.

"When it is all that thin, we are done."

Twyla tentatively reached in and then began pulling in earnest. Like most of the things at the candy shop, the task came easy to her once she had seen it done. In another fast fifteen minutes, they were done with the stretching and waiting for the brittle to harden. Emma made a pot of coffee while they waited.

By the time they finished their coffees, Emma said, "Twyla gets the hammer."

Twyla spun around to Emma, then to Jacob. "The hammer?"

"Yes, I suppose she has earned it," Jacob agreed.

Jacob reached into a drawer and pulled out a rubber mallet. "Do I need to explain how this works?"

"I think I can figure out I hit something with it. Is this how the brittle is made into pieces?"

"You got it in one guess. Hit it a few times—you will know to stop when the pieces are all around three inches by three inches or slightly smaller."

Twyla looked at the table of brittle reflecting the light off its shiny surface. She got a gleam in her eye and yelled, "Aaaahhh!" as she hit the brittle for the first time and watched it break up. True to its name, the brittle split apart and cracked easily. A few more hits were all it took to get the brittle to the desired size.

"That may have been too a bit too fun," Twyla said, setting the hammer down.

"I get the next batch," Emma said.

Jacob teased his sister. "I don't know. Twyla did it in fewer hits than you and seemed to enjoy it more."

"I wouldn't turn down another chance to do that," Twyla agreed quickly.

"Well, before we start worrying about next batch, let's get this sorted into eight-ounce and one-pound baggies and ready for sale."

The three of them did just that, then wiped down and cleaned up as the first customers lined up outside. Brittle was a town favorite, and folks seemed to know when it was being made.

Despite the very early start, Twyla was as pleasant and professional as always throughout the day serving what seemed to be a never-ending line of customers who wanted brittle and ... well, maybe a bit of chocolate to go with it.

For his part, Jacob spent the day making batches of white, green, and red hard candy he rolled into ropes, braided, then rolled the braided mix into a new rope, spun it making six-inch-wide circles, and then stuck a lollipop stick into them while they were still warm. He would be making hundreds of these white, red, and green colored suckers between now and Christmas—the sweets another town favorite.

At the end of the day, Twyla was given a pound of brittle, a lollipop, and the now customary "Great work today, Twyla." from Jacob.

Tearing open the bag, she said, "Ooh, I have wanted to try this all day." She put a piece of the brittle in her mouth and closed her eyes, savoring the flavor as it melted. "It tastes like it smelled—delicious!" she exclaimed.

"You sound like you have never tried it before," Jacob said, surprise evident in his voice.

"We only moved to town last year. Before that, we would come into Barnsville just before Christmas, and Dad would buy us a candy or two. I never even saw peanut brittle."

"It has been known to run out before Christmas week arrives," Jacob said.

"This is just wonderful," Twyla said, feeling her face warm. She hated that she blushed when talking to young men—she hated being the big girl with the red face. "I need to get home—my cat will wonder what became of me," she said looking for an exit. *Great, now I am the big crazy cat girl with the red face.* She walked away from the shop.

CHAPTER 3

Jacob sat at the head of the table and said the dinner prayer. To his left sat his mother, Connie, and then his sister. Tonight was macaroni and cheese night, his favorite.

As they ate, Emma asked "How do you like Twyla?"

"She seems to be working out well."

"Yes, but how do you *like her*?"

"She seems nice enough."

"But do you like her?

"You mean *like* her? I haven't really thought of her that way. Why do you ask?"

"She gets all flustered when she has to speak with you. I think she has a crush on you."

Jacob shook his head. "I think you are seeing things that aren't there."

"Maybe so, but maybe not."

Connie shook her finger at Emma, "Don't be starting gossip, girl."

"Yes, ma'am."

The next morning brought snow, not the kind that buries you, just the kind that makes you start thinking of hot chocolate and the coming holidays. Jacob stood inside the candy shop and stomped his boots to clean the dry snow off himself. He thought back to what his sister had said the night before and smiled. Would it be so bad if a nice girl liked him? Twyla was so full of happiness and energy he wondered if he could keep up with her. He decided he would look for any sign she was interested, then maybe if she was, he could ask to walk her home.

Snow did not slow the townsfolk from making it into the shop. Jacob sold hot chocolate mix with shaved chocolate in it that was the "go to" drink for snowy days. Tins of it flew off the shelves, and a pot was made to give samples to people as they came in from the cold.

Twyla was pouring out sample cups when a customer about her own age came into the shop and bumped into her.

"You oaf, watch what you are doing!" Rachel McAdams said angrily. "You've spilled chocolate on my new sweater!"

"I am so sorry. I was just filling up some hot chocolate cups when you bumped into me ..."

"So now you are saying it is my fault? Where is your manager?"

Twyla felt her face warming and knew she was turning crimson and looking guilty. "Jacob Wyse is the owner. I will get him for you." *Great there goes this job, and I really liked working here.* Twyla walked over to get Jacob. "Jacob, the woman in the sweater wants to speak with you. She bumped into me, I spilled hot chocolate on her, and she demanded a manager."

Jacob looked at Twyla oddly then left the glassed-in area and came out onto the sales floor.

Rachel McAdams stood with her arms crossed tightly. "So, you are the owner? What are you going to do about this? Your bumbling cow spilled all over my new sweater."

A small crowd had formed, much like sharks in bloodied waters, waiting to see what would happen next.

"I'm sorry," started Jacob. "But from where I was standing, it was pretty clear she was doing exactly what I had asked her to do, and you plowed into her, knocking the hot chocolate everywhere."

"Your father wouldn't have spoken to me that way." Rachel said.

"Well, I guess I knew him a bit better than you. Yes, yes, he would have spoken to you exactly that way if you wrongfully blamed one of his employees and then called them a cow."

"There are plenty of other places to get candy from."

Jacob pointed to the door. "I am glad you realize that—perhaps you should leave now and go to one of them."

"Whatever happened to the customer is always right?" Rachel fumed.

"No one is always right—you are surely old enough to realize at least that much."

The crowd went back to shopping for candy and gossiping among themselves. Twyla went to the candy-making area to speak to Jacob.

"Why did you lose a customer over me? Wouldn't it have been easier to have fired me and kept the customer? I am just a temporary worker here."

"She was wrong—she should have apologized."

"I am so glad you saw what happened."

"About that, I may have overstated what I saw."

"How much did you see?"

"None of it."

"But you said that you saw her bump me."

"That is what you told me. I have not known you to be a liar or to spin tales."

"But this store is your livelihood, you can't just believe people who say something."

"I had to believe her or believe you. I chose to believe you. Was I wrong?"

"No, but ..."

"She spoke rudely to you. I apologize that you had to go through that."

"I have heard worse than that about my weight. I am just built this way—I can't help it."

"There is nothing to 'help.' You look fine."

Twyla soared inside—that was the closest to a compliment she had ever received from anyone about her looks. She did something impulsive and hugged Jacob quickly. "Thank you for believing me!" As quick as it started, the hug was over, and Twyla went back to work.

Jacob for his part stood there, apparently shocked but pleased.

CHAPTER 4

Jacob looked out at the pans he had prepped, crushed walnuts a layer deep in each of them, the chocolate caramel ready to pour so it would lock the walnuts in place. Next was to cover the mix in fondant. While the caramel cooled, Jacob would make the fondant mixture.

Jacob scaled up the recipe, set all the ingredients except the vanilla into his pan and began warming it over a low flame. He stirred until the sugar had all melted then stopped, covered the pan, and waited for the temp to rise to 240 degrees. Once he had the 240 degrees, he removed the cover, added the vanilla, stirred, then spread the fondant over the caramel nut sheets and rolled the pans up jelly-roll style, wrapped them in wax paper, and left them to harden. Once hardened, the rolls would be cut on an angle creating Caramel Nut Rolls.

Jacob had just finished wrapping the last of the rolls when the bell for the door rang. Looking up, he saw that it was too early for his sister, who was always on time but never early. Making his way to the door, he was pleasantly surprised to see Twyla on the other side.

"Come on in. You are early, nearly a half hour."

"I wanted to thank you again for yesterday. People in my life generally don't stand up for me."

"You need better people in your life then."

"Yes, I probably do."

"Since you are here early, you can help me cut the caramel nut rolls—they should be just about hardened. Well, after you sign in and make us some coffee. We can't sample the candy without a good cup of coffee to wash it down."

Twyla smiled. "I will get right on that."

The two sipped coffee while slicing the nut rolls, and when finished, they ate the uneven end pieces as a reward for their efforts.

Putting a finger to his lips, Jacob said, "Don't tell Emma. I do this with all the candies I have to cut. She will start showing up and that means less for me."

"Don't you mean less for *us*? Now that I know your secret, I am sure to arrive early every day."

"I'd actually enjoy that. Why don't you start a half hour earlier, and I can show you how some of the candies are made."

Before she could answer, a ring at the door announced Emma's arrival. "I'll get it," Twyla volunteered.

"Good morning, Emma," Twyla gushed.

With a questioning turn of her head, Emma answered, "Good morning to you too. What has you so extra cheerful?"

"Jacob asked me to start a half hour earlier each day."

"You are celebrating losing more sleep?"

"No, that he is going to show me how some of the candy is made. I find the process fascinating."

Emma quirked her eyebrows. "Do you like Jacob?"

"Of course I do. He is a good person."

"No, I mean *like* him."

"Oh, I am not sure I ever thought of him that way."

"I think he likes you. He never has said good job to anyone else, and he goes out of his way to spend time with you."

"I am sure you are seeing something that isn't there. Jacob is a handsome enough guy—he wouldn't be interested in fat old me."

From the other side of the shop, Jacob asked, "What are the two of you talking about?"

Both girls looked up with faces that spoke of possible guilt. "Nothing," they said in unison.

Thanksgiving came and went. Jacob noticed the crowds growing nearly every day from that point on. Some folks wanted to keep candy in the house for visitors, and others got an early jump on their Christmas shopping. He looked over at Twyla, working her charm on a customer who was trying to decide if they should get the nut clusters or the caramel nut roll. He was not in the least surprised, with Twyla's helpful advice, that they bought both.

Waving her over to him, Jacob asked, "Twyla, can you take a minute and call our supplier for gummy bears and gummy worms? We need to order extra. Ask them to add 30% to our last month's order—that should get us past Christmas."

"Is their phone number on the Rolodex?"

"Yes, under gummy." Jacob laughed, and Twyla joined in.

"Well, you two seem awfully chummy," Emma said with an odd look in her eyes after Twyla had gone into the office to make the call.

Jacob shrugged his shoulders. "I enjoy working with her, that is all."

Emma giggled. "Sure it is. Sure it is."

Jacob stopped and thought. Nothing in Twyla's words nor actions led him to believe she was romantically interested in him, nothing. He shrugged and went on with his day.

Emma nudged Twyla when it got slow. "Jacob sure does rely on you more than anyone I have ever seen. Are you sure he isn't sweet on you?"

Twyla shook her head back and forth. "He hasn't said or done anything to make me think so. I just think he likes working with me, and that is fine. I enjoy working with him too."

"You just can't see how different he is with you than with any of our former employees."

"No, I can't see into the past, if that is what you are suggesting."

Emma laughed. "You can't see what is going on today?"

"Why are you so eager to get Jacob and me together?"

Emma twirled a loose strand of hair. "Well, if you two were together, you could work here year-round, and I wouldn't have to. I don't really like doing this every day and besides, I am of an age when a suitable man may come calling."

"Has any particular boy grabbed your eye?"

"Never-you-mind that," Emma said.

A new wave of customers cut that conversation short.

During the next week, Twyla learned to cut and wrap caramels, to stir fudge while it cooked, to order the items they did not make themselves, and she got to use the brittle hammer again.

Monday morning before the store opened, Jacob gathered Twyla and Emma. "Christmas is only three weeks away—things are going to get hectic in here. I usually call Mom in to help in the kitchen. I am thinking of having Twyla help me this year. Do you know if Elsa has a job? She wasn't terrible last year—it shouldn't take too long for her to get back up to speed on the register."

Emma looked at Twyla, then at Jacob. "I can ask her, or we could have Mom come in midday to take the register and cover the later hours so the days are not so long."

"Check with Elsa first. I'd like to let Mom stay home—she has plenty to do there without helping here all day and evening."

The next day, Emma showed up with Elsa, a thin, incredibly attractive young girl ready to go to work.

Elsa looked over at Jacob with a big smile. "I was so hoping you would ask me to come back this year."

Jacob bobbed his head from across the store. "We certainly can use the help—looks like a banner year so far. Sorry to start you so late."

Elsa looked at Twyla, and a quick look of scorn went across her face. "Oh, you have some help already."

"Elsa, this is Twyla. She is going to help me in the back area making candy this year."

That makes sense, I wouldn't want her to be greeting customers either. She reached out her hand to shake with Twyla. "Pleased to meet you, Twyla," she said with a smile that was just fake enough to be noticed.

Twyla shook her hand. "You as well. So you worked here last year?"

Elsa quietly replied, "Yes, Jacob trusted me with the register in the busiest time of the year."

Excusing herself from the catty conversation, Twyla said, "Speaking of Jacob, I guess I had best go find out what he and I are making today."

Elsa turned to Emma. "So, your mom isn't helping this year? It isn't like Jacob to let the hired help in the kitchen."

Emma shrugged. "Jacob runs the place; it is his call who he hires."

Elsa asked quietly "So ... is he seeing anyone?"

"No, I thought he was sweet on Twyla, but he hasn't made any kind of move."

With a look approaching horror on her face, Elsa gasped. "Twyla? Why on earth would he settle for her?"

"She is a nice enough person. Why wouldn't Jacob like her?"

"She is the size of both of us combined."

"She has a great personality and is good with customers."

"Whatever ..."

The week went by, and as expected, the shop was exceedingly busy. Elsa came back up to speed slowly on the scales and register while Twyla was an immediate help in the kitchen. With the extra set of hands, they were able to more than double the output and keep ahead of demand.

Friday evening at the end of the day, Jacob walked Twyla to the door. "Twyla, I just want to say what a huge help you have been this week. I was a bit worried you might not be able to get up to speed quickly enough, but you have exceeded my goals for you this week. I think we are so far enough ahead that we can make another batch of brittle. We usually have to run out to keep up with the rest of the chocolates."

"I am sure your mother would be more help back there than I am, but thank you."

"Well, yes and no. She knows most of the recipes already, but she doesn't always do things the way I like to do them. I try to run as efficiently as I can. Mom likes to do things the way she did with Dad. It can make for some minor clashes in the kitchen. We haven't had any of those this year."

"Well, I will try to keep doing things the way you show me. Was there anything else?"

Jacob was gathering his courage to ask Twyla to dinner when Elsa interrupted. "Oh, Jacob, what a day, huh? We should go and grab some dinner at Mario's. I know how you love Italian food."

"That's a great idea—we should *all* go for a celebratory dinner. Can you come, Twyla?"

Twyla looked and saw Elsa slowly shaking her head no. "I have some shopping I have to do, maybe some other night."

Elsa looked across the room. "Emma, we are going to Mario's—come with?"

"I can't, I have a previous engagement."

Jacob spun his head around to look at his sister. "Really? Do I know him? Is it serious?"

Emma laughed. "And that is why I never tell you anything, dear brother of mine."

Jacob and Elsa left for Mario's, leaving Twyla and Emma to lock up. Twyla turned to Emma. "OK, your brother is gone—do I know him?"

"I don't have a date. I just know that Elsa has her sights set hard on Jacob. I figured to give them a bit of time together." Then Emma noticed the look on Twyla's face. "Wait, you do like him, don't you? Why didn't you go to dinner with them? I would have gone if it was the four of us."

"She was shaking her head no at me. She didn't want me there."

"What about Jacob? Was he shaking his head?"

"No, but ..."

"Twyla, let me explain about Jacob. I love him like the brother he is, but I think he is incapable of asking a girl out. If you want to see him and have him see you, you are going to have to do what Emma just did—make it your idea."

"Well, it is too late to worry about it. I am sure that wisp of a girl is working her way into his heart already."

"Could be, but I know he resisted her all last year or maybe didn't notice her throwing herself at him. I just figured that was why he didn't bring her back this year and instead asked me to find someone new."

Listen to me, fretting about a boy that hasn't shown me an ounce of attention as if I could compete with a thin girl. Twyla made her way out the door.

The next day was chaos in the kitchen. Twyla and Jacob were not much talking with each other and kept bumping into each other. By the time the day was over, they were both glad for the end of it. Twyla said a quick goodnight and left without waiting for the "Good work today" she knew wasn't coming. *Why am I so worked up about him dating the twig? He had plenty of chances to ask me out. He clearly isn't interested in the fat girl.*

After Twyla and Elsa had left, Jacob walked towards the door only to find his sister smiling at him.

"What?"

"Please tell me you didn't notice?"

"Notice what?"

"Twyla was a mess today after you and Elsa went out last night. She thinks you two are dating."

"Why would she think that? I mean we just had dinner on a Friday night ... OK, I can see why she would think that except she was invited too. I was about to ask her to go to dinner when Elsa did it for me, then Twyla said no."

"Elsa was shaking her head no at Twyla."

"Great. You two left me to sit with that girl all evening and listen to her talk about herself."

"If you were going to ask Twyla out, you should do it. I don't know what you are waiting for."

"Sure, it is easy for girls. You just wait for a guy to ask, then you can say yes or no or maybe some other time."

"Yes, we wait, and wait and wait for the boy to man up with the courage to ask. That can be just as exasperating as well."

Jacob thought for a bit. "Yes, I guess it could be."

CHAPTER 5

On most Mondays, Jacob and Emma ran the registers, giving the hired help the day off. Today, they had Twyla there on a third register just to keep the orders flowing out of the store. Jacob could not recall a busier day in the shop's history. The volume of customers was constant throughout the day, leaving little time for much conversation at all other than the occasional "We are running low on Almond Butter Crunch" or the echo of "next in line."

As Jacob finally closed the door, an hour after the scheduled closing time, he looked over at Emma and Twyla, and after a moment, he started laughing. "Do I look as tired as you two do?"

Emma rolled her head on her shoulders to stretch her tired muscles. "I can't believe how busy it was—did you run an advertisement or something?"

Jacob shook his head "No, we never run ads this time of year. Foot traffic is heavy enough without. Can you imagine if I had?"

Twyla chimed in, "I just feel bad I was barely able to to restock the sample trays. They were always empty every time I made it out there. Same with the Hot Chocolate."

Jacob replied, "I never had a chance to leave the register to check on them."

Twyla looked at Emma and Jacob. "I was trying to make sure anyone who came in had the same experience I had years ago. This shop was magical to me."

Emma nodded her head. "You were great. I can't believe how you flew around the store helping people while still ringing up probably more than I did."

Jacob went to his small office to count the drawers and get the deposit ready—something he did each night to keep the money away from the shop when they were closed. He took about a half an hour to get the deposit ready while the girls cleaned up the shop and restocked the candies they had more of in stock.

"Wow, we are out of peanut brittle again," Twyla said to Emma

"That never stays on the shelves—we could probably just make that and still keep busy all day."

"Why don't we make more of it then?"

Emma yelled across the shop, "Jacob, Twyla wants to know why we don't make more peanut brittle?"

"I am only one man. I cannot keep up with the demand."

Twyla nodded. "With the two of us making it, I bet we could get another couple batches in."

Tuesday morning came early as Twyla and Jacob agreed to work an extra hour in the mornings to try to make room for more brittle. This morning was a similar product, Almond Butter Crunch

They melted the butter, added the sugar, syrup, and water while slowly raising the temperature of the mix. They took turns occasionally stirring the mix, watching for it to reach three hundred degrees. Once the candy hit three hundred, they quickly stirred in the coarse chopped nuts and spread the mix into ungreased pans. While still warm, the mix was covered with chocolate and sprinkled evenly with fine ground nuts. Once cooled, they turned the candy out of pans and broke it into pieces similar to Peanut Brittle.

They fell back into their rhythm and knocked out four pans of the almond crunch in harmony. They cleaned up and moved on to dipping some fondant, some caramels, and some creams into chocolate.

Wednesday came, and they made peanut brittle. Jacob walked Twyla through all the steps, and they were ready with a batch twice the size of normal when Emma and Elsa showed up to help pull it. Jacob never considered Elsa for the hammer job, instead he simply handed the mallet to Twyla and let her break the candy down.

Jacob looked at the broken candies "OK, let's get this bagged and ready for sale."

Twyla asked, "May I take a couple pounds and send it to our candy distributor as a Christmas gift?"

Nodding his head, he said, "Sure, I usually don't have any and send them a sampler box."

Hours later while she was ordering from the supplier, Twyla said, "Mr. James, I am sending you some of the Wyse peanut brittle. Let me know if this is something you might want to distribute to other candy shops."

"I have heard the rumors about that brittle. I will be glad to get a sample and let you know," Mr. James replied.

The two finished placing the order for the shop and arranged to have the delivery driver return the brittle to the distributor.

CHAPTER 6

The next two weeks flew by with chocolates being made, and chocolates being sold nearly as fast. The only drag on the operation was Elsa and her near nonstop flirting with Jacob. As the shop closed on Dec 22nd, Jacob found himself looking at the books after making the deposit ticket for the bank. This was already the best Christmas season the shop had ever known. and there were two more days to add to the total. Jacob normally gave the temporary employees a box of chocolates and a check for $50. This year he would be giving them a little extra.

The phone rang, a rarity for this hour of the evening. "Hello?"

Paul James replied, "Jacob, you have been holding out on me. That peanut brittle is amazing. How soon can you get me five hundred pounds of it? I have buyers waiting for your answer."

Quirking his brow, he said, "I hadn't thought about having you distribute it."

"Your new office girl, Twyla, seemed to think you were ready to go."

Smiling widely, Jacob replied, "I see, that sounds like Twyla all right. I will have to check the production schedule, but I am sure I can get that made and ready within a week to ten days."

"Perfect. Not everyone wants chocolate for Valentine's day. Merry Christmas, Jacob, to you and yours."

"Thank you, Paul, the same to you and your family."

Jacob sat for a minute and wondered how much to sell the brittle for in quantity and how much that meant they would be making for each shipment. They would need to order more bags with the shop name on them—it was Wyse peanut brittle after all. *How do I reward Twyla for finding a way to keep the shop busy during the slower seasons?* That thought would have to wait for the morning.

December 23rd started with Elsa being late by forty-five minutes. The shop had a line at the door when they opened, so Twyla went out onto the sales floor instead of helping Jacob make candies. That was more candy cooking than Jacob would have been willing to try alone. When Elsa did arrive, she had no real excuse for her tardiness. Instead, she just batted her eyes at Jacob, obviously assuming that would fix everything.

Jacob grabbed Emma and brought her to a quiet spot on the floor. "Do you have any other friends you can get to work New Years to Valentine's day?"

Emma's mouth dropped. "Jacob, you have never fired anyone. Why now?"

"It is one of our busiest day,s and she just floats in when she wants? That cannot be allowed, even for a friend of yours."

"I can ask around, but I don't know anyone off the top of my head who is looking for work. Are you really going to fire her at Christmas?"

"I did not choose the timing, she did."

Calling across the store, he said, "Elsa, please come see me in my office"

The office barely had room for two chairs and was the one place in the candy store that smelled like business instead of candy. "Sit down."

"If it is about the Christmas bonus, can't that wait for later? The floor is full of people."

The blood vessels on Jacob's temples throbbed hearing this. "Bonus? No, this is not about any bonus. This is about you not showing up on time to serve those people that are filling our store right now."

"I said I was sorry."

"Well, so am I. This was your last day. I would rather know I am a person down than have to find out and ruin another batch of candy because I had to let Twyla go out to help Emma."

"So, that pig ruins a batch of candy and you decide to fire me?"

Twyla was coming back to the office to let Jacob know she was headed back into the kitchen and overheard Elsa's comment. *Pig, Cow? Why am I always livestock? Can't they come up with anything original?* "Excuse me, Jacob," she called out from outside the closed door.

Jacob sighed, wondering how much Twyla had heard. "Yes, Twyla?"

"I just wanted to let you know we got that first big wave of people set, so I am going back into the kitchen."

"Twyla, I'm sorry to ask this, but can you stay out on the floor today? I will explain it later."

"You're the boss."

Turning his attention back to Elsa, he said, "You mentioned a Christmas bonus. I will pay you the $50 bonus the same as last year, but that is from my generosity, not something that you have earned."

Twirling a strand of hair, Elsa simpered, "Well now that we aren't working together, perhaps you could take a girl out to dinner?"

"Elsa, I keep telling you I am not interested in you that way. How completely inappropriate to bring that up now even as I am having to fire you."

"You are serious, aren't you? You need a pretty girl to keep the people coming in. They won't come in to see *her*."

Jacob folded his arms. "They were coming in record numbers before you graced us with your presence, and they will keep coming in for the best candy for miles, not for some self-proclaimed beauty queen. Go get me your timecard. I will write your last check now.

With the appropriate tear in her eye, Elsa said goodbye to Emma and promised they could still be friends regardless. Elsa had no words of goodbye for Twyla.

Jacob caught Twyla's eye and waved her over. "Twyla, my office, please."

Turning to Emma, she asked, "Are you OK out front alone?"

"I will be fine. Just try to rush him and for goodness sakes don't get fired too. I don't want to finish this year alone."

"Twyla, what on earth made you think to distribute Peanut Brittle?"

"I am sorry, I heard Emma say the shop could make just that and stay in business. It made me wonder if that was a way to take some of the cycling out of your business. Right now, you go crazy from before Thanksgiving to just after Valentine's Day, then get slow for the rest of the year. Well, Mother's Day and Easter excluded.

"I am not angry with you. It is exactly the kind of thing that we need. I am extremely happy with everything you have done this year."

"But?"

"No 'but'."

"You called me off a busy floor to say that? Good thing you don't have a boss, he would eat you up for that. You could have said that at closing this evening."

"I did not want to forget it if the day got crazy."

"Well, thank you. Maybe you can keep me on till Easter to help with the extra work?"

"That is not the worst idea I have heard today." Jacob laughed. "Now, get back to the sales floor—I hear it is busy out there. Good thing I don't have a boss watching over me."

CHAPTER 7

"Are you sure you don't need me today?" Connie Wyse asked her son.

Jacob turned and smiled, "No, I decided not to make candy today, which puts three of us on the registers. I may need you if Emma doesn't find us a replacement soon, though. Twyla has talked Mr. James into distributing our peanut brittle so the kitchen will be busier than normal for a while."

"Wow, your father once talked about doing that—he would be so proud of you."

"He'd be proud of Emma for finding Twyla, I think. Speaking of which, I am keeping her on until at least after Valentine's Day, maybe Easter. If the shop stays busy, I mean."

"You don't need to check with me on that. You run that business and run it well, I might add."

"Thanks, Mom. See you this evening."

Jacob put on his coat, hat, and gloves then stepped out into a light snow. This storm was expected to put two to five inches on the ground before it was done. There was already an inch or more on the ground as Jacob rounded the corner onto the street where the candy shop was. It was a short ten-minute walk most days, a bit longer today with the lack of traction in places. He was met at the door by Twyla, who always seemed to be early.

"Hello, Twyla, good morning to you."

"Good morning, Jacob. Looking forward to a busy day?"

Opening the door, Jacob replied, "We will be ready for whatever day finds us."

Twyla walked towards the kitchen. "I will start a big batch of hot chocolate."

"Careful not to spill it on anyone ..."

Looking over her shoulder, she said, "Still not funny, Mr. Wyse."

"I have become Mr. Wyse. Here I thought I was growing on you."

"And here I thought you had a decent sense of humor."

"Before anyone else gets here, can I speak with you?"

Twyla laughed quietly. "UH-OH. He got a taste for firing—looks like I am next."

"Well, that is part of what I wanted to talk to you about."

Twyla stopped what she was doing and walked over to Jacob. "What's the matter? Did I do something?"

Pointing to a nearby stool, he answered, "To be truthful, yes, yes, you did. Since you are here, grab a seat."

Twyla was silent, and the color seemed to have left her face.

"We usually tell the Christmas help they will be let go on New Year's Day."

"Oh, is that all? Yes, Emma explained that to me when I agreed to come here to work."

"Well, that is just it. I would like it very much if you could stay working here until Valentine's Day."

Twyla let out the breath she was holding. "Yes, I'd be glad to work an extra month or so. That is much better than the "You are fired on Christmas Eve" that you had me expecting."

"What? How could you think that? You have been a big part of our success this season."

"I joked about getting fired—you said that was a part of what you wanted to talk about."

"Oh, I meant keeping you on."

Twyla smiled. "You really need to work on your communication skills, Jacob Wyse."

Twyla got up and made a double pot of Hot Chocolate, went out onto the sales floor, stocked up the tins and canisters of hot chocolate mix around the display, and started a second batch of chocolate to keep the pot full past the early morning rush.

At eight-thirty, Emma arrived uncharacteristically early.

"Good morning, Emma."

"Good morning, Jacob."

"Hey, Emma"

"Good morning. Twyla, how has the morning gone so far?"

"Well, your brother told me he was firing me then changed his mind and asked me to stay on until Valentine's Day."

"Fire you? What did you do?"

"She didn't do anything, and I already apologized. I told her I needed to speak with her, and she joked about getting fired. I was so eager to ask her to stay that I wasn't thinking right and agreed that was what it was about.

Emma smiled. "You really need to work on your communications and people skills there, brother."

Jacob shrugged, "So I have heard."

The day flew by. People would come in, shake off the snow and the cold, grab a cup of hot chocolate and wish everyone a Merry Christmas as they walked out with bags of candy that were probably not on their list of things to buy today. Before anyone knew it, it was four-thirty.

Jacob stood back from the register, then said loud enough for all to hear, "Folks, as is our custom, Wyse Candies will be closing in a half hour for Christmas Eve. Please enjoy the hot chocolate and samples but remember to get your purchases to the register by then."

Emma walked over to where Jacob was ringing up the last customer in his line. "You sound so much like dad when you say that."

Jacob hugged his sister. "I wish he were here too, Emma."

"So did you ask her out yet?"

Jacob turned to look her in the eye. "Who?"

Emma shrugged and rolled her eyes. "Twyla. I can tell you like her, and I happen to know she likes you."

"I admire her as a person, but it is not the same, and I doubt she cares about me as anything other than a boss. A boss who needs to work on his communication skills."

Emma laughed quietly. "She told you that too, huh? Well, it sounds like she is comfortable speaking to you plainly without worrying you will get angry with her."

Jacob nodded. "Yes, I think she understands she is a big part of what worked this Christmas season."

"Why do you think that?"

"Well, I told her so when I asked her to stay on."

"You can say that, and you can't find a way to ask her to a simple dinner?"

"I will think about it. Not today though, the timing is all wrong."

"Really? Because who wants a New Year's Eve date anyway?"

Jacob shrugged and walked away from Emma

At five-twenty, the last purchase had been rung up, and the shop was closed. Jacob took the three register drawers to his office and began to do the daily cash out. They would be closed the next two days as they celebrated Christmas with immediate family and then the following day visiting extended family and friends. Emma and Twyla made short work of cleaning the store, washing the plates from the samples, and the hot chocolate pots and pans. They swept the floor and restocked the candies while Jacob was making out the bank deposit.

Jacob shouted out, "Emma, come into the office, please."

Turning the corner and stepping into the small space "Yes, brother dear."

"Here is your Christmas bonus."

Emma scrunched her eyebrows together. "We don't usually give ourselves Christmas bonus. Do we?"

"We haven't before, but this year has been extremely profitable, especially Christmas season. I am going to give Twyla the same amount."

Emma opened the envelope handed to her. "A thousand dollars?" she shrieked then hugged her brother.

"It has been a great year."

"Twyla!" Jacob yelled next.

Twyla came around the corner and joked, "Yes, Boss."

Handing Twyla an envelope, he said, "Emma and I want you to have this as an expression of our thanks for the work you have done and continue to do for us."

Twyla's shriek was louder than Emma's as she opened the envelope. "Thank you, thank you!" she said as she hugged first Emma then Jacob. Jacob's hug lasted a moment or two longer than Emma's as it seemed neither Jacob nor Twyla were eager to end it.

CHAPTER 8

Saturday, December 27th, came with another light snow and much chatter about the people visited and friends that came calling. For Jacob, it was another Christmas without his father and he was left feeling melancholy.

Seeing Jacob frowning, Twyla asked, "Is everything all right, Jacob?"

"I miss my father this time of year. His absence has taken much of the joy out of Christmas for me."

"I am sorry for that loss—I cannot begin to imagine it."

"Nothing to be done about it. I hear that time heals all wounds—I just wonder how much time that really takes."

Twyla shrugged. "Try doing something different—take a chance on something you wouldn't normally do."

"Maybe I will just try that, but for today, it is Pralines."

The two took out the brown sugar, regular sugar, cream, butter, and a huge bag of pecans.

"Now, we are going to raise this to the soft-ball stage."

"Why is it called soft-ball?"

"When you get between 235 and 245 degrees and spoon some of the sugar mix into a glass of water, the ball of candy will slowly flatten in your hand when you remove it from the water. We do that for soft candies and chewy candies instead of hard ball or hard crack like we do for brittle"

Twyla listened intently. "You sure know a lot about making candies. I guess that comes with owning a shop."

Jacob shook his head. "More like the fact I have made candy or helped make candy for as long as I can remember."

Twyla gave a genuine laugh. "That would help too."

They got the mixture up to temperature then spooned it out over an enameled table allowing the pieces to firm up. Jacob even took the extra time to show Twyla the process of how to check for soft-ball stage with water, as if he didn't have a candy thermometer available.

As they finished making the pralines, he asked, "Twyla, can you make us a pot of coffee? I am near certain we can find a couple of imperfect pralines in this batch that will need to be culled before we make them available to the public."

Twyla smiled and nodded. "It is a fine thing you are so willing to suffer for your customers, Jacob. So very noble of you."

Jacob shared the smile. "As my assistant, I expect no less from you."

Twyla flirted back. "The horrors of this job—no one understands the sacrifices made."

Emma came through the door and heard the tail end of the conversation. "'Sacrifices?' Ooh, what are you two sampling this morning?"

Jacob chuckled. "You know me too well, sister. We made pralines. I am guessing we can find an imperfect one for you as well."

"Imperfect? You pick them at random and call them that just so you can sample. You take after Dad that way. He always used to declare candy unsellable so that we could have some when he made it."

Twyla looked over at Emma. "I don't care who started the tradition, I am just glad to share in it."

Emma nodded. "I am glad both for the tradition and a happy reminder of Dad this time of year. Speaking of traditions, what are the two of you doing for New Year's Eve? Any plans?"

Twyla shook her head. "I am going to curl up with a good book and a warm cat and read—that is my New Year's Eve tradition."

"That is still better than mine," Jacob said. "I will be going to bed early. My internal clock is set. I will wake up at four a.m. even though we will be closed."

Emma shrugged. "You two are old fogies; I am going to the church singing they are having as a celebration of the New Year."

Twyla looked toward Jacob and seeing him looking her way immediately turned away. "Well, that sounds like fun, but I have already picked out my book."

Jacob's face flashed disappointment. "Well, these pralines are not going to eat themselves, let's get the bad ones eaten and the good ones ready for sale."

Wednesday, during work, Emma was all excited about the singing and who might be there. Twyla and Jacob were both silent on the matter.

"But, why don't you want to come, Twyla? Maybe some good-looking guy will want to drive you home."

Twyla shrugged. *No one wants a cow to ride in their cart.*

"Your loss." Emma sighed.

"What about you, Jacob?"

"I don't want a good-looking young man to offer me a ride home, thanks."

Twyla burst into laughter despite her friend Emma showing clear frustration.

The shop was quieter than before Christmas but still busy enough they couldn't talk about it much more.

At the singing, Emma saw Benjamin Lapp from across the lawn. More importantly to Emma, he saw her.

With a tip of his hat, he asked, "Did you want to play some volleyball?" barely able to meet her eyes.

"Why, thank you, I'd love to," Emma said and took Benjamin's arm, walking to the net.

They played for fifteen minutes and won. Benjamin proved himself an asset on the court, and Emma played well also.

"Let's cool off and get a drink," Emma suggested.

"That sounds like a great idea. I will go get them—wait for me?"

With a bit of dreaminess in her voice, she answered, "I will," but her mind was saying *I have been.*

They drank the punch, talked and talked. It turned out they had much in common, they both liked the idea of farming, they both preferred coffee to tea, and they both loved ice cream—vanilla fresh out of the churn best of all. When the singing had nearly ended, Benjamin slipped away from the other gentlemen and found his way to Emma's side.

"If it would not be considered too forward of me, I would love to drive you home tonight."

"I'd be delighted," came the swift reply, and the two made their way out of the home where the singing was held.

"Emma, I am not sure how I never really noticed you before, but would you consider letting me make you some ice cream this Saturday? I will bring the churn and the ingredients to your house."

"It is the middle of winter," Emma started, then continued, "And I would love to have some fresh churned ice cream." as she quickly caught herself.

Friday, January 2nd, there was a noticeable change in Emma—she was smiling and singing from the time she arrived for work. Both Jacob and Twyla teased her and tried to get her to tell, but she kept her news to herself until lunchtime.

"If you two must know, Benjamin Lapp drove me home from the singing ... and he is coming to the house tomorrow to make me some ice cream—vanilla just like I like it."

Twyla's face beamed. "Well, you should bring home some of the pralines to put on top—everyone loves pralines."

Jacob frowned. "Benjamin Lapp. Isn't he the youngest son on the Lapp farm? Won't he be a farmer?"

Emma couldn't look her brother in the face. "I suspect that he will be getting the farm ..."

"How could you work here and be a farmer's wife?"

Emma rolled her eyes. "I think it is a bit early to worry about that. He is making me ice cream, not asking me to marry him." *For now.*

CHAPTER 9

The first week of January brought cold temperatures and plenty of snow. The shop was less hectic than before Christmas but stayed busy enough to justify keeping Twyla working.

Twyla answered the phone, "Wyse Chocolates, Twyla speaking. Oh, hello, Paul. How did the peanut brittle go over so far? Really? Another five hundred pounds already? I will talk to Jacob and get it on the schedule. How soon did you want that? Next week should be fine."

Jacob overheard the conversation and was elated. The brittle was a success. He ran across the floor towards Twyla.

"That was Paul James?"

Twyla smiled. "Yes, it was."

"And he is already ordering more brittle?"

"Yes, he is. He said he hasn't seen a response like this in years for a product. He wants another five hundred pounds next week, then probably again two weeks later, but he will confirm that with you after this next batch is delivered."

Jacob was elated. He went over to Twyla and threw his arms around her, giving her a big hug. "Thank you. Twyla, this is all on you. You are the reason for this success.

Twyla, for her part, was also ecstatic. She was a vital part of a team for the first time in her life. And if Jacob chose to show his thanks with hugs, she was not of a mind to object.

"Let me go, so I can order the materials. I don't think we have enough glucose nor peanuts on hand to make that much. Should I order for five hundred pounds or the thousand?"

"Ask if there is any discount for the higher bulk. If we get at least five percent off, go ahead and have them ship a thousand pounds. We will need some for the store soon too."

Twyla was both relieved and saddened by him letting go. She found herself drawn to Jacob but did not want to get her hopes up. Fat girls don't get guys like Jacob, she told herself over and over.

"Jacob, do you keep track of what you sell by weight each month? How much of each item that is?"

"We haven't been. Why, do you think we should? What would the benefit be?"

"Well, since you are now also a wholesale kitchen, it would make it easier to make a schedule for production. Instead of waiting for things to go low, you can schedule to make them when they will just start to get low. Mainly the big items to begin with, then as time goes on and you have more information collected, you could schedule out a week or two and know that you won't run out of anything in the store."

"Is that something you would be comfortable doing, Twyla?"

"I can set it up for you. I think once you see it, it will explain itself so you can keep it going when I am gone."

"Gone? Where are you going?"

"It is only a few more weeks until Valentine's Day."

"That reminds me, can you stay on until Easter?"

"I would love to stay on another couple months— we can get the schedule working by then I think. Have

I mentioned that you really need to work on your communications skills?"

As Valentine's Day approached, they made heart-shaped chocolates, made extra chocolate covered caramels, creams, and fondants for sampler boxes. Each evening, Twyla went into the office with Jacob, and while he cashed out the register and made the bank deposit, she totaled the amount of each candy sold and kept a daily log. Her idea soon started paying dividends as there were days on the schedule that were able to be filled with making fudge that wasn't quite out yet but according to the sheets, would be in a few days. The more of this that happened, the more interested in the whole process Jacob became.

"So, it will eventually tell us when to schedule everything? I won't have to go around the store looking for what is low to know what I am making the next day or run out of items before I make them?"

"There will still be a need to mind your store, Jacob. This will, however, reduce the number of times you run out of anything that people come in to buy. Let's say we have to make brittle for two days next week, and the books show that by then, we will be out of Nut Rolls—we can schedule the nut rolls before the brittle and never run out."

"Twyla, you are a genius! How did I run this shop without you?" Jacob gushed.

"Quite well as I recall,"

"Not as well as now, you have to admit that. You have brought Wyse candies forward and helped us to grow."

CHAPTER 10

Valentine's Day brought news to the shop. Benjamin Lapp had asked Emma for permission to court her, and she had accepted. This normally would have been private, but as it affected her future in the shop, she felt obliged to tell her brother.

"What am I to do? Bring Mother back to the shop? She has finally been able to get back to her quilting—you know how she loves it."

"I think you are missing the obvious answer."

"I can't make all the candy and ring it up too."

"Brother, you are dense sometimes. You have Twyla. I bet she would love to work here year-round and be your helper. I bet if you ever got around to asking her, she would want to be more than that."

"I tell you, sister, that I have been watching, and she hasn't shown any signs of interest. I would hate to ruin such a great work relationship, especially now that you are in the process of wanting to leave."

"I will be around until summer's end anyway, maybe a bit longer. Just ask the girl to dinner already. I can't believe you let Valentine's Day get past you on this. What an easy ask that is."

"We were busy getting a production schedule together. It was Twyla's idea. She really has been a great help at the shop."

"Do you like her?"

"Well, sort of, but not enough to ruin the working relationship we have if she does not feel the same."

"I keep telling you, the girl is pining away for you."

"I highly doubt that. With her personality and cheerfulness, I bet she has many young men interested."

"Ach, brother, you are not like most men. Most see her size and stop looking. They don't want a personality or a brain or a great helper. They want a pretty girl."

"Like your Benjamin likes you?"

"Did my brother just call me pretty?"

"No, you must be hearing things."

"Jacob, you need to work on your people skills and communication. You can't even tell when a girl wants you to walk her home."

"Jacob, the production schedule shows we will be out of chocolate caramels in a couple days. Do you want to do a batch of those as well today?"

Jacob narrowed his brows in disbelief. "Caramels? Already? Let me go check the stock on those."

Jacob went over to the chocolate caramels and saw a few pounds of them waiting for sale. "I think we are good, there are a few pounds of them still."

Twyla explained, "Well, the schedule is full for the next six days with peanut brittle and then taffy. According to the way the caramels have been selling, we will go out of stock on them before the week ends."

"I guess it won't hurt to run a batch of them just to be certain."

"Trust in the process, Jacob. The schedule is your friend."

With a smile, Jacob replied, "It is starting to feel like the schedule is my boss and by the schedule, I mean it is beginning to feel like you are my boss."

"You have an odd way of saying, 'Thank you for getting a production schedule running, Twyla.'"

"I know, I need to work on my communication skills."

"Yes, yes, you do, oh boss of mine."

By week's end, they had made the now one thousand pounds of brittle that Paul James had ordered for the month and, sure enough, would have run out of chocolate caramels without Twyla's intervention.

"Trust in the process," Twyla reminded Jacob when he was checking the inventory of the caramels.

"We definitely would have run out a couple of days ago. I understand the English use computers for inventory."

"You don't need a computer, you have me. Well, until Easter."

"About that ..."

"Do you not need me till then?"

"Actually, the opposite. How would you feel about working here through the summer months?"

Twyla nodded her head and teased, "You are getting better at this—you didn't wait till the week before I was scheduled to leave before asking me. There may be hope for you yet, boss."

Summer came and went—the orders for brittle got larger and larger. Mr. James was up to ordering a ton of brittle a month now trying to stock it up for the fall and winter seasons. Emma was still running the register out front while Twyla and Jacob worked in harmony in the kitchen.

Early in August, Connie Wyse stopped by the store to get some chocolates for friends she was going to be visiting.

Connie finished her order, "... and some pralines."

Emma put all the selections in a big bag and brought her mother to the register. "Still no charge, but I have to list what we sell so Twyla can schedule when to remake things."

"She can do that already?"

"She can do anything, except to get Jacob to ask her out."

"Does Jacob know?"

"I keep telling him, but he refuses to see it. So does she for that matter."

"I can see it from here—they are a match. Look at them smiling and working together."

"I am going to have them both as side sitters at my wedding, maybe that will wake them up."

"Wedding, you say?"

"Well, I wasn't going to mention it this early, but Benjamin and I are planning to wed this fall. Nothing big or fancy."

"Does your brother know?"

"I am not sure how to tell him. He is not going to be happy."

"I am sure he will be happy for you."

"Yes, just not for himself nor the shop. I think he thought I would be here forever."

"I can come back to work here."

"I am not sure Jacob wants you to. He likes being the boss of the shop."

"He can be my boss as easy as yours."

"I am not his mother."

Across the dinner table, Jacob got the news of the impending wedding. "Do you have anyone who could come to work for us? With the brittle selling so well, I need Twyla in the kitchen with me. To keep up."

"I can still run a register," Connie responded.

Shaking his head no, he said, "You should be able to make your quilts and spend your time as you see fit, Mom."

"What if I see fit to check in on my son?"

"I just don't want to tie you down to the shop."

Emma muttered, "You were more than willing to tie me there."

"That was clearly a mistake on my part. I shouldn't have counted on you."

"I never missed a day nor was I ever late. You take that back, Jacob Wyse!"

"I mean I should have realized your long-term goals were not inside the shop."

"You really need to work on your communication skills, brother of mine."

CHAPTER 11

The chocolate shop was a flurry of activity as Jacob worked off the stress of losing Emma. Twyla, for her part, kept up with him step for step but only with much effort.

"Jacob, we have never tried to make so much brittle in a day. Can we really do two thousand pounds of it? That is usually two days on the schedule."

"After we break the brittle, I will start the next batch, you can clean the workstations, then wash the pots and pans. By the time you are done with those, I will need you again in the kitchen to help pour and stretch the next batch. I think we can do it."

Twyla asked the question he seemed to miss. "Who will bag the brittle?"

"Emma can. The register is not so busy right now, so she can keep an eye open for it as she wraps. It is not ideal, but it will be huge if we can run a ton of brittle in a day."

The three of them worked harder that day than any other in the history of the shop. When the day was done, the ton of brittle was bagged and ready for shipment.

Jacob turned to Twyla. "I knew we could do it."

"Let's never do that again ..."

Jacob teased, "You sound like Emma."

"That is because Emma is smart enough to know we need a fourth person in the shop to try that again."

Emma added, "My feet ache from running back and forth all day. Are you trying to punish me for leaving?"

"Leaving?" Twyla asked.

"Benjamin and I are to be wed this fall."

Twyla jumped up and down then hugged Emma. "That is wonderful! I am so excited for you."

"You and Jacob will be side sitters for me," Emma declared rather than asked.

Jacob turned to Twyla and she to him. "I would be honored, sister," followed by, "I've never been a side sitter before," from Twyla.

Later, when alone with Emma, she asked, "Isn't it more usual to have couples as side sitters?"

"You two are a couple, you just can't see it."

"I hope this doesn't make it awkward in the shop after."

Emma smiled. *For my brother's sake, I hope it does.*

CHAPTER 12

With the wedding now looming in the near distance, the shop was in full gear. There would be vanilla ice cream and pralines for everyone at the wedding to commemorate Emma and Benjamin's first date as well as sampler trays of chocolates at each table.

Jacob turned from his work. "Twyla, how is that batch of fondant coming? I have the nut rolls waiting for it."

Using her frock to wipe the sweat from her brow, she replied, "Should be ready to go in about five minutes."

"How are we going to account for all the chocolate we are taking from the shop?"

"I assume you are giving it to your sister and her new husband. Did you want to charge her for it?"

"No, no, no. I mean in your schedule. Won't this make a demand that doesn't reflect in the daily numbers?"

"You had me wondering there for a second. I am not going to count any of the chocolate leaving into the equation. We will just have to make a wide mix to restock. I think that is the best way. Otherwise, each year around now we will be flooded with pralines."

"What about the days we are closed for the wedding? How will you figure those?"

"I won't. I think the best way for that is to have the two days as no sales. It will all balance out in the long run."

"I trust you."

Twyla's face warmed, and she knew she was blushing. Such a simple phrase, but the three words made Twyla feel like she was where she belonged, where she wanted to be. "You are getting better at that whole communication thing, boss."

The wedding was now a scant week away. Jacob let Emma have the time off, not that an Amish wedding was as ornate and planned out an affair as an English one, but rather because the poor girl was giddy to the point of not being able to concentrate on what it was she was doing. Twyla stepped up and covered the sales floor while Jacob took care of production during business hours. Twyla was still coming in a couple hours early to keep production on schedule, and with the continued success of the peanut brittle sales, her wages were more than covered. Her staying on through fall was never in question.

"Twyla, what is on our must make schedule for this week?"

"We really should do a single batch of brittle, so that we are not behind when we return from the wedding. There are also a few of the regulars that are running low or will be by then. I will write them down for you—you can make them in whatever order you want."

Jacob went back into the kitchen and began a batch of chocolate caramels. He realized it was easier with Twyla in the kitchen to make enough for both loose caramels and for the nut rolls. *Everything is easier with Twyla.* He sighed and continued to stir the caramels.

With the wedding just a day away, the shop closed early, and Twyla put the 'closed for two days' sign up in the door. Most folks around here knew of the closing and the reason already, but it was good business to keep the clients informed.

"So, I will see you at the church tomorrow," Jacob said as they locked up the door.

"I will see you there. Oh, can I get a ride with you from the church to the reception? I don't know how long it will go, and I don't want to have my English driver wait too long."

"I could just pick you up at your house and drive you to the church and back," Jacob offered.

"If that wouldn't be too much trouble, I'd like that."

If Jacob saw the spark in her eyes, he never placed it.

CHAPTER 13

Jacob stopped the open carriage outside Twyla's home, and she came out before he could go and knock properly. "I am so excited," she said quickly, and her tone left no doubt to her honesty.

"Why, Jacob Wyse, picking me up in an open carriage. What will people say?" she teased.

"Mom and Emma wanted the closed buggy to keep their hair in place. Is the truth. I don't much care what people think is the rest of the truth."

He doesn't care what people think in general or doesn't mind what they think about us? He really does need to communicate better.

The wedding ceremony went perfectly, and the young couple left for the reception followed by a trail of buggies. Jacob and Twyla were near the head of the line as they had the honored responsibility of being side sitters— sitting with the newly married couple and enjoying their first meal together with them.

Twyla knew those spots were usually given to either newly married or couples that were at least dating. What Jacob knew, he kept to himself. Everyone enjoyed the meal and the conversation—the big hit was the dessert of vanilla ice cream with Wyse pralines.

Jacob was quick to praise Twyla for her part in making sure the pralines were available for the wedding, making her blush more than once when folks asked if there would be any more pralines left in the shop come Monday. Twyla's heart fluttered when she heard Jacob praise her work. No one had ever done that for her. She had always been OK or enough, never praiseworthy. She excused herself to wipe her eyes.

"What did you do to make Twyla cry?"

"I don't think I did anything. I was just telling Hershel how great it is to have her around the shop and how much easier she makes everything for me."

Emma gave a knowing look then a nod.

"Are you OK, Twyla? I am sorry if something I said made you sad."

"You really are bad at communication, Jacob. Those were tears of happiness. I have never had anyone brag about me to another."

"I find that hard to believe."

"Stop it, or you will get me started again."

Jacob scrunched his shoulders. "Uh ... OK, I guess."

As the reception wound down, aunts and cousins stepped in, stepped up and got the cleanup going. Jacob was politely told he was not needed for this part of the day, so he returned to Twyla.

"So, did you enjoy yourself, Twyla?"

"I cannot remember a better day in ages."

"Ready to head back home?"

"No, but it is that time."

The two walked over to the carriage, and Jacob held her hand as she climbed in. He went to his side and jumped aboard. A slow pull on the reins got the horse to step backward far enough to clear the nearby carts, and a quick flick of the wrist got the mare to slowly begin the ride home.

"I am happy for Emma," Jacob said, breaking the silence. "It must be something to find the person you are matched with."

Twyla looked at the distance between them in the carriage and said in a whisper, "It must be."

The rest of the ride home was quiet, broken up by Jacob talking shop and Twyla's short responses.

CHAPTER 14

Monday morning, back at work, Jacob handed Twyla a cup of coffee and asked her to sit a minute.

"I did not expect this when we met, but you have become invaluable here. I hope your plans include Wyse Chocolates for the next couple years anyway. I guess what I am trying to say is can you stay and work year-round from now on?"

"I'd love to. I really do enjoy working here with you, Jacob."

"We will probably have to get Mom to come in on busy days to help with the registers, or maybe you know some people looking for work for this fall through Christmas and New Year's?"

"I will ask around ..."

Thanksgiving came and went, and the business was even greater than the year before. Jacob hired two young girls to work out front and had Twyla train them. His mother worked the kitchen with him while Twyla was out teaching the new girls how to keep the samples stocked and still ring up orders and be friendly. Twyla was all smiles but all business when it came to the new hires.

During one of the training weeks, Twyla's parents came into the shop.

"Hello, Mom. Hi, Dad. Welcome to Wyse Chocolates"

"Hello, Twyla. We were in the neighborhood and decided to stop by and get a few chocolates. Do you know anything about them so you could help us, or should we get someone else?"

"I can tell you that with the exception of anyone with the last name Wyse, I know more about these than any person in the shop." Twyla tried to impress her parents.

Her mom whispered to her, "It is not proper to be boastful."

Twyla shrank her shoulders. "Yes, Mum."

Seeing this, Jacob came over. "You must be Twyla's parents. I am Jacob Wyse. I cannot begin to tell you how happy we are to have had Twyla here with us this past year. She has been instrumental in making us more successful and a friendlier place to visit. Pick out what you want—it is on me. I can't have my best employee's family paying for their chocolate, not when their daughter helped to make most of it."

Twyla's parents looked at Jacob, waiting for the punchline that never came. They then looked at Twyla, seeing her perhaps for the first time through the eyes of someone who appreciated her for who she was, instead of who she might someday become. Twyla just blushed and smiled.

At the end of the day, after cleaning the shop and restocking and tidying the inventory, Twyla walked back to where Jacob was finishing the deposit ticket for the day.

"Thank you."

Jacob looked up, confused. "Huh?"

"Thank you for today. My parents were impressed with you."

"They should be impressed with you. You certainly have earned my admiration."

"That is why I am thanking you. They were impressed with you, and you went out of your way to let them know that you are impressed with my work here."

"I hope that isn't what you think."

Twyla spun to face him. "You aren't impressed with my work here?"

"Well, yes, but more than that, I am impressed by you. You are ... well, sturdy."

"Jacob, you really do need to work on your people skills. When you say sturdy, a fat girl hears fat, not dependable."

"Fat girl? You? I mean you are no twig like Elsa, but you are not fat."

"Jacob, I know me better than you do. I am fat, large, big-boned to those trying to be nice."

"I guess I just don't see you that way. You are just ... well, you."

Twyla swooned inside and went out on a limb. "Jacob Wyse, would you walk me home tonight?"

"Sure, why?"

"Never mind."

"Wait, do you mean walk you home like ... *walk you home?* I'm sorry ..." Jacob hesitated. "... I have been trying to get up the nerve to ask you to dinner since you started here. I just didn't think you were interested at all."

"Perhaps you have heard this before, you really need to work on your people and communication skills."

"Well, instead of just walking you home, would you like to go to Mario's with me for a pizza or maybe an eggplant parmesan and spaghetti unless you'd like something else?"

"No, I love Italian, and I hear Mario's is great. I have never been there yet."

"We will have to fix that. We can walk to Mario's, then to my house to get the horse and buggy for the ride to your house."

"I don't live that far away—we can walk it."

"I don't want people to get the wrong idea."

"What do you mean?"

"I mean when a young man courts a woman, he drives her around—he doesn't walk her around."

"Do you mean ...?"

"Unless you think you see too much of me around the shop already, I would like to get to know you outside the shop as well."

"I would love to drive around with you, Jacob Wyse."

The two were inseparable from that point on.

Just before closing the shop for Christmas Eve, Jacob walked up behind Twyla and whispered into her ear, "Would you be willing to be a spring bride? I am not sure I want to wait longer than that to have you as my wife."

Twyla nodded her head yes. "Jacob Wyse, you certainly have been working on those communication skills."

CHOCOLATE CARAMELS

1 Cup Sugar
1 Cup Light Corn Syrup (Karo's)
3 Squares Baker's Chocolate
1/4 Teaspoon Salt
1 1/2 Cups Heavy Cream

Combine sugar, syrup, chocolate salt and 1 cup of cream. Place over a low flame and stir until sugar is dissolved and mixture boils. Continue to boil mixture until 238 degrees. Stirring constantly, add the remaining 1/2 cup of cream and boil slowly until the mix reaches 246 degrees. Keep stirring and pour into 8" x 4" pan. DO NOT SCRAPE the pan. Let stand until cool. Cut into squares. Wrap in wax paper.

CREAM FONDANT

2 Cups Sugar
Dash of Salt
1/4 Cup Milk
1 Tablespoon Light Corn Syrup (Karo's)
1/2 Cup Heavy Cream
1/2 Teaspoon Vanilla

Combine ingredients (except vanilla) in a pan over low flame. Stir until sugar dissolves and mixture boils. Cover and cook without stirring to 240 degrees. Pour fondant at once on a cool to lukewarm wet plate.

Work until white and creamy then knead in wax paper. "Ripen in Refrigerator" 24 hours. Makes one pound.

CARAMEL NUT ROLL

1 Cup Chopped Walnut Meats
1 Recipe of Chocolate Caramels
1 Recipe of Fondant

Sprinkle nuts into two slightly greased eight by eight pans. Prepare chocolate caramels mix and pour carefully over nuts in pans. When cool, remove from pan and spread fondant evenly on the plain surface of the caramel. Use half batch of fondant for each sheet. Roll and wrap in wax paper. Let stand for several hours to harden. Cut crosswise into quarter inch slices. Makes about 64 pieces.

ALMOND BUTTER CRUNCH

1 Cup Butter
1 1/3 Cups Sugar
1 Tablespoon Light Corn Syrup
3 Tablespoons Water
1 Cup Coarsely Chopped Nuts
4 1/2 Ounces or Large Bar of Milk Chocolate Melted
1 Cup Finely Chopped Nuts

Melt butter in a large saucepan. Add sugar, syrup, and water. Cook, stirring occasionally to hard crack stage (300 degrees) At 300, quickly stir in coarse nuts and then spread out in ungreased 13 x 9 1/2 x 2 inch pan. Cover while hot with the melted milk chocolate, then sprinkle with the fine nuts. Cool thoroughly then turn out of the pan and break into pieces.

PRALINES

1 Cup Light Brown Sugar.
1 Cup White Sugar
1/2 Cup Cream
2 Tablespoons of Butter
1 Cup Pecans

Cook sugar and liquid until boiling, add nuts and butter. Cook to a soft ball stage 235 degrees. Take off fire (stove). Stir but do not beat. Drop onto aluminum foil then let cool.

ABOUT AMOS WYSE

Amos Wyse was born in the Midwest. Spending a great deal of his youth around good, hard-working farmers, those who lived near them and worked with them. When writing, he keeps those people and the life lessons they taught close by.